BOOK ONE

CRIME CROWNED

MERCILESS Sinner

BELLA RAY

A DARK MAFIA ROMANCE

Copy Edit by: Rawls Reads Editing

Proofreading by: Evil Comma

ASIN: B0GHZJM57D

ISBN: 978-1-971395-02-9

CONTENT & TRIGGER WARNINGS

Merciless King is a dark mafia romance intended for mature audiences. This story contains graphic content and themes that may be upsetting or triggering to some readers.

PLEASE READ WITH CARE.

POSSIBLE TRIGGERS INCLUDE:

- **VIOLENCE** – including gunfights, physical assault, and on-page death
- **TORTURE** – references to past and present torture, both physical and psychological
- **BLOOD & INJURY** – depictions of injury, recovery, and the aftermath of violence
- **KIDNAPPING & HOSTAGE SITUATIONS** – on-page abduction, captivity, and coercion
- **THREATS TO FAMILY MEMBERS** – including murder threats and coercion
- **ORGANIZED CRIME** – mafia activity, corruption, and criminal enterprises
- **DARK ROMANCE DYNAMICS** – power imbalance, possessive behavior, obsession, morally gray decisions
- **GRIEF & LOSS** – death of a spouse, emotional trauma, and mourning
- **SEXUAL CONTENT** – explicit, on-page intimacy including dominance/submission elements
- **ATTEMPTED SEXUAL ASSAULT (FOILED)** – references to and depiction of a prevented assault

This novel explores dangerous power dynamics, morally gray characters, and intense emotional and physical situations. Reader discretion is advised.

DESCRIPTION

TEN YEARS AGO, THE MAN I LOVED VANISHED.

He abandoned me.

I survived.

I built a life without Massimo Manetti. Married the wrong man. Raised my son in silence. And buried the truth so deep, I almost convinced myself it didn't matter.

Then my world was torn apart.

My son and husband were taken.

And the only man powerful enough to get them back is the one man I swore I'd never face again. The man who doesn't know the truth: The child I'm asking him to save... is his.

Massimo rules Las Vegas with blood and control. He's ruthless.

Possessive. Dangerous. Most of all he's Merciless. Now he's demanding answers I'm not sure I'm ready to give.

Because saving my child means trusting the man I never stopped loving.

I won't beg.

I won't break.

And I won't lose my son.

As enemies close in and old betrayals surface, I have to decide if giving Massimo the truth will save us... or destroy everything.

Merciless Sinner is a dark mafia romance featuring second-chance

love, a secret baby, forced proximity, a powerful anti-hero, and a heroine who refuses to kneel.

* For readers who like their romance dangerous and possessive—with a hard-won HEA.

Day One...

Las Vegas looks best from above, and I've made a study of all its angles. From my penthouse, the Strip is a river of molten gold, lit with more electricity, money, and delusion than the rest of Nevada combined. Every pulsing LED flashes a promise and a threat. The city glitters so perfectly it camouflages its own filth, hiding the rot until you're close enough to smell it.

The tourists, drunks, adrenaline junkies, and the terminally lost see a playground, a second chance. Redemption, if they can find the slot machine or roulette wheel that tilts the universe in their favor.

I see only territory, a chessboard crowded with pawns and a few useful bishops. All I taste is ownership.

The moan of the woman, bent over the counter as I pump into her from behind, distracts me. It's a high-pitched sound that's supposed to get my attention, when really what it does is make me realize I don't even know her name. She's as faceless and meaningless to me as the rest of them.

Every casino worth bleeding for answers to me, whether its shareholders know it or not. Beneath the noise, each floor hums with the tension of my influence. There isn't a punter or a pit boss or a cocktail waitress this side of the border who doesn't know my face, even if they pretend otherwise. I own slices of this city most men never see: the back hallways where the real deals are cut, the penthouse suites where visiting dignitaries have their sins scrubbed clean, the cash rooms that never see daylight. There are elevators built for one-way trips, stairwells that lead to whole floors missing from the city's official memory, and doorways you open only with the correct combination of passwords, banknotes, and threats. These are my proprietary routes. The city runs on me, not on luck, and certainly not on karma.

You'd think people would remember that. But just this week, someone forgot, and I don't tolerate memory lapses.

Two nights ago, the first domino fell, a dealer from *The Lucky Seven*; less than three hours later, a club promoter from XS. By dawn, there were six bodies sprinkled through my domain, all dead from coke laced with something nasty, synthetic, and not even a little accidental. It wasn't a message. This was sabotage: noisy, public, expensive.

One of the dead got my attention. A potential news headline, the kind of name that floats on billboards and LED loops. A minor celebrity. When a man like that dies, it isn't just another overdose. It becomes a headline. A press cycle. A public outrage. Once the news hits the stream, it'll drag heat down on it. The shrapnel—gossip, panic, regulatory scrutiny—will do more damage than any single bullet ever could. Press becomes pressure. Pressure becomes investigations. And investigations turn over stones I've worked very hard to leave undisturbed.

If I don't choke this story at the root, I'll have feds nesting in every chandelier from Fortuna to the Lucky Duck. And right now, I cannot afford federal curiosity. Not with the Mexicans probing the edges of my territory, testing how thin the walls are. Not with half my recent cash still mid-launder. Not with Senator Kingsley sharpening his anti-drug crusade for campaign season. I have too many goddamn fires to put out already.

I pause, she moans again and tries to turn her head to look at me, but I grab her by the hair and direct her gaze back straight forward. She'll get a story to tell her friends, and my body gets the release it so desperately needs after the last few days.

She's a pretty thing, from Nebraska or somewhere cold. I don't remember. We didn't talk much. I was on my way to my penthouse when she caught my gaze. She smiled, and I bought her a drink. Ten minutes later, here we are in the men's bathroom, with my men outside to ensure our privacy by keeping anybody out.

My clothes are still on, her skirt is hiked up over her hips, and only the important parts are exposed. After the first few intimate encounters after my... accident, I got tired of women asking about my scars. Always the same questions. *What happened? Did it hurt? You must have been in so much pain*. For the past ten years, I made sure none of them saw me naked. The current position is my favorite. I have a firm hold of her hips, setting the rules and tempo.

She's close now. Good. I'm ready for my release, too.

But I'm nothing but a gentleman when it comes to women. Ladies first. Always. Then a quick goodbye.

"Ah, that was so good. My toes are still curling." She comes, and after a moment's reprieve, she gives me a cute look from under her eyelashes while putting her skirt back in place.

I toss the condom in the trash and wash up. "I'm glad."

"Well... call me?" she asks as I gently, but firmly, lead her out of the washroom.

"Sure, give your number to one of my men. Thanks, sweetheart."

By the time I hit the elevator that goes to my penthouse, I've all but forgotten about her.

An hour later, I stand in my office overlooking the Strip. My phone lies on the glass desk, screen dark until duty summons. I rest my palm on it, heartbeat steady, ready. At 1:42 a.m., Enzo's name blinks across the display. Two words:

ENZO:

We're ready.

The private elevator hums again, and I watch the city slide past the glass. Below, the casino floor swirls like a living tide. Hope and desperation walking hand-in-hand, the tourists flitting between stages, every slot machine yowling for attention, every blackjack table promising an upset. The hopeful believe they can turn their luck. They don't know the house is a living predator, me.

When the doors hiss open to the casino floor, the air thickens. Women turn, their hair tossing in practiced arcs, perfume meeting ozone. The smiles are always too bright, too eager, and never for nothing. They want to be noticed on their own terms or ignored entirely, but I am the one who writes the rules here. Men notice next, some stiffen, others shrink, a few keep their heads down and try not to look at all. My crew falls in around me as if conjured by magic. Six men, all in black, hands empty but never unarmed. They walk in a diamond formation, not because I ordered it, but because years of violence have trained them to move as a single organism.

Outside, three SUVs idle in the turnaround, engines rumbling. One door is already open for me, a courtesy. Luc, the driver, stands at parade rest, eyes scanning the lot for threats or paparazzi. The valet line is long, even this late at night. Customers will wait until my bulletproof Escalade pulls out. I'm halfway to the car when I see it, a flash of red hair in the crowd.

My heart hits my ribs with an old, unkind impact. For a second, the casino floor drops away, and I am twenty-two again, chasing a girl down Fremont Street, my hand closing around hers as she laughs, wild, reckless, impossible. The night had tasted like freedom back then. Like I could outrun consequences if I wanted to.

The woman in the lobby has the same fire-red hair, the same wicked curve at the corner of her mouth. But her laughter is wrong. Too sharp. Too fast. A hysterical staccato instead of something real.

Wrong woman.

Wrong era.

I look again, but now she's just a tourist, drunk, and propped up by her friends as they all move back toward the casino. Nothing special. I exhale slowly and get into the car. *Focus*. That girl from Fremont was my first lesson. The one I paid for in blood and silence. Never rely on a woman. Never trust a woman. Never confuse softness with safety.

Women cry. They plead. They promise. They make you believe mercy is possible, and then they teach you how expensive that belief can be. I learned that once.

I don't repeat lessons.

I don't do mercy anymore.

I don't do trust.

I do loyalty.

Earned the hard way.

And I sure as hell don't give women second chances.

I bury the thought where it belongs, drown it in a glass of bourbon, and lock it away with the others, sealed tight in the part of my mind that never opens. Because ghosts are dangerous, and she is the most dangerous one of all.

The interior of the SUV is cold, dark, and quiet. Luc drives fast but smooth, weaving through the city's arteries toward the east side. My crew says nothing. They all know the rules: no chatter, no questions, not unless I ask. I look out the window and watch the Strip fade, replaced by strip malls and tract houses, then the blank faces of tilt-up warehouses. No one's tailing us; I'd spot it if they were. I check my phone. No new messages.

The crematorium is twenty minutes out, buried in a wasteland of storage units, weed dispensaries, and wholesale furniture outlets. The building is deliberately anonymous: tan stucco, flat roof, no windows on the street side. I bought it two years ago, cash, and hired a crew that only speaks when spoken to. The sign out front reads *Nevada Memorial Services*, but we call it *The Oven*. Sometimes you need to erase a body from the earth; sometimes you just need to remind a man that you can.

Inside, the air is hot and chemical, the tang of disinfectant riding up the nose until it almost burns. The floors gleam. The walls are white as bone. Every surface is so clean it's unnerving, as if death itself must be sanitized before proceeding.

Enzo waits in the prep room, standing at attention. He's six-two and built like he could bench-press a Harley, but his movements are all discipline, never a wasted motion. His face is heavily disfigured by scars that put the fear of God into the most courageous man.

Which isn't Norm, who is lying on a steel slab, wrists and ankles cinched with leather restraints. He's balding, nondescript, one of those men who could disappear in a crowd, which is why I hired him in the first place. Now, his face is a rictus of fear, jaw clenched, eyes dry and darting. He's past denial, past bargaining, and well into the final stage: animal panic. Under the stretcher, another body waits, zipped and tagged. The legal one, the one scheduled for tonight's burn.

The gurney rails lead directly into the open mouth of the cremation oven. The heat is palpable, even from the doorway. Enzo opens a bottle of Stagg from my personal reserve, pours bourbon into a glass, and hands it to me.

I take a sip, and it burns going down. Good. Pain should mean something. I circle the table, shoes clicking on tile, and watch Norm the way a cat watches a mouse that's already caught.

Norm makes a show of tugging at his restraints, his head rotates as his eyes follow me, panicked. "What is this? Why am I here? Massimo, please, I don't—I don't—"

I raise a hand. The silence buries him.

"You laced the coke. Why?"

He blinks. Once, twice. He looks confused, like he's lost the thread of the conversation. "No," he pleads. "No, I didn't. I wouldn't. I swear to God." He looks to Enzo, desperate for an ally, but finds only ice.

"Six people are dead," I fill him in. "One of them a headliner. The news cycle is already on fire. The coke traced to you. If you didn't cut it, who did?"

Norm shakes his head, frantic. "I don't—I mean, it's the same stuff I always get. Same source. Same run. I even tried it like I'm supposed to."

Enzo steps forward. He's always preferred action to words. "How the fuck could you not notice? That's your job. You run the girls; you watch the product. If people die, you're supposed to call us before the press does."

"I didn't know!" Norm's voice goes up, cracks, splinters. "Nobody said anything. Nobody OD'd, not even the girls. I swear, you can check."

Enzo looks at me, a silent question. I nod. The gurney shifts forward, closer to the heat. Norm shrieks as his shoes start to melt, the rubber bubbling and peeling. One of my men steps forward and puts out the nascent fire crawling up Norm's pant leg, then steps back just as quickly. Even mercy is efficient in my house.

Norm is crying now, snot and spit pooling under his chin. "I didn't know. I swear. Please. Please, Massimo. You know me."

"Where did you get the coke?" I ask again, quieter this time.

Norm is shaking so hard the gurney rattles. "Same guy as always. Del."

I believe him. Del was the first man I questioned a few hours ago. But it doesn't matter who or what I believe. I finish my bourbon and set the glass down on the steel counter.

"Who had access to your place?" Enzo's voice is a rasp, the edge of a blade pressed against the moment.

Norm's jaw works as if he's chewing on nails. Bloodless lips open and close. He's already in shock, pain signals short-circuiting, but fear is the greater anesthetic. "My girlfriend," his voice sounds parched. "Ann. But she wouldn't—she doesn't—she never touches my work. She wouldn't even know what to—"

I flick my eyes to Enzo. There's a protocol here, a choreography. This isn't about the answer so much as the way it's delivered. The rhythm of the thing. Enzo's hands are folded, loose, but his thumbs are white at the knuckle, a tell. He's impatient. Norm is wasting our time.

The gurney slides forward, the steel wheels whispering over the tile with a sound that is somehow more chilling than a gunshot. Heat pours from the open oven in waves thick as oil; the flesh on Norm's calves is already pink, mottling with the first stains of burn. He jerks, tries to jackknife upright, but the restraints hold. The table slews a quarter inch to the left. Enzo's foot on the pedal brings it back into place. I could almost laugh at the neatness of it; the way the man's terror makes the room feel cleaner, sharper, as if fear itself is a disinfectant purifying the air.

Norm howls. It's a real, animal sound, scraping from somewhere deeper than words. Instantly, the white floor is splattered with tears, streaked with mucus, and covered with piss. I've seen men face death with less noise; I've seen them greet it as a favor, a relief, sweet—or at least necessary. But this is not that kind of death. This is the kind that makes people remember you, the kind that puts a rusty hook in the back of memory and drags it out for years. I let the noise fill the room. It's a good warning for the staff. The front clerk is probably already updating her résumé.

"I didn't betray you!" Norm yelps. The words are barbed wire, tangled, and raw. "I swear, Massimo! On my life! I never would!" He's cowering into the restraints, his spine arched so hard it looks ready to snap. For a moment, I consider the possibility: What if he *is* telling the truth? But then, truth is less important than effect. The story isn't about what happened; it's about what will happen next. Order is maintained not by justice, but by consequence.

Enzo pours me another bourbon, and I let it wash down my throat. Let the words hang in the chemical air.

"You don't need to betray me to destroy my business," I explain to Norm. "You fucked up the moment you stopped paying attention."

Norm goes silent. Broken, maybe. Or calculating. I walk to the slab, set my glass down, and lean so my face is inches from his. I want him to see my eyes, to understand the nature of the thing that's about to unmake him. I want him to know it's not personal; it never is.

"I'm sorry," he wails. "I'm so sorry, Massimo. I'll make it right. Please. I'll do anything."

Anything is already happening. The gurney slides again, and now his shins are blackening. I breathe through my mouth. Never let the body's last betrayals get to you. That's where sentiment lives.

I look at Enzo. "Do it."

Enzo presses the button, and the oven's jaws close around the slab. The hiss is monstrous, a sound that wants to be remembered, but the soundproofing does its job. The room goes oddly still, like the moment after a verdict has been read.

I pour myself another drink and watch the thin thread of smoke curl from the vent, dissolving into the recirculated air. Outside, Vegas lights up the horizon.

Inside, order is restored.

"Let's go find Ann," I say, opening a small hatch inside the oven door. Heat and a sickly smell engulf me. I finish the drink and toss the empty glass into the fire, where two bodies are already turning to ash.

It's an easy disposal. Clean. No questions asked. No one weighs ashes, and even if they did, the desert is generous with its silence. Ashes to ashes, dust to dust, as they say. Enzo is on the phone before the glass even settles, giving the drivers the new address.

It's going to be a long night.

We're out of the Oven in under two minutes, the smell of rendered fat clinging to my suit like a reminder. People think the violence is the hard part.

It isn't. The hard part is deciding. Once the decision is made, everything else is just mechanics.

Outside, the air is cooler. Dawn is beginning to carve a sickle of light along the mountains, thin and sharp. Our convoy waits, engines humming, as men already move through checklists on their phones. I slide into the Escalade, and we're rolling before the door even shuts.

"The address Enzo texted?" Luc asks, eyes flicking to the rearview, waiting for my nod.

We pass a billboard for a celebrity magician, his smile blown up to the size of a house, promising miracles to anyone stupid enough to believe in them. I wonder what it would take to make *him* disappear.

Enzo scrolls through contacts beside me, expression flat, calculating. He's already three steps ahead. I let him work. My mind drifts to the business at hand. I don't torture women.

Not because I'm kind. Because they break too easily. Tears come fast. Voices crack. Promises spill out before the pain even has time to teach them anything useful. There's no measure in it. No test. No dignity. And tears—God, I hate tears. They do something to my stomach. Open me up. Leave me exposed.

Somewhere behind my ribs, a memory shifts: green eyes, blood on tile, a sobbing sound from a woman who refused to be broken.

I shove it back where it belongs. Ghosts are dangerous. The woman who taught me that is the most dangerous one of all.

The city wakes up around us, not in the way the brochures promise, but in the hour of janitors and service calls, when the party ends, and the real business begins.

And tonight, business is far from finished.

A few hours later...

My phone rings at 5:43 in the morning. I feel the vibration before I hear the sound—a reptile's warning in the dark—my father's number pulses on the screen. He never calls me this early unless something is on fire, or about to be. I answer, propping myself up in the half-light, the air in my chest already coiling tightly.

"Jenna," he says instead of *good morning*, no warmth, no ramp, just the sound of my name as a pointed reminder. "Have you seen the news?"

I blink myself awake faster than I thought possible. "No." There's an undercurrent in my voice I hope he doesn't hear. "What happened?"

"A performer died overnight. Cocaine. Fentanyl contamination, most likely." A deliberate pause follows, just long enough for me to conjure the right amount of horror. "Very public. Very ugly."

I don't need to ask if it's someone important; he wouldn't care unless it moved the needle. A nobody dies, and it's a tragedy. A celebrity dies, and it's legislation. I fumble for my tablet, quickly scrolling to the headline. Being my father's PR director means I don't get the luxury of shock. I get angles. Talking points. Damage control. A job I never wanted. I studied English; I wanted to become a writer. But when Carter's accident happened and the sympathy wave hit, my father decided I was more useful beside him than anywhere else. I became the voice behind his speeches. The Collector of his crusades. The one who turns bodies into bills and grief into polling numbers. The grieving wife narrative tested well. So here I am.

The news is a slab of raw meat:

VEGAS ICON FOUND DEAD — SUSPECTED DRUG OVERDOSE

My stomach knots itself into something new and permanent.

"We need to capitalize on this." I can feel my father's glee through the phone, and I anticipate the words forming, neat and trimmed, already rehearsed in his mind. "Remind people what we stand for. Human trafficking was just the beginning. Nevada needs stronger drug legislation. We can make this a state issue."

I picture the latest campaign photos: his smile sharpened for the cameras, the handshake grip just short of a threat, the clean sweep of a landslide win. The banners with the word FAMILY in a font larger than his own name. He'd spent election night on camera, spinning a narrative about innocence and danger, about protecting people who couldn't protect themselves.

"What do you need from me?" I ask. My voice is small,

but that's the way he likes it. He wants a daughter he can keep in line, one far removed from the rebellious kid he brought to heel ten years ago. But for my son, Amauri, I'd go to hell and back if I had to. And again. He's worth every day, every hour, every minute of the debacle that has become my life.

"A statement. Something warm. Personal. You're good at that. The grieving wife angle still plays well."

It's not a question. It's an assignment. I close my eyes, trying to will the room into a different shape. I stare at Amauri's picture, and like always, the image of him grinning into the camera makes it all worthwhile.

"I'm not—" I start, but he cuts me off like a surgeon cauterizing a wound.

"I know," he says. "But perception matters. We'll have Carter echo it at the office today. Optics."

Optics. The word tastes like a pill I can't swallow, leaving a bitter shell dissolving on my tongue. He loves me playing the role of the devout wife. The loyal mother. The woman standing beside America's wounded golden boy. Carter in his wheelchair. Brave. Resilient. Beaten down by life but still smiling.

My father stands just behind him, hand on his shoulder, the champion of the common man. The man who understands tragedy because it happened in his own family. It polls beautifully. Every photo says the same thing: *I get you. I get your suffering. I am one of you.*

Voters eat it up. Carter loves it too. Loves the reverence. The sympathy. The way people look at him like he conquered something instead of surviving it. I play my part because I have to. Because in this family, safety is conditional. And I have a son to keep alive.

"Send me a draft," I resign myself, while my hands curl into fists under the covers.

"Good girl." He hangs up before I can respond, and I'm left staring at the screen, the headline boring into my brain like a screw.

COCAINE. VEGAS. DEAD.

This will play right into my father's newest bill about stopping drugs from coming into Nevada. With the success of his human trafficking bill earlier this year and this new one, he's on the road to becoming president. The only people who hate him are the criminals, but Dad has guards who shield him from that threat.

Something ugly and familiar creeps up my spine, a sense of a memory, of a time I've tried to layer over with better images. Before I can finish the thought, Carter yells from the other bedroom. "Jenna! I need you. Now."

I close my eyes and count to five. My bedroom is the only territory I ever managed to claim in this house, the only border he's ever respected. It's a truce, a partition of sorts: he sleeps in one room, and I in another. We move along parallel lines, never touching, rarely intersecting, maintaining the illusion of autonomy. As if I had any in the first place. As if my father wasn't the one who forced me into this charade of a marriage.

Carter is never cruel in ways people can see. He is careful about that. His bitterness leaks out in silences, in absences, in the way he makes me feel like I'm not important enough to notice. But the moment he needs me, he drags me back into his orbit.

I force myself out of bed and pad down the hall. Carter lies exactly where he always does, propped up like a miniature dictator: pillows fluffed, arms crossed, the unmistakable lines of rage already forming around his jaw. The wheelchair waits beside him, the silent witness to every one of our mornings.

He has an aide for everything—a therapist, an assistant, a helper—but he insists I do this part, claiming it's too private for anyone but his wife to handle. No matter whether I was a willing bride or not. Carter has an extraordinary talent for rewriting reality until it flatters him. In his version of our story, he's the injured hero. The betrayed man. The one who suffered most. Our marriage isn't something I was maneuvered into; it's something he salvaged. Noble. Necessary. In his mind, he *saved* me and Amauri. He believes that. Completely.

He's the kind of man who could drive drunk, plow into someone crossing the street, and wake up furious at the victim. *What the hell was he doing out at that hour? Why was he in my way? Now I'm the one paying for it.*

That's Carter. First, he sold me. Then he bought me back. And somehow, in his mind, he's still the one who was wronged. "You took forever," he snaps.

"I just woke up."

"Don't get smart with me." His gaze flicks to the digital clock, numbers ticking like a bomb; there is not a trace left of the charming boy I once thought myself in love with. "I have to be at the office by eight."

The office. The one my father built for him. The one with the windows and the oxygen-pumped air and the rows of expensive, meaningless awards. The one place Carter has been important since injury decimated his football career. He's my father's accessory. Even before the accident, he wanted Carter to be his son-in-law. He was malleable, easy-going, and America's Sweetheart. After the tackle that paralyzed him, his importance only grew in my father's mind. Carter had become the tragic story. A young man's life dream, abruptly halted; a man who should have given up, but who rose to the occasion. A hero not just on the football field, but all the way around. A role model for any young man. A message to everyone: *You can overcome anything.*

I change his urine bag without comment, my hands moving as if guided by muscle memory. He does not thank me. He never does.

"Careful," he hisses. "Jesus, Jenna, do you want to humiliate me?"

I clench my jaw, focus on the mechanics: clamp, unhook, reattach, rinse. "I'm being careful."

"Try harder."

I help him into his shirt and trousers. Up top, his body is still lean and hard, but below, there are no bulging muscles; they atrophied years ago. There is no gratitude in his face, only the momentary pleasure of being obeyed.

"You see the news?" he asks, the question a test.

"Yes."

He grins, teeth too white, too perfect. "Good timing, huh? Dad's gonna milk that for all it's worth."

Dad. Sometimes it feels like Preston Kingsley is more Carter's father than mine.

Like my father adopted him the moment he was broken and no longer of use to his own. Dad always wanted a son. Someone polished. Ambitious. Public-facing. Someone he could shape. Carter needed a patron, especially after the accident. My father needed a symbol. They found each other.

Carter worships him for it. For the office. The platform. The relevance he would've lost without him. And Dad loves having a wounded hero at his side, a living monument to perseverance. It plays well in photographs.

As for Carter's father? I like to think he knew what kind of man Carter really was and turned from him. He never had much of a presence in Carter's life to begin with.

"You know," he says, "people love a crusade. The more tragic, the better. Drugs. Trafficking. All that puritan bullshit." His smile gets meaner. "Almost makes you forget where the real money comes from."

My hands freeze.

He notices.

"Don't," he says, softer now, the edge of threat replaced by something almost gentle. "Don't pretend you don't know how this works."

I straighten up, feel the bones in my back clicking into place.

"You can finish getting dressed," I tell him.

He laughs. "Still playing the saint, huh? You know what happens to saints in this family, Jenna. They burn."

The threat is old, but it lands the same way every time. *Toe the line, Jenna, or we'll take Amauri from you.*

"You should be grateful," he continues, his tone almost affectionate. "I didn't have to claim that kid. I could've let your daddy clean it up some other way."

It's a story he tells himself that he did me a *kindness.* That I *owe* him for the life he's given *my* son, for every day we're allowed to pretend.

"He's my son," I say instead.

"Who's alive because of me," Carter agrees, as if it's obvious. "Don't forget that."

As if I ever could. As if he or father would ever let me forget it. So I finish dressing him, help him into the chair, and roll him toward the hallway. I do not cry. I do not scream. The tears are stored somewhere else, in a different body, a different life. A life that started and ended ten years ago. After I found out that I was pregnant; after the father of the baby left without ever looking back.

Carter never eats breakfast at the house, so I roll him straight outside, where Jason—his driver, private assistant, best friend, or whatever else Carter needs him to be that day—is already waiting for him to load him into the shiny Mercedes SUV. A gift from my dad for a job well done a year ago. They will stop at a fast-food place, or maybe a strip club, and eat on the way to the office. None of my business. Good riddance for the day.

As for me, I make my way into the kitchen to find the only person who makes all this worthwhile. Amauri is already there. He likes to wake up before me. He says it makes him feel grown-up. He sits at the counter, legs dangling, a bowl of cereal already half gone. He glances up at me, and his face is all light, no shadow, no apprehension, just the open trust of a child who has never had to doubt his place in the world. A confidence I will do anything in this world to protect, even by staying married to the man who sold me for playtime.

"Did you sleep good, Mummy?"

Mummy. He told me once I looked like the hot lady in *The Mummy*.

He didn't realize the movie was about a wrapped-up corpse, not someone's mother. He just heard the word *mummy* and decided it must be about me. I never had the heart to correct him. I know what he means; that's all that matters. The sound of it softens things inside me that I thought were fossilized.

"Yes," I say. "Did you?"

He nods, spooning cereal with the careful intensity of a scientist. "I dreamed I was a pirate."

Of course you did. I lean down and kiss his head. He smells like toothpaste and something bright, like summer sun on a new notebook. If I could bottle it, I'd wear it for armor.

"Mummy," he says, pushing his hair off his forehead, "is my hair ever going to be blond like Dad's?"

The question nearly undoes me. Carter's hair is blond, always perfectly styled. But Amauri's isn't. It's dark, heavy, with a stubborn wave that defies every brush and comb.

He doesn't know how close he comes, every day, to the edge of a different truth.

I smile, the way I've taught myself to. "It's genetics, honey. Your grandpa had dark hair when he was young."

"And my eyes?" He studies me with a seriousness that makes him look older than his almost ten years. "Dad's eyes are blue. Yours are green."

I want to tell him he's made of every secret I've ever buried. That before politics and wheelchairs and carefully staged photographs, there was a different life. A different man. A different future.

I want to tell him the truth about the night everything split in two. That he was born from a love I wasn't allowed to keep. That there was a man once who would have burned cities for him, or so I thought. That the world rearranged itself in one night, and I've been living in the wreckage ever since.

Not here, not now, not ever.

"Maybe one of our ancestors was a dark pirate a long time ago," I tease. "Ask your grandma. She knows all the stories."

He laughs, and the tension in my chest loosens just a little. He moves on to talk about his day, about the spelling test, and the kid in his class who says bad words. He is a good kid. He fills all the cracks in my life without even knowing.

I watch him, this boy who is more mine than anyone else's in the world, and for a moment, I almost believe in the lie of the family we've built. But the moment passes, and the truth seeps in like cold water: Amauri is already more of a man than Carter ever was.

How he gets himself ready without complaint. How he watches, listens, and adapts, calibrating his responses to the moods that animate our house, the silences and sharpness that form our family grammar. The way his eyes sweep a room before he enters, as if scanning for a threat or an opportunity, some evolutionary leftover from a lineage that's always had to watch its back. I see it. I see him learning every day how to move through a world that isn't built for the truth of who he is. I see it, and I love him harder for it.

I don't think about the lie holding all of this together. How every smile and bedtime story and lunchbox love note is mortared with silence, with what I don't say, with what I swear I'll never say. I don't think about the DNA, the inheritance, the man whose shadow brushes the edge of my son's face every time he laughs or wrinkles his little face in concentration.

I watch him walk toward his backpack, his posture a study in small confidence, straight-backed, steady, chin up but not arrogant, not yet. There's a grace to it, something practiced, even though no one taught him. He's already his own person, already in on the cosmic joke that everyone else is faking it too, that the world is mostly bluster and bluff. He smiles at me over his shoulder, and for a terrifying second, I wonder what will happen when Massimo finally notices him. What if he comes looking? What if Amauri, by just existing, calls him back across the years, across the secrets I've hidden in plain sight?

He opens his backpack, then looks up at me, the way he does every morning, and says, "You forgot your coffee again."

I blink. He's right, a full mug, still steaming, sits untouched on the counter. I cross the kitchen, ruffle his hair—he ducks, grinning—and pretend it was all part of the plan. "What would I do without you?" I ask.

"Probably die," he deadpans, but then he laughs, because he knows my father would never let that happen. For him, the world is still a good place.

I work very hard to keep it that way. I curate the illusion: the loving grandfather, the devoted father, the tidy family narrative that fits neatly into school forms and Christmas cards. Though I don't know how much longer I'll be able to.

He's getting older. Smarter. Observant in ways children aren't supposed to be yet. One day, he'll notice that the new teddy bear wasn't from Dad. It was from me. That Grandpa insists on photos not because he wants memories, but because he wants material. That Carter's smile only appears when a camera does.

He already senses the distance. I've seen it in the way he watches other fathers in the park, how they kneel, how they laugh, how they throw footballs until their shoulders ache. One day, he'll understand that Carter doesn't refuse to throw the ball because he can't. He refuses because he won't.

He'll figure out that missing the school play wasn't about illness. Or meetings. Or responsibility. It was about interest. Unless I called the press. Unless I dangled optics.

Which I have done. I'm not proud of it. But if a photographer means his father shows up and claps, I will make the call.

I just can't always make it work. The other parents already resent the extra cameras in the hallway. The principal smiles too tightly when a news van pulls up. I can't manufacture love. I can only stage attendance. And one day, he'll know the difference. "I'll be ready in ten," I tell Amauri, squinting at the clock. "Homework check. No excuses."

"Yes, Mummy," he says solemnly, already pulling out a notebook like it's a contract he intends to honor. His sense of responsibility is relentless; that, at least, is something he has in common with Carter. He's trying so hard to catch his *father's* attention, it hurts my heart every time.

I bolt upstairs, coffee in one hand, phone in the other, already thinking two hours ahead. I have precisely twelve minutes to make myself presentable. The shower is hot and brutal, punishment and reward all at once. I don't bother with my hair; there's no time. The mirror is fogged over, mercifully, so I don't have to see myself while I scrub. The routine is so second-nature that I can do it without thinking: moisturizer, a swipe of concealer under the eyes, mascara thick enough to create a shield, lipstick a shade too bold for the office, but I need the armor today. But when I put the deodorant on, I pause. Underneath my bra, the black-and-red lines of my tattoo poke out. I still.

I haven't gone down this particular rabbit hole in years.

Gently, I touch the black ink first, then the red. My

finger traces over the letter *F* for forever, the only one visible right now. The skull and the rose. Somewhere here in Vegas is a man wearing the other part of this tattoo. Does he think of me sometimes when he looks at it, too? Or has he forgotten me completely? I blink back a tear. He's the only person in the whole world who knows about this tattoo. The only one who matters. *Ten years*, I think. *Ten years, and the pain is still as fresh as the day* he *left me.*

Resolutely, I pull a blouse over my head, dressing for war. A pencil skirt comes next. Then high heels that force me to walk with purpose. I slip my wedding ring on last, a ritual I refuse to skip. It's a reminder. A reminder of all the lies my life has become.

In the hallway, I yell, "Purse... keys... I'm forgetting something... phone... what am I forgetting?" In the doorway, I stop, theatrical in my stance, and pretend to slap my forehead. "Oh, right. There should be a kid here somewhere."

Amauri comes around the corner, giggling, clutching his notebook and lunchbox. The joke is old, repeated almost daily, but he's still young enough to enjoy it, to believe that repetition is proof of love. He hands me my keys with a flourish, as if he's the only thing keeping this operation afloat. Maybe he is.

He slings his backpack over one shoulder with the easy athleticism of a kid already too big for his own body. "I'm ready."

Of course you are. You always are.

The drive to school is mercifully quiet. It's just Amauri and me. I try to savor it, every traffic light and crosswalk, every stretch of silence. He hums along to the radio; the sound is barely audible, more vibration than music, like the way cats purr when they're happy. I glance over at him; his profile is soft in the morning light. He looks nothing like me, not really. He looks exactly like an echo of someone else, someone who left a stamp on his DNA and then vanished.

The radio host clears his throat and switches gears, and I hit the brakes. My hands go white on the steering wheel. "—and in other news, casino magnate and philanthropist Massimo Manetti—"

"Mummy!" Amauri yelps, grabbing the door handle, panic in his voice.

"I'm sorry," I gasp, heart thumping so hard I can taste it. "Sorry, honey. I just—traffic. Someone cut me off." I try to laugh the lie off, but my mouth is dry.

Manetti.

Of course.

He's always on the news. Always in the background, a hum of gold and arrogance and something colder. Casinos, charities, city projects, his name stamped on everything that matters in this town. There are whispers of organized crime, but no one says it out loud. Not anymore. He's cleaned up, they say. Legitimate, they say. The American Dream. How am I supposed to forget him when his name is everywhere? When Vegas says it like a prayer and a warning all at once?

I force myself to breathe, to unclench my jaw, to keep my eyes on the road. Smile. Drive.

"Are we late?" Amauri asks.

"No," the word is but a hiss of air, before I add more gently, "We're fine. You'll be early, actually."

He nods, reassured, and goes back to his humming. Oh, to be a kid and be able to forget. I drop him off in the car line, kiss his cheek, and make him promise to text when he gets inside. I watch until he disappears through the doors, his backpack bobbing with every step. He's safe. He's out of sight. Only then do I let myself fall apart a little, hands shaking as I grip the wheel. When a car behind me honks, I take in a deep breath and drive to the office, my mind stuck in a loop. The radio keeps talking, filling the car with *his* name, *his* reach, *his* power. It's like there's no air in the city that isn't touched by him.

And all I can think is: *Fucking Manetti.*

As if forgetting him was ever an option. Even if it weren't for Amauri.

The office is on the twenty-third floor of a glass tower that overlooks the strip. On the elevator up, I catch my reflection in the gilt trim, lipstick intact, eyes steady, all signs of panic erased. I step out into the corridor, my heels echoing off the marble, and I make it almost to my office without incident, but at the last second, I see Carter through the glass wall of the conference room, already holding court, his expression filled with the same good old boy charm that made me fall for him. He spots me instantly and waves. Keeping up appearances.

I take a breath, smooth my skirt, and walk past, head held high, ready to play my part. Because if there is one thing my father and Carter and every man like Manetti has ever taught me, it's how to armor up and walk into the fire like you own the place.

The following meetings are a blur of talking points, media strategies, and not-so-veiled threats. Carter wants me to draft a press release by noon. Dad wants a personal statement ready for the evening news cycle. There's already a rumor that Manetti is hosting a gala in honor of the dead performer, and the optics are brutal. It's a chessboard of grief and leverage, and who can look the most moral for the cameras.

I nod, take notes, and promise the impossible. When the meeting adjourns, I slip away to the bathroom, lock myself in a stall, and give myself my sixty seconds of Massimo. That's what I allow myself when things go really, really bad. I think of Massimo and me ten years ago, before he just up and left. Sometimes I think about that night we met. The night I killed a man. It helps to remember that I was brought low before and rose. Granted, I had Massimo then, but I like to think I would have come out on top even if he hadn't shown up when he did. Sometimes I think of him and me in bed. Of how good his hands felt on me. His kisses, oh God, his kisses. No man has ever kissed me the way he did. So deep and full of confidence and possession. That's where I go now. I close my eyes, take a deep breath, and let myself fall into his imaginary arms. *I love you, he whispers in his deep, dark voice. I love you too, I reply, meaning it with every part of my soul. His arms are around me, strong and steady, holding me in a way that lets me know the world around us could fall apart, and nothing would happen to me because I have him. I breathe in his strength and feel it surrounding me like a heavy coat. We're at the Shark Reef aquarium, surrounded by filtered, bluish light, walking through an underwater glass tunnel. Big and small fish swim all around us, but I only have eyes for the man by my side. The most handsome man I've ever seen. The man who saved me in more ways than one. I still can't believe he calls me his. It seems as surreal as the under-the-sea illusion in the middle of the desert. And yet, here we are.*

I can almost smell the air from ten years ago. Just like I can almost feel Massimos' hand around mine.

The timer beeps. My sixty seconds are up. I fix my makeup, wash my hands, and get back to work.

The next day...

The Sovereign never sleeps. Its heart beats in time with the city, a pulse that thrums inside my own chest, making me as restless as the machine I've built. The casino is alive at all hours, all seasons, all states of the soul. No matter who you are or where you come from, if you step onto my floor, you belong to me for as long as I want you. You might not know it, but that's the only thing keeping you safe.

I had the Sovereign constructed for a single purpose: to be unbreakable and unbreachable, as inevitable as gravity. But even the best machine is only as good as the people who run it, and so every corridor, every secret camera, every reinforced door, and silent elevator is an argument against human error. I have spent years learning that no matter how you engineer a system, it's the flesh that betrays you first.

I step through the private entrance, the one guests never see, and take the elevator that requires both a thumbprint and a code that is changed daily. The world outside the elevator shrinks as I rise: the gaming floor, oxygenated and cacophonous, fades into nothing, replaced by soundproofed silence and the kingly monotony of carpet meant to last generations. By the time I reach the top, the only thing that matters is what's on the other side of the door.

The private conference room was modeled on a Roman triclinium, minus the louche decadence. Instead of couches, there are leather chairs. Instead of mosaics, there's a view: the entire valley, the Strip curling below like a neon necklace. The windows are triple-layered, bomb-resistant, and cleaned every morning before dawn by a man who never takes the same route to work twice. If you know where to look, you can see the penthouses where most of the major players sleep, the rooftop pools where their wives and mistresses get sunburned 'til noon, the little alleyways and garages where their foot soldiers and capos negotiate the price of betrayal.

These are not the things outsiders notice. But I notice everything.

I pause just outside the conference room, listening through the open door, just for the pleasure of knowing these men have already forgotten that nothing in the Sovereign belongs to them, not even their secrets.

"...I'm telling you, if I had that kind of luck, I'd start believing in God again," someone says, and the laughter that follows is sharp and genuine. I know that voice. Damiano Ferrante: raised in Summerlin, first arrested at twelve, a man who never met a rule he couldn't bend or break. His family is big in Vegas and disowned him when he turned eighteen; now he's a billionaire in his own right, buying out his family's businesses one by one. He's good with numbers, even better with people, but what sets him apart is the way he enjoys every minute. Most men in this business develop a death wish or a self-preservation instinct. Damiano managed both.

"Luck?" another voice scoffs. Alessio Vitali is the only man I've ever seen crush someone's windpipe with one hand and keep talking like nothing happened. His father is a low-level enforcer with the Black Mesa Reapers, an organized MC in Vegas that's overdue for a reckoning. Alessio's mother left when he was eight.

Raised by a volatile alcoholic with a permanent chip on his shoulder, Alessio learned early that emotions were liabilities. He buried his until there was nothing left to show. He dealt coke before he could legally drive. Killed before he could legally vote. Fear doesn't touch him, because the people who should have loved him already walked away.

Except us. We didn't. And that changes things.

"You don't have luck," he continues. "You have blunt force trauma and a short attention span."

"That's still better than being boring," Damiano fires back, never missing a beat.

"Gentlemen," a third voice intervenes, this one steady, the only one that matters if things get strange. Gabriel D'Amato: my consigliere, the only person in the world who can say exactly what he thinks to my face and survive. He's built like a swimmer, probably because he spends more time in the pool than at the gym. His voice is dry. "If either of you had luck, you wouldn't still be alive."

That earns another round of laughter, with an edge that's more respect than amusement.

The last presence in the room is silent, but I know he's there. He is always the last presence in every room, the one everyone else orbits around but never quite approaches. Enzo Carbone. Old enough to be any of our fathers, and sometimes he plays the role, only he's the kind of father who makes you dig your own grave as a lesson in character. In the old days, Enzo ran muscle. Now he's the last word on discipline. There is no sentimentality in him, only a kind of minimalist violence that cleans up after itself.

I watch their silhouettes through the glass, the way they lean in and out of the light. I know who will speak next, who will laugh, who will look away. We are all roughly the same age, except Enzo. Thirty-something, but with mileage. We grew up in parallel, tracing the same city blocks, learning the same lessons, breaking the same commandments. We knew each other long before money or blood or power made the distinctions permanent. Before bloodlines became weapons instead of bonds. Before the world decided some of us would be kings and some would be casualties.

I don't let myself get nostalgic. Nostalgia is for men who think the past won't come hunting.

I push open the door, and everything stops.

Not a chair moves, not a voice stirs. The air in here is always chilled to sixty-eight, and it's always a few degrees colder once I enter. They look up in unison, four sets of eyes tracking me the way predators track something that might be carrying a weapon. Or a treat. Enzo's expression is unreadable, but the other three show it: a flicker of tension, the tiny recalibrations, the way their hands go from idle to alert. It's an old dance, and everyone knows the steps.

Alessio elbows Gabriel, muttering, "Stalking again?" in a voice pitched just above a whisper. It's meant to irritate, and it does.

Gabriel's phone is out, casting a ghostly light onto the table; images reflect on the glass walls, changing too slowly for anything but obsession.

Damiano leans over and squints. "You serious right now?"

Gabriel doesn't look up. "Just tracking movement patterns."

"Bullshit," says Alessio, and this time the word hangs, inviting a fight.

Gabriel finally glances up, unbothered. "She's married."

"Yeah, that should be your first clue to leave her the fuck alone," Damiano points out, grinning.

"I'm not bothering her. I'm just making sure she's okay." Gabriel's voice is sharper now, something brittle at the edges. The way it gets before someone gets killed. I've never heard it before because of a woman.

"Right," Alessio says. "Like when you sent the Gucci purse a few weeks ago?"

Gabriel's jaw sets.

"Or when you paid for her car repair?" Damiano chimes in, as if it's a game and he's winning. I knew about the purse, but this one is new. "What did you tell her this time? *Congrats, you won a mystery contest? One you didn't know you entered?"*

Alessio laughs loudly. "You know, sooner or later, she's gonna run out of those. Or her husband will start to ask questions. That'll be fun."

Gabriel says nothing. He makes a show of turning the phone off, the screen going black with a decisive flick of his thumb.

"Fine," he snaps. "Fine."

He glares at the table, and by extension, all of us.

I've never had to worry about Gabe, but ever since he's become obsessed with *that* woman, he hasn't been himself. It started a few weeks ago, and it has only gotten worse. He's never been possessive of a woman or stalker-ish. This is new territory for him and me, and I'd better keep an eye on him. He has *that* look. The one I recognize that stared back at me in the mirror ten years ago. We might need to have a chat.

Enzo watches this with the calm serenity of a father, proud of his sons. In another life, we might have been exactly that. He lifts his glass and almost smiles, almost. Enzo doesn't really drink or smile. Not the way the rest of us do. But he appreciates the ritual. That's how you spot the old-school men: they understand that everything is theater, and that theater is also everything.

I don't know if he's ever enjoyed a single minute of his life. He wasn't built for pleasure. He was built for endurance. For decades, that endurance was tested. His wife ran out on him with their children when they were still small. No note. No goodbye. No trail. And no matter how much power Enzo amassed, no matter how wide his reach stretched, he never found her.

Not until recently.

One of his daughters, grown now, contacted a DNA testing company of all things, chasing answers, not knowing what she was setting in motion.

That was the stone at the top of the hill. Now it's rolling. And for the first time since I've known him, Enzo has been smiling. With reason.

"Relax," I tell Gabriel, realizing he's close to snapping. Unexplainably, this woman has gotten under his skin. "If you're going to do something stupid, at least do it clean." Gabriel's head snaps toward me. "Just shoot the husband," I continue. "Comfort the widow. Simple."

The words hang in the air for one, two, three seconds. It is not a joke.

Gabriel holds my gaze, and something in his face fractures. "I can't hurt her," he says, the words quiet but unmistakable. "She loves him."

I study him. Really look. I used to think the only thing that mattered was loyalty, but now I know better. The only thing that matters is restraint. Men like us, we're all born with a flaw—some to violence, some to greed, some to the need to be adored—but the one that gets you killed is wanting what you're not allowed.

"No woman gets that close," I declare. Not to men like us. Not without consequences. A memory flickers across my mind. Brief, uninvited, dangerous. A girl's hair stuck to my palm with blood, the smell of copper and perfume. I crush the memory before it gets any further. There's no room for sentiment here.

Alessio gives a low whistle. "You hear that, Gabe? Massimo just diagnosed you."

Gabriel doesn't blink. But he huffs a sigh that lets us know he's finished debating his private life. Just to be sure we understand, he asks, "Okay, so why are we here?"

I let the silence after the question expand, testing the air for any trace of disrespect, any hint that the men assembled here have forgotten where they are or who I am. But they know. We've all bled for this city, for this organization, and for each other. They were the men beside me when my blood turned against me. The ones who chose me anyway. I trust them to the extent that anyone trusts men like us, which is to say: until one of us stops breathing.

Enzo sets his glass down. The click is a trigger, resetting every set of eyes to him. "Because someone cut our coke, and six people died," he informs them.

The dull, echoing pain of it unspools through the room, invisible but absolute. Killings happen all the time in Vegas, overdoses, disappearances, bodies in the desert, or, if you're really unlucky, the Clark County coroner's freezer. But this? This is a violation. Not the deaths themselves, but the method.

Alessio curses under his breath, a creative string of Italian vowels that would have made my grandmother proud. "That's not a warning shot. That's a billboard."

"One of them was famous enough to get the fucking

press all over it," I add, my tone as flat and cold as the marble beneath my shoes.

Enzo meets my gaze with the wordless communication of soldiers: I have your back, and if you die, I'll kill the man who made it happen. Damiano leans back in his chair. His face is built for grinning, all sharp lines and cocky Mediterranean angles, but even he can't find anything funny about this. "So, what? Someone wants to make us look like chumps?"

"Someone wants us to burn," I say. "Not just me. All of us. They want us on the defensive. They want to see if we'll eat our own."

There's a moment of collective consideration, the kind that in other settings might pass for a prayer.

Enzo inhales. "The coke came from Del and Norm. Neither of them cut it."

Gabriel folds his arms and closes his eyes for a millisecond, then opens them razor-sharp. "Del was a pro. He wasn't stupid enough to contaminate supply, not even if he was paid twice what he's worth."

"And Norm," Alessio offers, "was a careless little shit, but he wasn't disloyal."

"Not until he roasted at eighteen hundred degrees," Damiano jokes. It's tasteless, but that's Damiano: he only ever jokes when he wants to draw blood.

The air in the room shifts. My mouth opens, but before I can speak, Enzo puts a hand on my forearm. I let him. If there's one man on this planet who can touch me in front of my own crew and not lose a finger, it's him.

"Easy," he warns. "We need clear heads."

He's right. I exhale once, then twice.

Damiano shrugs; the motion is all bones and bravado. "What? I'm just saying, that's one way to guarantee brand consistency." The others don't laugh, but I notice the smirks.

Enzo leans in, keeping his voice low and surgical. "This isn't a comedy hour."

"Ann cut the product," I throw out before this conversation deteriorates any further.

"Who the fuck is Ann?" Alessio asks, looking from one of us to the next as if the answer might be written on the back of Enzo's hand.

"Norm's girlfriend," Enzo supplies, no judgment in his tone, only the fatalist's acceptance that every man's worst undoing is a woman somewhere, sooner or later.

I correct him, "Ex. Briefly. She admitted it right before the last shovel of dirt hit."

Damiano's cocky half-smile vanishes. "She say why?"

"She got paid," I answer. "Cash. Hand-to-hand. No name, no face."

"Of course," Alessio mutters. It's always fucking cash, always someone getting paid to take out the middleman, or, in this case, poison the whole fucking supply chain.

"That's the problem," I meet his gaze, "they didn't contaminate the entire supply, only random doses."

Alessio isn't the only one cursing about that piece of information. It implies anything but randomness. Somebody wants to destroy our reputation.

"Any description?" Damiano is already reaching for his

tablet, his phone, whatever electronic leash he prefers today.

Enzo gives it to him. "Mexican-looking. That's all she gave us."

Alessio chews on that, working his jaw hard from side to side. "Cartels have been sniffing around. Wouldn't be the first time they tried to dip a toe."

Enzo shakes his head. "Doesn't feel like them."

I meet his gaze, and in that instant, we're back in a basement in Henderson, five years ago, the air thick with bleach and hornet-nest panic as we negotiated with a cartel rep who had more tattoos than skin. The cartel doesn't do subtle. They don't hide behind women, and they sure as fuck don't leave loose threads.

"No," I say. "It doesn't."

Gabriel—who has been patient, almost saintly, in the background—finally speaks. "They want us chasing the wrong people," he thinks out loud, as if reading my mind.

"Exactly," I reply, and it's almost a relief to hear him confirm it.

There are two kinds of men in this life: the ones who crave chaos, and the ones who surf its crest and never let it wet their shoes. The first group dies, eventually. The second group is the reason Vegas still exists.

These men? They surf. So do I.

"Someone wants fallout," Gabriel continues, eyes never leaving mine.

"Or wanted us chasing shadows," Damiano adds.

"Someone cut our coke to make us look weak, to force our hand," I summarize for the record. "They want bodies.

They want spectacle. They want to see if pressure makes us fracture." I let my gaze move around the table. "If the heat gets high enough, men start asking who failed. Who let it happen. Who's talking. They're betting we'll turn inward. That we'll start hunting each other instead of them."

Alessio, ever the pragmatist, cracks his knuckles and grins. "Are we going to disappoint them, Boss?"

I look around the table, at the faces that have passed through so much pain and so much money that the difference between the two is barely discernible. "No," I say. "We're going to salt the fucking earth with their blood."

Enzo pours himself another drink, but it's not a toast. It's the chemical necessity of a man who knows the score. "What's the play?"

"Damiano," I order, "pull every camera feed you can. Casinos, clubs, streets, back channels. I want every frame of Ann's movement for the last month."

He nods, already flicking through his phone. "I'll find her. And whoever paid her."

"Alessio," I order, "street level. Quiet questions. I want to know who's talking, who's spreading rumors, who's suddenly got more cash than sense. Any new faces, any old enemies crawling back out of the strip."

He smirks, the implication clear. "I'll listen with my fists."

It's Gabe's turn. "I want you on counter-surveillance. Anyone circling politics, law, media, anyone who profits from us fighting ourselves. Track every story, every leak. I want to know who benefits, and I want to know it before I read about it on the news."

Gabriel sits up straighter, as if the assignment is a benediction. "Already on it." He nods.

"And keep your personal life clean," I add, because it's not just a joke, and he knows it.

Gabe grins, sharp and tired. "Always do."

Enzo looks at me. "What about you?"

I look out the window, down at the river of neon and lost souls streaming through the Strip. Vegas runs because I say so. It's time to remind the city who's still in charge. "I'll take care of Manetti business; you take care of the rest."

There's a pause as the men process the end of the meeting, a ritual as old as the city itself. They don't get up, not yet. They wait for the signal.

I give it. A single nod.

The room breathes again.

Enzo stands first, not out of disrespect, but because he's earned it. He collects his glass, wipes the condensation away with the edge of a monogrammed handkerchief, and turns to Damiano. "Start with the west end. Use the new system. Less chance of a leak."

Damiano nods, already pulling up feeds. He moves with the wiry energy of a man who lives for the chase, a man who would be a serial killer in another life if not for a healthy respect for hierarchy and cash flow.

THAT SAME NIGHT...

It's almost dark when it happens. Tension has been in the air all evening, splinters of it working into the seams of every conversation. I'm rinsing a glass at the sink, half-listening to Jason, who stayed later than usual tonight, and Carter in the adjacent room. They're arguing about politics, but not really; what they're really doing is trying to one-up each other, as men do, about who knows more about the undercurrents, who's been reading the better sources, who's less naive. Carter, whose voice never drops below a certain volume even when he tries, has already managed to say *let's be realistic* twice in the past five minutes. Jason, whose smile always means he's angry, is goading him on, playing the part of devil's advocate with all the subtlety of a sledgehammer.

Amauri is at the small table with his math books, his elbows on the wood, feet swinging under his chair in time with whatever internal song he's composing. His tongue pokes out the side of his mouth, his brow furrowed with the grave importance only a fourth grader can bring to three-digit addition. He is the only one immune to the friction static in the room; he is the only one truly present, drawing pencil lightning bolts on the margins of his homework and humming to himself.

I'm watching the darkness fill the backyard through the window. There is a chill in the air, a subtle drop in pressure. I tell myself it's the weather, but there is a part of me that has known for hours that something is coming. It's the way the wind has gone still, how the birds have vanished from the powerlines.

The glass in my hand is still cool from the drink it held a few minutes ago. I hold it under the tap, watching the thin stream of water run over my skin, and I wonder how many times I've done this exact thing in my life. Rinsed a glass. Stood at the sink. Listened to my husband argue with his friend, caretaker, driver, therapist— whatever role the man filling the silence happens to occupy today.

How many times have I tried to perform normal? How often have I told myself that if I just keep moving—keep cleaning, keep smiling, keep managing—I won't hear the voice inside me screaming to get out. To take Amauri and run. To disappear so completely that no one can ever find us again.

My father can't force me to have an abortion anymore. Amauri is here now. He's ten years old. He exists. He breathes. He laughs. I could file for divorce like every other woman in the world. Only... I'm not every other woman, am I?

To the world, I wouldn't be just leaving a husband. I'd be abandoning a—the word flashes through my mind, sharp and cruel—a *broken man.* The shame hits immediately. Hot and choking. I swallow it down. A man in a wheelchair. A survivor. A hero. A symbol. The public adores Carter. They see the tragedy, not the cruelty. The accident that stole his future. The golden boy brought low. They don't see the way he uses his broken body like a weapon. They don't see how carefully he wields it. They certainly don't see the man who sold me to his coach when I was eighteen.

The man who said *call me* and walked away, leaving me behind to be raped. The man who spat *whore* at me when I finally broke it off.

If I leave now, my father will take his side.

Not because he loves Carter, but because he loves optics. Because Carter is useful. Because a loyal, paralyzed son-in-law looks better than a divorced daughter with inconvenient truths.

They would frame it as a concern. For Carter. For Amauri. They would talk about stability. About routine. About what's best for the child.

And they would try to take my son.

Not that either of them truly wants him, no, he's leverage, a symbol. Plain and simple. And because he's easier to control than I am. I could survive the press turning on me. I know exactly how it would go. After all, I'm the one who would orchestrate it if the roles were reversed. The headlines, the whispers, the think pieces. The righteous outrage. The woman who left the disabled hero. The ungrateful bitch.

I could live with being hated.

But Amauri couldn't.

How does a boy grow up when his classmates' parents whisper? When his mother's name is dragged through the mud, her face paraded across screens and papers? When kids repeat things they don't understand?

I know what a witch hunt looks like. I design them for a living. I'm the PR shield for my father and my husband. I know how stories are shaped. How truths are buried. How narratives are weaponized until there's nothing left but what people want to believe.

So I stay.

I stay in a loveless marriage with a man I despise. I swallow my anger. I manage appearances. I survive on scraps of peace. Because at least this way, I have Amauri. Until I can find a way to protect him, I'm trapped. I've managed so far, and I sure as hell will keep on doing so.

Suddenly, without warning, the power goes out. It doesn't flicker. It doesn't hesitate. One second there is light, and the next there is nothing but darkness. The sudden absence of light is so complete it seems to pull all the air out of the house. The refrigerator goes quiet. The A/C's hum dies. The clatter of Carter's voice is cut off mid-argument, and for half a second, nobody makes a sound.

Then the world erupts.

First comes the crash, no, not a crash, an explosion. The back door is obliterated inward, glass and wood splinters all at once. The shockwave throws me hard against the counter, the glass in my hand shatters, and water and blood mingle on my palm. I'm only dimly aware of the pain; the adrenaline is already pounding through my pulse, roaring, telling me to move, run, do something. But I am rooted by the sight of them: men, half a dozen at least, without masks, but all the more terrifying for it. No hesitation. No warning. They move as one, rifles up, bodies low and fast and technical, the kind of movement that comes from training, not instinct.

Jason is already moving. I see him in silhouette, throwing himself between Amauri and the chaos with a single, desperate leap. Amauri is screaming, but the shots drown everything out. The first round is so loud it feels like it cracks the bones inside my head. The muzzle flash lights the room in freeze-frame horror: Jason's face twisted, eyes wide, arms outstretched. He goes down immediately, the force of it knocking him back into the table, his body crumpling like a rag doll. Amauri falls with him, a tangle of limbs, and for a split second, I think maybe he's shielded, maybe he's okay, please God let him be okay.

The men are on top of them. They swarm like jackals, one grabbing Amauri by the collar—Amauri flailing, he's alive! Thank God—another man shoots a single round into Jason's head. They shout commands in a language I don't understand, but the violence is universal. I try to scream. I try to run. But a hand—a huge, gloved hand—snatches my ponytail from behind and pulls me off my feet. They scramble for purchase, kicking wildly, but the air is gone, and all I can taste is fear.

Carter is in the living room, his wheelchair wedged behind the couch. For a moment, I see him try to wheel himself out of the room, his eyes wild, jaw clenched. He throws something—a remote, a mug, whatever he could reach—at the men. It bounces harmlessly off one of their backs. The man turns and, without breaking stride, slams the wheelchair over, sending Carter sprawling. I hear the dull thud of his body on the floor, the air punched out of his lungs.

I taste copper, and it takes me a second to realize it's my own blood. I twist, I flail, but the hand in my hair is unbreakable. Another arm wraps around my waist, pinning my arms, and I'm dragged backward, heels against the marble. They haul me to the ground, face-first, pressing my cheek into the cold tile. Tears and blood blur my vision of the kitchen; my eyes land on the math homework scattered like confetti.

Amauri returns to my sight, tiny and shrieking, arms windmilling as he fights the man holding him. He screams for me, the word *Mummy* stretching into something raw and animal. He kicks, he bites, and for a moment I'm filled with pride—my child, my little fighter—but then the man clamps a hand over his mouth, and the pride curdles to terror.

I lose time, maybe minutes, maybe seconds. I don't know. There is a high buzz in my ears, a static that drowns out everything else. I'm vaguely aware of Carter being dragged out from under his wheelchair. I try to turn my head to see Amauri, but a boot presses down on the side of my face, grinding me into the ground.

They are talking to each other, rapid and clipped. One yells into a radio. Another flips Carter over with his boot and pats him down, efficient and dispassionate. They're not here for money. Not here for things. They're here for us. That realization is a hundredfold more terrifying.

Blindly, I reach out, and my hand finds the handle of a cast-iron pan that must have fallen to the floor. My fingers curl around it, slick with blood, and I swing it upward with everything left in me. A sense of déjà vu overcomes me—another time, another man—making me sick to my stomach, but there is no time to think about the past. The pan connects with the side of his head, and he lets go. Instantly, I'm on my feet, rushing forward straight for the intruder holding Amauri. Taking him off balance, his grip on my son loosens, and Amauri scrambles away, crawling toward me, but a third man catches him by the ankle and yanks him back so hard his sneakers slip right off his feet. He screams again, high and keening.

That's when Carter shouts. "You motherfuckers!" His voice is ragged, furious, and so loud in the silence that even the invaders pause. He's upright again, knuckles bloodless on the arms of his chair; his whole body is trembling. "Let me go! Do you have any idea who I am?"

The man nearest Carter smirks, orders two of the guys to lift Carter up, then punches him—hard—in the gut. Carter doubles over, held up on his useless legs by two men.

A fifth man grabs Amauri, who is still struggling, and throws him over his shoulder like luggage. I lash out again, this time with my fists, but I'm lifted into the air, a hand covers my mouth and nose until I can't breathe, until my vision goes white at the edges. I come back to myself in the grip of a man carrying me like a sack of flour. The world tilts and spins, and from above me, I can hear the whir of a helicopter. Everything still feels so surreal to me, like I'm dreaming, or maybe caught up in an action movie, like this isn't really happening to me. To us. But then I hear Amauri scream again, see him being carried into the hovering helicopter. A helicopter! In the middle of our yard! I struggle again, remembering bits and pieces of a few self-defense classes I took over the years, twisting hard in the man's grip, I somehow manage to drive my knee into his solar plexus. His legs buckle, and his grip loosens around me. Enough for me to twist some more and fall to the ground. The problem is, I can't seem to stop falling. I keep rolling. The ravine!

The backyard slopes sharply here by the terrace toward the ravine, and I'm tumbling down it. My body is no longer my own. And then there is pain. The world flips end over end. More pain. So much pain. A rock hits me in the hips, and my palm tries to grab on to something, only for it to be a cactus. My elbow hits a boulder, and for good measure, my knee decides it wants to make its acquaintance, too.

When my body finally comes to a stop, it takes me a moment to gather my wits. Above, the men scream in what I now realize is Spanish. I recognize the cadence of the language. Most of it is drowned out by the sound of the helicopter. And then I see it. I see it rising into the air, and I scream again. So loud, I nearly break my vocal cords. Amauri! They have Amauri. The helicopter lifts, a monstrous insect rising above the trees, its searchlights sweep across the ravine floor where I lie broken. Shots crack the night. It's only luck that keeps me from being riddled with bullets. I almost wish one would put me out of my misery.

When I finally open my eyes, the silence is absolute. And my son is gone.

Later that same night...

Blood dries fast under club lights. That's the first lie people believe about violence: that it lingers, that it stains, that it leaves some kind of mark that a mop and a rag can't erase. But the truth is, even the worst of it can be buffed away in minutes as if nothing ever happened, unless you know where, or how, to look.

By the time I arrive, the floor's already been mopped, the broken glass swept, the music back to its loud, predatory pulse. Neon breathes over polished chrome and tables, undulating across black tile as if the club was exhaling. The only thing that lingers is the chemical tang of bleach beneath cologne and spilled cocktails.

The manager stands rigid near the bar; his tie loosened, sweat painting a dark V down the center of his pressed shirt. He doesn't speak until I look at him directly.

"Two shots," he fills me in quietly, his words are rushed by apprehension. "Near the VIP stairs." He's trembling. He should be, the clusterfuck happened under his nose. In *my* club.

"Dead?" I ask.

"One. The other critical."

I nod and move past him. The smell is still there, more than just bleach, the copper tang of blood, the oily note of gunpowder, the sour adrenaline of panic. Even under the scrub of industrial cleaner, it's unmistakable. I follow it up the stairs, past a velvet rope and security men who stiffen into statues the instant I pass.

This is my club. My pride, my flagship, my fortress.

Neutral ground.

Someone violated it anyway.

Enzo joins me at the landing, Bello Capelli right behind him, both men cut from the same cloth, impeccable, disciplined, lethal. I read the situation in the way they stand: Enzo's jacket is unbuttoned, his hand never strays far from his holster; Bello's eyes track every movement in the room, cataloguing threats, calculating trajectories.

"This wasn't random," Enzo mutters, his jaw working a piece of gum to pulp. "The shooter knew the layout. The cameras were looped for ninety seconds."

"Inside help." I rotate my head to make the stiffness there less painful.

"Or borrowed access," Bello offers in a flat voice. He's Enzo's second-in-command, and I trust both of them implicitly. They've both been with me since the beginning. Bello had been my eyes and ears while I was out after the *accident*. "Either way, they were not amateurs."

We stop at the exact spot where it happened. Unless someone pointed it out, you'd never know. Fresh paint is already drying on the wall, the bullet hole perfectly patched, and a row of new glasses lines the shelf. That's how we do things here: not just clean, but immaculate, the illusion instantly restored.

Bello's sacrifice was more than just manpower; he'd burned favors to keep the cops out of this. Called in markers that will take years to repay. I make a mental note: that's loyalty, and it'll need to be returned.

"Who was the target?"

Enzo hesitates, just long enough to betray the weight of the answer. "Mia Pascale is the casualty. Her bodyguard's the critical."

"Fuck," I mutter.

Mia Pascale is a minor celebrity, a *social influencer*, the kind of woman with her own perfume line and a rabid horde of followers. The kind of woman who makes headlines if she so much as sneezes in public. *Just like the entertainer* runs through my head, and I file that thought under *later*.

My phone vibrates, the name on the screen makes my scalp tighten: Damiano.

"Is this important?" Already sensing it will be.

"Not sure yet." Damiano's voice is a little too level. "But I'm pulling chatter off the police bands and private lines. Something big went down tonight."

Enzo and Bello lean in, their attention shifting as if guided by an invisible string.

"Go on," I command.

"There was a home invasion in Summerlin," Damiano continues. "High-end neighborhood. A bodyguard is dead. The wife escaped, but the husband and kid were taken."

Nothing that public happens in my city without my knowledge, much less my permission.

"Names?" Enzo asks.

"They're keeping it quiet so far," Damiano says. "But the husband—he's political, state level."

The phrase people use about feeling like someone walked over your grave finally makes sense to me. I feel it now; it's like an electric chill in my molars. Someone's digging up something I worked a decade to bury.

"When?" I ask.

"About an hour ago. Same window as the club hit."

Two public strikes. Two violations. Different signatures. Same intent.

"This isn't noise," Enzo wagers.

"No," I agree. "It's a message."

"And it's sloppy," I add.

Enzo shifts his weight.

"They want us chasing smoke," I continue. "Cartels don't work like this. Locals don't either. This is someone who understands optics, not territory."

"Political," Bello guesses.

"Exactly."

"My screen's lighting up," Damiano says. "Sending you the address."

My phone buzzes with a string of digits: the Summerlin house, a sprawling estate in a gated community with twenty-four-hour surveillance and private patrols.

"Anything on the wife?" Bello asks.

"She's in PR," Damiano says. "High-level. Does comms for the husband and her father."

That stops me cold.

"Who's her father?" I keep my tone too careful as every nerve inside me tenses, and every muscle stiffens.

Damiano hesitates, but only for effect. He likes to make things dramatic. "A state senator."

Enzo snorts in impatience. "Name?"

"Preston Kingsley."

The name detonates in my inner ear. I don't show it. I've spent too long training my face to betray nothing, not even to myself. But something old and ugly stirs in my chest, a memory with teeth. Ghosts that don't want to stay hidden.

"Wait," Damiano says, "there's more."

He whistles, low, like a man witnessing his own funeral. "The husband is Carter Whitford."

The name has barbed wire wrapped around it. A symbol. A hero. The only man I ever failed to have killed. The one man who deserved it more than any other. If he could be called a man.

Damiano keeps talking, oblivious to my churning gut, the low burning fury that's simmering underneath my skin like a volcano about to erupt. "The wife is Jenna Whitford. And the kid they took is Amauri."

Son.

I never knew she had a son. Good for her.

I haven't spoken to her, haven't so much as Googled her in ten years. When her face flashes on a newsfeed, I change the channel. When someone mentions her name,

I walk away. That kind of distance doesn't happen by accident. It's built. Maintained. Enforced. Necessary.

Enzo is watching me, waiting for orders, reminding me that I don't have time for ghosts. Not now. Not ever. Whatever she was—whatever we were—it's dead. Buried where it belongs. And I have no intention of digging it back up.

"Get me everything," I press out, glad my voice is even. "Every dollar, every link. Who backs Kingsley. Who wants Whitford gone? Who profits from new drug laws?"

"What about Kingsley?" Enzo asks, with the caution of someone defusing a bomb, he knows me well enough to sense that I'm holding something back. Rightly so. I am. But this ghost I don't want to resurrect. Not ever. God have mercy on her if she ever so much as shows herself in my orbit. I'd love nothing better than to wrap my hands around her tantalizing neck and squeeze the life out of her lying body.

I force my mind back to Kingsley. The New York family owns him. Enzo has ties there. Ties that might come in handy.

"Later," I cut him off with a flick of the hand.

For a moment, we all just stand there, the club noise rolling up from the floor below, laughter and music and the illusion of safety. But what I hear is the clock starting, counting down to whatever comes next.

Someone just reached into my past and pulled out a ghost.

Deliberate?

LATER THAT NIGHT...

The world keeps tilting. Every time the limo hits a bump, pain explodes somewhere new: my ribs, my ankle, my head. I'm wrapped in a blanket that smells old and has stains on it that no amount of Clorox will ever get out. There's still blood on my hands. Dried now. Dark. I keep rubbing at it like it might come off if I try hard enough.

Dad sits across from me, his jaw clenched, his phone pressed to his ear until the moment the door shuts and the car pulls away from the police station.

Then he rounds on me. "What the fuck were you thinking, Jenna?"

I stare at him. The words don't land right away. They bounce around in my skull, looking for somewhere to stick.

"The police?" he snaps. "Are you out of your mind?"

I laugh. It comes out wrong, too high, too loud, almost hysterical. "Oh—oh geez, Dad, I don't know," I choke. "Maybe because my husband and my son were kidnapped?"

His eyes flick, sharp. Calculating.

"Lower your voice."

My son.

"Amauri," I sob, folding in on myself as the name tears out of my chest. "They took Amauri."

My body shakes violently now. I can't stop it. Every breath hurts. Every movement sends cactus spines deeper into my skin. Tiny needles still prick my arms, my legs, my scalp. I must look insane, bloody, torn, feral.

"They told me I had to go to the hospital," I manage between gasps. "They said—said my head—"

"You're not going to the hospital," Dad says flatly. "Not yet."

I stare at him again.

"Not yet?" My voice cracks. "Dad, I was beaten. I fell—I rolled down a—"

"I know," he says. "And it's unfortunate. But right now, a hospital creates records. Records create questions."

"My son is gone," I scream. "What questions could possibly be worse than that?"

He exhales slowly, the way he does before a press conference.

"Jenna," his voice softens, which is worse. "Tell me exactly what happened. Who did this?"

"I don't know," I cry. "I don't know who did this or why. They just came in. Guns. They killed Jason. They took Carter. They took Amauri. I fought—I tried—I—"

My hands shake uncontrollably. I hold them up like proof.

"They dragged him away," I whisper. "He was screaming for me. Dad, he was screaming for me."

Silence fills the car, thick and suffocating.

Finally, Dad speaks. "This was not random." I look at him, wild-eyed. Of course, this wasn't *random*! "I mean politically," he clarifies.

That word hits harder than any blow.

"They knew where you lived," he continues. "They knew who to take. They didn't kill you."

"They tried," I choke.

"But they didn't," he doubles down. "Which means you were part of the objective."

I stare at him, horrified.

"What does that even mean?"

"It means," his fingers rub his chin carefully, "that this was about leverage."

My chest tightens until I can barely breathe.

"Who would do this?" I whisper. "Why?"

He doesn't answer right away. Outside the tinted windows, Las Vegas blurs past, neon and darkness and distance.

"Jenna," he says finally, "you need to understand something."

I look at him, my father, the man who taught me how narratives work, how truths are shaped, how damage is controlled.

"This does not go public," he decides firmly. "Not yet. Not the way you think. You do not speak to anyone without me. You do not post anything. You do not make pleas."

"My son is missing," I scream. "What am I supposed to do?"

"You're supposed to let me handle it," he replies calmly.

The limo turns onto his street. His mansion looms ahead, gated and guarded, a fortress dressed up as safety. I curl inward, shaking, blood and cactus spines and terror pressed into my skin.

"They called the cops," I whisper again, like it's a crime. "The neighbors called the cops."

The limo pulls up at the grand entrance, and Dad shoots me his *keep your mouth shut* look, one I know all too well. Silently, I follow him up the large marble stairs to the big iron gate-like doors. They pull open as if by invisible hands, but it's only Jeffrey, one of Dad's servants.

"Sir," he nods at Dad. "Lady Jenna."

Lady Jenna! He's always called me that, like I'm some kind of nobility. He was imported from England to serve Dad's ego. I'm not in the mood, but I force a tired smile at him, "Jeffrey."

He looks like he wants to say something, but Dad pulls me straight into his office. The scent of leather, wood polish, and something sharper and cleaner meant to signal control envelopes me, bringing up memories, none of them good. I pull the blanket I have still wrapped around me tighter, unfeeling of its roughness. The door shuts behind us with a heavy click that feels final, like the world outside has been sealed off. Spent, I sink onto the edge of one of the chairs, my legs finally giving out. The pain catches up all at once; my ankle is throbbing, my ribs are screaming, and dried blood clings to my skin when I move. Hundreds, no thousands of sharp, spikey cactus spines are embedded seemingly in every part of my skin and scalp.

Dad doesn't sit. He goes straight to his desk, already reaching for the phone.

"Marianne," he orders when the line connects to his live-in assistant. "I need you in here. Now."

It's the middle of the night, or early in the morning, however you want to look at it, and he has no regard for waking his assistant. He doesn't even wait for a response before hanging up. I hug myself. My teeth are chattering, even though I'm not cold. Without a word, Dad pours two scotches and holds one out to me. Numb, I chuck it down. Grateful for anything to distract me, even momentarily, from the pain in my heart.

Marianne Hale appears less than a minute later. She must have been asleep—she's wearing a bathrobe, her hair hastily pulled back—but she still looks professional somehow. Tablet already in hand. Bare feet silent on the hardwood. When you are a live assistant with a sitting senator long enough, you learn not to ask *why*. Only *how fast*.

Her expression is carefully neutral until her eyes land on me. Then—just for a flicker—something human breaks through. "Jesus," she murmurs. "Jenna—"

"Focus," Dad snaps.

She straightens immediately.

"There's been an incident," he continues briskly. "Home invasion. One fatality. Two abductions. We are going to dictate the story on this."

"No," I croak. My voice sounds wrong, shredded. "No, I don't think so."

Dad finally looks at me. Really looks. Then he shakes his head once, decisive. "Find someone else to handle PR on this."

Marianne hesitates. "Sir—"

"She's in no condition," he cuts in. "And I won't have her anywhere near the press."

Marianne nods, already making notes. "Understood."

"Take care of the police," Dad continues. "Keep everything compartmentalized. And for fuck's sake, keep the press out of it."

"Yes, Senator."

Marianne pauses, glances at me again, softer this time. "I'll make sure you're taken care of," she promises quietly. As if I would ever trust her.

I don't answer. She leaves as efficiently as she arrived, the door closing behind her with another final click.

Dad exhales, runs a hand over his face, then finally sits across from me.

"All right," he tries his hardest to be calm and measured. But underneath it runs a current of calculation. "From the beginning."

I shake my head weakly. "I already told the police—"

"I'm not the police," he interrupts. "And this is not a deposition."

I swallow hard.

"I need to know exactly what you saw," he explains more patiently than I would have thought him capable of.

"What you heard. How many men? What they said. What they didn't say."

My hands start trembling again.

"They killed Jason," I whisper. "He stepped in front of Amauri, and they just—shot him. Like it was nothing." Dad doesn't react. "They took Carter. They tipped his chair, dragged him—" I go on, even as my voice is breaking. "Dad, they dragged Amauri. He was screaming. For me. I fought them. I bit one of them. I—I rolled down the hill. I thought I was going to die."

I start crying again, ugly and unstoppable. Dad watches me with an intensity that feels like scrutiny, not comfort.

"Did they say any names?" he asks.

"No."

"Threats?"

"No."

"Demands?"

I shake my head. "I don't know, I couldn't understand them."

Silence stretches between us.

Finally, Dad leans back, steepling his fingers. "That's a problem."

My stomach drops. "What do you mean?"

"It means," he says, "that this isn't about money."

A chill crawls up my spine.

"Then what is it about?" I whisper.

Dad looks at me for a long moment. And for the first time since the limo, I see something like uncertainty flicker behind his eyes.

"That," he says slowly, "is what we're going to find out."

"I think they were speaking Spanish," I remember. Talking hurts. I must have hurt my throat pretty badly when I screamed Amauri's name.

Dad's eyes sharpen.

"There was a helicopter. They came with it." I recall the moment it took off. The moment my heart broke into a thousand pieces when I realized Amauri was on it.

That does it for him.

He pulls his phone out again, fingers moving fast, turning away from me as if I've ceased to exist.

"I need flight registers," he demands without greeting or apology to whoever is on the other end. "Private, charter, med-evac, everything. Radar readings too..." A pause, "No, do not flag it. And absolutely do not let this go public."

I push myself up from the chair, pain screaming in protest. "What does that mean? Dad?"

He lifts a hand without looking at me. *Wait.*

I don't.

"I'm right here," I cry. "They took my family. You don't get to shut me out."

He turns back to me at last, phone still in his hand.

"We need to establish patterns," he sounds like he's just trying to pacify me. "That's all."

"Patterns of what?" I demand. "Who would do this? Why?"

Before he can answer, his phone dings with an incoming message. I see it before he can turn it away. Carter. Strapped into a helicopter seat, face pale, jaw clenched. A harness cutting across his chest. And beside him—

"Amauri," I whisper.

My son's eyes are huge, terrified, too bright in the harsh cabin light. His hands are clenched in his lap like he's trying very hard not to cry. Like he's being brave because he thinks he has to be.

A sound rips out of me. I don't recognize it as my own.

Dad's phone rings again, this time with an incoming call. When he answers, a heavily accented voice announces, "You know the drill."

Then the other party hangs up.

Drill? I stare at my dad, my vision tunneling.

"What drill?" I choke. "What are they talking about? What do they want?"

"I need to think." He turns away again, pacing now, keeping his voice low, controlled. I know that voice. It's his threat assessment tone. The one he uses when the threat is not directed at him and he thinks it will be useful. My heart starts pounding so hard it feels like it might tear free.

"Dad," I call. "Dad."

He doesn't answer. I step into his path, grabbing his arm despite the pain shooting up my side. My fingers dig into his sleeve like it's the only solid thing left in the world.

"You know who took them," I accuse. It isn't a question anymore. "You know."

He looks down at my hand like it's an inconvenience, something interrupting his train of thought. Then he looks at my face. He doesn't deny it. He cups my cheeks suddenly, firm hands on both sides of my face, forcing me to look at him.

"Jenna," he says. "Jenna. I need you to be reasonable right now."

Reasonable.

"Can you do that for Daddy?"

My legs give out. I don't remember deciding to sit, but the couch catches me as my knees buckle. The room tilts again, slower this time, like the world is sinking instead of spinning. He presses a glass into my hands. Scotch. Again. My fingers barely close around it when another thin cactus spine seems to push further in, invisible but impossible to ignore.

I shake my head. "Amauri—"

"Drink," he pushes gently. "You need it."

I don't argue. I swallow. It burns all the way down, and still, it doesn't touch the cold spreading through my chest.

"The Cartels," the way he says it sounds as if he's discussing zoning permits. "They weren't pleased with my latest proposal."

The words take a second to register. My mind scrambles, searching through half-heard conversations and headlines and dinners where I sat quietly while he talked shop.

"Your... proposal," I whisper.

"The one about the drugs," he explains, a hint of impatience mingles in his tone. His gaze is chiding, *you should know that*, it says. "Cocaine. Distribution. Penalties. Enforcement."

Images collide in my head. The bill earlier this year. The one he'd championed so proudly. The one that shut down trafficking pipelines nationwide. The applause. The interviews. The praise.

And then the next step.

He was going to try it out in Nevada first this time. Statewide. It was supposed to be a model. Because the drug money doesn't stop at cartels. It goes up. Into campaigns. Into committees. The police. If he cleans up Nevada, he becomes untouchable. A hero. Maybe more than that.

My stomach drops.

"They took my family," the words taste like blood, "to use them as leverage against you."

He nods gravely. "Yes."

The room goes very quiet.

"They want you to back off," I continue, my voice now eerily calm. "To kill the bill. Or stall it. Or make concessions."

"Yes."

"And if you don't?" The dread rises higher, restricting my breath.

He hesitates just long enough. "Then they'll remind me of what's at stake." My heart breaks open, but he doesn't notice; he keeps talking. "They made a mistake," Dad says calmly. "A critical one."

I stare at him, my ears are ringing, but I don't dare to allow hope to ignite. I know him too well. Know already where this is going, but I don't want to put it into a thought or words yet. "What mistake?"

"They didn't take *you*."

The words don't make sense at first. I shake my head slightly, like that might dislodge whatever he's trying to say. "I don't understand."

He smiles. Not wide. Not cruel. Just... satisfied.

"Don't you see?" He's nearly triumphant. "This is brilliant."

My stomach turns sour.

"We spin it," he continues, already pacing now, warming to the idea. "Senator's son-in-law and grandson kidnapped. Daughter barely escapes with her life. A home invasion. A martyr narrative." He gestures vaguely at me, as if I'm a prop. "The public will eat this up."

I feel like I'm going to be sick.

"What happens to Amauri?" I whisper. He doesn't answer immediately. "And Carter?" I add, because I *am* still, inexplicably, a decent person. "What happens to Carter?"

He shrugs. That small, dismissive movement lands harder than any blow.

"Don't you see?" he repeats, almost impatient now. "Up until now, Amauri was a ticking time bomb."

My heart stutters. "A what?"

He sighs, as if explaining something obvious to a child. "Manetti's bastard son."

The room tilts. For a second, everything goes distant and hollow, like I'm underwater. *He knows*. The realization blooms slowly, sickeningly. He's known. Somehow. Always. I never told him. I never said it out loud. But of course, he knows. Of course, he knows that Amauri is

Massimo's son. That thought barely has time to register before a dark premonition claws its way up my throat.

"What are you saying?" I ask, my entire body shaking. "That a dead grandson and son-in-law are worth more to you than if they're alive?"

He rubs his hands together. Actually rubs them.

"The Cartels played this beautifully," he beams. "Forced my hand without ever having to ask."

I stare at him. This man. My father. I've always known he was a bastard. Cold. Ambitious. Ruthless.

But this?

"He is your grandson," I remind him, and now my voice is breaking completely. "Amauri is *your* grandson."

He shrugs. "A bastard," he replies flatly.

The word drops into the room like a corpse. The air goes still. Heavy. Suffocating. I feel something tear loose inside my chest, something final and irreversible. My son is not a symbol. Not leverage. Not collateral damage.

He is a little boy who calls me *Mummy*. Who makes his own lunch. Who believes pirates are real and the world is mostly safe.

I stand up.

Slowly.

Every part of me is shaking, but my voice is suddenly very clear. "You will not sacrifice my child."

My dad's expression hardens. "Jenna—"

"No," I interrupt. "You will not turn my son into a campaign strategy."

"This is bigger than you," he snaps. "Bigger than your feelings."

I laugh. It's quiet. Broken. Unhinged. "You taught me how narratives work, how power is built. How people are used." I step back from him, like he might be contagious. "But you taught me something else, too," I continue. "That when men like you decide someone is expendable, they never stop at one."

His eyes narrow. "Careful."

"No," I whisper. "*You* should be."

Because in that moment, something else locks into place. A terrible, liberating certainty. If I stay here, my son dies. If I listen to my father, my son becomes a footnote. And if I want Amauri back, I will have to go to the one man my father never controlled.

I turn to the door.

"Where do you think you're going?" Dad tries to stop me.

"To get my son back."

My hand closes around the handle. I pull it open and look up. Two men stand in the doorway, filling it completely. Dad's bodyguards. Black suits. Earpieces. Impenetrable. Sean, my father's top security dog, is one of them.

Of course he is.

I laugh once, sharp and disbelieving. "Dad. Really? Seriously?"

"It's for your own good," my dad explains calmly, like he's soothing a child. "You're distraught. You're not thinking realistically right now."

I turn back to him. "I'm thinking perfectly clearly."

"You'll see," he continues, unfazed. "In time, you'll

understand this is the best way."

He nods once. Sean steps forward.

"No," I snap. "Don't you dare—"

Sean scoops me up with humiliating ease, his arms locking around me as if I weigh nothing. I struggle, kick, and pound at his shoulders, but it's useless. I'm too weak, too spent, and hurt in too many places. He grins as he carries me toward the stairs, his grip lingering where it shouldn't, his hands careless and proprietary. I don't even have the energy to be afraid of him right now.

"Make sure she takes the pills," Dad orders, staying behind us. "At least three of them."

Sean chuckles softly. "Of course, Senator."

He carries me up the stairs and into my old bedroom. Nothing has changed. The same furniture. The same muted colors. The same carefully curated childhood preserved like a museum exhibit. On the nightstand sits a glass of water and a small white bottle. Already prearranged. Neat. Orderly. Jeffrey or Marianne?

Even from here, I recognize the label: Xanax. *Daddy's* choice of drug for me. It's not the first time Sean has forced me to take them. He sets me down on the bed and steps back just enough to block the door.

"Well," he folds his arms, his eyes roam me freely now. "Are you going to be a good girl?" My stomach turns. "Or," he adds pleasantly, "do you want me to force them down?"

I pick up the bottle with shaking fingers, shake out three pills, and put on a show, tilting my head back, swallowing, sticking my tongue out. "See? Taken."

Sean watches me far too closely, his gaze crawls over

my face, my throat, my body like he's undressing me layer by layer. He's always looked at me like this. Since I was a teenager.

"Good," Sean approves at last. "Very good."

He lingers a second longer, then steps out, closing the door behind him with a heavy click. The lock slides home. I sit there, heart hammering, pills hidden between my molars and cheek, saliva pooling until it burns.

I don't swallow. I wait. Because if there's one other thing my father taught me, it's how to never give up.

The next day...

Morning comes without mercy. I don't remember falling asleep. One moment I'm staring at the ceiling, the next the light is wrong, too pale, too honest.

Vegas looks best at night. Daylight shows you what survives when the glitter shuts off.

I sit up, my jaw already clenched, my body already tight with a fury that never really leaves anymore. My phone has fallen off my chest onto the sheet, dark and silent. It never rang.

It never rang ten years ago either.

That's where my mind goes. Not to how we met. Not to her laugh, or the way she used to tuck her hair behind her ear when she was nervous. My memory doesn't give me those things anymore.

It gives me the asphalt. Headlights. Impact. The sound of my body breaking.

Then the engine again.

Twice.

Gabriel found me in the street, more dead than alive. Broken, twisted, unrecognizable. He told me later that I didn't look human anymore. That he thought I was already gone until he heard something, a breath, a moan, or maybe stubbornness.

I don't remember any of it.

I remember waking up weeks later, drifting in and out of darkness, pain so complete it erased everything else. A room that wasn't a hospital. Shadows instead of nurses. The smell of blood and antiseptic mixed with desperation.

Gabe couldn't take me to a hospital. My uncle would have finished what his sons started. Bello figured it out first. Confirmed it. The hit had been ordered from inside the family. High up. Clean. Efficient. Designed to look like an accident.

My father and my uncle built this empire together. When my father died, my uncle held the throne in trust. Long enough for me to grow into it. But regents don't always enjoy stepping aside.

He had sons of his own. Three of them. Two who enjoyed the crown's shadow. One who studied how to claim it.

"Don't move him," Bello had advised. "If he goes to a hospital, he dies."

So they found someone else. A butcher with a medical license. A man who asked no questions and made no promises. He kept me alive. Barely. Put me back together wrong, because wrong was better than dead.

When I woke, my body was a ruin. And still, it wasn't over. Years later, they had to break me again. Break bones that had healed crooked. Re-set joints that never aligned. Pain layered on pain so I could walk like a man instead of a reminder. It was worth it. Every fracture. Every scream. Every dark night I thought I wouldn't survive.

All of it was survivable.

All, except her.

What she and I had was a secret. Not an affair. A decision.

She didn't want anyone to know she was with me so soon after Carter. Not after the accident. Not while the world still treated him like a saint in a wheelchair. And I didn't want my uncle anywhere near her. Didn't want her touched, threatened, or leveraged. So we agreed. No names spoken out loud. No public traces. No claiming each other until it was safe.

I honored that promise, even when I was broken. Even when I was unconscious.

The moment I was somewhat coherent, I sent Bello to find her, to tell her to wait for me, then I waited until I was healed enough to go find her myself. I didn't have to look very hard. She was everywhere. The newspapers had her face on the front page. Glossy. Perfect. Smiling beside a man in a wheelchair.

HIM!

Carter Whitford.

In a wheelchair.

The man I'd failed to kill.

Her hand rested on his shoulder like devotion had always been her natural state.

GOVERNOR'S DAUGHTER MARRIES
LOCAL HERO

TRAGEDY, RESILIENCE, AND LOVE TRIUMPH IN LAS VEGAS CEREMONY

Her father was governor then. Just stepping into the national spotlight. The photos were immaculate. White flowers. Cameras angled just right. Carter looked brave. She looked... serene. Untouchable.

I stared at the article until the words stopped meaning anything.

Married.

Publicly.

Permanently.

Proudly.

No trace of me.

No hint I'd ever existed.

She hadn't waited.

I read every line anyway. Like a punishment I deserved. They wrote about her strength. Her loyalty. How she stood by Carter after the accident. How she represented everything good, and steadfast, and American. Had she lied to me even before? When she said she had broken up with Carter?

They didn't write about the promises she made in the dark. They didn't write about the blood under her nails. About the forever we swore wasn't optional.

Not the soft kind.

Not the hopeful kind.

The kind forged in blood and fear and guilt.

Forever in pain. Forever in death.

We even had it tattooed together.

Hidden beneath the ribs, just under her breast. It wasn't romantic. It wasn't pretty. It was a vow made by two people who already knew there was no clean way out. Ink burned into flesh the same way the promise burned into us, quiet, permanent, impossible to undo.

We buried a body together. Swore that if one of us went down, the other would carry it. That no matter what happened, we would never disappear on each other.

She vanished anyway.

What the asphalt couldn't do. What the engine couldn't do. What my uncle couldn't do.

She did.

I learned how to breathe again after that. Just not how to forgive. I broke a rule for her back then. I showed mercy. Not to an enemy, worse. To someone I cared about. I allowed sympathy into decisions that should have stayed sharp. I believed that loyalty could exist without control, that love could survive without leverage.

That was my mistake.

Mercy brings exposure. It teaches people where you're soft. And once they know that, they cut there first. Women aren't dangerous because they lie. They're dangerous because they make you want to believe them.

I believed once. And it nearly got me erased. So, no—I won't make that mistake again. Ever.

I'd rather die than let anyone see that part of me twice. Rather bleed out alone on concrete than hand someone the blade and trust they won't use it. Rather end her myself than let her do again what she did before.

I survived by cutting mercy out of myself. If she ever stands in front of me again, I won't hesitate.

I won't ask why.

I won't remember what we were.

I'll do what should have been done the first time.

The sun is already up, promising another scorcher when I leave the casino. One moment I'm surrounded by cool artificial air, the next I step into desert heat that even the misters can't keep at bay. My men peel off in practiced formation, clearing space without breaking stride. The SUV waits at the curb, engine running, door already opening.

Routine. Control. Just the way I like it.

"MASSIMO!"

The sound slices through everything. My blood, my cold heart, my flesh, every scar on and inside my body.

I stop.

Time doesn't slow—it *shatters.*

I turn.

She's there.

Right there.

For a split second, ten years disappear. The street becomes a locker room. Concrete becomes tile. Blood becomes blood. Her hair is loose, her clothes are torn, her skin is smeared and bruised, and everything about her is the same as it was that night. There is even the same raw desperation that knocks the breath out of me in her eyes.

The same look.

The same silent plea.

Like the decade between us never happened.

Then the present crashes back in.

She's reaching for me again.

Just like she did before.

And I remember exactly what it cost me to answer.

A man has her arm twisted tight in his grip. One of Kingsley's bodyguards, I bet. Big. Confident. Smug enough to believe he can touch what doesn't belong to him. Her fingers stretch toward me, trembling.

"Please," she gasps. "Massimo—"

Every instinct I own detonates at once. This is the moment. The one I swore I'd never face.

I can walk away.

I can let the senator clean up his own mess. Let her disappear back into the cage she came from. Let my rule stand.

No mercy.

Or—

I can step forward.

I can take one more breath and undo ten years of discipline. I can put my hands on a man who doesn't know what he's holding. I can shatter the promise I made to myself with my own blood.

If I move, everything changes.

If I don't—

She screams my name again.

And the city holds its breath.

Earlier that morning...

The door clicks shut. The lock slides home. Silence presses in, thick and suffocating. I sit on the edge of the bed, the glass of water still trembling in my hand. The pills leave a bitter and chalky taste in my mouth, and my gums are burning as I hold them there. I lean forward and spit them into the palm of my hand, one by one. My hands are shaking so badly that I almost drop them.

Daddy won't help me.

The thought lands clean and final.

Amauri will die.

Not because he did anything wrong. Not because I failed to love him hard enough. But because he's *inconvenient*. Because he's leverage. Because the wrong men decided he was expendable.

I press my fists into my eyes until sparks explode behind my lids.

Think.

I have to think.

My father has power. Influence. Men. Connections that reach into every dark corner of this city. Still, he won't save my son. Which means there is only one option left.

I've known it since the moment *Daddy* refused to save my son. But I'm afraid to breathe his name. Afraid that if I do, something will come for me. Afraid that saying it out loud will make it real, will wake something I buried a decade ago and swore never to touch again.

Massimo.

The name coils in my chest, tight and dangerous.

Of course, I know who he is now.

Everyone does.

You don't live in Las Vegas and *not* know his name. You don't work politics, don't spin narratives, don't bury scandals without running into his shadow sooner or later.

Back then, I knew too. I knew he was bad trouble.

Capital *B*. Capital *T*.

The kind of man other girls whispered about. The kind parents warned their daughters away from. Tattoos and violence, clinging to him like heat. A man who didn't pretend to be safe.

I should have run. But honestly, I was never given a choice.

Flash.

A locker room that smells like sweat and blood. My hands are shaking so hard I can't even scream. A body lies on the floor.

And him. He's there. Massimo. Checking for a pulse that's long gone.

Not panicked. Not cruel. Just... there.

Steady.

"It's okay," he says quietly, hands nowhere near me. "You're safe now."

No one else has ever said that to me, before or since, and meant it. How I wish somebody would do so now.

Another flash.

His jacket around my shoulders in the desert night. His eyes on the horizon like he's guarding the world itself. The way he never asks for anything. Never touches unless I reach first.

He was the only one who helped me. Not because he had to. Because he chose to. And he never asked for anything in return except my silence.

That was the easy part.

Even after he disappeared, I kept it.

The tattoo—an exact duplicate of his—still lives beneath my ribs. I see it every morning when I look in the mirror. These days, I have to lift my breast slightly to see it, because ten years... because a baby... because time is not gentle. My chest tightens until breathing hurts.

He's a bad man. I know that.

But he's the only one who never looked at me like a symbol. Or a bargaining chip. Or a liability. He looked at me like I was real. And now my son is gone. *Our son.*

I stare at the door, at the walls of my childhood bedroom, at the careful safety my father has turned into a cage. If I stay here, Amauri dies.

If I go to him... I don't finish the thought. Because I know the risk. Have calculated it before. A man like Massimo would want his son, no matter the consequences to the mother. He would take him from me. I have no doubt.

I slide off the bed, knees weak, heart hammering, and press my forehead to the cool wood of the door.

"I'm sorry," I whisper. To Amauri. To myself. To the girl I used to be.

Then, finally, I say his name. "Massimo."

The man who vanished. One day, he was waiting for me behind the bleachers. The next, he wasn't. Not the day after. Not the one after that. The disposable phone he'd given me stayed silent until it went dead. No longer in service. Weeks passed.

I was a governor's daughter. Pregnant. Alone. Carrying a secret that could get my child killed. So I chose survival. I married a man who betrayed me. I had my son. I lived a lie.

Then one day, I saw it on the news: *Vittorio Manetti and his three sons killed in apparent home invasion. Massimo Manetti swears vengeance.*

He was alive. Suddenly, his face was everywhere.

He wasn't dead.

He had simply... forgotten me. Ripped my heart out. Left me.

I swore I'd never reach for him again. And I didn't.

Until today.

Today, he doesn't get to disappear.

If there is one man who can bring my son home, it's Massimo Manetti.

My gaze moves through my childhood room. *Daddy* thinks he's clever. He isn't. This room was never a prison to me. It was a challenge. I learned its weaknesses years ago, back when I was a teenager sneaking out in borrowed dresses and filled with bad intentions, slipping past guards who underestimated a girl who smiled too easily.

The door is locked.

The window isn't.

The false security of the third floor.

I don't shower. Don't change. Don't look at myself in the mirror. Blood, dust, and cactus needles still cling to my skin and hair, but I don't care. All I see when I close my eyes is Amauri's face in that helicopter. Pale. Terrified. Looking for me.

I move on muscle memory alone. The dresser scrapes softly as I push it aside, just enough. The window opens with the same quiet complaint it always has. I swing one leg out, then the other, ignoring the protest in my ribs, the sting in my palms. Warm night air hits my skin as I lower myself onto the narrow ledge, fingers searching and finding familiar cracks in the stone. I used to do this barefoot. I still am.

Down the trellis. Over the ivy. Onto the gravel path that *Daddy* never bothered to light because no one was supposed to be back here.

I don't stop.

The outer wall looms ahead, high but not impossible. I scale it the same way I always did, knee, elbow, breath, patience. I drop down on the other side with a soft grunt, landing hard and steady. My body might be older, but hours in the gym finally pay off. I'm out.

Without looking back, I walk, realizing and regretting too late that I should have tossed a pair of shoes down before I started to climb, but I've long learned that regrets are ghosts that don't rattle chains, they just sit quietly beside you.

I force myself not to run, because running draws attention. Running looks guilty. Vegas' back alleys are bad enough. I don't need to draw more attention to myself than my bedraggled form already does. It helps, though, people think I'm just another homeless person, looking for a handout. I cut through side streets, past tourists too drunk to notice me, past valet lines and neon reflections in puddles of spilled drinks. The Strip rises ahead of me like a mirage—lights, noise, excess—a city that eats people alive and calls it entertainment.

I disappear into it.

His casino dominates the block, all glass and steel and calculated arrogance. I slip into the shadows across the street, ignoring the way my heart is hammering and my breath is too shallow. Because even after all these years, even after the reason why, my stupid, stupid heart still flutters at the thought of him. He was more than a teenage crush. I tried to tell myself over the years that it was normal to pine for the father of my child. That it was normal to love him still. Only... what I feel for him is so much more than love.

I find a dark corner where no valet will see and chase me off. I wait. Bruised. Dirty. In pain. A woman who should know better. A woman out of options.

I stay here, in the dark corner, and wait for him to appear. He has to, at some point. Everybody leaves to go to work or the gym, or a date, or whatever else men do. I hate the waiting. Despite the pain in my feet, I move back and forth on them. If anybody sees me, I'll look like one of the drugged-out, crazy women I always give a wide berth.

There is no way in hell anybody would let me into the casino looking like this. So I wait.

Time stretches the way it only does when fear and hope share the same space in your chest. Minutes thicken. My palms won't stay dry. I press them against the cool stone of the building just to feel something solid. The casino never really sleeps, but it does change its rhythm. Gamblers drift in and out beneath the towering glass façade, dressed in linen and silk and tailored confidence. Laughter spills from open doors, bright and careless.

I pull my thin sweater tighter around me. I'm hyper-aware of every passing glance. Of security at the doors. Of the way the bouncers scan faces without seeming to.

The clink of chips carries on the air like music every time the entrance doors open. Each time they part, my pulse spikes. Not yet. Not him. Not for me.

A woman in a designer dress glides past with a man whose face I recognize—some actor. Someone whose smile is worth millions.

I haven't slept. I can feel it in the way my jaw aches from clenching. In the way my spine won't relax. I stand too straight, like I'm bracing for impact. If he doesn't let me in... If he won't see me... I swallow hard and wait.

The Strip hums, alive and hungry. Above me, the misting system hisses to life, and a fine spray settles over my skin. At first, it's a relief. The desert heat has been building slowly, sneaking up while I wasn't paying attention. But then the dampness sets in. My hair begins to frizz; curls loosen and cling to my neck. Fabric sticks to my ribs, tracing bruises I haven't had the luxury of acknowledging. My blouse darkens slightly, the thin material pressing closer with every breath. I shift my weight, pressing deeper into the shadows, feeling exposed anyway.

Everything about this place is designed to seduce: the way the lights reflect off the polished stone, the scent of expensive perfume, cold air, and money. The casino looms behind me, elegant and ruthless, a monument to control and excess.

I feel small.

And then a car pulls up. Black. Immaculate. My stomach drops so fast it feels like falling.

No.

Please—

My father's car.

He found me. I almost scoff at my own stupidity. One plus one and all that. He didn't become a senator because he underestimates people. Not even his own daughter. The car stops. The back door opens. Sean steps out.

The sight of him makes my skin crawl. He scans the area with lazy confidence, already knowing what he'll find. His gaze lands on me like a spotlight. I try to melt into the wall, to become part of the shadow, but it's pointless. He smiles at me, walks up to a valet, and says something, pointing at me like I'm misplaced luggage. Then he comes straight toward me.

My pulse roars in my ears. There's nowhere to run. The crowd is too thin here, the security too tight, the exits too far.

"Don't," I say, my voice shaking despite myself. "Don't touch me."

He grabs my arm anyway. His grip is iron. Possessive. Familiar in the worst way. I twist, and panic floods me. My head turns in a desperate plea to find someone, anyone... and then my eyes fall on *him*.

Everything stops.

He's stepping out of the building, surrounded by men who move with purpose, with deference. The morning light catches him just right, outlining broad shoulders, sharp lines, the controlled violence in the way he holds himself.

He hasn't changed the way I feared. He's older, yes. Harder. Time hasn't softened him; it's refined him. The dangerous aura around him is unmistakable, heavier now, earned. The pictures of him didn't prepare me. Not even close. He's breathtaking.

Maybe because my body remembers him before my mind can catch up. Maybe because the world tilts slightly toward him, like it always did. Maybe because I've been holding my breath for ten years without realizing it.

Sean tightens his grip, muttering something sharp, impatient. Before I can stop myself, before I can think, I scream.

"MASSIMO!" The name rips out of me, raw and desperate and full of everything I never said.

This is for Amauri, I tell myself. For my son. But it's a lie. Because even without Amauri—even without fear—if I had ever been this close to him again, I would have screamed his name all the same.

Time stops. Not slows. It simply stops. All of it. The noise of the Strip fades into something distant and unreal. The clatter of chips, the murmur of gamblers, the hiss of the misters, all of it dissolves until there is only him.

His eyes find mine. For one impossible fraction of a second, I see him. The old Massimo. Not the Don. Not the monster the papers write about. The man who used to look at me like the world had narrowed down to one fragile, impossible thing.

Me.

His gaze softens. Just a crack. Just enough.

I love you.

The words aren't spoken. They don't need to be. Never had. They whisper through my mind the way they always did, the way they used to sound against my skin in the dark.

My chest caves in with the memory of it.

Hope flares, bright, stupid, lethal.

Then his face shuts down.

It's like watching steel slide into place. His jaw tightens. His eyes go flat. The softness disappears so completely that it's as if it never existed at all.

He's going to turn.

I know it.

He's going to turn away from me. Walk back into his fortress of glass and power and leave me exactly where I am, dirty, bleeding, held by a man who isn't afraid to hurt me. Something inside me screams before my mouth does.

Sean tightens his grip, muttering something sharp and

impatient, his fingers digging deeper into my arm like a warning.

I scream again. "MASSIMO!"

As the sound echoes between us, I feel it, the moment my heart understands something my mind refuses to accept. If he turns away now,

I don't just lose my son. I lose the last lie that's kept me alive.

The morning holds its breath, waiting to see what he'll do.

MASSIMO

I STARE AT HER. FOR A HEARTBEAT, THE WORLD FRACTURES. She shouldn't exist here. Not like this. Not torn and bleeding and shaking in the morning light like something dragged straight out of my past and thrown at my feet.

An apparition.

A ghost.

Mercy.

If anyone in this world ever had the right to ask that of me, it wouldn't be her. She looks like she's been through a blender. Hair wild, clothes ruined, skin marked with dirt and blood and fear. Bruises already blooming beneath her eyes, on her arms, on her throat.

Just like the last time.

The memory slams into me without warning, *locker room tile cold under my boots, blood everywhere, her shaking so hard I thought she'd break in half if I touched her wrong.*

I hadn't turned away then.

I was a kid. Stupid. Soft enough to believe some things were worth bleeding for. I paid for that mistake. I tell myself I'm not that man anymore. I tell myself I'm stronger now. Smarter. Hard enough to survive anything.

But then I see the hand on her arm. That motherfucker's grip is wrong. Possessive. Tight enough to leave bruises she'll carry long after today. I can see his fingers digging in, claiming space that isn't his to take. My jaw locks. Anger surges fast and violent, cutting through every careful rule I've built my life on. I remind myself I'd step in for any woman. Any woman being handled like that in my territory would earn my intervention. That's order. That's control. That's not mercy.

So why shouldn't I do the same now?

Why shouldn't I do what I'd do anyway?

Except I know the truth.

This isn't about territory.

It's about *her*.

About the way she's looking at me like I'm the last solid thing left in a world that keeps tearing itself apart. Like she's already lost everything and still reaches for me.

Again.

That terrifies me more than any enemy ever has. Because I feel it, the old pull, sharp and dangerous and stupid. The instinct to step forward. To put myself between her and the world. To break the rules that I carved into my flesh just to keep breathing.

I swore I'd rather die than make that mistake again. But God help me, seeing that motherfucker hurting her makes my vision go red.

I take one step. Just one. Already knowing there's no walking away from whatever comes next.

The city exhales.

The morning doesn't hold its breath anymore.

It already knows the answer.

The eyes of the man who is holding her widen. It's subtle. A flicker. The moment he realizes the wrong man has noticed him. I stride forward. Unhurried, my gaze now firmly on my prey.

"This is none of your business," he snaps, squaring his shoulders, tightening his grip like that will save him. "Step back or—"

I would have loved to hear the end of that sentence, because, or.... *What*? What would that glorified bodyguard have done to me? I'm too enraged, though. I interrupt, setting him straight. "You're on my property, and you're hurting a woman," I cut in.

My voice is low. Flat. Deadly.

The words land harder than shouting ever could. My men shift behind me. Ready to finish whatever I start. I lift one hand without looking back.

Stay.

I don't need them.

The rent-a-bodyguard laughs, sharp and brittle. "You think you—"

I step into his space. Close enough that he can see it in my eyes. Close enough to smell his cologne, his fear, the stale confidence of a washed-out special ops asshole who thinks the world still owes him respect. He doesn't get to finish the sentence. My fist does it for him. It connects with a dull, meaty crack that vibrates up my arm. Bone meets bone. The sound is wrong, too solid, too final. The man's head snaps to the side, his grip breaking as his body folds like someone cut his strings.

He goes down hard. Knees first. Air explodes out of

him in a wet gasp; hands scramble for balance that doesn't exist. He doesn't even try to get back up. He just stares at the ground, stunned, blood already spilling from his mouth onto polished stone.

The Strip keeps moving.

Someone screams.

Someone films.

Security freezes.

Jenna sways.

I'm there before she hits the ground. She looks up at me like she's trying to focus through water. Half broken. Bruised. Exhausted beyond reason. Her eyes search my face like she's afraid it might disappear if she blinks.

My jaw tightens.

"Jenna," her name comes out in the same way you greet someone at a dinner party. Calm. Polite. As if the world isn't on fire.

"Massimo," she whispers in the same tone she used before she fell asleep in my arms or when she woke up.

Her eyes roll back.

"Fuck."

I catch her as she collapses. Her body goes limp against my chest, a sudden, terrifying weightlessness that hits harder than any blow. She's lighter than she should be. Too light. As if the world had already been carving pieces out of her while I wasn't looking. Too fragile. Not for what she's endured.

For what's coming.

My arm locks around her instinctively, holding her upright as if she belongs there. As if she's always belonged there. Her head falls against my shoulder, warm breath ghosting across my collarbone, her pulse flutters weakly beneath my fingers. For a second—just one—I feel the echo of something dangerous. Then I crush it. Because no matter why she's here. No matter why, my body moved before my mind could stop it. No matter why, seeing another man's hands on her made something in me snap—

She's on *my* casino ground now.

My territory.

My world.

And God help her—because nobody else will—I'll have my revenge on her. Fate. Gods. Whatever cruel, cosmic joke dragged her back into my orbit didn't do it out of mercy. Not for her. Not for me.

This isn't salvation.

This is judgment.

I carry her past the waiting SUV, my grip firm, unyielding, already claiming what the city dared to hand back to me. Around us, my men move with brutal efficiency, sealing off space, erasing witnesses, restoring order like this was always meant to happen.

Maybe, I think sardonically, *this is divine justice*. Not the kind that absolves. The kind that balances the scales with blood. Maybe this is my turn. My time to collect.

I take her back into the casino, and people gasp, hands fly to their agape mouths. I barely notice any of it. Not really. My guards push people out of the way so I can take Jenna back up to the penthouse. The moment the glass doors close and the outside disappears behind tinted glass, one truth settles cold and final in my chest: Whatever she came here seeking—

Protection.

Help.

Redemption—

She's going to pay for what she took from me first.

"Get a doctor. Now," I bark.

On the way to the elevator, as her head rests against my shoulder, I know one thing with terrifying clarity: There's no going back from this.

Not for me.

Not for her.

She stirs as the elevator hums upward. At first, it's just a breath, a faint shift of weight against my chest. Then her lashes flutter, long and dark, trembling as consciousness creeps back in. She frowns slightly, as if waking from a dream she doesn't want to leave. Her eyes open. Green. Still too bright. Still a weapon. They find my face and lock there instantly, as if no time has passed at all. A smile curves her lips. Soft. Dazzling. Familiar enough to cut straight through muscle and bone.

"Massimo," she murmurs.

My spine turns rigid. That smile has ruined men. I know that now. I know what it does. How it disarms, how it makes you forget where you are, who you are, what you swore never to be again.

Sirena. Like the creatures of myth who don't drag men under by force. They sing. They make you step into the water willingly. And by the time you realize you're drowning, it's already too late. The name coils through my mind, bitter and precise. She looks at me like I'm salvation. Like she's been lost at sea and finally found land. Her eyes light up, wet with relief, hope spilling out of her so freely it almost takes my breath.

Almost.

I harden.

I don't smile back. I don't soften. I don't give her anything. My glare is cold enough to freeze steel. Her smile falters. Confusion flickers across her face, quick and fragile. Her brows knit together. She searches my expression like she's looking for something she misplaced. Then she sees it. The wall. Her lips part slightly. Tears well, fast and treacherous, pooling in her eyes like she's trying not to cry and failing anyway.

The sight should do something to me.

Once, it would have undone me completely.

Instead, it makes me colder.

No.

I won't let her do this again.

I won't let her wreck me with a look, with a smile, with that quiet way she has of making herself seem small and breakable when she wants something. I know what she is now. I tighten my hold on her, not to comfort, but to keep control, keeping my arms firm around her like a restraint. The elevator continues its ascent, smooth and silent, sealing us into a narrow box of glass and steel.

"Don't," I order flatly.

The word lands between us like a blade. Her breath catches. A single tear escapes and slides down her cheek.

She doesn't wipe it away. She just looks at me, wounded, bewildered.

Good.

Let her feel it.

Because whatever she thought this was—

Whatever hope she let herself believe in—

It ends here. I won't be pulled under by a siren again. Not ever.

JENNA

He sets me down on the couch like I'm fragile cargo he doesn't want to drop. The penthouse is all glass, angles, and restrained excess. Everything is expensive. Everything looks controlled. It smells like leather, cold air, and power. Nothing here that gives a hint of the man standing before me.

He steps back immediately. Leans against the wall and crosses his arms like he wants to bring as much distance between us as possible.

"Talk." The word is flat. A command issued by a man used to being obeyed. It's not an invitation. I swallow.

My head feels thick and cottony, like the world hasn't quite snapped back into focus yet. From the pain, the loss of my son, the lack of sleep, the fight with my father, the long walk. Take your pick. I search his face for something —anything familiar—but it's unreadable. Closed. Distant. Like he's already gone somewhere I'm not allowed to follow.

"I'm—" My voice cracks. I clear my throat. "My house... There was a home invasion." The words crumble as soon as they leave my mouth.

I press my lips together, but it's useless. Tears spill over anyway, hot and humiliating, sliding down my cheeks faster than I can wipe them away.

"They killed Jason," I whisper. "They took Amauri and... my... husband." I bite my lower lip, wondering if I should have said the last word or not. Massimo always hated Carter, ever since that night... He wanted to kill him, but I talked him out of it, and then fate intervened, and... I can't say Carter got what he deserved, that's too cruel, his fate is one I wouldn't wish on my worst enemy, but... There is a part of me that... *Stop! Now is not the time to psychoanalyze your fucked up relationship with your ex-boyfriend/husband. Amauri,* I remind myself. *Amauri.* My chest caves in, and I break, folding forward, hands fisting in my lap as sobs tear out of me. He doesn't move.

"I heard," he says, but doesn't step closer. Doesn't soften. Doesn't even flinch.

I look up at him through blurred vision, disbelief creeping in through the grief. What happened to him? This isn't the man I knew. Not even the version I was afraid of him becoming. This is... emptiness. Ice. Like he carved everything human out of himself and left nothing behind.

I didn't exactly expect a warm welcome.

But this?

This feels like hate.

And it hurts more than I'm prepared to admit. Why is he looking at me like that? *He's* the one who left. *He's* the one who vanished without a word, without a goodbye, without even the courtesy of an explanation.

And it's been ten years.

Ten!

Is it really so easy for him to dismiss me like this? Like I'm nothing more than an inconvenience that wandered into his life again?

Fine.

If this is how he wants it... I wipe my face with the back of my hand and straighten my spine. He's going to be cold? I can do cold, too. I've had practice.

"They took my son." The words come out clearly. No more shaking. No more tears.

Something flickers. Just a crack. He exhales slowly, his jaw tightens, his eyes darken with something that isn't anger.

"I heard that too." A pause. Then, quieter, "I'm sorry."

The words land heavier than anything else he's said. I don't know why, but they almost undo me all over again. I realize with terrifying clarity that whoever stands in front of me now isn't the man I loved. But he might still be the only one who can save my son. The old Massimo would already be on his knees in front of me, asking what he could do. How fast. How far. Who needed to bleed.

This one—this one doesn't move. He watches me like I'm a variable in a science experiment. I don't know what to say. That's the scary part. I've spoken to presidents, donors, and media sharks with smiles like knives. I know how to spin a room, how to bend a narrative until it breaks in my favor.

But this man?

I don't know how to reach him anymore. Most terrifying of all is that Amauri's life is ticking away while I hesitate. The thought turns my stomach. I hate myself for what comes next, for the way my mind shifts into survival mode. For the cold, ugly realization that this is no longer about truth or fairness or what anyone deserves. It's about leverage. And I have none. He doesn't need any money. There is no power he doesn't already own. No secret, at least none that would scare him.

He tilts his head slightly, eyes cutting, dismissive. "So why are you here?" he asks coldly, gesturing vaguely around the penthouse. At the glass walls. Himself. "Daddy doesn't have enough reach?"

The words sting more than I would have expected. My throat tightens, but I force myself to breathe through it.

"My father knows who took them," I tread carefully. "And he's choosing not to help."

That earns me a flicker of interest. Not sympathy. Calculation.

"He thinks it's... advantageous," I continue, hating every syllable. "To let this play out."

Massimo's mouth tightens, just a fraction. "That's cold, even for the old bastard."

I swallow hard.

"I don't have anyone else," I admit. And this time I don't dress it up. Don't strategize. "You're the only one who can get my son back."

Silence stretches. I can feel the weight of the city pressing in through the glass, all that power and violence and consequence humming just beneath the surface. I meet his gaze, even though it hurts.

"I know you don't owe me anything," I add quietly. "I

know you hate me. But Amauri is innocent. He didn't choose any of this." My voice breaks despite my best efforts. "And if you don't help me," I whisper, "he will die." I hold his eyes, refusing to look away.

He turns away from me. Moves to the bar like this conversation is nothing more than background noise. It's early—too early—but he doesn't hesitate. He reaches for a bottle that looks expensive and dangerous, pours himself a generous amount, and drinks it down like a man dying of thirst. The muscles in his throat work as he swallows. If I didn't know any better, I'd think he was stalling. Hope flares anyway. Stupid. Desperate. *Please,* I beg silently. *Please, please, please.*

He pours another glass. Slower this time. Turns it in his hand once before drinking again. Then he faces me. His eyes are cold. So, so cold.

"And what would you do," he asks evenly, "if I got your son back?"

The answer comes without hesitation and in one breath. "Anything." The word falls out of me like a confession.

His mouth curves, not á smile. Something sharper.

"Anything?" he repeats. Mocking now. "You do know who you're negotiating with."

I nod. I do. God help me, I do.

"I'd do anything for him," I say. My voice shakes, but I don't stop. "For him."

"Him?" he echoes.

I nod again. "My son."

He lets out a short, humorless chuckle and turns back

to the bar, pouring another bourbon like he needs it to keep himself upright. Ice-cold ants climb around inside my stomach, freezing me, and I wrap my arms around myself. I've never seen him like this, not even when we buried...

"You know what I find interestingly disturbing?" he throws over his shoulder, interrupting my thoughts.

I hold my breath. Shake my head. He sets the glass down with deliberate care and walks toward me. Every step tightens something in my chest. More ice ants begin to move through me, spreading from my stomach.

"You haven't pleaded for your husband yet," he says calmly. "The man you couldn't wait to marry."

He might as well have slapped me; that's how much the words sting. He stops in front of me and then—slowly—lowers himself down until he's eye level with me. Kneeling. Controlled. Intentional. He takes my face in his hands, and I stiffen. He's not rough. But he's not gentle either. It's a precise vise. The contact sends a jolt of electricity straight through me. My skin remembers him before my fear catches up. And then the fear hits anyway—sharp and paralyzing—because there is *nothing* in his expression. No warmth. No anger. No mercy.

Just a void.

For the first time in my life, I'm afraid of him. "Please," I whisper.

His thumbs press lightly into my jaw, forcing me to meet his eyes.

"Please, what?" he demands.

The question is a blade.

"Please save my son and my husband," I rush out, the words tumbling over each other.

He tilts his head, studying me like a problem he already knows the answer to.

"Or," he continues for me, keeping his voice dangerously calm, "please save my son and let my husband rot?"

My breath stutters. I can't answer. The truth is already written all over my face. And he sees it. Every last piece. I don't know what he wants. That's the worst part. If he wanted money, I'd find it. If he wanted blood, I'd cut myself. If he wanted obedience, silence, a signature—anything concrete—I would give it to him. But he's looking at me like I'm a puzzle he already solved and discarded.

His thumb brushes my lower lip. It's barely a touch. Accidental, almost. It's enough for my body to betray me in the worst way. Heat curls low in my stomach, slow and treacherous, a pulse I haven't felt in years waking like it was never gone at all. It chases the cold from my limbs, spreads in places I don't have words for anymore. Shame crashes into me instantly. I hate myself for it. But my body doesn't care about pride or timing or betrayal. It remembers *him* the way smoke remembers fire. The way muscles remember a movement long after the mind forgets.

I don't have a reference point. I never did. He was my first and only. There was only ever him. I've never slept with anyone else. Never wanted to. Never needed to. And maybe that makes me pathetic, or naïve, or weak, but I know, deep in my bones, with terrifying certainty, that no man will ever make me feel the way he did. He ruined me for everyone else. My body knows it. Remembers.

Something flickers in his eyes. He sees it too. Whatever I hoped for dies instantly. Disgust floods his expression, sharp and unfiltered. Like I've confirmed something ugly he already suspected. He jerks his hands away from my face and rises abruptly, as if staying close another second might contaminate him.

"You don't have anything I want," he says coldly. The words land like a death sentence. "You wasted your time."

My chest tightens, and panic claws its way up my throat. "If your father doesn't want to interfere," he continues, turning away from me like I'm already finished, "then he must have his reasons."

The room feels suddenly enormous. Too quiet. Too empty. My heart hammers, every instinct screams at me that this is it, that if I don't say something *now*, I'll lose everything. Including my son.

Most shameful of all, somewhere beneath the terror, beneath the grief, beneath the humiliation, my body still leans toward him, and I realize, with sickening clarity, that he knows exactly how much power that gives him.

My heart hardens. It's ugly. It's feral. It has nothing to do with dignity or pride or fear anymore. It has everything to do with my son.

"You have to get him back," I demand. My voice doesn't shake this time. "You have to."

He lets out a short laugh. Sharp. Disbelieving. "I don't *have* to do anything. This has nothing to do with me."

Slowly, I stand up. My knees are no longer weak. My

body isn't cold anymore. It's actually getting hotter as fury rises inside me, the kind of fury only a mother knows when her young are in danger. I glare at him, every ounce of fear burning away under something hotter. "You're wrong."

His eyes flick to me, irritated.

"It has *everything* to do with you. He's *your* son." The words detonate between us. The second they leave my mouth, I know I've made a mistake.

A terrible one.

The silence that follows is violent.

He stares at me like the world has tilted off its axis. Like I've just rewritten something fundamental inside him without permission. The glass in his hand flies. Not dropped. Thrown. It whistles through the air like a missile and explodes against the window behind me, bourbon and shards raining down in a sharp, glittering spray. The sound is deafening. Final.

I flinch but only barely. I don't step back. I don't scream. I don't apologize. I stand there and let the storm come.

He's on me in a heartbeat. Too fast. Too close. His face is inches from mine, his eyes are blazing, his jaw clenches so hard I can see the tendons in his neck strain. Veins stand out along his throat. His chest rises and falls like he's fighting something inside himself with everything he has.

His lips move. But no sound comes out. For a second, I think he might kill me. And if this is how it ends—fine. At least he knows. At least Amauri isn't a ghost anymore. At least the truth is out there now, breathing between us, impossible to take back. I stare right back at him, heart hammering, spine straight. Because even if I don't know him anymore—even if the man in front of me is a stranger carved out of rage and scars—I know men *like* him. Men like him don't abandon their blood. Men like him don't leave their sons in the hands of kidnappers. And whether he wants me dead and gone, or broken for daring to say it, he won't let Amauri die.

Not now. Not ever.

He knows it. I know it. And soon, Amauri will too.

MASSIMO

I DON'T DOUBT HER. NOT FOR A SECOND. THE MOMENT THE words leave her mouth, the truth hits me with a force that has nothing to do with reason. It doesn't ask for proof. It doesn't pause for logic. It settles deep, heavy, and final, like something my body has always known but my mind refused to touch.

My son.

The rage that follows is immediate and visceral, so sharp it steals the air from my lungs.

MINE.

Not metaphorical.

Not imagined.

Not a lie meant to corner me.

Mine in a way that reaches back through blood and bone and instinct. I'm in her face before I remember moving. So close I can see the pulse beating wildly at her throat. So close I can smell fear, sweat, the faint trace of her soap, something soft and domestic that does not belong anywhere near what she's just done to me.

My vision tunnels.

My son.

The words detonate again, louder this time, ripping through me with fresh violence.

MY SON!

Mine.

The realization hits like a second betrayal layered on the first, cutting straight through bone. She didn't just leave me. She didn't just disappear while I was broken, drugged, stitched. She took my blood. She took my heir. She took ten years I will never get back. Ten years of first words. First steps. First scraped knees. Ten years of my son learning how to exist in a world that didn't have me in it because she decided I didn't deserve to know.

The rage is so intense it goes white-hot. I've killed men for less. I've burned empires for less. My hands curl into fists at my sides, because if I touch her right now, I don't trust myself to stop.

"How," I grind out, my voice sounding barely human, "could you do that?"

The question isn't curiosity. Its disbelief sharpened into something lethal. How could you look at a child who was half me and decide I wasn't worthy? How could you let another man raise him? Put my son in another man's house, give him another man's name, another man's lies? Carter fucking Whitford, no less! How could you keep him from me?

Every instinct in me screams to end her. Not quickly. Not clean.

But I don't.

Because killing her now would be mercy. It would let her

escape the weight of what she's done. Let her avoid the reckoning she owes me. I want her alive. I want her to feel this. To understand exactly what it means to steal something sacred from a man like me and live long enough to regret it. My jaw locks so hard it hurts. I lean closer, straining to keep my voice low, shaking with barely contained violence.

"You didn't just betray me," I snarl. "You erased me."

My chest heaves, my breath burns as I fight the urge to tear the room apart with my bare hands.

"You took my son and never told me." My eyes burn. I've never felt this furious. Not at my uncle. Not at the men who tried to kill me. Not even at the city when it turned its back. This is different. This is personal. This is raw.

This is a wound that never had the chance to scar over because I never knew it existed. I pull back a fraction, just enough to keep myself in control.

"Pray," I tell her coldly, "that killing you isn't the easiest solution."

Because right now, it's the only thing keeping her alive. She opens her mouth. I see it, the instinct to defend herself, to explain, to carve space for survival out of whatever scraps I'm leaving her. A knock at the door spares me. The sound is jarringly normal. Max, my top guard, sticks his head in, "Doc is here."

Finally.

I turn on her with a sneer sharp enough to cut. "Patch her up," I snap, jerking my head in her direction like she's a problem that needs managing. Not the reason my world is tearing itself apart. "Then get her out of my sight."

She flinches. The doctor nods quickly, already moving, already choosing obedience over questions.

I can't breathe. The air in the room feels too thick, too heavy, like it's pressing in on my lungs. There's a stone table nearby, marble, obscene, meant to impress men who don't know the cost of anything real. I grab it and tip it over with a sound that feels like a rupture. It crashes to the floor. Marble explodes. The expensive flooring fractures beneath it. I feel nothing.

My fist hits the wall.

Again.

And again.

The pain is sharp, grounding, a clean line through the chaos. Skin splits. Blood runs. I welcome it because it's simple, because it makes sense, because it doesn't lie.

I hear a sound I don't expect. A whimper. Instinctively, I turn. She's staring at me. Not defiant now. Not strategic. Just... small. Her eyes are wide, tears pooling without spilling, like she's watching something she can't understand and is afraid to name.

The doctor has edged closer, cautious, eyes flicking to my knuckles, to the blood dripping onto the floor.

"Your hand—" he begins.

"In the guest room," I snarl, not looking away from her. "Now."

The doctor thinks about saying something else. I can see it. Then he thinks better of it. He guides her away gently, one hand at her elbow, his body instinctively positioning itself between us. His instincts are right.

The door closes.

Soft.

Final.

The silence after is unbearable. I stagger to the bar and pour another bourbon; my hands are shaking now, and the glass rattles against the counter. I drink it like it might drown what's clawing up my throat. It doesn't.

The bottle leaves my hand without conscious thought. It shatters against the wall, glass and liquor spraying like a second, lesser explosion. The glass follows. Then another. The penthouse takes the abuse in silence.

I stand there amid the wreckage, blood dripping from my knuckles, chest heaving like I've run miles instead of standing still. Ten years.

Ten years stolen.

And now the truth is here, bleeding into everything I touch, demanding payment. I press my forehead briefly to the cool wall, jaw clenched so hard it aches. This isn't over. This is the beginning. God help anyone who stands between me and what was taken from me, because nothing is going to survive what comes next.

The door opens without ceremony. Max must have heard the noise and called him, because Gabriel strolls in like he owns the place, jacket half open, posture loose, that familiar swagger like nothing in the world could truly surprise him anymore. He takes one look at the room.

The shattered marble. The glass embedded in the wall. The blood dripping steadily from my knuckles onto the ruined floor. He lifts an eyebrow.

"What?" he asks mildly. "Did you see a mouse or something?"

I stare at him. For a long, suspended moment, I'm ready to tear him apart. My body is still humming with violence, muscles tight, breath ragged, rage looking for somewhere to land. Then something breaks. I laugh. It rips out of me, harsh and ugly and uncontrollable. The kind of laughter that bends you forward at the waist, that scrapes your throat raw, that sounds more like a man choking than anything resembling humor. I laugh until my chest hurts. Until tears sting my eyes. Until the room spins just a little.

Gabe watches me without flinching. Doesn't reach for a weapon. Doesn't crack another joke. He just lets it happen. He's always had that effect on me. When the laughter finally burns itself out, I straighten slowly, wiping a hand across my face. My breath is still uneven. My knuckles still bleed.

Gabe nods once, like this all checks out.

"Rough morning," he wagers.

"You could say that."

He moves closer then, careful but unafraid, his eyes flick briefly to my hand before meeting my gaze again. There's something steady there. Familiar. Earned. We've been through hell together. He dragged me off the asphalt when I was more dead than alive. Kept me breathing when my own family wanted me erased. And when his twin sister was taken—when they found what was left of her—I was by his side as we waded through blood. We distributed vengeance together. Clean. Thorough. Final.

Some bonds don't need words.

He gestures at the wreckage. "Want to tell me what caused this? Or should I guess?"

I exhale slowly, the last of my laughter fades into something heavier.

"She's here," I state simply.

Gabe's expression changes. Just a fraction. Enough.

"The ghost," he murmurs.

"Yes."

He doesn't ask which one. He's always known there was a woman in my past. Just not who. When men spend as much time together as we do, they see things. They notice things they don't see. He never asked. I never told. He nods again, like this explains everything it needs to.

"And?" he asks quietly.

"And she dropped a truth on me," I say, voice flat now. Dangerous. "One that changes everything."

Gabe studies me for a long second, glances toward the guest room from where small noises betray a presence. He cracks his neck once, slow and deliberate, like a man settling into familiar work. He reaches under his jacket, pulls his gun, and checks the chamber with practiced ease.

Anyone else in this room—even Enzo—would already be disarmed and bleeding for a move like that. Not Gabe. I just watch him.

He meets my eyes, calm as ever. "Okay," he says. "Who do we kill?" He pauses, then adds thoughtfully, "Please say we can do it slowly. I'm in the mood for slow."

I don't answer right away. I don't need to. Gabe knows better than to rush me when my silence sounds like this.

He's got his own ghosts. Always has. That's why he stalks a woman instead of asking her out like a normal human being. Married or not, morals were never the obstacle. Gabe takes what he wants. Who he wants. When he wants. Except this time.

"Whoever took Carter and Amauri Whitford," I finally spit out. The wrong last name burns my mouth. My jaw tightens around it.

Gabe's head snaps up. "Come again?"

I don't look at him. I can feel his mind working, fast and lethal, grabbing for threads, trying to weave something coherent out of what I just said. He comes up empty. I sigh and turn toward the kitchen. The faucet hisses as I shove my hand under cold water. The sting distracts from my mood from the mess of emotions I don't know what to do with. My knuckles throb, the split skin burns as blood swirls down the drain in diluted ribbons. Gabe follows without a word. He opens the freezer, grabs a bag of frozen peas, and presses it into my hand like this is just another morning after a bad night. I take it. Hold it against my knuckles.

"They took my son," I say quietly.

Silence follows. The kind that isn't empty, just stunned. Gabe doesn't move. Doesn't speak. I can feel the shift in him anyway, the way something heavy settles into place.

"Whitford isn't your name," he states slowly.

"No," I reply. "It isn't."

I lean back against the counter, eyes closed for a brief second, the cold biting into my skin, grounding me.

"She never told you," Gabe guesses.

"No."

Another beat.

"And now?"

"Now," I say, opening my eyes, "someone put my blood in a helicopter and thought I wouldn't come for it."

Gabe's mouth curls into the cold mask he's famous for. A mask that has made grown men cry and shit their pants.

"Okay," he says calmly. "Now we're talking."

His mind is already recalibrating, already moving pieces on a board only men like us can see.

"Then," he adds, dropping his voice an octave, "we don't just get them back."

I meet his gaze.

"No," I agree. "We don't."

No questions are voiced. No explanations are given. There are a thousand things hanging between us—how, when, why, what she knew, what she didn't—but none of them matter right now. Those are wounds to reopen later. Right now, there's only one direction.

Gabe nods once. That's it.

He pulls his phone out, already moving, already five steps ahead. His voice shifts, not louder, just colder. "I need everything you have on the Whitford kidnapping," he orders into the phone. "Timeline. Footage. Air traffic. Cell pings. Shell companies. Anyone who breathed near that helicopter."

He listens for half a second, then cuts in. "No filters. No delays. I don't care who it pisses off."

He ends the call and looks at me again. "War?"

I don't hesitate. "Yes."

The word lands heavy. Final. Gabe's mouth curves, sharp and satisfied, like a blade finding its groove. He starts tapping messages, fingers flying. I know what that means: doors opening that don't usually open, people waking up to find their phones ringing with names they don't want to see.

I straighten slowly; the frozen peas slip from my hand and thud softly onto the counter. "They touched my blood. They took him."

Gabe's eyes darken. "They just signed their death warrants."

Outside, the Strip keeps glittering. Inside, something ancient and merciless unfurls its wings. This is what happens when men like us stop reacting and start hunting. Somewhere in this city, people are still breathing who won't be by nightfall. The war doesn't announce itself.

It just begins.

I'M SO TIRED IT FEELS LIKE MY BONES ARE HOLLOW. NOT THE kind of tired that sleep fixes. The kind that seeps into your marrow and stays there, humming. My head throbs in slow, punishing waves, and pain pushes the medication the doctor gave me. Every blink feels like an effort.

My hands are wrapped in thick, layered white gauze, making them clumsy and foreign. Earlier, the doctor picked tiny rocks and cactus spines from my palms one by one, apologizing each time his tweezers pinched skin instead of thorn. I cried the entire time. Silently. I couldn't help it.

My hands look like a wrapped mummy, which just makes me think more of Amauri. Of how small his hands looked wrapped in mine when he was learning to walk. How he used to press his palms flat against my cheeks when he wanted my full attention.

"Anything else hurt?" the doctor asks.

Nothing he can fix, so I shake my head. "No," I whisper. My throat tightens anyway.

"Just scrapes and bruises," he diagnoses, almost kindly. "You were lucky. Nothing sprained. Nothing broken."

Lucky. The word lands wrong. I start crying again, silent and shaking, my shoulders fold in on themselves. Lucky that my son was taken. Lucky that my husband was dragged off. Lucky that I escaped just far enough to watch it happen.

The doctor watches me with a detached sympathy that feels practiced. He's older, gray at the temples, eyes dulled like someone who's seen too much suffering to react the way people expect. He pats my shoulder once, awkward but not unkind.

"Take care of yourself now," he suggests.

It's probably the closest he'll come to comfort. He opens the door to leave, and voices drift in from the other side. Low. Male. Controlled. Massimo isn't alone anymore.

The door closes softly, cutting the sound off, but it's too late. The knowledge settles in, heavy and unavoidable. I just want to curl up on the bed and disappear in this immaculate room that is too perfect. Cream-colored walls, dark wood accents, sheets so crisp they barely wrinkle beneath me. Everything smells faintly of clean linen and something sharper underneath, money, power, order.

Before he wrapped my hands, the doctor let me shower. The bathroom is obscene in its luxury. Marble everywhere, warm beneath my bare feet. Water that came down in a steady, enveloping sheet, hot enough to sting, then soothe. I stood under it longer than necessary, letting it pound against my scalp, trail down my back, carry dirt and blood and fear down the drain.

For just a moment, I closed my eyes and forced myself

to forget. To forget helicopters, forget the screams, forget the look on Amauri's face. It lasted maybe thirty seconds.

Now I'm wearing a shirt I found in the walk-in closet. Too big. Soft. It smells like Massimo: clean, masculine, and unmistakable. The scent wraps around me like a memory I didn't ask for, makes my chest ache in a way I don't have the energy to fight.

I know I need to go out there. I know I need to face him again. Whatever comes next. Whatever punishment or bargain or war he decides on. But I'm so tired. So bone-weary.

I sit on the edge of the bed, staring at my wrapped hands, breathing in the scent of him, and wonder how much more a person can lose before there's nothing left to take. With effort, I force myself off the bed. Every step feels like wading through water, but I keep going anyway. The door opens without sound, and the living area stretches out before me, glass and marble, city rising beyond the windows like a living thing.

Just like I thought, he isn't alone. There's a stranger with him now. Tall. Dark-haired. Broad shoulders under a jacket worn like armor. He's handsome in the way men who live close to violence often are—sharp lines, controlled posture—but there's something cruel carved into his features. Not flashy. Not theatrical. Just... permanent. Like he's learned exactly where mercy fails and never bothered looking for it again. Then again, Massimo wears the same mark now.

"Jenna," Massimo announces flatly without looking at me. It hurts anyway. "Gabriel," he adds, turning slightly.

"Gabe," the other corrects mildly.

"Gabe," Massimo finishes, then gestures toward me without warmth. "Jenna."

Gabe's gaze settles on me, curious but not invasive. Not sexual. Not dismissive. He assesses me the way a soldier sizes up terrain, cataloging, measuring, and noting damage. I feel Massimo's eyes on me too, heavy and unavoidable, but I don't let myself look at him. I know what I look like. My hair is still wet, clinging in darkened curls around my face. No makeup. No shoes. Hands wrapped thickly in white gauze. The too-big shirt that hangs off my shoulders because I have nothing left of my own. Which is exactly the truth.

Pitiful.

The thought snaps something sharp and angry into place inside me. I straighten my shoulders, lift my chin. If we're at war, I won't back down. Gabe nods once, as if acknowledging the shift. Something like respect flickers across his face.

Massimo finally speaks. "What does your father know about this?" he demands. Ruthless and calm. "Do not leave anything out. No matter how inconsequential you think it is."

I swallow. My throat tightens, but I push through it. "He knows who took them," I fill him in. Saying it out loud still feels like swallowing glass. "He knew almost immediately."

Massimo's jaw tightens. I don't miss it. "Who?"

"He didn't tell me." Finally, I meet his gaze. I need him to know that this is the truth. "He said that plenty of people were angry about his latest proposal, mostly the Cartels," I continue. "About the drug bill. He thinks they're using Carter and Amauri as leverage. To force him to back off."

"To stall," Gabe murmurs.

"Yes," I agree, nodding. "Or kill it entirely."

Massimo's silence is a weight pressing against my ribs.

"He also said..." My voice falters. I force it to steady. "He said it was... advantageous. Politically. That this could be spun. That the public would sympathize, rally."

Gabe lets out a low whistle. Massimo still won't look at me.

"And you?" he asks. The question lands heavier than the rest. "What did he expect you to do?"

My hands curl uselessly inside their wrappings.

"He expected me to stay," I say quietly. "To be sedated. Managed. Out of the way."

Gabe's eyes flick to my bandaged hands, then back to Massimo. I can feel Massimo now. Not just watching but *measuring*. Like he's trying to decide what I am to him in this moment. Liability. Weapon. Weakness.

Every part of me reacts to him anyway. My pulse stutters. My skin tightens. Even now, even after everything, he pulls at me like gravity. I hate that. I also need him.

"So I left," I finish. "And I came here."

Silence stretches.

The city glows behind them, indifferent. Massimo's gaze finally lifts. It hits me like a physical thing. Cold. Dark. Unreadable. A shiver moves through me at the thought that whatever happens next, he's already decided I'm part of it. Whether I survive it or not is still up for debate.

His phone rings. He exhales sharply. "Not now, Enzo."

A beat passes. His expression shifts. His brow wrinkles, his jaw tightens as he listens. He glances at Gabe, who meets his gaze instantly, alert and focused.

"I'll be right there." Massimo ends the call.

He looks at me like he's memorizing a problem he doesn't have time to solve. "Get some rest," he orders. "I need to go." Then, to Gabe, without lowering his voice, "You stay here. Make sure she doesn't do anything stupid."

"Yes, boss," Gabe replies easily.

Without another word—without another look—Massimo turns and storms out. The door closes behind him with finality. The absence he leaves behind is louder than the destruction earlier.

Gabe shifts his weight and looks at me, the edge of danger softened just slightly by practicality. "Hungry?"

I shake my head. The idea of food feels impossible.

"I'll go," I say quietly, "and try to get some sleep."

He nods once. Doesn't argue. Doesn't follow. The guest bedroom welcomes me back in its sterile luxury. I close the door, lean my forehead against it for a second longer than necessary, then cross the room and sit on the edge of the bed. I don't think I can sleep. I don't think my mind or the pain in my chest will let me. When they say your heart bleeds, they weren't lying, and it hurts. Exhaustion, however, doesn't ask permission. I lie down, the sheets cool against my skin, and inhale Massimo's scent that still clings faintly to the shirt I'm wearing. Against all expectations, I fall asleep. Not peacefully. But deeply. As if my body knows the war has begun and is stealing what rest it can before everything breaks loose.

"So I left," she concludes. "And came here."

The words land harder than they should. Jenna Whitford doesn't run *toward* safety. She runs toward fire and hopes it burns the right people first. I'm about to ask the next question. The one that matters. The one that will decide whether I throw her out or lock her in. When my phone rings. Enzo. *Shit, I don't have time for this.*

"Not now, Enzo," I snap, irritation flaring hot and sharp. I turn slightly, half-present, my attention still split. Part of me is still tracking her posture, the way she's holding herself upright by force of will alone, the other is already bracing.

He must hear the impatience in my voice, my distraction, because he throws the words at me like bumper stickers to catch my attention. "We found more laced Coke. Same signature. Fentanyl."

My jaw tightens. My brow furrows as the words come through the line, precise and methodical, slotting into place like teeth on a gear.

"I'll be right there." I end the call. Whatever else is happening, this needs my immediate attention.

I stare at Jenna, the urge to pull her into my arms

collides head-on with the urge to crush the life out of her. Both instincts are sharp. Both feel earned.

I settle for, "Get some rest. I need to go." Turning to Gabe, I order, "You stay here. Make sure she doesn't do anything stupid."

"Yes, boss," he replies easily.

Trusting him, I pull the phone back out and dial Enzo as I exit my penthouse and enter the security antechamber, where my guards instantly stand to attention. One presses the elevator button, and the other six fall in line.

"Stay here, Max. Nobody in, nobody out," I order.

"Yes, boss."

"Boss?" Enzo answers.

"Where?" I bark out, pushing the casino level button.

He gives me the address of one of our dealers who was found dead a few minutes ago. He gives me more details on my ride down and on my way to the valet area, where three SUVs are already idling.

"And Massimo," Enzo adds, "this was done *after* it left our control."

I close my eyes for half a second.

That's when I feel it, the pressure from both sides. My empire is bleeding in places people can see. And a few stories above me, a woman is wrapped in my shirt, looking like she might break if someone touches her wrong. Two wars. One distraction.

"I'm on my way." I end the call.

The city slides past the tinted windows in streaks of light and shadow, Vegas breathing neon like nothing is wrong. Something is very wrong. This isn't random. It never is. Someone is moving against me with intention, touching my product, poisoning *my* reputation, testing how far they can go without forcing my hand. They're not trying to burn my empire down. They're trying to make it *turn* on me. That's what I should be thinking about. About the structure. The routes. The men who might be wavering. The pattern forming just beneath the surface.

Instead, I see her.

In my shirt.

Fuck.

The memory hits uninvited, vivid as a bruise. The way the fabric swallowed her frame, how it slipped off one shoulder because she was too tired to notice. Bare legs. Wet hair. Wrapped hands. She looked like she'd been pulled out of a wreck and set down somewhere she didn't belong. I didn't give her options. I know that. She took what she could find. Still, why did it have to be *that* shirt?

I grip my jaw, irritation flaring hot. It's ridiculous. A shirt means nothing. It's fabric. Cotton. Replaceable. Except it isn't. She shouldn't look like that in anything of mine. She looked... fragile. Beautifully broken.

The thought turns sour immediately. I wanted to fix her, just like back then. The instinct came fast and dangerous, the urge to pull her into my arms, to press her head against my chest and promise her that everything would be okay. That I would make it okay. That nothing else would touch her. God help me, I still want that. The pull she has on me is uncanny. Even knowing what I do about her. Sirena. What they didn't tell you in legends is that even if you manage to walk away, their allure will never leave you. Eventually, they'll get you.

Then Amauri cuts through the fantasy like a blade.

My son.

The word snaps me back into place, rage surges hard enough to wipe everything else clean.

She kept him from me.

For ten fucking years.

Every mile the car eats up feeds the fury, sharpens it into something useful. I don't forgive. I don't forget. Wanting her doesn't change what she did.

But wanting her matters. That's the problem.

She wasn't my first. I've never pretended otherwise. Desire has never been scarce in my world, and I've never been a man who denies himself what he wants. But Jenna—

God.

She was different. Innocent, at least at first, until I ruined her, then she wasn't fragile. She burned. She *answered*. She didn't just take what I gave, she met it, matched it, undid me in ways no one else ever managed to. My body remembers her without asking permission, a low, dangerous pull.

I hate that I want her.

Physically. Viscerally. Enough that the thought of anyone else touching her makes something ugly coil in my chest. Enough that I can already feel the justification lining up, neat and merciless.

Maybe I don't hurt her. Maybe I make her pay another way.

She can't be punished like a man. Not really. And no matter how much I want to tear into her for what she did, I can't bring myself to destroy the mother of my child. That leaves... alternatives.

A widow is still useful.

A woman bound to me, whether she wants it or not, is leverage I understand very well. Or maybe I don't decide yet. Maybe I keep her close. Where I can see her. Touch her. Where she can't disappear again. Where every breath she takes reminds her who she belongs to now.

Because a son needs his mother.

Whether I hate her or crave her—or both—Jenna is no longer someone I can cut loose without consequence. I don't need to decide what I feel. I need to decide what I *do*. She's mine to do with as I please. When I please.

The plan begins to take shape quietly, methodically, the way all good ones do. Not mercy. Not revenge.

Leverage.

The most dangerous part?

I don't know yet whether she's the weapon or the reward. Or the mistake I'll make anyway, because I've never been very good at resisting the things that ruin me.

The car slows as we near the address Enzo gave me, and security lights sweep over steel and glass.

Someone is trying to make me look weak. They picked the wrong moment. Because if there's one thing I still know how to do better than anyone, it's turn obsession into power.

The car pulls to a stop, and the noise in my head goes quiet as utter focus settles in. The dealer's name was

Steven. Young. Careful. Ambitious. Exactly the kind of man I prefer working for me, smart enough to stay alive, hungry enough to listen. He picked up the coke from Pablo, one of my lieutenants. Pablo was there when the shipment came in. I was there too.

I remember it clearly.

We tested it together. Clean. No smell of chemicals. No bitterness on the tongue. Nothing raised alarms. From there, it went straight to Steven. No stops. No middlemen. Which means the contamination happened during transport. Someone got to it after it left Pablo's hands.

I step out of the car as Enzo joins me; his expression is already grim. The building Steven lived in rises in front of us, new construction, glass and steel, trying hard to look more expensive than it is. Decent. Clean. The kind of place a man rents when he wants to project success without drawing attention.

Exactly what I encourage.

Our dealers don't look desperate. They don't look flashy. They blend into high-end gyms, rooftop bars, and charity galas. They deliver to clients who pay more because they expect better. Dead clients ruin that illusion.

Inside the apartment, Enzo's people are already busy cleaning. The furniture is modern and neutral. No clutter. No chaos. Steven was careful, even in death.

"Timeline?" I look to Enzo.

"Somewhere between three and eight in the morning," he fills me in. "Security cameras show him leaving around nine last night, coming back around one."

"Was he out doing deliveries?"

"Checking right now," Bello holds up what I'm guessing is Steven's phone.

I walk slowly through the living space, cataloging details. Windows. Door locks. The counter where the product would have been set down. This wasn't a smash-and-grab. This was intimate.

"He trusted someone," I venture.

"Yes," Enzo agrees. "Or someone made sure he didn't notice."

I stop near the kitchen, staring at the empty counter; the absence is louder than anything else in the room.

"This wasn't meant to wipe us out," I continue. "If it were, they'd have laced the entire stash."

"They want fear," Enzo speculates. "Selective damage. Bodies that point back to you."

I nod in agreement. "They're not attacking my money. They're attacking my reputation."

That fact alone is telling. This isn't random violence. This is someone who understands how power actually works. Someone patient. Someone with history. Someone who wants me looking everywhere at once.

I think of Jenna again, but this time, I push the thought aside deliberately.

Later.

Right now, I have a trail to follow.

"Lock this place down," I tell Enzo. "Find out who Steven saw in the last forty-eight hours. Anyone who touched that product. Anyone who breathed near it."

He nods. "Already in motion."

Bello clears his throat as he enters. "There's something else."

I turn slowly, giving him my full attention. Bello doesn't interrupt unless it matters.

"The entertainer," he continues. "And Mia Pascale. Both are low-level famous. Enough name recognition to get press. Enough relevance to raise eyebrows."

I agree. "I've been thinking along the same lines."

Steven's death looks different on paper. A dealer overdosing on his own product reads as an accident, tragic, unfortunate, forgettable. The other two don't. Their names travel. Their faces circulate. They make noise.

"Three incidents," Enzo says. "Three different optics."

"Exactly," I reply. "This isn't chaos. It's deliberate sabotage. They want the inside and the outside looking at me." I step closer to the counter, bracing my hands against the cold stone, letting the pattern settle into place. "They're not flooding the streets," I muse. "They're not torching entire shipments. They're lacing *portions*. Randomized enough to avoid detection. Controlled enough to steer the narrative."

Bello nods grimly. "Enough to make people wonder which batch is safe."

"And whether buying from us is worth the risk," Enzo adds. "Or dealing."

"Fear," I agree quietly. "But selective. Intelligent."

This isn't a brute-force attack. This is a man—or group—who understands how power erodes. How reputation rots before it collapses.

"They want everyone guessing," I continue. "Dealers

watching each other. Buyers hesitating. Our own people doubting the chain of custody."

"And you," Bello says. "Distracted."

I straighten. "They're not trying to take my empire. They're trying to hollow it out. Turn it against itself."

Silence settles over the room.

"Which means," Enzo suggests slowly, "they'll do it again."

"Yes," I agree. "And not where we expect."

I push away from the counter with a decision fully crystallized. "Lock down transport routes," I order. "New protocols. Rotating escorts. No solo runs. Anyone who deviates gets flagged."

Enzo nods without hesitation. I drum my fingers once against the stone. "You two talk to *everyone* who had contact with that last shipment. All the way down from Pablo. And I want every ounce tested before it goes out. No exceptions. This stops now."

"You've got it, boss," Enzo agrees.

Good.

Because whoever thought they could poison my streets and walk away is about to learn something very simple: I don't miss patterns. And I don't forgive lessons taught in blood.

The drive back to the penthouse is a blur of calculations. The laced coke isn't isolated; it's coordinated. Selective contamination. Enough to spook buyers without triggering full shutdowns. Then the club shooting, clean, precise, timed for maximum visibility. Different methods, same message.

Pressure.

They want me to react. To chase smoke and make mistakes. They want me looking *anywhere but inward.* I won't give them that satisfaction.

By the time the car pulls into the valet lot, I've already mapped the next steps: audits disguised as loyalty checks, sudden reshuffles, silence where noise is expected. Let them think I'm distracted. Let them think I'm soft.

Moving through the casino is like second nature, so much so that I don't even notice the stares, the flirting, the sudden tension. The elevator ride up is quiet. My men are well-trained and pick up on my mood.

The doors open into the security antechamber, and the guards straighten as I pass. Everything is as it should be. Controlled. Contained.

Then I hear it. My name. Not spoken. Not called. Screamed.

"MASSIMO—!"

The sound rips through the penthouse, raw and terrified, echoing down the hall like a gunshot. I don't stop. I don't even slow. The sound of my name doesn't paralyze me; it flips a switch. Fully alert, purposefully, I stride towards the guest bedroom, gun out, safety off. My senses take in my surroundings instantly: dimmed lighting, sharp neon from outside, nothing moving in the shadows, a slight shuffling sound now that the scream has died out; the only things I smell are bourbon and Gabe's cologne.

Gabe is already there, halfway out of the guest room, hands lifted slightly when he sees me. His expression is sharp, alert.

"I didn't touch her," he says immediately. "She's having a nightmare."

Another scream, broken this time. Hoarse. Desperate. My name again.

I don't answer Gabe. I shove him to the side and move past him, into the room. She's thrashing on the bed, sheets twisted around her legs. Her bandaged hands claw at the fabric; her breath is coming in short, panicked bursts.

"No—please—don't—"

Her body curls inward, bracing for something that isn't there anymore. I don't touch her. I stand there, watching fear own her even in sleep. This isn't theater. This isn't manipulation. This is real. Suddenly, the war outside my walls feels secondary to the one happening right here, in this room, one I never planned for and don't know how to fight. She screams my name one last time, then gasps awake.

Her eyes fly open, wild and unfocused, and they lock on me. Time stops.

The city keeps breathing outside the windows. My empire keeps bleeding quietly in the dark. Standing at the foot of her bed, listening to my name echo out of her terror, I understand something with brutal clarity: Whatever this war becomes, it's already deeply personal.

LIGHT. TOO BRIGHT. IT HUMS. NOT LIKE MUSIC, THIS IS electric, alive inside the walls. It crawls under my skin, makes my teeth ache. My feet slide on cold tile. Smooth. Slippery. I know that sound, the faint squeak of skin moving too fast. I'm not steady. I try to stop, but my body doesn't listen.

I become aware of hands. Hands around my throat. That's why I can't scream. The hands are suffocating me. *On your knees, little girl,* the voice snarls into my ear, raising revulsion, fear, and anger simultaneously. But something else too. *Betrayal*! He betrayed me in the most vicious way possible.

Your boyfriend sold you out. In the end, they all do.

The words burn deeper than the fingers around my throat. It doesn't make any sense, but I hear a door closing, laughter. I know where I am, and yet it doesn't look at all like it did then. Lights flicker, adding a horror-movie touch—as if the situation needs it.

On your knees, little girl, he repeats. The word disappears into the hum. I look for another door. There isn't one. Another sound reaches me, becomes louder and louder until I want to throw my hands over my ears. It takes a moment to realize it's the sound of a helicopter. It's taking something away. Something important. My back hits hard wood, and the impact knocks the breath out of me. My hands scramble for balance, slide, fail. My heart slams against my ribs so hard it hurts.

My pulse roars in my ears. My chest burns. I try to breathe deeper, but the air won't go where it's supposed to. Panic rises fast and hot, clawing up my throat. Hands again. On my arms. On my shoulders. Stronger now. Guiding. My skin crawls.

"Please," I try.

My mouth opens. No sound comes out. The lights blur. A flash of someone turning away. A familiar shape. A promise already broken. It's Carter. He left me. He left me there for his coach to rape so he could get playtime on the field. The realization hits harder than the hands ever could. Left. I was left. My chest caves in. I fold inward, my arms wrap around myself as if I can disappear into my own ribs, into bone, into nothing.

"No," I sob. "No—please—"

The words lodge in my throat and won't come out. My breath stutters. My body trembles, helpless, braced for something I can't name but know is coming. The sound of rotor blades grows, drowning out everything else. With it, my desperation heightens. My mouth opens again. And this time, one name breaks free. The one name I didn't know to call out ten years ago, but who was there nevertheless.

"Massimo."

It rips out of me, raw and desperate, like a lifeline

thrown into black water. Like the last thing I have. My body jerks. Air floods my lungs in a sharp, painful gasp. My eyes fly open. Darkness. A ceiling I don't recognize.

My heart hammers wildly, my skin is slick with sweat, the sheets are twisted around my legs like restraints I can't quite escape. It takes a second—two—for the present to crash back in. Then I see *him.*

Standing at the foot of the bed.

Emotions crash over me too hard to describe, too many to decipher. Crawling out of *that* particular nightmare is always hard. But with the added sound of the helicopter taking Amauri away, it feels like I'm not simply suffocating, but being eviscerated at the same time. Sweat drips down from every pore in my body. I can feel my hair plastered to my skin, not that I care. My heart is pounding so fast and hard inside my chest, it feels impossible that it's still going. Breathing hurts, like it did back then... like I had been choked in real time. My eyes meet Massimo's, and the déjà vu moment robs me of my last breath. I can't help it, though, because hope collides with fear as hard as it did back then. Only now my hands are sticky with sweat, not blood.

Time seems to halt completely as we stare at each other. Like the years are moving backward in the blink of an eye. I don't know if he feels what I feel, but for me, it's as if all the emotions that happened in the following months after that day have been balled up and stuffed down my throat. Hope, love, betrayal, secrets, laughter, tears, all of it tumbling through my head like laundry in a dryer.

Most of all, there is need. A primal, deep-rooted, lonely need. Besides Amauri, nobody has hugged or embraced me in ten years. I haven't kissed anybody, haven't made love to anybody in ten years. And my traitorous body chooses this moment to remind me of how Massimo excelled at making it sing.

It's more than desire, though. A sob rips from my throat, lonely, desperate, if he would hold me, just hold me for one moment—a minute, that's all I'm asking—I know I'd find the strength to fight on. I always do. I know my eyes are pleading, the raw hunger in me for anything, any kind of human contact, anything to make me feel anything else besides pain. I don't even have the energy to be ashamed of it. He steps closer, just one step, it's all it takes to make my breath hitch, to make my heart stumble in its own impossible rhythm. His dark eyes turn darker. I know that look. That burning hunger. The desire. I've seen it so many times. One of them created Amauri. He wants me as much as I want him. If time felt like it stopped before, it's now gone entirely. Time doesn't exist. It's just him and me. No present, no past, no future. Nothing. We're suspended in this room.

Another step.

He's so close, the air between our mouths is nothing but hunger, the invisible thread that has always tied us together jerking taut without warning. I feel it snap me forward—an electric, involuntary spasm—and suddenly his gaze is so intense it's not just a sensation, it's a physical presence on my skin, like the heat of a fever. I'm dizzy and alive, more alive than I've been in years, and I realize I've been half-asleep for a decade, sleepwalking through my days with a part of me cordoned off, preserved like some delicate, unlabeled tissue sample: *Do Not Disturb*. Now he looks at me, and the echo of my desire takes form again, recalibrating itself in the new, post-Massimo world, unable to distinguish between survival and annihilation.

He leans in, slow and deliberate, as if he's savoring every millisecond of my anticipation, the way a lion might savor the stuttering heartbeat of prey before the kill. His knee lands on the edge of the mattress with the heavy inevitability of fate, the mattress tilts under his weight, and a low moan of protest from the frame punctuates the silence. His hand is on my waist, shockingly warm, the briefest flex of his fingers lighting up every dormant nerve ending from my navel to my spine. His thumb traces the thin band of skin above my waistband, and I shudder with the certainty that I have been waiting, unconsciously, for this precise moment since the last one ended.

He pulls me forward, and my body—traitorous, grateful, starved—melts into the space he makes for me. I crash into his chest, the old familiar solidity of it, that slab of muscle and bone and memory, and the last shreds of my composure evaporate. His lips are on mine, and I know instantly that the intervening years were a fabrication, that time is not, after all, real. This is the first kiss, and the last, and every desperate, whispered promise in between. His mouth is hot, demanding, his teeth nipping my lower lip as if to say, *Don't you dare leave me again*. I whimper, actually whimper, and his answering growl is the sound I used to live for, the sound that told me I was seen, claimed, wanted so deeply it could almost be mistaken for hate.

My hands move up his back, the broad, muscular stretch of it now mapped by age and violence and the kind of gym devotion that never fades. His hair is shorter than I remember, softer, and I wind my fingers through it, anchoring myself lest I float away entirely. The kiss deepens, his tongue finds mine with a slow, devastating certainty, a choreography so familiar my body falls into it like muscle memory. My mind, that old traitor, tries to keep pace: *This is wrong, this is dangerous, this is Massimo, you are not the girl you were*. But his mouth and hands and breath are an argument that drowns out everything but the drumbeat of *now, now, now*.

His other hand slides to my lower back, urging me closer, and I'm aware of the heat of his skin through the thin cotton of my shirt, the blunt pressure of his thigh between mine. My body responds with a reflexive hunger, that white-hot ache I thought I'd cauterized years ago now roaring up through my pelvis, raw and unashamed. He kisses along my jaw, my throat, dragging his teeth over the skin and leaving a trail of goosebumps in his wake. I tip my head back, surrendering, baring my neck like some offering.

"Jenna," he breathes, my name. I gasp, and he smiles against my skin, knowing exactly what it does to me.

The years collapse and expand simultaneously. I remember the first time we kissed, I remember the last time, too, though I didn't know it was the last, didn't know he'd disappear and take half of me with him. But memory is powerless now; the present is too overwhelming, too urgent. I want him to consume me, to erase the years of loneliness and longing with the brutality of his touch.

He tugs at my shirt, and I lift my arms, letting him peel it away. For a second, he pauses, just looking at me, his chest rising and falling like he's trying to memorize something essential. His hand cups my jaw, his thumb slides along my cheek with a tenderness that undoes me more than the hunger ever could.

"You're still so fucking beautiful," he murmurs, and I want to laugh, or cry, or both, but there's no room for anything except the way he's looking at me, as if I'm the only thing in the world worth the trouble.

His mouth finds mine again, rougher this time, his hands move greedily along my ribs, my hips, my thighs. I am desperate to touch him, to verify that he's real, that this is not some delirious hallucination conjured by a lonely, overworked brain. My palms move up and down his back. Somewhere in the back of my mind, I notice raised skin, but when he takes my breast into his hand, the shudders moving through me nearly kill me, and I forget all about it. I'm so close to coming, just from his kiss and touch.

The pad of his thumb caresses my nipple, sending more sparks through me, ready to ignite the charge already spreading through me. I arch my back, he looks up at me, then down, his eyes catch the tattoo poking out from underneath my breast, and he stiffens.

With a groan that could be the moan of a dying animal, he pushes back. "Fuck!"

The word tears out of him, rough and unguarded, he's breathing hard, his chest is rising and falling like he's just run a mile instead of crossing a room. So am I. We stare at each other, suspended in the wreckage of what almost happened. His hands are still on me, one at my waist, fingers digging in like he's anchoring himself, the other braced against the mattress. I can feel the tension coiled in him, every muscle locked tight, his body fighting an order his mind is screaming.

His eyes flick over my face like he's cataloging damage. Tears. Sweat. The way my lips are still parted, still chasing the echo of his. Confusion burns through his expression, sharp and ugly and real. Desire is there too—I can see it, feel it—but it's tangled with something darker. Rage. Guilt. Fear. Control slipping. He shakes his head once, hard, like he's trying to clear it.

"This—" he starts, then stops. His jaw tightens, his teeth grind against each other. "This can't happen."

The words land like a slap. I flinch, just barely. "I didn't —" My voice breaks. I swallow and try again. "I didn't mean to—"

My hands fumble for the shirt he took off me, pulling it around me like a shield.

"I know," he snaps, too fast, then reins it in. His voice drops into something rougher. "That's the problem."

He stands abruptly, creating space like it's the only thing keeping him upright. His hands rake through his hair; he paces once, twice, like a caged animal.

"I come home and hear you screaming my name," he mutters, not looking at me. "I walk in and find you drowning in a nightmare. And then you look at me like that—" He turns back, eyes blazing. "Like I'm the only thing keeping you from falling apart."

My throat tightens.

"Because you are," I whisper.

That stops him. Not cold. Not fully. But enough. He closes his eyes briefly, as if the weight of that sentence presses straight through bone. When he opens them again, something has hardened.

"This is not comfort," he warns quietly. "This is not mercy. And it is definitely not forgiveness." He looks at me like he's memorizing every crack in my armor. "This is a mistake waiting to become a weapon."

Silence stretches between us, heavy and charged and unfinished. I sit there, shaking, hands clenched in the sheets. Forgiveness? What does *he* have to forgive *me* for? He turns toward the door, then stops.

Without looking back, he orders, "Get some sleep." Then, softer—so soft I almost miss it—"And don't scream my name like that again unless you mean to tell me why."

The door closes behind him. I collapse forward, forehead resting against my knees, my breath comes in ragged pulls. Because now I know the truth. I didn't just *wake* from a nightmare. I stepped right into another. Into the one where Massimo hates me for unknown reasons. Forgiveness? If anybody has anything to forgive, it's me. It was he who walked out on me. Wasn't it?

For the first time, I'm starting to wonder. Did he really leave me, or did something happen? But what? And why wouldn't he have contacted me?

Later that day...

The gym still smells like iron, sweat, and old violence. I need it. The weights. The burn. The punishment my body understands better than thought. Alessio and I go at it hard—pads first, then sparring—until my muscles scream and my lungs drag fire. He's good. Always has been. Fast, brutal, smart enough not to get sloppy when emotions are in play.

Doesn't stop him from reading me anyway. He steps back, rolling his shoulders, sweat running down his spine. "So," he says casually. Too casually. "A son?"

I snort, wiping my face with a towel. "Word spreads fast."

He grins. "You run a family. Gossip's part of the benefits package."

I don't bother denying it. There's no point. They'll all know soon enough.

"Yeah," I say. "Amauri."

The name feels strange in my mouth. Heavy. Permanent.

Alessio's expression shifts, not soft, but respectful. "That changes things."

"Everything," I agree.

He nods once. "Damiano find anything yet?"

"Not yet," I fill him in. "If he doesn't by tonight, I'll pay Senator Kingsley a visit myself."

Alessio's jaw tightens. "You want backup? I'm here." No bravado. Just fact.

I nod. "I know."

He said the same thing the first night we ran from cops into a Russian bar that didn't take kindly to boys carrying the wrong last names. We weren't brothers then. Not even close. Just reckless, territorial, and too proud to back down. He didn't owe me anything. He took the first punch anyway.

Outside, several SUVs idle, engines low and patient, waiting for us to step back into our roles. Men straighten when they see us. Doors open. The world slots back into place. I sink into the back seat and lean my head against the soft leather, eyes closing for half a second. Big mistake.

Instantly, I see green eyes. Wide. Shattered. Wanting. Her mouth still parted. The way her breath hitched. The way she melted into me like the last ten years never happened. The kiss. Her soft skin.

Fuck.

My body reacts instantly, traitorous and unforgiving. My cock turns painfully hard, like I'm twenty again instead of a man who should know better. Like she didn't rip something out of me and leave me bleeding in the street.

I exhale through my nose and adjust my hips, irritated beyond reason. Fuck her. I should be thinking about fentanyl-laced coke. About betrayals and transport routes and a senator who thinks he's untouchable. Instead, I'm thinking about the way she felt in my arms. That's a weakness. And weaknesses get you killed.

I open my eyes as the SUV pulls away, the city sliding back into motion outside the window. I'll deal with her later. Right now, I have an empire to protect. And a son to get back. As if on cue, my phone lights up. Enzo.

"I might have a trace," he dives in without preamble.

I straighten slightly. "On who?"

"A guy moving between Pablo's level and street distribution. He's sloppy. Thought himself invisible."

I smile without humor. "No one is invisible."

A pause. Then, "I'll have him ready."

"Take him to the warehouse."

That surprises him, and he goes quiet for half a beat. "The warehouse?" He exhales. "Not the Oven?"

"No." Not today. This needs to be close. Personal. What I don't say is that I need to hit something. Someone. I need to lose myself in the kind of violence that empties the noise out of my head and leaves only breath and bone and consequence.

"Got you. I'll have him there in an hour." If anybody gets me, it's him. He has his own ghosts to contend with.

I end the call and lean back as the SUV eats up the road, the city blurs past tinted glass. An hour. Enough time to get home and take a shower. To scrub her scent off my skin. Or try. I close my eyes for a second too long. Green eyes again.

The kiss.

The way she fit against me like my body remembers something my mind wants to erase. My jaw tightens. Fuck. I open my eyes and stare straight ahead as the car turns toward the Strip. Whatever happens in that warehouse will be clean. Simple. Pain in exchange for answers. Blood for balance. I can handle that. It's the things waiting back at my penthouse that are going to cost me.

Vegas slides past the windows in neon streaks. I don't see it. I'm counting seconds instead. Time wasted. Time stolen. Time my son is somewhere I can't reach yet. Enzo's last call still sits heavy in my ear. The SUV slows. Stops. I step out into the valet area, adjust my cuffs, and force my shoulders down. Don. Emperor. A man who does not unravel. Mask on.

The private elevator waits.

I strip off my jacket as I step inside and drape it over my arm without thinking. The motion feels wrong halfway through, like some part of me already knows tonight will not be clean. The doors close. Up. Each floor passes too slowly. My mind keeps circling back to her—Jenna. She'll be exhausted. She'll be wrecked. She'll cry. I can handle that. I expect her to come apart the way people always do when they finally run out of places to hide, out of lies to spin. To fold inward. To apologize for leaving me the way she did. For keeping my son from me. I expect tears, shaking hands, and lowered eyes. Begging, maybe. A quiet kind of repentance dressed up as regret.

I know what to do with that version of her. I'll let her speak. I'll let the guilt drain out of her until there's nothing left but relief and dependence. Until she looks at me like I'm the authority in the room. The man who decides what happens next. I expect her to crawl back to the place I left her, grateful I'm still standing here at all. Yes. That's the version of her I can live with.

The elevator stops. The doors slide open. I make my way through the antechamber and nod at the security guards. Gabe left five minutes ago after I told him I was on my way. Max opens the door to my penthouse.

She's standing there.

Not asleep.

Not curled up.

Definitely not broken.

Standing barefoot on the marble, eyes blazing, wrapped in my shirt like she chose it *on purpose*. She's on me, before I can say a word. "Where have you been?"

The sound hits me square in the chest. I barely step out before she's already moving toward me.

"Do you have any idea how long I've been waiting?" she snaps. "Do you think I slept? Do you think I can sleep while my son is missing?"

This is wrong. This is not the version I prepared for. "Jenna—"

"No." She cuts me off, jabbing a finger at my chest. "No. You don't get to say my name like that and expect calm. Where is Amauri?"

Her voice isn't breaking. It's worse. She's close now. Too close. I can smell her, soap, adrenaline, fear. My shirt hangs off her shoulder, collar stretched, sleeves too long.

She needs to be wearing something else. The thought

flashes sharp and irrational. I need to fix it. I don't know why. I just do.

"Have you found anything yet?" she demands. "Anything at all? Or did you just disappear again?"

Again?

The word lands harder than a slap.

"I'm working on it," I growl, irritated with her attitude.

Her mouth twists. "*Working on it*," she repeats, disbelief sharpening every syllable. "That's what this is to you? A delay?"

She shoves my chest. Not hard. Enough.

"You promised me," she nearly shouts, and now her eyes shine, furious and wet. "You looked at me and promised me you would bring him back."

I did no such thing, but I'll entertain her for a moment. Because even I know a mother can be irrational in a situation like this. "I will," I vow instantly, without hesitation.

She laughs, short and bitter. "Then why are you standing here with nothing?"

The jacket slips from my arm and hits the floor. I don't look down.

"I haven't gone after anyone yet," I chose my words carefully, deliberately. "Because I don't know who has *them*."

I stretch the *them* because, for some reason, she seems to be forgetting about her husband. I wish I could do the same. Carter fucking Whitford.

Her breath stutters. "So you don't have him," she states flatly.

"No."

The word costs me. Her shoulders rise and fall once. She doesn't scream. She doesn't cry. She just looks at me like I'm something she's deciding whether to trust or break.

"I don't care what you have to do." There is a fire in her eyes I've never seen before, not even after she killed Coach and threatened to kill me next. "I don't care how ugly it gets." She steps closer, close enough that I feel heat through my shirt, close enough that my body reacts before my mind can stop it, recognition, possession, memory. The instinct to pull her in hits hard and fast, immediately followed by the urge to shove her away. "Just don't come back without my son."

My son.

The words slam into me, delayed, violent.

My son?

The thought fractures outward, splintering through everything I've been holding together. How dare she? How fucking dare she stand here—barefoot, in *my* home, wearing *my* shirt as if it belonged to her—making demands like I haven't already lost ten years I didn't even know were mine. She didn't just keep Amauri from me. She erased him. No, worse. She erased *me*. I didn't know she was pregnant. I didn't get a choice. I didn't get a chance to protect him, to claim him, to fail *or* save him. She decided all of it for me, and now she's standing here invoking him like a weapon.

My jaw tightens until it aches. She doesn't get to do that. She doesn't get to withhold my blood from me and then tell me how to bleed. Anger roars up, fast and vicious, hot enough to scorch everything in its path. A decade of absence crashes into me all at once, first steps I never saw, nights I never guarded, a childhood lived without my name backing it. And still—

I want her.

That's the part that almost breaks me. I want her even as I resent her. Even as the word *son* detonates inside my chest and rearranges my entire sense of self. Even as every instinct I have screams to take control, to assert ownership, to remind her exactly who she's standing in front of. She looks at me like she's daring me to say it. Like she's daring me to deny him. Something ugly coils low in my gut, not just rage, but fear. A new kind. Sharp. Exposed. Because now there's something I can't afford to lose.

And she fucking knows it.

I step closer, not touching her, not yet. Just close enough that she has to tilt her chin up to keep looking at me.

"*My* son," I repeat quietly, tasting the words like they might cut me back.

Her breath stutters. Just once. Good.

I hate her for this.

I need her for this.

Somewhere beneath the fury, beneath the entitlement and the loss, something irreversible locks into place: Whoever took Amauri didn't just declare war on my empire. They touched my blood. And there will be no version of ugly I won't embrace to get him back. But first, I need to deal with the man waiting for me in the warehouse. The man who has no idea what's coming for him, because my fury is unleashed as it has never been before, and nobody will have mercy on him, least of all me.

I leave Jenna seething in the living room, slam the door to my bedroom in her face, and step into the shower, daring her to follow me. She doesn't.

The water is scalding, just the way I like it. I let it burn, let it scrape the night off me; the sound of Jenna's voice still ricochets inside my skull. *My son.* The words won't settle. They don't belong to the past anymore.

I'm bracing my hands against the tile when the phone rings. For one moment, I contemplate just letting it ring, but my sense of responsibility wins out. Ten years ago, I fought for my life to become the Don of the Vegas family, and I'm not about to jeopardize it. Not for her. Not for anybody.

I reach for the towel on the warmer, wrap it around my hips, and grab the phone from the vanity where I left it. For a moment, I catch my reflection in the mirror. The scars pitter-pattering all across my chest and arms, twining around my torso onto my back and legs that are currently, mercifully, hidden. Did Jenna feel them earlier when her hands roamed my back? I wonder what she would think of my body now. A sardonic smile curves my lips.

I hit answer and put it on speaker so I can keep drying off. "Talk."

Damiano is on the other end. Like always, he doesn't waste time. "The chopper," he says. "I traced it."

My spine goes still. "I'm listening."

"Venezuela."

The word lands wrong. Heavy. Out of place. Venezuela? "That doesn't make sense."

"I know," Damiano replies. "Tail numbers are clean, though. It's run through a shell company out of Curaçao. Fuel logs match."

I wrap a towel around my waist, my mind already moving.

"I don't buy from Venezuela," I say.

"No," he agrees. "*You* don't."

Venezuelan coke is trash. Flood product. Chaos supply. The kind of shit that burns cities fast and dirty. Which means this isn't business. At least not related to mine.

"What else?" I ask.

Damiano exhales. "The timing lines up with Kingsley's bill."

That's how the pieces click. A choked laughter bubbles out of me. This has nothing to do with me. But EVERYTHING with Kingsley. The Venezuelan fuckers have no idea what kind of hornet's nest they just hit. This is about Senator Kingsley. His clean hands. His public crusades. The trafficking bill that gutted entire pipelines. The next one aimed at drugs: *Nevada first*.

"This has nothing to do with us then," I say out loud to hear the finality.

"That's what it looks like," Damiano agrees. "This is about Senator Kingsley and his drug bill. They wanted leverage, they got it."

Only that they don't have Jenna. The only one who might have swayed the senator to do their bidding. He doesn't give a shit about Carter or Amauri. I doubted he would make an exception for his daughter even if the Venezuelan's did put their hands on her. But they don't know that. Which means they'll be coming after Jenna harder once they realize their leverage is shit.

That shouldn't bother me as much as it does.

"I'll have Enzo work on the New York angle." I fill Damiano in.

Kingsley is fully in the pockets of La Famiglia in New York. I don't know what kind of leverage they have on him, and I don't want to know, but I do know that touching him could cause waves with New York.

I wouldn't have given a shit six months ago, and I still won't hesitate if it becomes necessary, but Enzo has family ties with them. His new son-in-law is a capo to one of the biggest families. It's easier to work together than to be at war, so I'll give them the courtesy of talking to them first.

After we hang up, I take a deep breath. This drama is taking up more of my time than I want it to. My empire is on fire from within, and I'm distracted by a son I didn't know about and... his mother. Fuck.

I need to get my head in the game and focus on the jackass that Enzo's got strung up first.

I PACE. NOT BECAUSE I'M NERVOUS. BECAUSE IF I STOP moving, I might break something. The hallway in front of Massimo's bedroom is too clean, too quiet. The marble under my bare feet is cool, the soft lighting meant to soothe. Nothing about this night should be soothed.

I drag a hand through my hair and exhale hard through my nose. *Get it together.*

I was ready for this. I *prepped* for this. I built myself up brick by brick while he was gone, told myself exactly what I would say, exactly how this would go.

Fuck him.

Fuck him for vanishing ten years ago like I was nothing. Like what we had was disposable. One day he was there—dangerous and intense and real—and the next he was just *gone*. No explanation. No goodbye. Just absence.

Poof.

And now he has the audacity to stand there and look at me like *I* committed some unforgivable crime because I didn't bring a baby to his doorstep while he was off doing whatever he was doing?

I didn't *withhold* Amauri. I protected him.

The memory sharpens my spine instead of softening it.

I didn't know where Massimo Manetti went. He was like a ghost. We had disposable phones we only used to contact each other, and his went silent just like him. So yeah, fuck him. He walked out on *me*! I didn't know if he'd ever come back. My father gave me two choices. Marry Carter or get an abortion.

So yes. I chose.

I chose my son. And three months later, I was married to Carter. If that makes me guilty in his eyes, he can choke on it.

I stop pacing long enough to plant my hands on my hips and stare at his bedroom door. He's in there now. I can hear the shower running. I can almost see the steam fogging up the glass like this is just another night, another problem he'll wash off his skin before going out to solve his problems with violence and money.

Good for him. I don't get that luxury.

I don't get to be distracted, especially not by the infuriating fact that my body still remembers his. The way he fills space. The way my pulse reacts when he's too close. No. I shove that thought down hard.

I don't get to be horny.

I don't get to be nostalgic.

I don't get to want him.

Amauri is missing.

Everything else is noise.

If Massimo decides this is too complicated, too political, too slow—if he starts talking about strategy while my son is somewhere terrified and alone—

I'll do it myself. I have connections. Not like his. Not armies or empires or warehouses full of men who kill on command. But I'm not powerless. I know people who owe my father. I know people who owe *me*. I know how to move quietly when I must. If I have to burn bridges to get Amauri back, I will. If I have to walk into hell without Massimo, I will. He doesn't get the moral high ground. He doesn't get to decide how this goes.

The shower shuts off. My heart kicks once, hard, traitorous. For a moment, I wonder if he still likes it as hot as he used to. Then I straighten my spine and still myself. Whatever comes out of that room isn't a savior. He's either an ally—or he's in my way.

I will not hesitate to remove obstacles.

I've killed a man before. Not in anger. Not for power. I did it because he didn't stop. I'd do it again. Now more than ever.

The door opens. Massimo steps out. Fully dressed. Black suit, cut sharp enough to look like it could draw blood. Black shirt beneath it, no softness anywhere, no concessions. A red tie at his throat. Dark, deliberate, like he put it on knowing exactly what it does to people. To me.

His hair is dry now, dark brown so deep it's almost black, brushed back in that careless way that isn't careless at all. His face is all hard lines and control, his eyes piercing, unreadable, dangerous. He looks like a gangster. Not the myth. Not the romanticized version. The real thing.

The kind of man mothers warn their daughters about and daughters dream about anyway. Every inch of him is confidence, power, violence wrapped in tailoring that probably costs more than most people's cars.

My body reacts before I can stop it. Heat. Low and traitorous. A sharp pull in my stomach that has nothing to do with fear and everything to do with memory. God help me, he's been the star of my wet dreams more times than I want to admit; I want him even now, even like this. I hate that. I clamp down hard on the feeling, like slamming a door on a draft. Not now. Not him. Not when my son is missing.

Massimo's gaze flicks over me once, fast and assessing, like he's taking inventory. I can't tell if he notices my reaction or if he's just cataloging threats the way he always does.

"Have you eaten?" he asks.

The question throws me more than anything else tonight.

"No." It confuses me enough to counter, "Have you?"

A pause. Fractional. Honest. "No."

I fold my arms. "Then don't start."

"You need to eat," he replies calmly.

"So do you." I refute.

His mouth tightens, not irritation. Something else. Like he hadn't expected the mirror.

"I will," he almost smirks.

"When?" I ask.

He meets my eyes. Holds them. "After I know where *our* son is."

The word lands: *our*. But I don't give him the satisfaction of seeing it. He doesn't get to play the martyr.

"Then we're both starving," I grind out. "Congratulations. Very productive."

A ghost of something crosses his face. Not a smile.

"Stubborn," he accuses.

"Takes one," I reply.

Silence settles as we both remember the old times we used to banter. But it's different now. Combative. He's still watching me intently when his lips move again. "I know where the helicopter went."

Just like that, we're back to business. Back to war. My heart steadies. Focus snaps back into place. "Where?"

"Venezuela."

The word doesn't make sense.

"Venezuela?" It takes me a moment to connect the dots. "So, my father was right. This is about the bill. About drugs."

"Looks like it," he agrees.

I press my arms against my chest, grounding myself, ignoring the way the suit moves when he shifts, how everything about him looks like it was designed to command attention.

"Kingsley's bill will hurt them. Nevada, New York, Chicago, and L.A. are their primary markets," Massimo explains.

I frown. "It's a good bill."

"Depends on where you stand," he disagrees. "Drugs are a lucrative business; they bring in a lot of money, and money is important to a lot of very powerful people."

I draw a slow breath, grounding myself. "Drugs are evil. They ruin lives. They kill people. They rot everything they touch."

Massimo watches me like I've just said something interesting, not naïve.

"People ruin themselves," he replies mildly. "Drugs just show them how."

"That's bullshit," I snap. "They need to be stopped. They shouldn't be coming into this country at all."

He laughs then. Not loud. Not cruel. Almost fond. "And you think your father is the right man to stop that?"

"Damn straight I do." As his daughter, I might not be his biggest fan, but this I can say without hesitation. "He believes in it. He's spent his entire career trying to clean things up."

Massimo nods once, slow. Considering. "Sweetheart," he says gently, and the word lands heavier than any insult ever could, "politicians are the ones who benefit the most from drug money."

I stare at him. "That's not true. They're the ones trying to stop it."

This time, he laughs out loud. The sound cuts through the room, sharp and unapologetic. He shakes his head like he can't believe I still think the world works the way it's supposed to.

"Do you really believe," he asks calmly, "that if the full power of the United States government wanted drugs out of this country—if the DEA, the FBI, the military, every alphabet agency you can name actually wanted them gone—they would still be here?"

I open my mouth. Nothing comes out. I close it. My mind whirls. Is he right?

"Borders are suggestions," he continues. "Ports are owned. Cartels don't move without permission. Nothing that big survives without protection."

I feel cold all over.

"Trust me, Sirena." His tone is not condescending, which makes it worse. "The men you vote for are the ones getting rich." My stomach twists. "And I'm fully on board," he adds, without shame, "with benefiting from the same system they pretend to fight."

Silence crashes down between us. I don't agree with him. I've always known my father could be cruel. Ambitious. Calculating. But I thought the crusades were real. That the causes meant something. That underneath the strategy, there was conviction. If that isn't true—

I swallow. "My father—"

"—has enemies," Massimo cuts in calmly. "And protection."

The words scrape.

"You don't know him," I deny. "He's difficult. He's cold. He's obsessed with appearances. But he's not corrupt. Not in the way you are thinking."

The word hangs between us. I'm not naïve about my father. He knew what Carter did to me. He knew. And he still pushed the wedding forward. For his campaign. For the optics. For control. I don't pretend that was kindness. But ambition isn't the same thing as corruption. My father truly believes in what he's fighting. Human trafficking. Drug cartels. The men who profit off addiction and broken girls. I've seen the files. The late-night strategy calls. The anger that isn't performative. He wants to stop it. He just believes the world is only saved by people ruthless enough to reshape it.

And sometimes, reshaping it requires collateral. I was collateral, I accepted that. What I can't accept, what I can't forgive, ever, is his willingness to sacrifice Amauri. Still, objectively, that doesn't make him corrupt. It makes him... an asshole. A very egocentric, egomaniacal asshole. Massimo studies me for a long moment. Not dismissive. Almost careful.

"I'm not saying he sold himself," he admits quietly. "I'm saying someone found a way to hold him still."

The temperature in the room seems to drop a few degrees. "That's not the same thing."

"No," Massimo agrees. "It's worse."

I shake my head. "You're reaching."

"If I am," he challenges, "prove it."

That stops me. He steps closer—not crowding me, not touching—but close enough that I have to tilt my chin up.

"New York doesn't invest in politicians out of admiration," he continues. "They invest because they get something back. Silence. Timing. Restraint." My stomach twists. "And when a man with a clean public image becomes untouchable," Massimo continues, "it's usually because touching him would expose something."

He's giving me a challenge. "You're thinking my father is in the New York mafia's pocket. You want me to look and find out why?"

"Yes."

"You want me to investigate my father."

"See what he's protecting," Massimo reiterates.

I swallow.

"For Amauri," he adds.

The word lands differently now. Not as leverage. As alignment. I look away, jaw tight, thoughts racing. If someone has something on my father... if this isn't about money... if this is about reputation, or history, or a mistake buried deep enough to rot quietly... it would almost make sense that he's ready to sacrifice his grandson. Not to me. But to his fucked-up mind.

"What if there's nothing?" I argue purely on reflex, years of conditioning.

"Then we clear him," Massimo replies without hesitation. "And we remove anyone who thought our son was acceptable collateral."

My chest tightens with something I refuse to name.

"And if there is something?" I ask quietly.

Massimo's eyes darken, his tone merciless. "Then we use it. And we get Amauri back."

I straighten, spine locking into place. "Fine," I agree. "I'll look."

He nods once. No triumph. No gratitude. Just war, advancing.

As he turns back toward the exit, I realize something chillingly clear: He didn't ask me to make myself useful. He assumed I would. And for the first time in a long time, I don't feel deployed. I feel valued.

THE NEXT DAY...

Enzo doesn't sit until I tell him to. That alone tells me he already knows this isn't a normal meeting. The office is quiet, the blinds are half drawn, Vegas is still pretending it's just another morning. I stare at the strip outside. By daylight, the city looks like a beautiful whore without makeup. No shadow. No illusion. Just harsh angles and exhaustion you're not supposed to notice. Cracks in the paint. Stale air. Regret clinging to everything like smoke that never quite clears.

This is why we build without windows. Why we run tunnels under the city.

Why we dim the lights, blur the edges, and keep the clocks out of sight. People can't see reality and keep losing money. They need darkness. They need noise. They need to be drunk enough on light and sound and promise to forget that the magic is manufactured.

So we keep them inside. We keep them distracted. We keep them wanting.

Vegas only works if you never let it wake up. I stand at the glass anyway, watching the city stripped bare by the sun, and think about my son somewhere far away, exposed to men who don't bother with illusion at all.

I don't care if this city falters while I'm gone.

Illusions can be rebuilt.

Blood cannot.

Enzo knows me well enough to sit in the silence until I break it. "I'm going to Venezuela."

He doesn't blink for a few seconds. "Venezu-*fucking*-ela?" he curses. "What the hell for?"

"I have to get my son," I state simply. The words hang there, heavy, undeniable.

Enzo frowns. Just slightly. "Your... son?"

I watch the way the pieces shift behind his eyes, rearranging themselves into something that finally makes sense. Kingsley. The helicopter. The boy.

"Oh," he says quietly. Then, "Fuck me."

"Yeah," I agree. "My son."

He drags a hand down his face, exhales hard. "Kingsley's grandson is—"

"Mine."

Silence detonates between us.

"That's why," Enzo says slowly. Not a question. "That's why this isn't negotiable."

"Gabe's already moving," I fill him in. "Boots on the ground. Intel. I'll be in and out. Two days. Max."

"No, you don't want—," Enzo snaps. He reins it in fast, but the damage is done. "This will send the wrong message. You disappear now, and every vulture in this city will smell blood."

"I won't be disappearing."

"You'll be out of the country," he points out sharply. "That's the same thing."

I lean back against my desk, grabbing the headrest of my chair. Calm. Deliberate. "I have to get my son, Enzo."

Enzo exhales hard, scrubs a hand over his face. "I'll go."

I don't answer.

"I know the terrain," he presses. "I have the contacts. I can get in and out without the entire underworld lighting up."

"It has to be me."

"Why?" His voice cracks just enough to give him away. "Because it's personal?"

"Yes."

"That's exactly why you *can't* go," he fires back. "You're the king. You don't chase. You don't expose yourself like this."

I stand. The chair slides back quietly. Final. "As you already pointed out, this is not negotiable."

"And what happens to everything you've built if you don't come back?" Enzo asks. "If you die—"

"I won't."

He laughs. Short. Bitter. "You sound like every man who ever thought love made him invincible."

I step closer, lowering my voice. "No, this isn't about love. Love hesitates."

I meet his eyes. "This is about responsibility. About my son."

That does it. Enzo bows his head. Just a fraction. Submission, not defeat. "What do you want me to do?"

"I want you to reach out to New York. Quietly. Find out if they're willing to remind Kingsley how much he owes them. I want everything he knows, before I land."

Enzo pulls out his phone. He's loyal. He always has been. I won't punish him for fighting me; that's his job.

"What do I tell them?" he asks.

I don't hesitate. "As little as possible."

Enzo nods once, already dialing, already shifting into motion. He stops at the door.

"You think this has anything to do with the poison?" he asks. "With what's happening on the streets?"

I don't hesitate, "No. This is separate."

He turns back, searching my face. "You're sure."

"The Venezuelans don't play games like that." I'm positive on this. This is nothing but a coincidence, bad timing. "They don't undermine markets. They flood them. Whatever's poisoning my product is someone else's work."

"And Venezuela?" he presses.

"They have no idea what they started."

Enzo absorbs that, then straightens. "While you're gone?"

"You watch everything," I order. "Every shipment. Every test. Every whisper. I want eyes on the distributors, the warehouses, the drivers. I want to know what the streets are saying about me."

"And if the rumors start moving?"

I reply, "You don't chase the mouths. You find who's feeding them."

He nods. Once. Final.

"I'll keep the city steady," he promises.

"I know."

He leaves to make the call.

I don't sit. I call Damiano.

He answers before the second ring finishes. "I was just about to call you, boss."

That alone tightens something in my chest.

"Talk," I say.

"There's noise," he tells me. "Not loud. Not yet. But it's old."

I stop moving. "Old how?"

"Like something that remembers," he picks his words carefully. "South side. A few guys saying Mexico's stirring. That a debt nobody talks about is waking up."

A familiar cold settles under my skin. "What kind of debt?"

Another pause. Damiano chooses his words like they might detonate. "Blood. From long ago. Maybe your father."

I close my eyes for half a second. Not in surprise. In calculation. Mexico doesn't move on ghosts. Cartels move for profit. Territory. Opportunity. Not memory. Blood from long ago isn't a cartel problem. It's a lineage problem.

Vendettas don't need announcements. They don't need flags or press or noise. They just need time. And time is something my family has never lacked.

"Who's saying this?" I want to know.

"Nobody specific. Which is what makes it dangerous."

Nobody specific means it isn't rumor. It's circulation. Whispers that test the temperature before the knife comes out.

"Keep listening," I tell him. "Don't move."

"Yes, boss."

The line goes dead.

I stand alone in my office, the city humming outside as if nothing is wrong.

Venezuela is a problem.

But this?

This feels like the past deciding it's done waiting. And I've learned the hard way—when old ghosts stir, they never come alone.

MASSIMO'S OFFICE SMELLS LIKE HIM. EXPENSIVE, dangerous. Something dark and mysterious. I sit at his desk, keeping my spine straight, forcing my hands to steady, preparing to use his computer like it's a weapon I'm still learning how to hold.

He opened an incognito window for me before he left. He didn't say a word about it. Just stepped aside, tapped two keys, and walked out like privacy was something he granted, not something I had to ask for.

The chair is heavy, built for a man who doesn't fidget, who expects the world to adjust around him. I move the mouse, and the screen wakes instantly. No password prompt. No hesitation. Just access. For a moment, I just stare at it. At the quiet arrogance of it. At the assumption that no one here needs permission. Then, because I'm human, because I'm standing in the center of a man's world and pretending I'm immune to it, I let curiosity win. I know I shouldn't. But I try anyway. I click where his profile should be. Or I try to. The bandages make it harder than I expected. My fingers are clumsy inside the gauze, thick and uncooperative, at least on my left. The right is better. Not good. Just... usable. The cursor jerks across the screen in uneven jumps, mocking me. I exhale sharply.

"Of course," I mutter.

For a second, I consider giving up. But that's not my style. I glance around the desk until I find a small pair of scissors tucked into a drawer. I drag them closer, awkward with the bulk of my wrapped hands. I wedge one handle against the desk and force my fingers through the other. It's ridiculous how hard this is. But carefully, snip after snip at the tips of the bandages, I free my fingers. Just enough. The soft cotton loosens, exposing the pads. I flex them once. Better. Usable. I reposition my hand on the mouse; if I'm going to stand in this world, I'm not doing it helpless.

And there they are, user settings. Private directories. Anything that might say Massimo Manetti. The cursor spins once. Then stops. Access denied. Not dramatic. Not locked down with flashing warnings. Just... absent. Like the door was never there to begin with. His world doesn't exist on this machine. Not personally. Not digitally.

What's here is infrastructure. Calendars without context. Files stripped down to function and purpose. No photos. No emails that aren't operational. No trace of a man, only the shape of power. I feel a strange flicker of something. Not disappointment. Respect, maybe. Or the quiet understanding that this is a man who learned a long time ago that the safest place to keep himself is nowhere at all.

Whatever Massimo Manetti is—whatever he fears,

wants, remembers—it isn't stored on a hard drive. It isn't accessible. Not even to me. I pull my hand back from the mouse like I've brushed against something sharp. Then I turn back to what I came here for: My father.

I start where it hurts least. Public records. Safe territory. Familiar. My father's voting history scrolls past the way it always has, clean lines, predictable arcs. Committee memberships. Co-sponsorships. Appearances. I've seen all of this before. Grew up with it. Dinner-table conversations dissecting policy. Talking points rehearsed before interviews. Press strategies discussed like chess. This is the version of my father I've spent years defending.

I click through donations next. Campaign finance reports. PAC disclosures. Everything filed on time. Everything properly categorized. No red flags. No obvious irregularities. Nothing illegal.

My stomach clenches, slow and unmistakable, as if a buried part of me has always understood what this means and is bracing for impact: Everything is too clean. Bills that should have stalled glide through with barely a murmur. Opposition that should have fought tooth and nail quietly disappears. Amendments that should have sparked outrage never materialize. Names that should raise eyebrows don't, at least not on paper.

It's not corruption.

It's lubrication.

The kind that keeps things moving so smoothly, you don't notice the hands applying pressure. I lean back. My burning eyes take in the screen without seeing the words any longer while my mind starts to work, but before anything can settle, I hear a knock on the door. Soft and polite.

The door opens before I answer. A bear of a man steps in, closing it behind him with practiced discretion. He moves like someone trained to clear rooms, not enter them, broad shoulders, compact power, the kind of stillness that comes from knowing exactly where every exit is. He looks like the kind of man you see in recruitment posters or action movies. Black Ops. GI Joe. The kind of soldier who doesn't talk about what he's done because he doesn't have to. He meets my eyes without staring, assessing without being obvious.

"Max," he says. "Head of security for Massimo."

Not at the casino. Not for the building. For Massimo. That alone tells me everything.

"There's a Sean here," he continues. "He wants to see you."

My head snaps up. Sean. My stomach twists. The timing is almost funny. Almost. I should have expected my father to send him or someone, maybe Marianne, sooner rather than later. Instead of trying to call me or coming himself.

"Do I have to?" I hate that my voice isn't steadier, that even now it gives away the kind of vulnerability I always feel around Daddy's bodyguard.

Max doesn't hesitate. "Not if you don't want to."

For all I know, Max might be a cold-blooded killer, but right now, the way he looks at me is nothing but reassuring. It tells me that he has my back, that one word from me and Sean will disappear, no questions asked. For a moment, I wonder what Massimo did to inspire that kind of loyalty in a man. But it's quickly replaced by a feeling of power that I haven't felt... ever? The dangerous part is that I like it. Very much so.

"Then tell him to go fuck himself."

Max's mouth twitches. Then he grins, slow and unapologetic. "It'll be my pleasure, ma'am."

He turns to leave without another word. The door closes. Silence rushes back in, thicker than before. I turn back to the screen, to the immaculate rows of numbers and names and approvals, and feel the unease settle deeper, colder.

I'll be the first to admit I've never been my father's biggest fan. I've always loved him; I mean, he's my father. I think I always will in one form or another. Love doesn't disappear just because you start to see someone clearly. Love, I'm discovering, can live hand-in-hand with hate. It's just... thinner now. Like a photograph that was left out too long in the sun. The shape is still there, but the color isn't.

Looking back, I realize the clues were there. He's always been ambitious. Relentlessly so. Work came before everything else, before birthdays, before dinners, before quiet moments that didn't serve a purpose. The world beyond our front door always seemed to matter more than the one inside it.

I never fully appreciated before what that ambition cost my mother. Publicly, he adored her. He never missed an opportunity to praise her resilience, her grace, her strength in the face of her medical issues. He spoke about her like a testament, like proof of his own decency. Friends admired him for it. The press loved the story, a devoted husband standing by a fragile wife. But love isn't what you say when people are listening. Love is what you protect.

He never protected her from the quiet accusation that lived just beneath the surface: she had failed him by giving him only one child, and a daughter at that. No heir. No legacy in the way he'd imagined it. Her body had betrayed him, and he blamed her for it.

He never said it outright, of course. But he never corrected the assumptions when people joked about him needing a son. Never shut down the speculation. He let the silence do the work for him.

Even as a child, I felt it, the way conversations would subtly shift, the way his pride dimmed when the subject turned to family. The way my mother would smile a little too tightly, as if she were apologizing for something no one should ever have to apologize for.

She died a year after Amauri was born. But in that short time, she was an amazing grandmother who loved him fiercely. She held him like something miraculous. Like a second chance she hadn't been given.

I miss her sometimes. Or maybe I miss the version of her I built in my head. Because the truth is, she wasn't the mother she should have been. Not to me. Not when it mattered most. The day I confided in her—terrified, pregnant, unsure—she told my father. Before I was ready. Before I could decide what that meant for my life. For my child. I told myself she was scared. That she thought she was protecting me. Protecting us. But something in me knew protection shouldn't feel like betrayal.

Even now, I don't know which memory to hold onto: the woman who rocked my son in the quiet hours, or the one who handed my secret to the man who she knew would use it. Maybe that's where I first learned how treachery rarely announces itself. How it slips in quietly and calls itself protection. How professions of love can look like loyalty while serving something else entirely.

His betrayal of her wasn't in the words he used. It was in the ones he didn't. Once you notice that kind of absence, you can't unsee it. Not in a marriage. Not in a family. And not, I'm beginning to realize, in a political career built on immaculate appearances and carefully curated truths.

Clean doesn't mean innocent. Clean doesn't mean untouched. Sometimes it just means someone else took care of the mess.

I still refuse to believe my father would work with the mafia. Or take bribes. Despite all his failures as a husband and parent, there has always been one truth about him that anchored me: he believed in doing the right thing. In changing the world for the better. That the needs of the many outweigh the needs of a few. That mattered to him in a way nothing else ever did. Maybe that belief started as a child's justification, something I told myself to make it easier to accept how cold he could be. But it didn't disappear when I grew up. Not even when I went to him for help, and he told me to marry Carter or get an abortion, even then, I found a way to excuse him. I told myself he had to stay clean. Untouchable. That sacrifices were necessary if he was going to do any real good. Even now.

And the evidence is there. Look at his record. In a single year, he successfully pushed through legislation that all but erased human trafficking from the United States. Not weakened it. Not slowed it down. Destroyed it. That doesn't happen without conviction. Without someone willing to take the hits and keep moving.

So no—whatever my father is, he isn't corrupt. He's a decent man. A moral one. That has to be true. I *need* that to be true.

Yet, the doubt is there. Simmering and festering. One question keeps entering my mind as I stare at the evidence of a world that never pretends to be innocent: how long has my father been protected? And by whom? And why. Hesitantly, I open a second tab. Campaign donors. PACs. Cross-reference addresses. New York pops up more than it should. I swallow, not willing to go there yet. *Amauri*, my heart screams. Amauri. Whatever this is, whatever I find, whatever of my illusions get destroyed, this isn't about me. This is about finding my son.

To stall, I open my email.

YOU ENTERED AN INCORRECT EMAIL AND PASSWORD COMBINATION. PLEASE TRY AGAIN.

I don't panic. I take a deep breath and try again. Slowly, I enter the required letters, making sure my fingers are steady and not hitting the wrong buttons.

You entered an incorrect email and password combination. Please try again.

I'm pretty sure I know where this is going, but I try to reset the password anyway.

Access Denied

My bandaged fist slams on the desk. *Really, Daddy? Really?*

I try his login.

You entered an incorrect email and password combination. Please try again.

I don't bother to try again. I went slow and steady when I entered the required information. Marianne Hall is next on my list.

You entered an incorrect email and password combination. Please try again.

The anger doesn't leave when I push away from the desk. It just changes temperature. Heat cools into something sharper. Sharper turns restless. I know the feeling well enough to recognize the danger in it. This is the part where my thoughts start running faster than I can keep them in order, where questions multiply instead of resolving. I need to move before I spiral. Before the noise in my head gets loud enough to drown out what little control I still have.

I stand. Pace once. Then stop again in front of Massimo's desk, my hands curl into fists at the edge. The surface is charcoal-gray marble, smooth and cold beneath my fingertips. The wood beneath it is dark, almost ashen. The desk itself isn't ostentatious. Not oversized. Not curved into dominance like so many executive desks I've seen in my father's offices over the years. It's just a long, elegant piece of furniture positioned against the side wall, angled so it faces both the entrance and the window at the same time.

No blind spots.

The rest of the office follows the same philosophy. Dark leather couches arranged for conversation, not comfort. Chrome tables, minimal and sharp. A bar tucked neatly into the corner, stocked but not flaunted. Nothing extravagant. Nothing unnecessary. Everything is deliberate. The entire space screams one word: control.

My gaze drifts back to the desk. Control. I need some. And leverage. For Amauri. As much as I want to sink into the false comfort of hope—to tell myself that Massimo will do what men like him do best, that he'll unleash violence and retrieve my son from wherever he's being held—I can't afford that kind of passivity. He's already made it perfectly clear that, under different circumstances, he'd like nothing better than to kill me.

I don't doubt it.

Even though I'd make that sacrifice without hesitation if it meant saving Amauri, I'd still very much like to stay alive long enough to raise him. To be part of his life. To watch him grow into something more than collateral damage in a war he never asked to be part of. That means I need information. Not just about my father. About Massimo, too. Power doesn't belong to the man with the biggest gun. It belongs to the one who knows where the pressure points are. I've spent too long being pliant. Too long letting other people decide what I'm allowed to know, what I'm allowed to survive. Complacency kept me breathing. It won't save my son.

The old Jenna—the one who questioned, who pushed back, who refused to accept neatly packaged truths—she didn't disappear. She just learned how dangerous it was to exist. It's time she returns. I turn my attention to the desk and start opening drawers. The first slides out easily, perfectly aligned pens, a spare phone, nothing personal. The second is the same. Documents, neatly clipped. Clean. Efficient. A man who leaves nothing behind by accident. The third drawer doesn't open. I pull again, harder this time. Locked.

I stare at it for a second longer than necessary. A challenge. The corner of my mouth twitches despite myself. I kneel, inspecting the lock, irritation bleeding into focus. Once upon a time—before Carter, before politics swallowed my name whole—I wanted to be a writer. I'd started a thriller, convinced I was going to be brilliant at it. I never finished the book, but I finished the research.

Lock picking had been part of it. I practiced on my father's desk and my mother's vanity.

I straighten a hairpin against the desk edge—while

cursing the remaining hand wrappings—my fingers move almost on instinct. Tension. Pressure. A careful twist, and the lock clicks open. I still for a moment, surprised by how easily it came back to me. Then I pull the drawer open. Inside, beneath a thin stack of papers, is something soft and worn at the edges. An envelope, folded too many times. I recognize it instantly. A photo booth strip.

My breath stutters.

I pull it out slowly, like it might disappear if I move too fast. It's us. Massimo and I are pressed together in a too-small frame, laughing, kissing, foreheads touching like the world had already narrowed down to just that space. My hair is longer. His expression is unguarded in a way I'd almost forgotten existed.

God.

We were so happy.

This was taken just days before he vanished. I trace the edge of the photo with my thumb, my chest tight. I was pregnant then. I didn't know it yet, but my body did. Looking at the picture now, I can see it on my face. The softness. The quiet certainty I'd mistaken for happiness alone. And the way he's looking at me—

That's love.

Not possession. Not hunger. Love.

The kind that settles. The kind that stays. He doesn't look like a man who would disappear without a word two days later.

"What the hell happened?" I whisper.

To him. To us. The question hangs there, unanswered, and something inside me shifts. Love like that doesn't vanish. It feels like a hot poker enters me; it sears and burns, but without pain. A love like that doesn't stop.

It's interrupted.

Taken.

The ache in my chest sharpens as the implication lands, not grief, not yet, but the slow burn of realization. Whatever tore him out of my life didn't just steal time from me. It stole choice. It stole truth.

And now it's doing it again.

My breath steadies. My pulse slows. The pain hardens into something colder, more precise. Anger. Not wild. Not blind.

Purposeful.

Whoever thinks they can stand between my son and me—I don't care if it's Daddy, the Cartel, Massimo, or the devil himself—if they think locked doors and erased records and carefully applied leverage will stop me. They have no idea what's coming.

They want war?

They'll get it.

I shove the drawer closed and stand, the sound final, decisive. My thoughts fall into line the way they always used to when I stopped reacting and started planning. I need to put the past behind me, forget who Massimo used to be, who we used to be. I need to see him as a tool to get my son back. Nothing else. A tool that needs to be controlled. Just like I need to control Daddy.

I stare at the screen again, sink back into the chair. The login screen is mocking me. I could try Carter's access, but if I'm locked out, he's locked out for certain.

He's a liability now. A problem already contained, wherever they're holding him.

But there's one more thing. One thing I hope they've forgotten. Hell—I almost forgot it myself. Before I became Jenna Whitford, I was Jenna Kingsley. For reasons I never understood, the IT department at my father's office could never merge the accounts. They couldn't simply change the name. So they created a new login instead.

What if they never deleted the old one?

I turn back to the desk, the computer waiting patiently in front of me.

I type it in.

JennaKingsley

Followed by my password. For a half second, nothing happens. Then the screen refreshes. I'm in. I laugh, short, breathless, disbelieving. My hand curls into a fist before I can stop it, a stupid, triumphant gesture I haven't made in years. Yes. My fist pounds the air.

Finally, something goes my way.

It's ridiculous how good it feels. Vindication buzzes under my skin, adrenaline snaps my spine straight. I want to dig immediately, dive into the files I know are waiting in the cloud, years of archived correspondence and internal memos that were never meant to follow me into marriage and exile.

But instinct stops me. Always check the inbox first.

It floods in faster than my eyes can track. Subject lines blur together.

I'm so sorry.

Are you okay?

If there's anything I can do...

Hope this finds you well.

Long time no see.

Friends. Acquaintances. Former colleagues. People who barely know me but smell opportunity, obligation, or both. Some want to help. Some want favors. Some just want to be seen doing the right thing. I scroll, detached, already numb to it. Until I see her name: Marianne Hall.

No subject line. Just her name, neat and composed, sitting there like it owns the space. My pulse skips. I click.

JENNA,

I'M SO SORRY TO HEAR WHAT HAPPENED. I WANT TO HELP IF I CAN. WOULD YOU BE OPEN TO MEETING?

—MARIANNE

That's it. No explanation. No reassurance. No performance. Interesting. Either Marianne doesn't know I still have access—which feels wildly unlikely given her position—or she does know, and she chose not to shut it down. I don't know which possibility unsettles me more. Still, I don't hesitate.

YES. WHEN AND WHERE?

The reply comes almost immediately, like she'd been waiting.

I can come to the Sovereign, if that's easiest for you.

Of course she can. She is free to roam all over the place, unlike me, who has been confined to a cage at the mercy of a man who hates her. I have no idea what she wants from me. But I'm not about to shove an ally off the board before I know what side she's playing.

I CROSS THE PENTHOUSE WITH PURPOSE, ALREADY SORTING logistics in my head—passport, weapons, timing—I feel her before I see her. Her presence presses into my spine like a blade, familiar and infuriating. I didn't expect her to still be awake. I definitely didn't expect her to still be wearing my shirt. Like it has every encounter since she reappeared in my life, the sight of her hits me harder than it should, soft fabric hanging off her like she belongs here, like she never left. Like the last ten years didn't happen. Heat coils low in my body, sharp and unwanted, my cock hardens, a visceral response I don't give permission to. Fuck.

"Where are you going?" she demands.

I don't slow. "Out."

"What are you doing?"

Packing.

I keep moving because if I stop, if I turn too soon, I'll remember the kiss. The way her mouth fit mine like it never forgot. The way my body betrayed me before my mind could catch up. I'm angry at her. Angry because she kept my son from me. Angry because she made that choice without me. Angry because I want her.

That's the real problem.

Desire rises, hard and unwelcome, tightening my control like a vice. I hate it. Hate that she can still do this to me without trying. Hate that my body reacts before my reason does. I push into the bedroom and head straight for the closet. If I let myself look at her too long, I'll either rip the shirt off her or lose my temper entirely. Or both.

Neither option is acceptable.

"You're not answering me," she snaps, following.

I reach the back wall and open the false panel. The lock disengages with a muted click, and the wall slides aside. Her breath catches. I don't look at her. I don't need to.

"Oh my God," she says. "Are those—are those grenades?"

"Yes."

I start selecting what I need, methodically and in control. The weapons steady me. They always have. Tools don't lie. They don't provoke. They don't look at you like you're both salvation and sin.

"You're going to war," she wagers.

"I'm going to get my son."

I turn just enough to catch her reflection in the mirror. Bare legs. My shirt. The echo of something domestic I never allowed myself to want. It makes my jaw tighten.

"Fuck," I mutter under my breath, not desire this time, but restraint. She needs clothes. Armor that isn't me.

"I'll have Max take you shopping downstairs," my voice is sharp. "You need to change."

Her eyes flash. "If you're going to get my son, I'm coming."

"No."

The word is final.

She steps closer, defiance radiating off her. "You don't get to decide that."

I turn fully then, letting my anger bleed into the air between us.

"Yes," I contradict her quietly. "I do."

"That's not fair."

"This isn't about fair."

Her voice drops. "You don't get to disappear again."

Again with *again*. The word lands deep, scraping something raw. But I'm too angry to care or second-guess her words. "I'm not disappearing, I'm going to get our son." That stills her, but I can't help but jab, "And your husband." That stops her completely. Because she understands what I'm willing to walk into to bring them back.

"You're not coming," I continue. "You stay alive. You dig. You don't become another variable I have to control."

"And if I don't listen?" she challenges.

I step closer, lowering my voice until it cuts. "Then you become a liability too. I don't carry liabilities into war."

Her jaw tightens. She hates this version of me. Too bad. It's the only one she'll get to see from now on. I turn away, reaching for the panel, for the familiar click of control—

"No."

The word snaps like a gunshot. I freeze.

"You don't get to do that," she contests. Her voice isn't

loud, but it's worse for it, tight, shaking, pulled from somewhere deep. "You don't get to decide everything and walk away like the rest of us are just... debris."

I turn back slowly.

"What did you think this was?" I ask, my voice already rising. "A conversation? A negotiation?"

She doesn't answer fast enough. That's a mistake. I take one step toward her. Then another. The air changes. Even I feel it, the way the room tightens when I stop pretending restraint is a choice instead of a discipline.

"You're standing in my territory," I continue, voice dropping, gaining weight. "In my house. Wearing my clothes. Telling me how this is going to go." Her chin lifts, defiant, but I see it, the flicker of awareness. The moment she realizes I'm not the man she used to argue with. I am the man men fear.

"You think you get a vote because you're angry?" I snap. "Because you're scared? Because you finally decided to stop being polite?" I'm right in front of her now. Too close. My shadow is swallowing hers. "This isn't a democracy," I add quietly. "It's not a court. It's not your father's office, where words get work done." I lean down just enough to capture her gaze. "This is my world."

Her breath stutters. She doesn't step back. Brave. Stupid. Both.

"You don't get to raise your voice at me," I continue, low and lethal. "You don't get to issue demands. And you don't get to mistake my restraint for permission."

Her hands curl into fists at her sides. "You don't scare me."

The lie is immediate. Her posture says otherwise. The way her shoulders tense. The way her breathing turns shallow. The way her eyes track me instead of holding my gaze. She's afraid. The realization lands hard, and to my surprise, it brings no satisfaction. No triumph. Just something dark and uncomfortable twisting low in my chest. I don't like it. Not the fear itself. The reason for it.

I step closer anyway, crowding her space until the wall is at her back and there's nowhere left to retreat. I don't touch her—not yet—but the threat of it hums in the air between us, unmistakable. She swallows. There it is.

Naked fear.

And damn it, some weak, buried part of me wants to ease it. To tell her she's safe. That I won't cross that line. I crush that impulse instantly. She needs to be afraid of me. After what she's done. After what she took. I brace one arm against the wall beside her head, close enough that she can feel the vibration of it, close enough that escape is no longer an option. "Don't insult me," I warn quietly. "I can see it."

Her jaw tightens. She doesn't look away. Brave. Or reckless.

"Good," I continue, keeping my voice low and controlled. "Fear keeps you alive." My tone is menacing. "And right now, you need to remember exactly who you're standing in front of."

For a moment, everything is balanced on the edge of a blade: her defiance, my restraint, the history burning between us. Then I step back. Because if I don't, I'll either break something I can't fix or prove her fear right in a way I never intended.

"Change your clothes," I say flatly. "Max will take care of you."

I turn away before my anger finds another outlet. Some lines, once crossed, can't be uncrossed. And despite everything, I won't become that man. I straighten, letting the full weight of me settle back into place. Don. King. Executioner when necessary.

JENNA

THE PENTHOUSE FEELS CAVERNOUS ONCE HE'S GONE. Too much space. Too much quiet. My footsteps echo as I pace, back and forth, the silence pressing in until I can't stand it anymore. Massimo's presence lingers everywhere, in the air, in the furniture, in the way the walls seem to expect him to fill them.

My thoughts won't slow.

Massimo.

Amauri.

Carter.

I push through the glass doors and step onto the terrace. The night air hits me, sharp and still warm. A pool stretches out before me, black and glassy under the lights, a hot tub steams quietly in the corner like it's waiting for someone who isn't coming. The city sprawls beyond the railing, all neon and illusion, pretending nothing is wrong.

My hands grip the stone edge as my mind races ahead of itself. Amauri is somewhere far away. Massimo is walking into hell. And Carter—

The memory comes uninvited. I hadn't seen him in

months when my father arranged the meeting. He was already in a wheelchair by then. Pale. Bitter. Reduced. Daddy had smoothed everything over the way he always does, press statements, medical silence, a neat narrative about an accident no one was allowed to question.

Carter looks up at me when I walk into the room, eyes sharp with spite.

"Well," his voice is tight and venomous. "Looks like you're going to marry me after all."

I broke up with him the day after he pawned me off to his coach for playtime on the field. A few weeks later, he had the accident on the football field. Naively, I'd thought: Karma.

"And I'm supposed to raise Coach's bastard," he continues, lips curling. "Funny how things work out."

I don't correct him. I let him believe it. It's his punishment, just in case there's any conscience or decency left in him.

Him.

The man who tried to break me. For everyone who thought my body was something they could use and discard. Carter didn't deserve the truth. In his bitterness, in his humiliation, he clung to that lie like it was the only power he had left. I turn away from the pool, heart pounding, chest tight. God, I was so young then. So tired. So determined to survive that I didn't care who I hurt as long as my baby was safe. I stand by the railing and stare out at the thousands of lights that rule Las Vegas every night. How many times have I seen this view? From how many different angles? How many versions of myself have stood exactly like this, pretending the city wasn't swallowing me whole?

But only one memory matters now. My wedding night. Or what passed for one. Carter was still recovering from surgeries, his body broken in ways no one was allowed to talk about, so there was no honeymoon. No travel. Thank God. Just a suite high above the Strip and the expectation that we would play our parts convincingly.

Which, perversely, was a relief.

I didn't need romance.

I didn't need touch.

I didn't need lies dressed up as love.

Most definitely not from him.

That weekend, I learned how to take care of him. Not as a wife or a partner, more like a nurse, as a penance. I learned how to help him dress and undress. How to lift him just enough to change the sheets. How to empty his urine bag. How to place a catheter without flinching, without crying, without letting my hands shake. He told me he was impotent. I was relieved. Not that I would have slept with him either way, still, it was a relief.

I did all of it without complaint.

Because that was the deal.

He married me because he needed a wife. Because he needed legitimacy. Because it was the only way he could claim a child as his and keep his political future intact. A man like him needed a family. And how convenient was it anyway that America's Golden Boy did get his happily ever after? Especially after the horrendous accident on the field that broke his spine.

I married him because it was the only way I was allowed to keep my baby. I never doubted my father would have made good on his threat. I could see it in his eyes when he said it, how easily he would have dragged me, kicking and screaming, into a clinic if I forced his hand. How small my pain was compared to his ambition.

So I agreed.

I smiled.

I survived.

But that night—hours after I said my vows—I stood on the balcony of a different hotel, staring out at a different sea of lights, and all I could think about was Massimo.

Where he was.

Why he had left me.

How he could have vanished without a word.

I cried then. Not for the first time. Not for the last. Up until the moment I walked down the aisle, I'd been hoping—stupidly, desperately—that he would appear. That he would interrupt the ceremony. That he would take one look at me and end the farce.

When the priest said the words *or forever hold your peace*, my lungs locked. I held my breath through Carter's careful, chaste kiss. Through the applause. Through the congratulations and well-wishes and the sound of my own name changing forever.

I knew—I knew—that the moment I allowed myself to breathe freely, I would fall apart.

So I didn't.

I held it in until I was alone on that balcony, high above a city that never cared who it destroyed, and only then did I let the tears come. They came hard. Silent. Uncontrollable. I cried for the man who didn't come. For the life I wasn't allowed to choose. For the girl I had been that morning, who still believed someone would save her.

And now, standing here again, years later, staring at the same glittering illusion, I realize something that makes my chest ache even worse. I've been holding my breath ever since. I press my hands to my face, drag in a breath, then another. Tell myself over and over that I'm not the girl who stood on that balcony anymore.

That girl learned how to endure.

This woman?

This woman is done enduring.

Amauri needs more than my survival now. He needs my teeth. My memory. My willingness to burn whatever stands between us. I straighten, the city lights blur for a moment before sharpening again. Whatever this war becomes—between Massimo's world and my father's, between the past and the present—I'm already in it. But I'll be damned if I let them move me around like a pawn any longer. I'm a fucking Queen, one who doesn't need a king, and they will learn that.

My hand drifts to the band on my finger. Carter's ring. Heavy. Cold. A symbol that never fit, no matter how many times I tried to convince myself it did. I stare at it for a long moment, remembering the girl who slid it on, telling herself she was being practical. Strategic. Protecting her child. I was surviving. Not living. Slowly, I twist it free. It leaves a faint indentation behind, pale against my skin. A ghost of pressure. For a second, I just hold it. The weight of it. The lie of it. It was supposed to make me safe. Instead, it made me small. I step closer to the balcony railing. The night air brushes cool against my face. Maybe it'll bring luck to whoever finds it. God knows it didn't bring me any. And then I let it go. It disappears into the dark without a sound. No ceremony. No regret. Just release.

I turn back inside. Massimo's office waits exactly where I left it, cool, controlled, expectant. I grab the laptop from his desk and carry it with me like something fragile and dangerous at the same time, then sink onto the couch. The leather is soft and expensive. My stomach growls, loud enough to startle me.

When was the last time I ate?

I can't remember. It feels like forever. The thought of real food turns my stomach, but I know better than to ignore it. I push myself up and head for the kitchen. The fridge is stocked like a fantasy: fresh fruit, charcuterie, leftovers plated like they were never meant to be reheated. Food that would make anyone else's mouth water. It does nothing for me. I stare at it, detached, then reach for a yogurt. Simple. Manageable. From the wine fridge, I grab a bottle without looking too closely at the label. I don't bother with a glass.

Back on the couch, I eat a few spoonfuls, take a pull straight from the bottle, and feel the edge of the world soften just enough to breathe. The laptop warms on my thighs as it wakes. I open my email first. The inbox refreshes. I'm done holding my breath. Now I'm hunting.

I don't open Marianne's email again. Not yet. I don't know how to respond, or where I'd even meet her. I could tell her to come here—if Sean is any indication, this place runs on Massimo's permission, and mine by extension—but I look down at myself and snort softly.

I can't meet her in his shirt.

The thought of asking Max to take me back to my house to get some of my things makes my chest seize. I have no idea what condition the house is in. I'm not ready to step back into that yet.

Morning, then. I'll deal with Marianne in the morning.

Massimo mentioned something about Max and shopping. I'll use that. I close the email and force myself back to the work I came here to do. The files are endless. Campaign records stretching back years. Decades. I start at the beginning—before the Senate, before the spotlight—when my father was just a lobbyist, learning how power moved. Donations trickled in at first. Small checks. Predictable names.

It's tedious. My eyes burn. The wine bottle grows lighter in my hand. Payments to printers. Marketing firms. Consultants. The occasional plumber, a painter, and maintenance invoices that make sense on paper. The kind of expenses no one ever questions. I still do my due diligence, though, and Google every single name. Some repeat over and over, making them a bit easier; others only appear once. A cell phone repair shop that's still in business. I look at the storefront. Granted, five thousand sounds high for a cell repair, but from the looks of it, they sell computer equipment too. Still, this is how you hide truth, bury it in the ordinary.

I scroll. And scroll. Hours pass without meaning. My eyelids grow heavy. My head dips forward once, twice. I consider closing the laptop, calling it a night, telling myself I'll see clearer in the morning—

My eyes fall on an entry.

Thirty thousand dollars.

My spine straightens.

The name isn't familiar. Northstar Advisory Group. The business doesn't ring any bells. I've seen so many like it; I have contacted them myself. Everyone thinks they can run a campaign, and sometimes it doesn't hurt to give an upstart a chance. You never know what ideas they might come up with. But we never started with thirty grand. Fifteen, maybe, to see if they were a good fit. Thirty is pocket change for an established company, one we've done business with several times, but not for a first timer. I'm glad I started from the beginning now, so I know I haven't seen that name before.

I switch the screen to Google and search. The company closed eight years ago, two years after we paid them. Ten... my spine tingles and I know I'm on to something. Ten years is the magic number. I click on more details about the company, and my pulse races. The owner's name remains: Sean Carpenter. I stare at the screen, then at the name. Sean. Yes, that Sean. My father's bodyguard. My breath leaves me in a shallow rush. I toggle back to the other screen, to the payment that was made one day before Massimo disappeared. Thirty thousand dollars.

That's not a campaign expense. That's not maintenance. That's not printing costs or consulting fees. That's payoff money. That's shut-up-and-go-away money. My hands start to shake as I lean back into the couch, and the room tilts slightly around me. Thirty thousand dollars to make a man vanish.

Is that all I was worth to him?

Is that all *we* were worth?

I picture Massimo's face from the photo booth, soft, in love, unguarded. I picture his smile. The way he looked at me like I was something sacred.

And my father?

My father would absolutely write that check.

Clean. Quiet. Efficient.

Did he buy Massimo off?

My chest caves in. That would explain how he knew who Amauri's father was, even though I never told him. The tears come before I can stop them, hot, humiliating, unstoppable. I clutch the laptop to my chest like it might anchor me, but it doesn't help. The sob that tears out of me is ugly and raw and ten years too late.

Thirty thousand dollars.

To stay away.

To disappear.

To leave me standing alone on that balcony, waiting for a man who was paid off. My body curls in on itself as exhaustion finally wins. The wine bottle slips from my fingers, rolling empty and harmlessly against the couch.

The laptop tilts, the screen dims as my eyes close. I cry myself to sleep with one thought burning itself into my bones: If my father did this—

If he stole Massimo from me—

Then I will destroy whatever he used to do it.

And I won't accept money as an answer.

MASSIMO

The jet hums beneath my feet, steady and inevitable, as we climb out over the desert. Venezuela. The word sits wrong in my mouth. The Venezuelans don't steal children. They move product. They flood markets. They burn through cities and leave rot behind. Kidnapping a senator's grandson is sloppy. Loud. It invites attention they don't want.

I drum my fingers against the table and take a sip of coffee. I need to be clearheaded for this. There are only two explanations: either the Venezuelans are desperate, or someone pointed them. Someone who wanted leverage.

I lean back in the seat, my jaw so tight it hurts, and my fingers drum faster before I still them. My thoughts drift where they shouldn't, away from strategy, away from logistics.

To him.

My son.

I should have asked her for a picture.

The thought irritates me more than it should. I won't ask Jenna for anything. Not after what she did. Not after ten years of silence wrapped around a lie I never got the chance to confront. Curiosity wins where pride shouldn't.

I pull my phone out and type their names. Jenna Whitford. Amauri Whitford. I expect curated smiles. Political gloss. Carter's shadow all over it. What I don't expect is the punch to the chest. Amauri's face fills the screen, mid-laugh, caught off guard. Dark hair. My nose. My mouth when I forget to control it. Something sharp and unmistakable in his eyes.

Mine.

I go still.

Fuck.

I scroll. Another photo. A school game. He's taller than he should be for his age, all limbs and momentum, a basketball tucked under one arm like it belongs there. My stomach drops. Basketball. It hits me all at once. Amauri Strout! He was my favorite player. The realization is so sudden it steals my breath.

Fucking Jenna.

What was she thinking?

She named our son after my favorite basketball player.

The memory shifts, unbidden, to when she searched me out a few days after *that* night.

Her eyes are frantic; her hands shake when she wraps them around a coffee cup like it's the only solid thing left in her life. She's asked around, probably heard the rumors that I'm on campus to sell coke for my uncle. She's not looking for comfort. She's looking for silence. For reassurance that what she did—what she survived—will stay buried. I can't be seen with her, especially not in the state she's in. I can't take her to my place. I'm still living under my uncle's roof, where every wall listens, every move is watched. So I take her for a drive.

I can tell she's scared. Not just of what happened, not just of what we did, but of me. The desert stretches out ahead of us, empty and endless.

Weeks later, she confessed that she thought I'd kill her.

As if I ever could.

The realization hits me now like a fist to the gut.

Fuck.

The memories come faster.

We learn how to exist together in pieces. First restaurants off the Strip where nobody asks questions if you tip well. Long walks through parks at night, neon bleeding into green, pretending the world is softer than it is. Museums. Quiet bars. Public spaces where hands brush instead of entwine, because discretion matters. It's not supposed to matter. A few weeks. A way for her to breathe again. Instead, we fall.

Not loudly. Not foolishly.

Deeply.

She laughs more with me than anyone I've ever known. Sleeps as the nightmares loosen their grip when she's pressed against my chest. Trusts me in ways I don't deserve. I book the best suite, not to impress her, but because I want her to feel safe. Chosen. Like she deserves beauty instead of an aftermath. She trusts me with her virginity, and the weight of that settles into my bones immediately.

She's my first real commitment. And I think—arrogantly, foolishly—that I'll be her last. I start making plans. Quiet ones. Dangerous ones. How I'll introduce her to my family. How I'll shield her from what I'm becoming. How we can carve out a life that belongs to us instead of obligation.

And now, here we are. She is in my hotel; I'm on a plane to fucking Caracas to get our son back. What the hell happened?

The question loops in my head like static as I watch the landscape blur beneath us through the small oval window. We're hours out, time enough for a whole life to shuffle itself around and leave me here with nothing but questions and half-baked regrets. I press my forehead to the cool glass for a breath. Let it wash over me. I don't expect answers. Just enough peace to think without the knot in my chest strangling every thought. I close my eyes. The hum of the engines is steady, too steady. It starts to burrow in, a low rhythm that dulls sharp edges. My eyelids feel heavier by the second.

I should be hashing out a strategy. Route, contacts, worst-case scenarios, contingency plans. But my brain has wandered back to her again. The way she used to look at me, unguarded. The sound of her laughter, the way it filled space I didn't know needed filling.

Sleep comes quietly at first. A heaviness behind my eyes. Then deeper.

I drift.

Not into peaceful dreams. Not exactly. More like a fugue, fragments of memory and fear tangled together. A hotel room. Her hair, falling over the pillow. Her first laugh at something dumb I said. The way she trusted me with her silence. And somewhere beneath it all: Amauri's face.

That sharp, unmistakable trace of me in his expression.

I don't sleep long, but long enough. A few hours. Enough that when I wake, my head is clear, the edge honed instead of dulled. My back aches when I straighten. I should've gone to the bed in the rear of the jet, but sleep was an accident I never intended. Memory dragged me under and only let me go when it was done with me. A flight attendant appears quietly and sets a tray in front of me. Eggs. Fruit. Bread. And most important of all, coffee, black. We're still over the ocean. The map on the screen confirms it, the curve of the earth stretching beneath us. My timer tells me what I already feel in my bones: one hour to landing.

I eat because discipline matters. Because bodies fail when you forget the basics. I drink the coffee slowly, letting the bitterness settle me back into the present. Then I work. I pull my phone from my pocket and open the files Gabe and Damiano sent while I was asleep. Photos. Satellite images. Security layouts. Names.

Aurelio Valverde. Officially, he's the Don now. Young enough to believe the title belongs to him outright. Smart enough to let people think that. Unofficially, his father still casts the longer shadow. Silvestre Valverde. I've met them both. Once, in Vegas. At a private event dressed up as charity. Crystal glasses. Tailored suits. Smiles that never reached the eyes. Aurelio was polite. Measured. Watching everything. Silvestre barely bothered with conversation, just studied me like I was a variable he hadn't decided how to solve yet. Ruthless men. Both of them.

Their cartel isn't subtle. They don't need to be. Their methods are effective because they're feared. Violence as communication. Excess as warning. If they've touched even a hair on Amauri's head... I stop the thought there. They won't have. Because if they have, none of this ends cleanly. Not for them. Not for anyone who helped.

I scroll through the compound layouts. Outer perimeter. Guard rotations. Internal structures. Living quarters separated from operations, smart, but predictable. I mark ingress points, potential blind spots, and places where arrogance creates gaps. Damiano's notes are precise. Gabe's intel confirms what I suspected. The Venezuelans didn't choose this target. Someone hired them. Someone made a mistake big enough to trace.

The plane begins its gradual descent, and the engines shift pitch. I lock the phone and lean back, rolling my shoulders once to ease the stiffness. Almost there.

Gabe waits for me on the runway with an old, nondescript jeep.

"How was the flight?"

"Tolerable." I don't waste time with pleasantries. We both know why we're here, and the sooner we can get it done, the better.

Gabe turns the jeep away from the city. We pass through neighborhoods that look like nothing, no landmarks, no excess, no reason to remember them. The kind of place that survives because no one ever thinks to look twice. When we finally stop, the house is exactly what it should be. Nondescript. Quiet. Forgettable.

The door opens before we knock. Inside, the living room is gone. In its place: screens, cables, laptops humming low. One wall is covered in satellite images;

another in floor plans, guard rotations, and timestamps. Red marker circles. Blue lines. Photographs pinned like accusations. In short, a war room.

Gabe shuts the door behind us. "This is everything we have so far."

I don't answer. I don't need to. My eyes are already moving. Aurelio Valverde's compound dominates the central screen. High walls. Tiered security. Too much money spent on making the perimeter untouchable.

"Perimeter's a fortress," Gabe confirms what I'm seeing. "Smart sensors. Thermal. Rotating patrols. Four-hour shifts."

"Expected," I reply. "He wants people to look there."

I step closer, studying the timestamps scrolling on a side monitor. "What's the cycle?"

Gabe pulls it up. "Every hour. Every ninety seconds, there is some weird power fluctuation."

I narrow my eyes. "That's not a fault."

"No," Gabe agrees. "We thought it was at first. Grid instability. But it's too clean. Too consistent."

"So something switches," I propose. "On purpose."

"Or something opens," Gabe counters.

I don't look at him, but my mouth curves slightly. "Find out."

I shift focus inward. Interior layouts. Residential wing. Operational wing. Aurelio keeps them separate, smart again. Silvestre isn't on-site full-time, but intel says he'll be there tonight.

"They're consolidating," Gabe says. "Too many eyes on them. Too much heat."

"They know someone's coming," I predict.

"They don't know who."

I tap the image of the main gate. "We don't go through the front."

"Obviously."

"We don't hit the perimeter at all," I continue. "Too loud. Too slow. They'll move the kid the second the alarms trip."

Gabe nods. "So we wait for movement."

"No," I correct. "We force it."

I bring up another screen, local infrastructure. Old maps layered over new ones. My finger traces lines most people would ignore.

"Compounds like this don't exist in isolation," I say. "They rely on something. Water. Power. Waste. You cut one, the others react."

"Power's too obvious," Gabe says. "They'll have backup."

"Exactly," I reply. "Which means the switch matters."

Gabe exhales slowly. "So we watch the cycle."

"We exploit it," I nod. "Ninety seconds isn't an accident. It's a window."

"But we don't know where it opens," Gabe says. "Yet."

I straighten. "Then we build everything else around that unknown."

He looks at me. Waiting.

"Teams staged, not committed," I continue. "Silent insertion options only. No explosions. No gunfire until we're inside."

"And the kid?"

"Primary objective," I say flatly. "Alive. Untouched. Everything else is secondary."

Gabe hesitates. "And the men holding him?"

I meet his eyes. "They live until he's breathing safe air."

That settles it. Gabe nods once. Loyal. Ruthless. Clear.

"So," he says, glancing back at the power data, "we're missing one piece."

"Yes," I agree. "But we know where it belongs."

I turn back to the screens, to the compound, to the steady pulse of that ninety-second fluctuation. Gabe is about to say something when my phone vibrates. Damiano.

The name alone tightens something in my chest. He doesn't call unless it matters. I take it. "Talk."

"Boss," he sounds clipped and strained. "We have a complication."

I don't look away from the screens. "Define."

A beat. Then, "New York has arrived in Caracas."

That gets my attention. "New York?"

"In Caracas," he confirms. "Just landed. Private arrival. Two names you're going to want to hear."

I straighten. "I'm listening."

"Stephano Conti and Raffael DeSantis."

For a fraction of a second, everything goes still. Then my mind starts moving. Conti first. Stephano Conti isn't a capo yet. His father, Gustave Conti, still holds that seat. Old-school. Careful. Their family doesn't run territory or muscle; they run fraud and cybercrime. Digital pipelines. Financial ghosts. The kind of money that never touches hands.

From what I know, Stephano is the real weapon. One of the best programmers in their circle. Quiet. Precise. Dangerous in a way that doesn't leave bodies until it's far too late. He doesn't pull triggers; he reroutes consequences. If he's in Caracas, someone needs something erased, rerouted, or made untraceable.

Then there is DeSantis.

Raffael DeSantis is newer. A shadow that didn't exist six months ago and now casts a long one. My intel is incomplete, but enough of the pieces line up to make him interesting and dangerous. Before he became a capo, he ran a vigilante outfit called Umbra Arcana—the hidden truths. Dramatic name. Effective execution. He built it to expose rot—cartels, traffickers, corrupt officials—then burned what he found. He recently married Sophia Giuliano, widow of a Giordano capo, and took over the branch. Drugs. Prostitution. Human trafficking. Except—according to every report worth trusting—human trafficking is effectively shut down. Prostitution dismantled. The money streams redirected or killed outright.

And Sophia's first husband?

DeSantis killed him. Not in a power grab. Not for territory. Because the man was abusing his wife. That detail sticks. DeSantis doesn't operate like a traditional mobster. He doesn't tolerate mess. Or hypocrisy. Or men who mistake power for entitlement. Which makes one thing very clear. If he's here, this isn't about money.

I listen as Damiano relays their movements, instruct him to continue surveillance, and end the call.

I look at Gabe. He's already piecing it together.

"This isn't a turf war," he concludes.

"No," I agree. "It's a convergence."

Conti brings infrastructure. DeSantis brings execution. Together, they don't destabilize cities; they surgically remove what doesn't belong. I look back at the compound on the screen. At the layers of security. At the careful arrogance of it. Then I think about what isn't happening.

Valverde didn't send anyone to the airport. No welcoming committee. No armored convoy. No public show of alliance. Conti and DeSantis landed quietly and disappeared into the city like men who weren't expected or wanted. And they're not staying anywhere that matters.

Second-rate hotel. Mid-tier security. The kind of place you choose when you don't want to be seen, and you don't want anyone mistaking you for a guest. That's not hospitality. That's distance.

Valverde keeps allies close. Enemies closer. But outsiders? He makes a point of reminding them whose ground they're standing on. He didn't do that this time.

Which tells me two things.

First: Conti and DeSantis didn't come at his invitation.

Second: Valverde knows they're here.

But he doesn't want them under his roof.

I don't say it out loud yet. I don't need to. Gabe's eyes narrow in the same direction my thoughts are going. I sit back, steepling my fingers, watching the power cycle blink again on the screen. Ninety seconds. Like a heartbeat.

"If they were negotiating," I continue, "they'd be housed like kings. If they were partners, Valverde would be showing them off."

"And if they were targets," Gabe finishes, "they'd stay invisible."

I nod once. That explains the hotel. The silence. The separation. Conti doesn't put himself in a position where he can be controlled. DeSantis doesn't sleep under the same roof as the man he might have to kill. Which means Valverde isn't just holding my son, he's pissed off a lot of other people. I glance back at the compound on the screen. At the power cycle. At the unseen door we haven't located yet.

"So," Gabe states carefully, "they're not here for you."

"No," I reply. "But we're about to be in each other's way."

And that makes this dangerous. Because men like Conti and DeSantis don't go to war unless someone makes a mistake large enough to attract predators. I intend to make sure that mistake isn't mine. I don't like sharing a battlefield. But if Conti and DeSantis think they walked into Caracas to run the board, they're about to learn whose game this actually is.

AT SOME POINT, I MUST HAVE DRIFTED OFF TO SLEEP AGAIN on the couch—it's way too comfortable. Because I don't ease into panic. I wake up in it. It's there the moment my eyes open, coiled tight in my chest, squeezing before I can even draw a full breath. Amauri.

The name is a pulse, a drumbeat, a scream I keep swallowing down because screaming doesn't get sons back. Before I even have a plan, I'm up and through the penthouse, swinging the door to the antechamber open and staring into six pairs of eyes. Six men who are built like linebackers, wearing the expressions of killers. Normally, I'd be intimidated; today, I'm not. I'm far too furious.

"Where is he?" I demand, voice already sharp, already past polite. My eyes level on Max, the only one I know in the group. He looks up from where he's standing near the elevator door, massive and immovable, like panic is something he's trained to absorb. "Morning to you, too, ma'am."

"Don't," I snap. "Don't do that. Where is Massimo?"

He exhales slowly, like he expected this. "He's not available."

My hands curl into fists. "That's not an answer."

"You know where he went," Max says carefully.

"No, I don't." I fire back. "I want to talk to him. Now."

"Jenna—"

"No," I cut in, stepping closer. "You don't get to soften it. You don't get to buffer me. He left me here with no information, no timeline, and a whole lot of silence. I want to know where he is, what he's doing, and why no one seems to think I deserve to be told."

Max holds my gaze. I see the calculation there, the judgment of how much truth I can handle without breaking. It only makes me angrier.

"He said you'd do this," Max finally allows. "Pace. Spiral. Try to insert yourself into things that aren't safe."

"That's convenient," I reply coldly. "Did he also tell you I'd be right?"

His jaw tightens. That's answer enough. A beat passes, a beat during which we measure each other to see who folds first.

Then Max nods once. "Penthouse. Now."

He doesn't give me a choice; his massive body moves forward, and if I don't want to be overrun, I have to move with him, back into the penthouse. He closes the door once we're inside, continuing on until we're standing in the middle of Massimo's living room with my heart in my throat and nowhere to put it.

Max holds out a phone. "We'll call him."

I snatch it. It rings once. Twice.

Then Massimo answers. "What," he sounds irritated, "is so urgent it couldn't wait?"

I don't bother with hello. "Where are you?"

Silence follows for a few seconds. Controlled. Dangerous. "Jenna?"

"Where are you? Where is my son?"

He exhales slowly, as if fighting with patience. "You have to trust me. I will get him back. And I will let you know the moment I have him."

Trust him? The words explode inside my skull.

"The last time I trusted you," I snap, "you—"

I stop myself. Bite my tongue so hard I taste blood. Not now. Now is not the time to tell him I know about the thirty thousand. About Northstar. About how close I am to believing he sold me out just like Carter did, maybe not with the same cruelty, but with the same result.

Gone.

Silent.

Paid for.

My chest aches like it's caving in.

"I need more than that," I press out instead, my voice shakes despite everything. "I need to know you're not playing a game with my son."

There's a breath on the other end of the line. Just one.

"I don't play games with blood," Massimo vows quietly. "Especially not mine."

Mine.

The word lands heavy. Complicated. Too late and too real all at once.

"You don't get to disappear again," my voice softens into something more dangerous. "You don't get to shut me out and expect me to just... wait."

"I'm not disappearing," he replies. "I'm working."

Another silence follows. Thicker. Taut. Then, clipped, "Stay where you are. You're safest there."

The line goes dead. I stare at the phone, my reflection warped in the dark screen.

Max clears his throat behind me. "He'll bring him back."

I laugh once. Sharp. Broken. "They all say that."

I hand the phone back slowly. My hands are shaking now that the adrenaline has nowhere left to go.

Trust.

The word feels like a weapon someone else keeps handing me, even though every scar I have tells me exactly how dangerous it is. But Amauri doesn't have the luxury of my doubt. So I swallow it. For now. And pray that, this time, trust doesn't cost me everything.

Max clears his throat. "Let's go shopping," he suggests, looking at me like he expects those magic words will make everything better. Will make any woman jump up and down in joy. No matter the circumstances.

I turn on him, ready with something sharp and ugly—something about retail therapy not resurrecting sons or soothing panic—but the look in his eyes stops me cold. He doesn't look impatient or mollifying; he looks like a man offering the only move he has left. And beneath it, something else: concern. Real. Unshowy. The kind that doesn't ask permission.

And then there is the small fact that I'm standing here, in front of him, barefoot and only wearing Massimo's shirt. So I swallow whatever was about to come out of my mouth. I do need clothes and shoes. I nod once. Max doesn't say anything else. He shrugs out of his jacket and settles it around my shoulders with careful hands, like I might shatter if he moves too fast. The weight of it grounds me more than I expect.

"Come on," he invites softly.

He walks me back into the antechamber, one hand lightly at my elbow, not guiding, not pushing, just present. He nods to one of the men, who immediately calls the elevator. Two more fall in behind us. Security.

The doors slide open, and we step inside. It's... crowded. Four of us in close quarters. All of them tall. All of them solid. All of them the kind of men magazines build fantasies around. This should be a girl's wet dream, alone in an elevator with three dangerous, beautiful men. Instead, my chest tightens. Because all I can think about is Massimo. Massimo and the kiss.

God—the kiss.

The way it blindsided me. The way it reopened places in me I'd sealed away and labeled survival. The way my body remembered him before my mind could argue. The way it wasn't gentle or careful, but desperate, and angry, and real. Like everything we never said collided at once. I grip Max's jacket tighter around myself. I thought I'd buried that part of me. Locked it away with the rest of the things I couldn't afford to want. But one kiss—one reckless, unforgivable moment—and suddenly I'm aware of my pulse again. Of hunger. Of longing. Of how much it still hurts.

The elevator hums as it descends. No one speaks. The men are statues around me, eyes forward, bodies angled subtly outward like a shield. And all I can do is stand there, surrounded by protection, feeling more exposed than ever. Because the one man I want—the man who woke everything I thought I'd lost—is somewhere far away, walking into danger with my heart clenched in his fist.

The doors open. The noise hits me like a wall. Sound, light, movement, all of it crashing together at once. Laughter, too loud, too sharp. Slot machines screaming in metallic joy. Waitresses weaving through the crowd, voices shrill as they call out drink orders—cocktails, cocktails—like a chant, like an incantation meant to keep the city alive. For a moment, I just... stop. My body hesitates at the threshold like it doesn't know how to exist in this version of reality. The air smells like perfume, alcohol, and electricity. Heat and sugar and desperation wrapped in glitter. Max is at my side instantly. Not touching, but close enough that I feel him, an anchor in the chaos.

"You okay?" he murmurs.

I nod, though I'm not sure it's true. This feels like an out-of-body experience. I haven't been alone in Massimo's penthouse that long. Not really. But it's been long enough to forget this, the pulse of Vegas, the way it never stops moving, never stops demanding attention. The way it swallows people whole and spits them back out smiling.

Someone brushes past me. A shoulder bumps mine. Before I can even react, one of the bodyguards steps in, firm hand to the man's chest, moving him aside with a warning look that needs no words. Not gentle. Not subtle. The man is drunk; he raises his hands in apology, nods at me, mouths, *sorry*, and stumbles away. The guards tighten their formation around me. I feel curious glances directed at me. Three guards, I must be someone special. Someone important. It hits me so hard, I almost laugh. Not because it's funny, but because it's absurd. I don't know what time it is. I don't even know what day it is.

Which makes me no different from every other tourist wandering this casino, untethered and disoriented, chasing something shiny without knowing why. The thought lands oddly comforting and deeply unsettling all at once.

The lights reflect off polished floors, off sequined dresses and gold watches, off faces flushed with luck or loss. People cheer at tables. Others stare blankly at screens, feeding machines that promise everything and deliver nothing. Life goes on. Here.

Even when mine feels like it's paused mid-breath.

I feel Max's presence next to me. Warm, safe. Reminding me that I'm not alone, even if the man I want to hear from is thousands of miles away, somewhere between danger and silence.

. . .

WHEN I STEP OUT OF THE SHOWER, I ALMOST RECOGNIZE myself again. Steam clings to the mirrors, softening the sharp edges of my reflection. My hair is damp and clean, my skin warm instead of chilled all the way through. I pull on the clothes I bought, tailored trousers, a soft knit top, shoes, understated but expensive in the way that doesn't beg for attention.

Decent. Normal. Human. And with my hands back. I don't need the stupid wrappings anymore. A couple of band aids do the trick just fine.

I'd expected the boutique in the casino to be all sequins and desperation, Vegas costumes for women trying to become someone else for a night. Instead, it was quiet. Polished. A high-end luxury space that catered just as easily to ballgowns as it did to stockholder-meeting wardrobes. Clothing for women who needed to be taken seriously in rooms full of men who underestimated them. I hadn't known how badly I needed that reminder.

Back in the penthouse, the silence no longer presses quite so hard. I make coffee—strong, grounding—and carry the mug into Massimo's office. The laptop waits where I left it, patient, complicit on the couch.

I sit.

Breathe.

I don't think I have the guts yet to dig further into Daddy's shit. I'm still digesting my last find. Not even the thought of Amauri can get me to open those folders. I call myself a coward and accept it. At least for the moment.

I stare at my emails: Marianne.

Now that I have decent clothes, I can meet her, but meeting her here would be a mistake. Too exposed. Too much Massimo in the walls. The city isn't an option either. I don't want to be alone out there, not yet.

A thought enters my mind: the boutique.

Neutral ground. Public enough to discourage theatrics. Private enough, with the right appointment, to talk. And Max will take me there whenever I ask, no explanations required. The plan clicks into place cleanly, and with it comes a small, fierce spark of control. I open my email and start typing.

Marianne,
I'm available today. If you're still willing to meet, there's a boutique at the Sovereign casino I trust.
It's private.
Let me know what time works for you.
—Jenna

I reread it once. No tells. No emotion. No vulnerability she can exploit. Then I send it. The laptop hums softly as the message disappears into the ether. I lean back in the chair, fingers wrapped around my mug, and wait. I don't know what Marianne wants. I don't know what she knows. She and I have never had the kind of relationship you'd call friendly, but we're not enemies either. She's just a fixture in my father's life. One he bangs on the side. *Yes, I know about that, Daddy.* At least he had the decency to wait until Mom died. *I hope. I don't want to know.* Five minutes later, my email dings.

I CAN MEET YOU THERE AT FIVE.

Three hours. My pulse steadies instead of spikes. That's new. Fear has burned itself down to something more useful.

"Alright," I murmur to the empty room.

I take a deep breath. In through my nose. Out through my mouth. Slow enough to convince my body we're not running anymore, we're planning. Let's do it.

Three hours to sit here and wonder... or do some research. *Come on, little girl, man up.* I open the file folder on the laptop again, fingers moving with purpose now. No more spiraling. No more doom-scrolling. The thirty thousand dollars sits there like a bruise I can't stop pressing, but I force myself to zoom out instead of drilling deeper into it. Context first. Patterns. What surrounded that payment, not just financially, but geographically.

Travel logs.

I pull them up and start scrolling.

New York.

Again.

And again.

And again.

Some of the trips look clean on paper. Meetings with the governor. Fundraisers. Panels. Conferences with names so bland they could hide anything. Those don't surprise me. New York is where deals happen. But then there are the others. Friday to Sunday. I can't find any official schedule. Any logged meetings. No entourage. Just... trips.

Pleasure trips, if the accounting language is to be believed. My stomach tightens. I've always known he went to New York more than necessary. It used to bother me in a vague, distant way, the kind of unease you file under 'not my business.' I'd chalked it up to networking. To ego. To the kind of ambition that requires constant stroking.

Now, looking at the frequency, the timing, and the lack of documentation? It doesn't feel like politics. It feels personal. I scroll further, and my eyes catch on a familiar category: Consulting fee.

The amount isn't outrageous. Carefully chosen. Enough to be meaningful without being memorable, still, something bugs me about it. The check was made out to a Louise Keller.

The name means nothing to me. Which makes me pause, because now we've entered a time where I was very active in Daddy's campaigns and daily routine. I click. Nothing else is there. Only that one-time payment. Just like it had been for the Northstar Advisory Group.

My stomach tightens again, and I open a browser window and type her name. Too many results. Authors. Professors. Realtors. A jazz singer. Too many to individually check out. That's okay. I can narrow it.

Louise Keller Kingsley.

The screen refreshes. And there it is. My breath catches. The name opens a door I didn't know existed. I keep digging. Louise Keller. Stripper. Twenty-three at the time. Arrest record for public intoxication. A few modeling shots buried under a dozen tabloids that never bothered to spell her name right. A few social media tags, nothing big, until: The article is old. Buried deep. Two clicks from obscurity.

SENATOR ACCUSED OF SEXUAL ASSAULT BY MANHATTAN DANCER.

My vision narrows. She accused him of beating her. Of raping her. The press in New York had a field day. A senator. A stripper. The kind of story that practically writes itself. They quoted anonymous sources. Questioned her credibility. Dug into her past with surgical cruelty. Grain of salt, one headline read. Troubled woman seeks payout, another implied.

Two days later, Louise recanted. There is a teary-eyed one-minute clip of her from a TV network. She sniffs through most of it. I have to replay the tape a couple of times just to understand what she's mumbling. She looks drunk. Or high. She says she'd made it all up, she apologizes, mistaken identity. The senator visited her, and she realized her mistake. It wasn't him.

The apology statement is dated the day after the check was issued. I stare at the screen until my eyes burn. My stomach turns, sharp and immediate, like my body understands before my mind finishes catching up.

I didn't know. The thought lands, heavy and sickening.

I didn't know, and that feels impossible.

By then, I'd been married to Carter for over a year.

Amauri was already born. I was working full-time, juggling motherhood, optics, and exhaustion. I'd wanted to stay home with my son—we could afford it—but Daddy and Carter had insisted I work.

"It looks better," they'd said. Like motherhood was a campaign accessory.

Which means I should have known about Louise. Yes, I was exhausted at the time, taking care of an infant and a man in a wheelchair takes its toll, but I did have help. I got enough rest so that I don't get to say those years were spent in a fugue state.

I read the news back then. I followed politics. I cared. Or at least, I thought I did. But somehow this slipped through. Or did I let it?

No, I shake my head. I wouldn't have. I might have taken Daddy's side, but no, this is not something that would have slipped by me. This was intentionally withheld from me. But why? The amount he paid her wasn't outrageous. Enough to disappear, not enough to scream guilt. And the story could have been made up. That's the poison of it. That's how men like my father survive. Plausible deniability.

But something in me recoils. Because God help me, I can see it being true. I can see his temper. The way his voice sharpens when things don't go his way. The coldness when disappointment sets in. The way women are always... secondary. Useful. Replaceable. The way he said he'd drag me, kicking and screaming, into a clinic if necessary.

I press my palm to my mouth, breathing through the

nausea. If he did this—if he hurt her and then erased her with money— then everything I told myself about him being a good man was a lie I helped maintain.

I hate myself for thinking it. After all, he is my father. But enough is enough. That get out of jail free card has expired.

No matter how much I may want to deny the ugly truth, he told me himself the kind of man he is. His exact words were: We spin it. Senator's son-in-law and grandson kidnapped. Daughter barely escapes with her life. A home invasion. A martyr narrative. The public will eat this up.

Followed by: Manetti's bastard son.

And ending with: Don't you see? Up until now, Amauri was a ticking time bomb.

I stand up, shaking my head to clear it. I can't dwell on that right now; it's too much. What I can think about are Massimo's words, how the New York family has something on him. I might not want to, but I can see that, too. And the one thing stands out clearer than all the rest, sharp as glass: whatever loyalty I owed my father ends where my son begins.

Thankfully, my timer beeps. It's five 'til five. Time to go see what information Marianne has.

MASSIMO

Tourist trap is the first word that comes to mind. Not a cheap one, no. This is the upper ceiling of what the middle class can afford. The kind of place people save for. Splurge on. Brag about afterward. High-end enough to feel special, accessible enough to stay full year-round. I know this tier intimately. I make a fortune off it.

The lobby is a riot of shine and noise. Polished brass everywhere. Oversized chandeliers dripping light meant to overwhelm rather than illuminate. The floors are composite stone veined to suggest luxury. Convincing at a glance. A lie if you look twice.

Where my hotels use real marble—cold, heavy, cut clean—this place uses imitation. Already scratched if you know where to look. Scuffed along the edges where rolling suitcases have chewed through the illusion. Corners dulled, chips hastily filled and buffed smooth under aggressive lighting designed to hide wear. It almost works.

The people complete the picture. An international assortment drifts through the lobby, phones always out, skin sunburned instead of pale. Families instead of escorts. Couples in matching outfits, children tugging on hands, voices loud with excitement. They think they've arrived somewhere important. That's the trick. My properties don't try to impress. They don't have to. Real luxury doesn't announce itself. It doesn't beg to be believed. It settles into the bones. It makes you feel small without ever telling you why.

This place does the opposite. Everything is overstated. Gaudy. Designed to convince the middle-class tourist that they've crossed a line into exclusivity. That they're brushing shoulders with wealth and power. It's an illusion. Which is why it matters.

Conti and DeSantis didn't choose this hotel because it was convenient. They chose it because it disappears into noise. No Valverde welcome. No armored convoy. No visible alliance. Just anonymity wrapped in gold paint. They didn't want to be hosted. They wanted to be overlooked. Everything about this place says one thing clearly: they didn't come to Caracas for comfort. They came for blood.

I move through the lobby without slowing, cataloging exits, sightlines, and reflections in mirrored columns. The illusion hums around me, loud and oblivious.

I reach the floor with Conti's and DeSantis' room. A guard answers my knock. He looks more Russian than Italian. Curious. Recognition flickers in his eyes, quick, instinctive. He doesn't know me personally, but he knows of me. Men like him always do. Before he can say anything, movement behind him catches my attention. Raffael DeSantis strides forward like he is already on his way out. He stops. Stares at me like he's just seen a ghost.

For a fraction of a second, I enjoy it.

"Massimo?" he says, disbelief threading the word.

"DeSantis," I reply evenly, like we're passing each other at a charity gala instead of colliding in a city soaked in cartel blood.

I step inside without waiting for permission. Two of my men follow. The others remain outside; it's a deliberate move. I don't want a war, but I'm willing to wage it. This isn't a show of force. It's a statement of confidence. If this turns violent, it won't be because I brought an army.

The Russian stiffens behind me. Uneasy now. He doesn't like surprises, and I'm very clearly one.

Raffael lifts a hand slightly, palm down. "Easy, Sasha," he says, almost amused. "I think he's friendly."

Friendly. I don't correct him. He gestures me further in, and I let him, eyes already moving, cataloging. It's exactly like the rest of the hotel. Designed to impress at first glance. Faux satin drapes catch the light just enough to look expensive from a distance. Gold-toned accents that are a shade too bright. Furniture with curves meant to suggest indulgence, not comfort.

Everything here is staged. Luxury as performance. There's no personal imprint. No art. No books. No signs anyone intends to stay longer than necessary.

My eyes flick to the woman on the sofa. At first glance, I categorize her the way I've categorized a hundred others over the years: decoration. Beautiful. Placed. The type of woman a powerful man keeps nearby because she looks good in the frame and knows when to stay quiet. The kind who orbits money and violence without ever touching either directly.

She's dressed for it, too. Effortless. Controlled. Nothing accidental. Raffael's, maybe. Or Conti's.

That assumption lasts exactly one second too long. Because she doesn't avert her gaze or try to flirt with me. She watches me openly, chin tipped just enough to be curious, not deferential. There's no hunger there. No calculation of what I might give her. No practiced softness. Instead, there's something sharp. Alert. A gleam of danger in her eyes that doesn't belong to women who exist to be entertained. That gives me pause.

I adjust the mental box I'd put her in, slide it aside entirely. She doesn't fit. Not quite. And I've learned the hard way that when something almost fits, it's usually the thing that cuts deepest. Interesting.

For now, the air is thick with recalculation. Raffael's surprise has already cooled into interest. The Russian's hand hovers near his weapon, unsure. The woman's gaze lingers, measuring.

They didn't expect me.

That plays in my favor. Because that means whatever they're planning, I just walked into the middle of it. No one here yet knows whose blood will actually flow this night.

Stephano Conti is the next person I clock. Relaxed posture. Watchful eyes. The kind of man who doesn't look dangerous because he doesn't need to advertise it. He stands dead center, like he owns the place. That alone irritates me.

"What the fuck," I snap before the door even closes, the words leaving my mouth sharp and unfiltered, "are you doing in this dump?"

Classic Vegas diplomacy. I don't soften it. There's no point. I scan the room automatically. Raffael's hand hovers near his holster, good instincts. Sasha's positioning is tight. The woman still looks like she's on vacation, which makes her the most dangerous person here by default. My gaze catches on her again.

"Who's she?" I demand.

Stephano answers without missing a beat. "My wife. Mrs. Conti."

She smiles. Sweet. Tooth-rotting. Fake. "Pleasure to meet you."

She's lying. Stephano getting married is news to me. I didn't expect an invite, but I do try to keep up with the other families' affairs. "You got married?"

"Yes," Conti's voice is clipped, proprietary. The new Mrs. Conti means something to him. "Try to keep up."

"And you brought your wife," I huff, "to Caracas."

"She insisted."

"She always insists," she corrects lightly.

I stare at her longer than necessary. Something about her doesn't sit right. Not just confidence, precision. Like she's cataloging everything while pretending not to care. I don't have time for puzzles.

Raffael steps forward. "What are you doing here, Manetti?"

I round on him immediately. "What am I doing here?

What the hell are you doing here? All of you? In my war zone?"

The words are out before I can stop them. My war zone. Interesting, the way it sounds out loud.

Raffael tilts his head. "We have business with Valverde."

Valverde is mine, and they better understand that right fucking now. "No. You don't."

Mrs. Conti raises a brow. "We don't?"

I don't know what business they think they have here, and I don't care. Whatever this is, it's noise. Secondary. The kind of amateur theatrics men mistake for power when they're playing at war instead of waging it. This isn't their stage. I don't have the time, patience, or inclination to let a second-rate, imported spectacle interfere with what I came here to do.

I point at her. Then Conti. Then DeSantis. "You. And you. And definitely you. All three of you need to get the fuck out of Caracas before you turn a controlled situation into a fucking crater."

"Controlled?" Conti echoes, incredulous. "Don't tell me you're in bed with the Venezuelans."

I step into his space deliberately, close enough that he can smell the tension on me.

"No," I growl calmly. "I'm containing them. There's a difference."

I hear the truth in my own words. Containment isn't submission. It isn't partnership. It's pressure applied so precisely that the target doesn't realize it's already trapped. You let the poison move. You let the money flow.

You watch who touches it, who skims, who panics when the tap tightens by a fraction.

That's how you learn where the rot is.

He scoffs. "Funny way of doing it, considering your casinos are laundering their money."

My mouth curls, not a smile. Of course, he knows. Because men like Stephano Conti don't make accusations unless they're certain. Because laundering leaves fingerprints, no matter how clean you think you are. And because if you run drugs long enough, you learn to recognize the difference between money that moves through you and money that belongs to you.

I don't deny it. There's no point. They do pass money through my houses. Not because I need it. Not because I answer to them. But because it's easier to watch a river when it flows through land you control.

My casinos are mirrors. Everything that enters them reflects back eventually: patterns, alliances, betrayals. One hand washes the other. The difference between laundering and leverage is intent. They think they're using my infrastructure. They don't realize I'm mapping theirs. Now Conti stands here, throwing the word laundering at me like an accusation, when it's really a confession of his reach. Which tells me one thing very clearly: He didn't come to Caracas blind. He came because he's been watching the same currents I have. And he thinks we're playing the same game. I hold his gaze, calm, unblinking. Let him wonder how much I've already seen. Let him wonder whether the valve he thinks I opened is the same one I'm about to close.

"Funny thing about leverage. Sometimes you let it flow so you can see where it goes. And sometimes you wait until everyone forgets whose hand is on the valve." I drop my voice. "You want blood, take it somewhere else. If you light this city on fire now, you don't just create chaos, you create collateral damage."

Collateral damage, I scoff. My son isn't collateral *anything*.

Raffael smiles. Not wide. Not friendly. The kind of smile that means he's just spotted the wire in a bomb.

"Collateral damage," he repeats thoughtfully. "Yeah. That's the part that gets messy."

He gestures toward the city beyond the glass. "But if what you actually need is two extractions—clean, alive—no explosions, no headlines, no congressional phone calls—then blowing up Caracas isn't the move."

That gets my attention. How the fuck does he know this?

"Careful," I warn.

"I am being careful," Raffael replies easily. "That's my point. Silvestre and Aurelio don't just hold cartel leverage. They hold people. People they think make them untouchable."

For one clean, tempting second, I imagine pulling my gun and shooting all three of them. Not in anger. Not wildly. With precision. One shot each. Center mass. End the conversation before it metastasizes into something I don't control. The thought isn't rage, it's reflex. Violence as punctuation. As reset.

But it would be messy. Too many variables. Too many

consequences. Too much noise in a city already primed to explode. And more importantly, too many unanswered questions that would die with them. So I don't move. I don't even blink. Instead, I let the weight of what Raffael just said settle.

People.

Not product. Not territory. Not routes.

People.

I already knew that, of course. I wouldn't be here otherwise. But hearing it framed that way—out loud, from another predator—sharpens it. Confirms it. Makes it undeniable. That's the real leverage. Always has been. My jaw tightens as I clock the room again. Conti's expression shifts; it's subtle, but there. A flicker of something like recalibration. His wife's gaze sharpens, confusion giving way to interest. They didn't know. Not fully. They understood the economics, the infrastructure, but not this.

I meet Raffael's gaze. He knows he just escalated this. Knows he crossed from implication into certainty. He's waiting to see if I flinch. I don't. Because careful isn't about avoiding violence. Careful is about deciding when it becomes inevitable. And thanks to him, the list just got very, very short.

"Vegas," Conti states flatly, and I narrow my eyes at him. "Of course."

Emotions flicker over his and his wife's expressions as if they've both just figured out why I'm here.

"You want them alive long enough to give something back," Raffael continues. "We want them dead. Those goals don't have to compete."

Silence stretches. Heavy and loaded. Inside it, my thoughts move fast and cold. I want the Valverdes dead. Father and son. Not someday. Not symbolically. Erased. Aurelio first, screaming if possible. Silvestre slower. Men like them don't get quick endings; they get lessons carved into them so the next generation remembers. I don't share kills. I don't divide vengeance like territory. I don't subcontract blood. What's mine, I take myself, and I don't leave witnesses who think they had a hand in it. That's the rule.

Nobody in this room has earned an exception yet.

Still, this isn't a clean situation, and I know it. As much as every instinct in me snarls at the idea of coordination, these three didn't wander into Caracas by accident. Conti doesn't leave New York unless the math is airtight. DeSantis doesn't follow unless something has already gone wrong. The woman is still a wild card. They're here because something pulled them. Something big enough to justify exposure. Which means whatever Valverde is sitting on—my son included—has consequences that reach beyond this city or mine.

That doesn't make them allies. It makes them a complication. A complication that can be exploited. I don't need their firepower. I don't need their permission. But I'm not blind enough to ignore the possibility that they've already seen pieces of the board I haven't yet turned over. If letting them believe they have a seat at the table buys me information, access, or time, I can allow the misunderstanding. For now. I keep my face neutral. Controlled. Give nothing away. "You're suggesting a joint operation."

They want blood. I want my son. If those paths intersect tonight, that's circumstance, not partnership. And when this is over? They'll learn exactly whose war this was.

"I'm suggesting we remove your problem first," Raffael clarifies. "Clean. Quiet. Then we deal with ours."

"And if I say no?" I ask, testing the edges.

The room tightens. Even the air seems to wait. Raffael doesn't blink. "Then we do it our way. And whatever collateral damage happens after?" He shrugs lightly. "That's on the men who chose to sit on leverage instead of handing it over."

There it is. The threat, dressed up as inevitability. He's telling me that if I don't allow this, he'll burn the board anyway—loud, indiscriminate—and dare me to recover what's left. He's betting I won't risk my son in the fallout.

He's right.

And he's just made himself a problem. I study him for a long beat, committing his face to memory. DeSantis thinks this gives him leverage. Thinks he's forcing my hand. What he doesn't understand—what none of them do yet—is that I'm not choosing between options. I'm choosing the order of executions. If I allow this, they get their moment. Their illusion of relevance. Their belief that this was ever shared ground. If I don't, they'll move without me, and I'll still walk through their wreckage to retrieve what's mine.

Either way, the Valverdes die.

The only variable left is how many bodies stack up before Amauri is breathing free air. I straighten slowly, letting the silence stretch just long enough to remind them who they're dealing with. Because this isn't about whether I'll work with them. It's about whether they realize—soon enough—that they're only being tolerated.

Conti steps closer. Close enough that I can't ignore him.

"If this were just about money," he states evenly, "you'd have sent men." A flicker crosses my control. "If it were about politics, you'd have sent lawyers." His voice lowers. "You came because the people taken mean something to you."

My jaw ticks. "Who told you that?"

"We have our sources."

Bullshit. I don't bother saying it. I'm still weighing Raffael's threat when Conti's wife chooses that moment to remind us she exists. She lifts a hand. Not tentatively. Not defensively. Bright. Cheerfully so. Entirely out of place.

"It was me. Hi." The timing is so wrong it almost works. I turn my attention to her fully this time. Really look. She's smiling like this is a dinner party she's hosting instead of a room full of armed men circling a cartel war. There's no fear in her posture. No nervous tells. She's not clinging to Conti, not posturing for approval. She's enjoying herself. That alone disqualifies her from being a decoration. I stare at her, measuring.

"What are you?" It's not an insult. It's an honest question.

She grins wider. "Complicated."

Sasha mutters from the doorway, unimpressed, "Psychotic."

"Jealous," she shoots back without even looking at him.

I almost smile. Almost. For a brief second, the tension fractures into something surreal. Like I've walked into the wrong play, missed a door, and ended up in a dark comedy instead of a bloodbath. But then I remember and turn deadly serious.

"This is just a courtesy visit because of the family ties, but make no mistake, if you won't don't leave within the hour, I will have you removed." No theatrics. No raised voice. Just a simple statement of fact.

I won't tolerate interference in my operation. I don't know them. I don't trust them. And I don't allow unknown variables near my blood. That should be the end of it. It would be, with anyone else. But his wife doesn't argue. She doesn't challenge me. Doesn't bristle. Doesn't defend. She shifts. Barely perceptible. A shift in posture. A recalibration of the room itself. She smiles—not brightly now, but knowingly—and tilts her head as if she's considering me, not the threat I just issued. There's no fear in her gaze. Just interest. That alone is disconcerting.

"Alright," her voice is still cheerful, as if we're discussing seating arrangements instead of forced removal, "why don't we all take a deep breath, drink a vodka, and talk like adults and not like testosterone-fueled macho mafia bosses? Let's find out if we have any common ground here first, and if we don't..." she trails off, shrugs, "then we can start making threats."

The words are flippant. The timing is not. She's not negotiating terms. She's buying time. And the room responds. I feel it before I see it. Raffael doesn't interrupt.

Conti doesn't assert himself. Even the Russian by the door eases by a fraction, like the pressure dropped a degree. I don't move. But I notice. This woman isn't just surviving proximity to power. She's managing it. Steering momentum sideways instead of blocking it. Creating space where there shouldn't be any. That's rare. And extremely dangerous.

Who the hell are you?

The room goes quiet. Too quiet. Raffael breaks it first.

"Before we start," he asserts, lifting a hand, "I want to make one thing clear."

He pauses. Smiles faintly. "Well... two things."

Everyone looks at him.

"First: I'm not drinking vodka." He points at her without looking. "I hate that stuff."

She gasps like he's insulted her ancestors.

"Second," he continues, eyes cutting back to me, "Aurelio is mine to kill."

My shoulders roll back slowly, muscle memory kicking in. The room tightens again.

"You can have him, DeSantis," I lie evenly, not intending to give up on my revenge at all. "I don't give a shit who fucks Aurelio's corpse so long as he dies screaming. I'm here for someone else."

Silence follows. Long enough that I consider whether I've misjudged this pause, whether this is where things fracture instead of align. But then Conti heads for the bar and starts pouring. Civilization, apparently, still exists. I watch him work with mild contempt and reluctant curiosity. Top-shelf vodka for his wife. Blue Label for Raffael and himself. An expensive bourbon for me. He hands it over.

I take it without thanks and swallow half of it down like water. The burn does nothing to settle me. But it does buy me a moment. And in that moment, I decide to level with them. At least for now. "Valverde took my son."

The room shifts instantly. Raffael blinks. Once. Genuinely surprised.

"I didn't know you had a son," he swirls the Blue Label in his glass.

"Yeah," I reply, running a hand through my hair before I can stop myself, "well. Neither did fucking I."

The admission costs me more than I let show. It cracks the edge of my control just enough to be noticed. By her. She props her boots on the edge of the sofa, posture casual, expression anything but.

"So," she says with bright cheerfulness that is one hundred percent fake, "we're all on the same page, then. We go in, get Massimo's son, get our answers from Silvestre and Aurelio, kill them, and go home. The end."

I stare at her again. Longer this time. I'm curious. "Seriously, who the hell are you?"

Conti answers for her, amusement flickering behind his eyes.

"My wife," he says, savoring it. "Is far too modest to say it out loud." He tips his head toward her. "She's Metelitsa."

The name hits like a blade between the ribs. I nearly choke on my drink. Of course I've heard of the famous Russian assassin. They call her the Blizzard; she comes in like the cold, hits like a blizzard, and leaves only corpses in her wake.

"Metelitsa?" I echo, sitting up straighter. "La Tempesta di Sangue? Oksana Arsenyev?"

"Oksana Conti," she corrects mildly. "I prefer Oksana, but yes."

I go still. Not shocked. Recalculating. That explains the posture. The timing. The way she bent the room without ever touching it. It also changes the map. Both Conti and DeSantis have a reputation for ruthlessness, but with her on board... it might change how I approach the outcome of this operation. I nod once.

"Alright," my mind is already working through possibilities. "Now we're speaking honestly."

Raffael lifts his glass. "Cheers."

I look between them—Conti, Oksana, DeSantis—and see it clearly now. A nightmare alliance. Not one I asked for. Not one I trust. But one that exists whether I like it or not. I exhale.

"Alright," I drink the rest of the bourbon. "Fuck it. We talk."

I set the empty glass down.

"This is how it's going to work. Aurelio has my son." My gaze flicks away, already done with the admission. "And someone who came with the package."

I look back at them. "I'm not staying in Caracas. Whatever we do, we do tonight."

Oksana's eyes narrow, curiosity sharpening into something lethal.

"Silvestre isn't sleeping at his usual residence," I

continue. "He moved two weeks ago. Quietly. No announcements." I do what I've never done before; I lay my cards on the table. "But he'll be at Aurelio's compound tonight. They're consolidating. Too much pressure. Too many loose ends."

Just like here, too many people in this room who want answers. I don't trust them. But it wouldn't hurt to know why they're here.

My words get DeSantis's attention. "Both of them?"

I nod once. "Same roof. Different wings." I let the implications hang for a beat before adding, "They've doubled external security and rotated guards every four hours." I watch their reactions closely. "Which means," I finish, "they're worried about the perimeter."

Which they should be.

Conti folds his arms. "Good. Because we're not coming through it."

My gaze snaps to him. Sharp. Interested. "You have an entry vector?"

Raffael's mouth curls back into that familiar smugness. "We do. Underground. Old infrastructure that they still rely on."

Something inside me clicks. Of course, the Valverdes would have tunnels. It also explains, "That explains the power cycling. We clocked a ninety-second fluctuation every hour. Thought it was a fault."

Oksana speaks before anyone else can. Calm. Certain. "It's not." She meets my eyes. "It's a door."

The board is finally making sense. The doubled perimeter. The rotations. The nervous consolidation. Men who believe walls keep them safe always forget what's beneath their feet.

"Then we stop circling each other," I propose.

I look between them—Conti, DeSantis, Oksana—voice cool, final. "I don't care who claims which corpse. We can argue about spoils and grudges after my son is safe and their leverage is dust."

Conti nods once. "You get your boy. We get answers. And blood."

Oksana lifts her glass again. "Efficient. I like it. Let's retrieve the child and remove the men who thought this was clever."

I stare at her. Longer this time. And—damn it—impressed.

"...Fine," I mutter. "I'll take the help."

But even as the words leave my mouth, I know the truth of it. Men like me don't share vengeance. We don't divide it. And we sure as hell don't forget who put hands on our blood. Aurelio and Silvestre didn't just cross me. They took my son. That kind of debt doesn't get negotiated. It gets erased. Not later. Not diplomatically. Completely.

But that reckoning can wait. For now, we're aligned, temporary allies with overlapping targets and a shared deadline. Tonight, we get inside. Tonight, we take back what was stolen and burn their leverage to ash. After that?

We'll see whose war this really was.

And whose it becomes.

It's really simple. I walk into the antechamber and tell Max, "I forgot something."

He studies me for a beat, doesn't ask what, and nods. He gestures toward the elevator, and just like earlier, two more guards join us, making the spacious area that wasn't meant for three linebackers suddenly feel cramped.

This time, the casino level doesn't hit me as hard as earlier. I still register the noise, but ignore it, just like the *Cocktails? Cocktails?* calls from the waitresses. I'm also prepared to sidestep the drunken asshole we encounter, sparing him the humiliation of being manhandled by one of the guards, not that he notices.

The boutique is still quiet, immaculate, and insulated from the chaos of the casino outside. Soft lighting. Plush carpet. Sales associates who know when to disappear. My eyes scan the shelves and rows of clothing racks until they land on Marianne. She's browsing silk scarves like she belongs here, fingers trailing over fabric with idle familiarity. Polished. Composed. Effortless in a way that makes my teeth itch. She looks up at exactly the right moment, surprise blooming across her face just slowly enough to feel practiced.

"Jenna," she says warmly. "What a coincidence."

I smile back. The kind you learn young. Pleasant. Unrevealing. "Marianne. Small world."

I feel Max stiffen, but ignore him as I walk over to Marianne, and we embrace each other, pretending surprise, pretending this isn't deliberate. She takes me in quickly: the clothes, the posture, the absence of strain. I do the same. She looks no different than always. Untouched by consequence. Her gaze flicks, just briefly, to Max.

"Your security?" she asks, chin lifting in his direction.

"Yes," I reply easily. "Massimo insists."

I watch her eyes at the name. Just for a fraction of a second, something sharp flashes there, interest, not surprise.

"Of course he does," she murmurs. Then adds, "I'm so sorry about Amauri and Carter."

The names land carefully, like she practiced the order. Child first. Husband second. Optics before emotion.

"I want you to know," she continues, lowering her voice just enough to feel confidential, "that I'm doing everything I can."

I let my shoulders soften. Just a little. Enough to invite her closer.

"Do you know who took them?" I need to know.

Her answer comes too quickly. "Yes." She nods once, then glances around the boutique, eyes flicking to the mirrors, the sales associates, the corners, like she's worried we're being watched. "The Venezuelan Cartel."

This confirms what Massimo told me.

"Your father is talking with them," she adds quietly.

The words slide under my ribs and twist.

"What is he saying?" I ask, holding myself back in an effort not to look too eager. "Did he change his mind? Is he backing down?"

We drift from shelf to shelf, holding up a shirt here or a skirt there for the other to look at, pretending intimacy, close enough to share warmth, far enough to keep secrets. Her perfume is subtle. Expensive. Controlled. She tilts her head toward me, sympathy carefully calibrated, shaking her head slowly, compassion settling into place like a practiced expression. "I'm afraid not. He's determined not to allow anybody to blackmail him. Your father is a very stern man."

Yeah, I think. Don't I know that. I study her for a beat longer than politeness allows, deciding to be direct, "So why are you here? What do you think you can do for me?"

Marianne takes my hands. I notice Max inching closer. "Whatever you need," she promises smoothly. "Information. Discretion. I can arrange a safe place for you to stay, if you're feeling... uncertain."

Safe from whom? She doesn't say it out loud, but the implication hangs there, heavy. Massimo.

"Anything," she adds. "I want to help."

I tilt my head, mirroring her posture. Matching her tone.

"Can you find me men," I ask evenly, "to get Amauri and Carter out of Venezuela?"

Her reaction is too quick, like she's been waiting for this exact question. "Of course. I know just the right men."

Unease settles through me. I'm not sure how to respond. I wasn't prepared for that answer, so quickly. My pulse spikes at the thought that maybe I can turn this around and be the one who gets Amauri out. As if sensing my apprehension, she leans in, lowering her voice like she's sharing a secret meant only for me. "Why don't you come with me and meet them in person?"

Something cold slides down my spine. There it is. Not rushed. Not forceful. No grabbing, no threat. Just the promise of solutions and the suggestion of movement. Get her isolated. Get her off familiar ground. Away from witnesses. Away from security. Away from control. Textbook.

I've seen it before, not like this, not dressed up in silk and concern, but the mechanics are the same. Offer help. Create urgency. Make staying feel unreasonable. Leaving feel logical. My pulse kicks hard, but my face stays smooth. Because this isn't panic territory yet. This is a confirmation. Marianne never wanted to help me; she is still and always will be loyal only to my father. She's here by his orders to get me out. It shouldn't bother me that he's not coming himself. I should be used to it. But there is still a small part inside me that slightly stings.

I don't even have a chance to come up with a response before everything goes wrong. Not loudly. Not like it did when they stormed my house. Right now, it's just a shift. The boutique doors don't slam open. They open normally. Too normal. Two men step inside, wrong clothes for the room, wrong posture for shoppers. Their eyes don't wander. They don't browse. They lock. On me. My blood turns to ice. Max moves before my brain catches up. His hand clamps around my elbow, not yanking, not panicked, controlled. Protective. Already pivoting my body, already angling me away from the mirrors, the exits, the glass.

"Now," he says quietly into my ear.

One of the men reaches inside his jacket, and that's when everything explodes. A sales associate screams. Glass shatters. People scatter, shrieking, bodies colliding as panic detonates through the boutique. One of the men lunges, not at Max. At me. Shouting something in the same language I heard at my house. Something inside me snaps, and in that instant, I see them as the men who took my son. I don't think. I don't hesitate. I grab the first thing within reach—a heavy marble display base—and swing with everything I have. It connects with a wet, sickening crack against the man's head. He goes down hard, collapsing like his strings were cut. Blood splashes across the pristine floor. For half a second, I just stand there, chest heaving, staring at him. Max shoves me behind him as more gunfire erupts, sharp, deafening, and contained. More men flood the space like they were waiting for a signal. They move with purpose, no shouting, no hesitation. Guns up. Angles covered. It's surgical. Ruthless. The kind of response that tells me this wasn't luck. This was anticipated.

One of the attackers bolts. He crashes through a rack of dresses, silk tearing, hangers screaming as he barrels toward the back. Max brings his gun up in one smooth motion, already tracking the shot.

"No!" I'm on my feet before I realize it, grabbing his wrist and yanking it down. The gun discharges anyway—deafening, wild—shattering a mirror instead of a spine. Max whirls on me like I've just stabbed him. My hands are shaking. My heart is trying to break out of my chest. I shake my head, hard. "We need him alive."

A split second. Then it clicks. Understanding blooms behind his eyes, sharp and immediate. He snaps his head to the side. "Tony. Hawk. Get that bastard—alive."

Two men peel off instantly, sprinting after the fleeing assailants. He's trapped himself inside a forest of fabric, panic shredding his precision. Dresses whip aside as he thrashes, trying to hide where there is nowhere to go. Everything is happening too fast. Shouting. Crying. The smell of gunpowder and expensive perfume collides in my throat. I haven't even looked for Marianne yet—

So I do. And my blood turns to ice. She's gone. Already halfway across the casino floor, slipping through a line of slot machines like she's done this before. A hand tight around her arm, guiding her forward with quiet urgency.

Sean.

Of course, it's Sean.

They don't look panicked. They look practiced. Coordinated. Like this wasn't the plan, but it was always an option. Max is at my side again in an instant, his eyes raking over me, searching for blood, for damage, for anything he missed. "Are you hit?"

"No," I breathe. "I'm fine."

It's true. Somehow. He checks me once more anyway,

thorough, unyielding. Then his hand closes around my arm, not rough, not gentle. Certain. "Let's go."

I don't argue. I don't resist. I let him pull me away from the chaos, from the glass and the screams and the blood staining the boutique floor. While we move, one thought pounds louder than the rest: They came back for me. And now they know exactly where to find me.

NIGHT IN CARACAS SETTLES HEAVY, LIKE A HAND CLOSING around a throat. The Valverde compound squats on the hillside below us, too large, too arrogant, all glass and water and artificial calm. A fortress dressed up as luxury. Mirrored pools reflecting lights meant to impress men who confuse excess with safety. Lit up like a fucking Christmas tree, or at least it was lit. Until Sasha triggered the EMP.

I don't hear it, but I feel it. A ripple through the air, subtle and violent at the same time. The kind of power you don't see but respect immediately. Every light across the estate dies in unison. Cameras blink out. The soft glow of security evaporates. Radios choke. Systems collapse. Blind. Just like that.

"Show-off," Oksana murmurs somewhere to my right.

Sasha smirks behind his mask. "I learned from the best."

The darkness shifts. Becomes something else. Alive. Predatory. The kind of dark that doesn't hide danger, it is the danger. They know we're coming. And we know they know. Perfect.

I check my rifle one last time. Solid. Familiar. The

weight grounds me. This isn't ceremony. It's function. Every piece of gear has a purpose tonight. Nothing ornamental. Nothing wasted.

Raffael is beside me, calm in the way only men who've killed too many times can be calm, wiping his knives like this is maintenance, not prelude. Stephano stands a few paces ahead, unmoving, his people forming instinctive cover around him.

I don't waste time wondering how Oksana convinced Conti to let her come. Then again, let isn't a word that applies to a woman like her. You don't grant permission to a force of nature. You either adapt around it or get flattened.

Still. If the roles were reversed—if my wife were standing here in the dark with rifles and knives and men who smell like blood and jungle rot—I'd have tied her up if I had to, hauled her off, and locked her in the safest room I owned. Concrete. Steel. No windows. No exits. Alive.

The thought hits harder than it should.

My wife.

The word flashes uninvited, sharp as recoil. I almost trip on it.

Wife.

It doesn't fit. It never has. Not cleanly. Not legally. Not after she walked out of my life and straight into another man's name. She chose Carter. Married him. Built a life without me. That's the story I've carried for ten years, worn thin from repetition but never fully questioned. Easier to believe she left than to interrogate why she didn't stay. Easier to harden around betrayal than crack open old silence.

And yet—

The word won't leave.

Wife.

Not because it's true. Because somewhere deep, unreasonable though it may be, a part of me never stopped thinking of her that way. Not possession. Not entitlement. Something quieter. Something that settled before I had language for it. Something dangerous.

I shove it down where it belongs. This isn't the night for fantasies or rewrites. Whatever she was to me, whatever I thought she did, whatever choices she made after me, that's blood already dried.

Oksana's presence unsettles me more than it should. She moves like someone who understands the cost of loving a man like Conti and still chose it anyway. Not blindly. Not foolishly. With eyes open. With teeth. I don't just respect that. I envy it.

I don't let myself think any further than that, because this isn't the night for ghosts or hypotheticals or the luxury of regret. This is the night I get my son back. Everything else—love, guilt, the dangerous pull of words like wife—can wait. If they survive me. We pull our radios from the Faraday cases. The click feels loud in the silence.

"Positions," I murmur.

No hesitation. No questions. I move to cover the flank, rifle up, sightline clean. Raffael melts into the foliage like he was never there. Sasha flashes two fingers, path clear. Conti nods once, jaw set. Then we move. The descent down the ridge is quiet. Boots kiss dirt. Leaves shift. Somewhere below, backup generators stutter, trying to claw power back from the void. Futile. The air is thick with humidity, rot, and metal. My breath feels heavy in my chest, but my mind is clear. Sharper than it's been in days. I think of Amauri.

I don't picture his face. That would fracture me. I picture distance. Obstacles. Men who need to stop breathing before I can reach him. That's manageable. We reach the north ridge patrol. Four guards. Panicked halos in night vision, clustered too close, radios useless in their hands. Amateurs.

Conti lifts two fingers. His men flow around him like water. He moves. One second, he's still. The next, he's gone. A hand clamps over a mouth. A body disappears into the brush. Bone breaks with a muted crack.

The other three spin. Too late. They never get a chance to fire. Stephano is on them like a hurricane, slitting their throats before I even have a chance to step forward. He turns back to us, moving without anger. Without flourish. Without even breathing hard. What gets me isn't the violence. It's the icy control. This isn't rage. This is precision. Contained fury. The kind that doesn't burn itself out, it executes.

"Holy fuck," I mutter before I can stop myself. "You married that?"

"Jealous?" Oksana whispers.

I snort. "Terrified."

It's only half a joke. Sasha meets my eyes and gives a single nod in Stephano's direction. Respect. Rare. Earned.

Raffael reappears like he stepped out of the dark itself. "One guard tower down. Two left."

Conti nods. "West side first. They'll bottleneck once they realize we're inside. Sasha, left flank. Oksana—"

She arches a brow, dares him to finish his order. He corrects himself immediately. "Right flank."

A short sound escapes me before I can stop it. Not quite a laugh. Not quite disbelief. Amusement. That's... unexpected. When was the last time I was in the field like this? Not delegating. Not directing from behind glass and screens. Not watching dots move across maps while other men bled for my interests. Here. In the dirt. In the dark. With the air thick and the stakes real.

And worse—I'm enjoying it.

Oksana and Conti move together with a precision that borders on obscene. Not rehearsed, not showy. Instinctive. Brutal. Like they're sharing a language no one else in the room speaks fluently enough to interrupt. They don't look at each other much. They don't need to. Adjustments happen mid-motion, a shift of weight, a raised brow, a fraction of a second shaved off a kill. It's intimate in the way only shared violence can be. A savage symphony.

I should want them dead. Men like me don't like witnesses. Don't like variables. Don't like other predators operating in the same dark. But instead, something else stirs, recognition, maybe. Or respect. The kind that only comes when you see someone else do the thing right. Clean. Controlled. Joyless in execution, but alive in motion. I almost feel like I don't want to kill them. That thought alone is dangerous. Because enjoyment like this dulls the edge. Makes men forget why they came. Makes them linger instead of finishing the job. I force my focus back where it belongs. This isn't art. This isn't camaraderie. This is a means to an end. But as we move—silent, lethal, perfectly aligned—I can't deny it: for the first time in years, I don't feel like a king watching war. I feel like a soldier inside it. And I remember exactly why I was feared long before I was crowned.

The closer we get to the villa, the more the tension compresses. Gunfire cracks somewhere below. Shouts. Footsteps scrambling uphill.

"They're regrouping," I whisper.

"They're panicking," Oksana replies calmly.

She's right.

"Good."

We round the terrace garden, stone pillars, bougainvillea, and narrow sightlines. A choke point dressed up as beauty. Valverde taste. I adjust my grip on the rifle. This is where men die, thinking they're still in control. And somewhere beyond this, my son is breathing air that belongs to me. No one here survives forgetting that. Conti slows. I know that stance. The fractional shift in weight. The way his shoulders lock without tension. He's sensing something. The dark answers first.

A single guard explodes out of it, blade raised, breath ragged, desperation driving him forward. I bring my gun up instinctively, but Conti is already moving. It's clean. A wrist twist so precise it looks rehearsed. Bone pops. The blade clatters away. A palm strike to the sternum drops the man like air leaving a lung. He folds, wheezing, eyes wide with shock. Conti steps in and knocks him out with the butt of his gun. No sound. No flourish. Ghost work.

"Not bad, Conti," Oksana murmurs.

He glances back at her over his shoulder, calm as a man correcting a line of code. "Trying to impress you."

"It's working," She grins back at him.

I groan quietly. "Please shoot me."

"Keep talking," Raffael mutters, "I might."

We move. The inner courtyard opens before us, vast, moonlit, framed by arches and broken fountains. Beautiful. Deadly. A kill zone disguised as elegance. Waiting for us at the far end, stepping into the moonlight like a man welcoming guests into his home, is Silvestre Valverde, a rifle slung over his shoulder. A smirk in place. He knows he's surrounded. He knows he's lost. His guards are dead, and he's one of the last men standing. Tall and proud. Old school. If he hadn't laid hands on my son, it would be admirable.

Gunfire echoes deeper in the compound, short, violent bursts. Our men are tearing through what's left of his crew. Silvestre spreads his arms. Mock-grand. "Welcome, friends."

Conti stiffens. DeSantis goes still. Oksana whistles. I snarl low in my throat. Silvestre's gaze slides to me, assessing, measuring. He holds his rifle loosely, like this is a negotiation instead of an execution waiting to happen. I don't wait. I push past all of them, fury rolling off me in waves I don't bother containing.

"Where is my son?" I demand.

Silvestre lifts his rifle. The barrel settles against my

chest. My men tighten their circle, metal whispers from holsters, safeties click off. The night compresses, breath held by too many killers in too small a space.

"I have no beef with you, Manetti." Silvestre sounds surprised to see me here. Whatever calculation I walked in with incinerates.

"You have my son," I snap.

Silvestre blinks with raw emotions; he's not posturing now. Real confusion creases his face. "Your... what?"

I step forward. I don't care that the muzzle presses harder into my chest.

"Senator Kingsley's grandson," I spit. "And his son-in-law."

I watch it land. Confusion first, then recognition. Then something close to horror.

"Massimo," Silvestre pronounces slowly, each word placed like a brace against collapse. "I swear to you, I had no idea."

Gunfire rattles again in the distance. I wait until the echo fades. Then I laugh. Once. Low. Empty.

"Why the fuck would that matter to me?" I growl.

I draw my gun, and it hits him in the forehead hard enough to snap his head back an inch. No warning. No hesitation.

"You took my son," I snarl. "That's the only part of this story that counts."

That's when the shitshow starts. Conti steps in, gun up, pressing hard against the side of my head. "Don't," he snarls. "He's mine."

Of course. Across the courtyard, weapons rise in reflex,

Gabe first, then the rest of my men, barrels swinging toward DeSantis, Conti, Oksana. Their people mirror us instantly. The air goes razor-thin. One twitch. One breath too loud. And this place becomes a slaughterhouse. Silvestre stands frozen between gods and guns, sweat beading at his temple where my barrel kisses skin.

"Everyone—" he starts.

"Shut up," I snap. "You don't get to talk your way out of this."

Conti's finger tightens. I feel it in the pressure against my skull. "You pull that trigger," his voice is cold, "and you die with him."

I don't flinch. "Then we all bleed."

For a heartbeat, no one moves. Too many grudges. Too much blood already promised. I glance sideways just enough to catch the storm burning behind Conti's eyes. He wants Silvestre dead. Desperately. I recognize that kind of restraint; it hums like a live wire. This isn't an alliance anymore. It's a powder keg. Silvestre sees it too. His eyes flick, counting barrels, exits, distances. Survivor first. Kingpin second.

"It wasn't my idea," he blurts, his voice is cracking just enough to sound real. "Someone hired us."

Gunfire cracks again, closer now. I press the barrel harder into his forehead. "Who?"

He swallows. "Let me live," he bargains. "And I'll tell you."

Conti laughs. Not loud. Not amused. "Nice try. We'll make you talk."

Silvestre's gaze darts from Conti to DeSantis to

Oksana. He sees the truth written plainly: pain later. Answers first.

She steps in then, calm, deadly. Like before. "Look. I get it. He took your son."

I don't look at her. My breathing is heavy now, my chest rising like a bellows, my fury barely caged.

"If someone hired him—someone bigger, cleaner, smarter—you go after that man," she continues. "Let us have him. And his pathetic son. I swear to you, he won't find an easy end."

Her words cut through the red. She's not asking for mercy. She's talking strategy. I don't lower the gun. But I listen. Because the only thing that matters more than how Silvestre will die is why Amauri was taken in the first place. And who ordered it. The math snaps into place almost immediately. Not trust. Not agreement. Delay.

Right now, if a shot is fired, nobody walks away. Too many guns. Too many men with reasons. Too many overlapping grudges pressed into too small a space. This courtyard turns into a tomb the second someone twitches.

That matters. I'm not afraid to die, but Amauri is still breathing somewhere beneath this estate, and I refuse to let my temper bury him with me. So I shift, barely perceptible. A fraction of a degree. Enough to change the equation without announcing it.

I let my eyes move and take Oksana in. Not as a woman. Not as an ally. As a variable. A weapon. Someone dangerous enough to matter. I can almost hear the numbers ticking through my head as I reassess the board.

Less mess later beats total annihilation now. I look back at Silvestre.

"If I promise not to kill you," I order flatly, "you tell me who the fuck hired you."

His nod is immediate. Too fast. Desperate. "Yes. Yes."

"Now."

He hesitates, tries to bargain. "Get me out of here first," he pleads, a sly gleam slipping into his eyes. He thinks distance equals leverage. He thinks breathing buys him control.

"Non-negotiable," I stare coldly into his eyes. "You could be caught in the crossfire."

Every gun in the courtyard rises another inch. I feel it more than see it, the collective inhale, the tightening grips, the shift of weight. DeSantis is ready. Conti is ready. My men are already ahead of me. Silvestre sees it too. The gamble sharpens.

"I want your word," he presses, voice tight now. "Not to kill me. And to get me out of here alive."

I roll my eyes. This is worse than negotiating with a five-year-old. Then I nod once. Sharp. Final. Having no intentions of following through. "Yeah."

The word tastes like poison. Every instinct I have screams to put a bullet through his skull right now. End it. End the lies. End the variables. This is going to be ugly no matter what. But ugly later still beats dead now.

Silvestre straightens, just a fraction. Enough to tell me he thinks he's won. "The people who hired me," confidence creeps back into his voice with every syllable, "they're Mexican cartel."

That lands more than he understands.

"They're shielding someone," he continues quickly, lifting his hand as if to ward off the curse he knows is coming. "I don't know who, but whoever it is, they're positioning. Vegas. They want to take it."

He hasn't given me a name, but his words align. Did they know Amauri is my son? No, I dismiss that thought almost instantly. They would have sent demands or a finger; they took him because of Kingsley's bill. They want the road cleared to bring in their drugs from Mexico and push me out of the picture. The truth hits. This is all about Vegas.

My jaw locks. Vegas isn't just territory. It's blood. Infrastructure. Legacy. A city I bled for until it knew my name. My crown. Something hard clicks into place behind my eyes. I still want Silvestre to suffer. That urge doesn't vanish just because I choose not to indulge it. It coils tighter, sharper, promising patience instead of release. Silvestre deserves pain measured in hours, not seconds. Deserves to understand exactly what it means to touch my blood. And that's the one currency I don't have right now. Time.

But the others do. Even if they're New York. Even if I don't like them. Even if trusting them feels like swallowing broken glass. After last night, after watching Conti and DeSantis move, after hearing the way they speak about vengeance, not as spectacle but as obligation, I know their grudges are as personal as mine. This isn't business for them either. It's debt. Old, intimate, unforgiving.

As far as Oksana is concerned... she has an iron or two

in this fire. I saw it in her eyes when Silvestre spoke. Not sympathy. Not mercy. Calculation sharpened by experience. She understands what I'm only just finishing mapping: Silvestre is a node, not the collector.

He didn't design this.

He was hired.

Which means there's another man out there who thought he could orchestrate this from a distance. Thought he could hide behind cartels and borders and plausible deniability while my son paid the price. That man matters more than Silvestre ever did. I can let the old bastard suffer at the hands of others—thoroughly—and in the meantime, I gain something far more valuable than blood on my hands tonight. I gain momentum. I gain allies who will bleed him for their own reasons. I gain time to turn and face the one who masterminded this.

Silvestre is just the door. The real enemy is waiting on the other side. I lower my gun. Silvestre exhales like a man clawing his way out of a grave. I turn my head and look at Conti.

"A deal is a deal," I say evenly. "He's all yours."

Relief moves through the courtyard like a sigh. Guns lower. One by one. The air loosens.

Silvestre's face drains of color. "No—no, you promised!" he wails. "You said—"

I step forward and drive my fist into his gut. Hard. The sound is wet. The kind of hit that empties lungs and dignity in one blow. He folds with a strangled sound, retching. I lean down, in a voice laced with malice, and I spit, "I don't make promises to child snatchers and blackmailers."

Then I straighten and snap my fingers. "Enough. Let's go get my son." I turn back to Silvestre. "Where are they?"

He blinks. He knows he's lost. "In the basement," he croaks.

That's when DeSantis steps forward.

"I know where it is," his certainty hums with lethality beneath the words. "Follow me."

My men fan out instinctively. Gabe is at my shoulder, others flanking left. Conti's hand flexes once, like he's deciding whether diplomacy officially dies tonight. I notice Gabe pulling out his phone, staring at a message. We move as one. The villa's stone hallways swallow us, emergency lights flicker, and gunfire echoes faintly in the distance as what's left of Valverde's army is erased.

DeSantis leads us through a grand foyer. There is a staircase to the right. A corridor to the left.

He turns left.

A door opens onto a narrow stairwell. Gabe leans in close, his mouth near my ear, voice pitched low enough that only I hear it. "Boss. The Mexicans made a move. They tried to snatch Jenna."

The world narrows to a pinpoint. My stomach churns so hard it feels like a fist closing inside me. "Max got her out," Gabe continues quickly. "Nobody got hurt. We grabbed one of theirs. Alive. Enzo's standing by, wants to know if you want him questioned now."

For half a second, everything inside me turns to molten lava. Someone dared touch her. Not threaten. Not circle. Touch. The urge to turn around—to abandon the stairwell, the basement, Silvestre, Valverde, all of it—and burn Vegas to the ground with my bare hands roars up so fast it almost breaks containment. I see red.

Pure. Blinding. Unapologetic.

With a herculean will, I force it down, knowing I need to restrain myself. "Tell Enzo to start," I murmur. My voice doesn't shake. That alone costs me effort. "I want names. Routes. Who gave the order. I want it all before I step foot back on my plane."

Gabe nods once and peels off without another word. My pulse is still hammering. The Mexicans didn't move out of fear. They moved because they understood something before I did. Whitford and Amauri ceased being leverage the moment they realized Jenna mattered more. And the Venezuelans? They were already written off.

Which means two things: first, the Mexicans knew the Venezuelans were compromised before I put a knife to their throat. That timing isn't luck. That's foreknowledge. Someone talked, either from my house or from La Famiglia's. A rat doesn't need to sell me out completely. He just needs to whisper once, at the right moment.

Second: they abandoned the Venezuelans without hesitation. Cut them loose like excess weight. No warning. No extraction. Just silence.

Whitford was a placeholder. Amauri was pressure. They realized Jenna was the real prize. If they pivoted this cleanly, this fast, then they weren't reacting to me. They were planning around me. Kingsley won't bend without his daughter. And now they know she's under my protection. Which means this stopped being transactional. This is personal now. Bloody.

I'm almost grateful DeSantis, Conti, and Oksana are here to finish the Valverdes. Let them bleed. Let them scream. I have other fires to put out, fires that will scorch entire supply chains and leave nothing standing where confidence used to live. Something else rattles beneath the rage and strategy; it settles heavy and undeniable. Jenna.

I try to frame it cleanly. Rationally. She's the mother of my son. That should be enough. It isn't. The truth presses in whether I want it or not. The thought of her being taken—of her being touched by men who would use her like leverage, like currency—does something violent to me. Something that has nothing to do with legacy or bloodlines and everything to do with possession that I don't want to name.

I don't say it out loud. I don't let myself dwell. But the realization is there, sharp and immovable: she means more to me than I'm willing to admit. Which means that whoever is orchestrating this—whoever thought they could test my borders by reaching for her—they didn't just declare war on my empire. They signed their own death warrant.

We descend the stairs. The basement waits.

And somewhere far from here, someone just made the worst mistake of their life.

We kill the night vision and switch to headlights. The beam cuts through the dark, and the smell hits immediately. Damp metal. Old blood. Rust. Something sour, a residual of ruined humanity that never fully leaves a place once it's been soaked in pain. Humiliation clings to the air like a residue you can't scrub out. The kind that seeps into stone and waits. My jaw tightens. This is where they're keeping him. The thought lands heavy and immediate, like a blow to the chest.

My son.

These fucktards dragged a child into this place. My child. I don't need to be told what happened here. I recognize it the way you recognize a language you were raised speaking. This is a place where men learned how much a body could take before the mind followed. DeSantis walks ahead of us like a man entering a grave he intends to desecrate. Whatever drives him, it's not business; it's personal.

. Silvestre trails behind, quiet now. Smaller. He doesn't run. He knows better.

At the bottom, the space opens up into a wide room carved from stone and cruelty. Cabinets line the walls, too many of them, too orderly. The floor slopes subtly toward a drain at the center, stained dark despite years of scrubbing. A rope hangs from the ceiling, frayed at the ends, swaying slightly in the stale air.

DeSantis points toward a row of doors along one wall. "Which one, old man?"

I don't take my eyes off them. Because one of those doors is between me and my son. And nothing in this world is going to survive standing in that space much longer. Silvestre points. I don't look at him. I shoulder past him and kick the door open. The stench hits first. Rot. Sweat. Fear. Bleach layered over blood like someone tried

—and failed—to erase what happened here. It claws its way down my throat, settles behind my eyes.

Inside, two shapes hover in the dim light. One man, barely alive. Sunken cheeks. Bruised wrists. His lips are split and dry, his breathing is shallow, like every inhale might be his last. I recognize him instantly ,even before Oksana exclaims, "That's Carter Whitford."

The way the man looks, it's more like she's naming a corpse. Satisfaction burns through me. Years ago, I tried—unsuccessfully—to have him killed. Instead, he earned himself a punishment that some might call harder than death. Still, it irritates the fuck out of me that he lived. And yes, it infuriates me that it's him Jenna married. But seeing him like this, here, now, it almost settles the old score. Almost.

He takes second place in no time, because beside him, holding his hand, sits a boy. My boy. He's huddled on the floor beside the man who isn't his father, dirt smeared across his face, shoulders tight, eyes too old for his age. He doesn't cry. Doesn't scream. Doesn't reach. He just watches us. Cautiously and assessing. Like a child who has learned the hard way that attention can be dangerous. In stark contrast to Carter, who proves he's alive by groaning and mumbling words that sound like pleas. I tune him out. My entire world narrows to the boy. My son. My chest tightens so suddenly that it steals my breath as the realization hits: he doesn't know me.

Of course he doesn't.

I turn to Conti because if I don't speak, I might do something irrevocable. "Do you need backup?"

"We've got it," he answers without hesitation. "Go. Get your people out."

I nod once. Respect passes between us, silent, mutual. Two men who understand exactly what it costs to stand in places like this and still walk away breathing.

"Good to see you again, Conti," and, surprising myself, I mean the words. "Let me know when you're in Vegas." My gaze flicks to Oksana. "It's been an honor, Metelitsa."

She inclines her head, sharp and knowing. My men are already moving, two of them on Whitford, efficient, gentle only in comparison to what they could be. I step past them. Toward Amauri.

His eyes track me as I approach, calculating, wary, intelligent in a way that hurts. Carefully, I lower myself so as not to scare him until I'm crouched at his level. I keep my hands visible. I keep my voice steady. I don't do gentle, haven't in a long time, but hearing my voice, I could almost call it that. "I'll take you to your mamma." The word tastes strange and right all at once. "What do you think?"

He blinks at me. No recognition. No relief. Just stunned silence. My heart breaks anyway. I remember the words I said earlier, laughing them off like they didn't matter.

Neither did I.

I reach out my hand, palm open. Not demanding. Not commanding. An invitation.

"Come on, little man," I say quietly. "Let's go home."

For a second, I think he won't. Then his hand lifts—shaking, filthy, brave—and slides into mine. The contact detonates something inside my chest. A sensation like nothing I've ever felt before. I close my fingers around his, careful. Protective. Absolute.

I stand and make my way to the door. My son's hand in mine. Whitford carried behind us. The door to the torture chamber closes on screams, on ghosts, on Silvestre Valverde. I don't look back. Because everything that matters is walking forward with me now. And anyone who stands between this child and me will not die quickly.

THE PENTHOUSE IS TOO QUIET. NO SCREAMS. NO GUNFIRE. No alarms. Just the hum of the city far below and the echo of my own pulse pounding in my ears. I pace, barefoot, back and forth. Too fast. Like if I stop moving, everything that almost happened will catch up to me. I almost got kidnapped.

Again.

My hands shake when I realize that part still hasn't landed properly. Not a misunderstanding. Not security theater. Men walked into a boutique with guns and intent, and eyes locked on me. The same men who took my son. The thought makes my vision blur red. I drag a hand through my hair, breathing hard, trying to slow my thoughts and failing spectacularly. Because it's not just them.

It's Marianne.

And Sean.

Sean.

My stomach turns at the memory of his hand on her back. Familiar. Possessive. Like they'd rehearsed it. Like they were comfortable in each other's space in a way that had nothing to do with chance. What the hell was he doing there?

I stop pacing long enough to press my palms against the window. *Think.*

My father must have sent them. That's the reflexive thought. The safe one. The one that still wants him to be the villain that I understand—controlling, cold, obsessed with optics. He can't be bothered to call me, but he sends his lackeys after me.

But that doesn't explain the attack. That doesn't explain guns in a casino boutique. That doesn't explain why men would risk an international incident to grab me.

Unless—

My chest tightens. Unless Amauri and Carter aren't enough anymore. Unless they realize something I'm not prepared to face yet. That I matter. Not politically. Not symbolically. But tactically. I laugh once, sharp and humorless.

Congratulations, Jenna. You've been upgraded from collateral to asset.

The thought should terrify me. Instead, it makes something ugly and determined settle into place. I turn back to the room, eyes scanning Massimo's office like it might answer me if I stare hard enough.

Marianne wasn't trying to help me.

She was trying to move me. Get me alone. Get me out of Massimo's orbit. Get me somewhere she controlled. Sean was the contingency in case she needed force. My pulse spikes again. I don't know how he fits into this yet. I just know he does.

The worst part?

Somewhere deep down, past the fear and the rage and the betrayal, something colder clicks into place. They came for me because my father didn't bend. I already knew that, but part of me was still hoping... it makes me wonder, would he bend if they had me too? If I thought that for a second, they wouldn't have to abduct me. I'd run to them screaming, arms waving, saying *take me, take me.*

I wish I could still say that my father does the things he does for ideological reasons, because he truly wants the drugs off the streets. A few days ago, I believed that. Not today, though. Not after the paper trails I've found. Not after seeing the gleam in his eyes. After seeing how much the idea of playing the martyred man who lost his family appeals to him.

A knock on the door interrupts me. "Come in."

Max sticks his head in. "Just wanting to check up on you. Do you need anything? Changed your mind about the doc?"

"I'm fine," I assure him. *As fine as I can be.* "I don't need a doctor, I wasn't hurt, which, by the way. Thank you." I don't think I thanked him yet.

He did save me.

"I just did my job."

I force a grin. "And a good one at that. I'll tell Massimo to give you a raise." But even I don't believe that I have that kind of power.

"By the way, next time, if you want to meet someone, just tell me." He winks, but it doesn't look friendly. "No need to play charades."

I hold his gaze. "Noted."

Our eyes hold for a few more moments, then he nods. "Alright then, if you don't need—" He's about to close the door and leave when a thought strikes me.

"The men? You did get one alive?"

"That was smart thinking on your part. Yes. He's alive, we have him."

I don't even know what I want yet, or why I'm curious. "Where is he? Will he be questioned?"

Max looks more than uncomfortable now. "Uhm..." he runs a hand through his hair. "You shouldn't bother yourself with that."

But I am bothered. I am bothered that this man is part of the group of people who came into my house and took my son. What gave them the right to do that?

I straighten, the pacing inside me slowing into something sharper.

"Where is he?" I ask again.

Max exhales through his nose. Not annoyed. Not dismissive. Careful. "Jenna—"

"I'm not asking to hurt him," I cut in. I don't raise my voice. I don't need to. "I'm asking where he is."

A beat. He studies me like he's reassessing the terrain. Like he's deciding whether I'm glass or steel.

Finally, "Not here, at a safe place. Enzo's handling it."

I have no idea who Enzo is, but I assume he must be more important than Max. I also have no idea of the hierarchy in the mafia, so I don't know what title Max or anybody else holds. I'm more of a corporate kind of girl.

It doesn't matter; what matters is, "Is he being questioned?"

Max hesitates just long enough to be an answer. "Yes."

I nod once. That confirms what I already suspected. Before I even know what I'm requesting, the words pop out of my mouth, "Take me to him."

Max's head snaps up. "No." It's automatic. Reflex. Protective. He looks almost apologetic about it. He back-paddles, "This isn't something you should see. It's not—"

"—clean?" I finish for him. "Comfortable? Easy to watch?"

His jaw tightens. "It's not for you."

I meet his eyes. Hold them once again. "He might have been part of the group that took my son," I explain quietly in case he didn't get the memo. "I think that makes it very much for me."

He doesn't argue immediately. That tells me everything.

"I won't interfere," I continue. "I won't touch him. I won't make this harder. I just want to be there."

"To do what?" he asks.

"To look at him," I say. "And ask him one question."

Max rubs a hand over his face, frustration bleeding through his control. "Jenna—"

"I almost got taken today," I interrupt. "Again. While I was shopping for clothes."

That lands.

"They didn't miss," I add. "They just didn't get me."

Silence stretches between us. I can see the calculations behind his eyes now. The ones Massimo taught him. Risk. Fallout. Control. Damage. He exhales. "I'll call Enzo. But if he says no—"

"I'll accept it," I lie.

Max doesn't look convinced. But he nods once and pulls out his phone, stepping just outside the door. I stand there alone, heart hammering, my reflection staring back at me from the dark glass. This isn't about revenge. Not yet. This is about reclaiming something they took when they decided I was leverage instead of a mother. And if Massimo's world thinks I'm going to stay upstairs, wrapped in glass and silence, while the men who hurt my son talk in rooms below... they don't know what a mother is capable of.

I hear Max's voice, low and tense, through the door. A pause. Then another. When he comes back in, his expression has changed.

"Enzo says... five minutes," he tells me. "You don't speak unless he clears it."

"That's fair," I agree.

He searches my face one last time. "Once we walk out that door, you will do whatever I tell you to do? And if I think it's too dangerous to move you right now, we come back here."

He's serious about it. I nod. Because my being taken is not in the best interest of my son.

We leave through a private elevator, then through the casino floor, which is, like always, packed with people. I notice six men are guarding me now, including Max. Max's eyes shift from left to right, then right to left. Never resting. He takes in everything around us, leaving nothing to chance.

The SUV is already waiting by the valet entrance,

engine running, doors opening before we reach it. Two cars fall in behind us as we pull away from the casino's artificial glow. Seconds later, Vegas blurs past the tinted windows, neon bleeds into concrete, thins, then disappears altogether.

The city gives way to industrial nothing. The drive is quiet. Nobody says a word as I stare out the window at the darkening sky. The day is finally coming to an end. I wish I could just roll up in bed, pull the sheets over my head, and forget everything. But that's a luxury a mother doesn't have. Not when her child is in danger.

The building appears without ceremony. Low. Squat. Forgettable. A crematorium. My stomach drops.

"Oh," I murmur before I can stop myself. "Fuck."

Max doesn't look at me. "They call it the Oven."

Of course they do. Genius, really. Heat. Finality. No questions asked. But still... fuck. The SUV stops. The air outside is still warm, heavy with the faint metallic tang of ash and old smoke. We walk through a nondescript door into a nondescript room. A man stands by another door, leading into the back. His hands are folded in front of him like a man standing guard at a church or a slaughterhouse.

He's bigger than I imagined. Broader. And his face, oh my God, his face. It takes effort not to flinch. Scars map him like a history written in flesh. Not one clean line, but many. Burns. Knife work. Damage layered on damage until the man underneath feels almost secondary to what's been done to him.

He watches me carefully as I approach. Waiting for something. Before I can step past him, he lifts a hand.

"Enzo."

I assumed so, but I take it anyway; it looks like manners matter here. "Jenna." Which he probably already knows, too.

"Before I let you in there," he states calmly in a surprisingly gentle voice, "I need to know you have the stomach for this."

I don't rush to answer. I force myself not to look away from his face, not to soften my gaze, not to offer pity or revulsion or polite avoidance. I've worked with disfigured people before, men and women broken by accidents, illness, violence. I learned early that most of them wanted one thing above all else: to be seen as normal. To be spared the stare.

Enzo is not one of those men. He wants me to look. He wants to see whether I'll blink. So I let my eyes travel—slowly, deliberately—over the minefield of his face. I don't rush it. I don't apologize with my expression. I don't pretend not to notice. Then I look back at his eyes.

"I'm probably not cut from the same material as you," I choose my words carefully. "But a mother can take a lot of shit when her child is in danger." I pause, then add, softer but steadier, "More than she ever thought she could."

Something shifts. It's subtle. A minute easing in his posture. The smallest nod, almost imperceptible, like a lock clicking open.

"Alright," Enzo says.

He steps aside and gestures toward the door.

"Welcome," he adds dryly, "to the part of the world most people pretend doesn't exist."

The door opens. Heat breathes out to meet me. I step inside. I thought I was prepared. I really did. I'd braced myself for blood, for screams, for something crude and cinematic. This is worse.

The smell hits first, burned flesh, melted plastic, scorched fabric. It crawls into my throat and sits there, thick and oily, refusing to move. My eyes sting. My stomach flips hard enough that I swallow twice just to stay upright. The ovens dominate the space. Wide open. Roaring. Fire rolls inside them like a living thing, hungry, relentless, utterly indifferent. The heat presses against my skin immediately; sweat blooms at my temples, under my arms, along my spine. The air hums. The flames breathe. There is something horrifyingly beautiful about it.

The way the fire moves. The way it consumes without judgment. Mesmerizing. Hypnotic. I hate myself a little for noticing.

Then I see him. The man on the stretcher is tied above a corpse. The living man's chest heaves violently, and sweat pours down his face, soaking his shirt. His wrists strain uselessly against restraints.

His feet, my breath stutters. Gone. Not entirely, but close enough. Melted leather fused to skin. Plastic embedded where bone should be. Blackened flesh blistering upward, angry and wet. The damage crawls higher than I expect; the heat has done its work slowly. Methodically.

His eyes are what threaten to undo me. Not

monstrous. Not cruel. He's terrified. Wild, frantic eyes dart between us; his pupils are blown wide, reflecting the raw animal panic of someone who understands exactly what's happening and knows he can't stop it.

He's young. Too young. Early twenties, maybe. Barely more than a boy. Pity wallows up inside me, but then I think of the panic I felt, the panic Amauri felt and is likely still feeling. And everything inside me locks. My pulse roars in my ears.

"If you want to leave," Enzo offers quietly beside me, his voice steady and professional, "no one will think less of you."

I shake my head. The movement is small, but it's final. I step forward instead. The heat intensifies immediately, licking at my skin, soaking my clothes. Sweat beads along my upper lip. My insides feel like ice and fire at the same time, cold dread wrapped in burning fury.

This man helped take Amauri. This man stood in my home. This man is part of why my son cried himself to sleep somewhere far away from me. And, up close, all I see is fear. Not innocence. Not absolution. Just fear. I stop a few feet away. Close enough that he can see my face clearly.

"Has he said anything yet?" I want to know, my voice sounds steadier than I feel. "About who sent him? Who ordered the kidnapping?"

The man's eyes snap to mine. Recognition flashes there. Something ugly and desperate. He knows who I am.

"No," Enzo answers before the man can speak. "He's been... resistant."

The flames roar louder, as if on cue. The man whimpers. A broken, animal sound that twists low in my gut. He's shaking now, teeth chattering despite the heat, tears cutting clean lines through soot on his cheeks. I'm not a medical professional, but I know that if he goes into shock, he won't be of any use to us.

I don't look away. I can't. Because this, this is the truth of it. This is what my son was dragged into. This is the world that reached into my life and took him like a bargaining chip. I don't know yet what I'm going to ask. But I know one thing with terrible clarity: I am done being shielded from the ugly parts of this war.

I don't rush him. I can tell that surprises Enzo. Men like this are used to shouting. To fists. To pain that comes fast and loud. They steel themselves for it, build walls around it. But silence—real silence—gets inside. Instead, I step closer until the heat kisses my skin, until sweat beads along my collarbone. He watches me with those frantic eyes, his chest is heaving, his breath hitches every time the flames surge. I crouch. Bring myself down to his level. He flinches, just a little, when our eyes meet.

"You're young," I state quietly. My voice doesn't echo. It doesn't need to. "I expected someone older," I continue, almost conversational. "Someone who'd already ruined their soul enough to sleep through this."

His lips tremble. He shakes his head once, violently, like he's trying to clear it. I glance at the tattoo on his neck again. Let my gaze linger there.

"You came into my house," I keep my voice calm and soft. "You walked past my child's room. You took him."

His breathing stutters. "I didn't, senora, I swear, it wasn't me."

I don't believe him. "I want you to understand something," I go on, steady as a metronome. "What's happening to you right now? This isn't revenge."

That makes him look at me properly.

"This is consequence." I straighten slowly and gesture toward the oven, not dramatically, just enough. "These men," I say, not looking at Enzo, but knowing he hears me, "they know how to hurt bodies." I look back at the boy. "I don't."

His eyes widen. Confused. Hope flickers there for half a second.

"And that," I add gently, "is why I'm the one talking to you."

I lean in, close enough that he can see the tears in my eyes, not falling, never falling, but there. Real. Burning.

"My son cried when you took him," my voice breaks slightly. The words scrape out of mc, raw now. "Not loud. He's not loud when he's scared. He goes quiet. Did you notice that?"

A sound breaks out of him, half sob, half denial. "I never saw your son, senora, I swear."

I ignore it. Even if he wasn't with the men who broke into my house, he's still a man who knew about it and chose to do nothing. "I don't know your name," I continue, relentless but soft. "But someone does. Someone who sent you. Someone who will sleep tonight believing you're strong enough to keep their secrets." I shake my head slowly. "They're wrong."

I reach out, not to touch him, but close enough that he feels the intention.

"You don't owe them anything," I point out. "They won't save you. They won't remember you. But if you tell me who ordered this—if you say the name—I will make sure one thing happens." His eyes lock on mine, desperate now. "I will make sure your mother knows what happened to you," I promise quietly. "And why."

That does it. It's like the last beam inside him collapses.

"No," he sobs. "Please—please—"

"You don't have to be brave," I tell him. "You just have to be honest."

Silence stretches. Then his mouth opens. And the truth finally starts to bleed out. Enzo shifts beside me, and something like awe tightens his scarred face. Not because of what I did, but because of what I didn't do.

I don't look back at him. I keep my eyes on the boy. And I listen to him break. Not all at once. Not theatrically. It's a slow collapse, like something inside him has finally given up the pretense of strength.

"Joaquín," he whispers hoarsely. "Joaquín Beltrán."

The name doesn't mean anything to me. I turn my head slightly, just enough to catch Enzo's eye. A silent question. *Does that mean anything?*

Enzo nods once. Grave. Confirming. *Yeah. It does.*

Good. I look back at the boy, because that's what he is, really. A boy who made a series of terrible choices and ended up here. He's shaking now, his breath is coming in ragged pulls, and his eyes are glassy with pain and fear.

"You did good," I tell him. The words surprise him. They surprise me too. "Thank you," I add, because it matters. Because I said I would treat him like a person, not an object.

I step closer. Every instinct screams at me not to touch him, not to cross that final line, but I ignore it. I force my hand to move. I brush a kiss to his forehead. It's brief. Almost ceremonial. His eyes fill.

"Tell me your name," I request softly.

He swallows. "Luis," he whispers. "Luis Herrera."

I commit it to memory.

"I'll tell your mother," I promise. My voice doesn't waver. "I'll tell her that at the very end, you did a good deed."

Something breaks in his expression. Relief, maybe. Or absolution. Or just the knowledge that someone will remember him as more than a mistake. I straighten. I don't look at him again. I turn to Enzo and nod. Just once. No words. He understands.

When I step back, the heat swells behind me. The roar grows louder. I don't watch. I don't need to. The decision has already been made, and that's the part that changes me, not the death, but the authority of choosing it. I walk out of the room with my spine straight, my hands steady, my heart beating slow and hard.

Somewhere inside me, something has gone quiet. And something else—something sharper—has taken its place. I step out into the corridor, and the door closes behind me with a heavy, final sound. The heat fades immediately, replaced by cool concrete and the faint echo of machinery deeper in the building. Only then do I realize my hands are shaking. Not badly. Just enough.

I'm drawing a breath when a weight settles on my shoulder. Enzo's hand. It's not possessive. Not restraining. Just... grounding. I look up at him.

"That," he praises, almost thoughtful, "was quite impressive."

I blink, caught off guard. There's no mockery in his tone. No indulgence. Just acknowledgment. The kind that isn't given lightly, if at all. I get the sense Enzo doesn't hand out compliments like that to anyone. I nod once, accepting it for what it is. Before I can say anything back, the door at the far end opens. My body reacts before my mind does. A cold shudder slides down my spine. Bello Capelli steps inside.

Time does something strange. The hallway feels narrower. The air heavier. I know that face. I've seen it before, years ago, in a different life, when hope still had sharp edges, and I thought words could fix things. Bello's face blurs at the edges, and suddenly I'm not here anymore.

I'm ten years back, standing at iron gates so tall they blot out the sky, fingers wrapped around cold metal that stains my palms with rust. A mansion rises beyond them, too big, too grand, all stone and shadow and secrets. This is where Massimo lives. The place I was never meant to see. My chest aches with every breath. I've already swallowed my pride to come here. I've argued with myself all the way up the drive. Turn around, Jenna. Go home. He made his choice. *But I don't leave. I can't. I just need to know why.*

Security tries to send me away. I don't go. I wait. I stand there in the sun, heart pounding, palms sweating, dignity fraying, thread by thread. Eventually, someone gets tired of me. They call him.

Bello introduces himself. He comes out like the gate itself has learned how to walk, solid, immovable, eyes flat with disinterest. He looks at me like I'm a problem already solved.

"What do you want?" he asks.

My voice shakes, but I stay upright. "I want to speak to Massimo."

He studies my face, something clicking into place. "You're Jenna."

It isn't a question. Hope flares so fast it almost knocks me over. He knows who I am. That has to mean something. Right? My heart lurches painfully against my ribs.

"Yes," I nearly yell. "Please. I just want to talk to him. I just want to understand."

Bello shakes his head. Once. Decisive. Final. "He doesn't want to see you." His voice is firm and cold. "Go home."

The words land like a slap. My throat tightens. I taste blood where I've bitten the inside of my cheek. "Did you ask him?" I whisper. "Did you tell him I was here?"

His eyes harden. "You're not welcome."

Something in me fractures then, but not all the way. I straighten. Wipe my face with the back of my hand. Force my shoulders back even as my chest caves in.

"Tell him," my voice shakes, and I take a deep breath, "that I came. Tell him I waited. Tell him—"

"Never come back," Bello cuts in, stepping closer, crowding

me back toward the gate. "This is over. Whatever you thought it was—forget it."

The gates loom behind me, unforgiving. I don't cry. Not there. I won't give him that. I nod once. Then I turn away on legs that feel borrowed, on a heart that feels like it's been torn loose and left bleeding in the gravel. But even now—even at my lowest—I don't beg. I leave with my spine intact.

The memory snaps closed. The hallway rushes in around me. The present reasserts itself. Enzo's hand is still on my shoulder. Bello is still standing just inside the door. His eyes land on me, and he freezes in pure, naked shock. Like he's just seen a ghost that he buried himself.

I meet Bello's eyes—really meet them—and whatever he sees there makes him swallow hard, and all the color drains from his face.

I'm not the girl at the gates anymore.

And this time? I didn't come asking.

Before he can recover. Before he can lie, I greet him. "Long time no see."

His mouth opens. Closes. He looks afraid. But I'm too shaken to try to figure out why. Enzo's hand tightens—just a fraction—on my shoulder, his attention sharpens. He looks between us, his eyes narrow just enough to be dangerous.

"You two know each other?" he asks, frowning.

The question hangs there, heavier than it should.

I don't look at Bello. I don't need to. "We met once, a long time ago."

Bello clears his throat. "Years ago," he adds quickly, too quickly. Like he needs to get ahead of something that's already breathing down his neck. Enzo's gaze flicks to him. Lingers. The scars on his face seem to pull tighter as his expression shifts from curiosity to calculation. He doesn't say anything, but I can almost hear the mental note being filed away. Interesting.

Suddenly, the day catches up with me, and I'm so tired it feels like my bones have weight.

"I want to go home." Whatever home is these days. My voice cuts through whatever Enzo was about to ask next. Not pleading. Just done.

Enzo studies me for a beat longer, then nods once. "Max will take you."

I turn away before Bello can say anything else. Before he can try to explain or apologize or—worse—pretend none of this mattered. I walk down the corridor and feel it again. That familiar pressure behind my eyes. The ache that comes from holding too much inside for too long. Behind me, voices resume. Low. Controlled. Dangerous. But I don't look back. I've had enough ghosts for one night.

The distance between Caracas and us is growing as the jet takes us back home. I don't relax. I won't. Not yet. A doctor hovers near Whitford, already fussing, checking vitals, murmuring reassurances, and cataloging damage like a man afraid of what he'll find.

"Look at the boy first," I order.

It's not loud. It doesn't need to be. The doctor blinks, startled, then nods and pivots immediately. Smart man.

Amauri sits on one of the seats, legs dangling, hands folded tightly in his lap like he's afraid to touch anything. His eyes track everything—the doctor, the equipment, me—quiet, observant, too old for ten. Too much like me. The doctor moves gently, methodically. Checks pupils. Palpates ribs. Notes the bruises blooming along his arms and shins. Old fingerprints. Careless ones. My jaw locks.

"No broken bones," the doctor assures me. "Some superficial bruising. Dehydration. No signs of internal injury." He hesitates, then adds more carefully, "Psychological trauma, most likely. Nightmares. Hypervigilance. But physically, he's unharmed."

Unharmed.

The word lands wrong. Like calling a house intact after it's burned down.

"Thank you," I tell him anyway.

He nods and turns back toward Whitford, who is already complaining loudly.

"My back," Whitford snaps. "My legs—check my legs. I can't feel anything. I need to know they're intact."

He hasn't changed. The accident didn't humble him in any way. If anything, it made it worse. It's always about him.

I don't wait. If I do, I might finish the job I started ten years ago.

"Come," I invite softly, crouching in front of Amauri. I keep my voice even, calm, the way Enzo taught me to speak to skittish animals and frightened men. "There's a shower in the back. Hot water. Clean clothes."

He studies my face with interest. Interest. As if he's deciding something. After a second of deliberation, he slides off the seat and follows me without a word.

The back cabin is quieter. Smaller. Private. I open the bathroom door and show him how everything works, controls, towels, and where the clothes are laid out. Sweat-pants. A soft shirt. Sneakers. Things that won't itch or bind.

"Do you need help?" He shakes his head, and I assure him, "You can take your time. No one will rush you."

He nods. After a moment of consideration, he looks up at me.

"My mummy?" he asks.

The word hits me harder than any bullet ever has.

"She's fine," the lie comes immediately. No pause. No doubt. "She's safe. And you'll talk to her soon. I promise." That part is true. I'm not so sure about the first.

He watches my face the way children do when they're deciding whether to believe a lie. Whatever he sees there seems to satisfy him. "Okay."

Not *thank you*. Not *are you sure*. Just *okay*.

I close the door gently behind him and lean my forehead against the bulkhead for half a second longer than necessary. My son. Only a few feet from me. A little person I didn't know existed just a few days ago, and who has already taken up permanent residence in my chest. I take a few deep breaths before I turn back.

Whitford is still talking. Still demanding. The doctor reassures him, checks his reflexes, and explains things Whitford doesn't want to hear. I ignore them until Amauri steps out a few minutes later, hair damp, clothes clean, looking smaller somehow without the grime and fear clinging to him. He walks straight to Whitford.

"Dad?" his voice is tight with apprehension, as if he's worried about the other man but not sure how he'll be received. I ball my fists. I'm only a hairsbreadth away from killing the bastard. Amauri is the only thing stopping me.

Whitford looks at him, annoyed, distracted. "Not now," he snaps. "Can't you see I'm hurt?"

Amauri's brow furrows. He steps closer to Whitford's seat, worry etched into his face.

"He needs water," Amauri says, turning to me. "And food. He hasn't eaten properly. He gets dizzy."

My chest tightens. Maybe I can have the flight attendant add some poison to the food and drink. It takes some willpower, but finally I manage to press out, "He'll be taken care of, I'll make sure of it."

Amauri considers that. Then nods once, satisfied. He climbs back onto the seat across from Whitford, close enough to keep watch, but far enough not to be snapped at again. He buckles himself in carefully, like he's been doing it alone for a while.

I take the seat opposite him, ignoring Whitford, who is eyeing me suspiciously. Amauri glances at me, then away. Then back again.

"You don't look like the bad guys," he finally decides.

I swallow. "I guess not."

He accepts that, too. Outside the small oval window, the sky lightens, and dawn bleeds slowly into the night. And for the first time since this began, I let myself think it: I have him. I have my son.

And the ones who made him learn how to be this brave? They will pay for it in ways no doctor can ever fix.

A flight attendant appears like she's afraid to disturb something sacred. She sets down a tray—chicken nuggets cut small, fruit, juice in a glass—and withdraws without a word. Amauri brightens at the sight of food.

"Dad," he calls to Whitford. "You have to eat. And drink. You're shaking."

Whitford barely glances at him. "I need a shower," he mutters. "I smell like—Christ—"

"You can have one," I cut in. I don't look at him. "They'll help you."

I nod once towards my men. Two of them move immediately. Efficient. Professional. Whitford bristles, starts to protest, but they're already lifting him carefully, carrying him toward the rear cabin. I don't spare him another thought.

Amauri watches them go, then turns back to his food with the seriousness of someone fulfilling a responsibility. He takes a bite, chews, swallows, and drinks juice. Only then does he look at me again.

"That was scary," I say, because silence feels wrong and I have no clue what else to say.

He nods, mouth full. "Yeah."

I shift, uncomfortable. I've interrogated men. I've negotiated wars. Talking to a ten-year-old feels like walking blindfolded across a wire.

"They were scary," he continues. "I didn't understand them. But Dad did." He pauses. "He said Grandpa would get us out of there."

My chest tightens.

"Did Grandpa send you?" he asks suddenly.

I don't know why I answer the way I do. I don't calculate it. I don't soften it.

I just shake my head. "No. Your mummy did."

Amauri's face lights up instantly. He giggles. An actual giggle. Like the world hasn't taught him yet that those can be stolen.

"I knew it," he nods proudly as if this had been a given fact all along. "You think she looks like that lady, too, huh?"

I frown. "What lady?"

He gives me a look, patient, indulgent. "The one from The Mummy. Duh."

I blink. He goes back to eating like that explained everything.

"This is good," he says between bites. "I knew Mummy would come for us." He nods to himself, completely certain.

I swallow hard. "Your mummy is..." I search for a word, feel clumsy reaching for it. "Nice?"

He looks at me like I've just said the sky might be blue.

"She's the best," he confirms firmly.

And then he starts talking. Little things. School. How she makes grilled cheese just right. How she pretends not to notice when he sneaks snacks before dinner. How she sings badly on purpose to make him laugh when he's sad. His voice slows. His eyelids droop. He finishes the last bite, wipes his mouth with the back of his hand, and leans into the seat with a small, contented sigh. I stand before I can think better of it. Carefully, I unbuckle and lift him. He doesn't resist. Doesn't flinch. Just tucks in against me like it's the most natural thing in the world.

I carry him to the couch and lay him down, pulling a blanket over him, tucking it in around his shoulders the way I've seen women do. He murmurs something unintelligible and curls onto his side. He's asleep. Just like that.

I stand there longer than necessary—resisting the urge to kiss his forehead because, God help me, he looks so much like me—watching him breathe. The rage I carried onto this plane—the tight, coiled thing that's lived in my chest since she said my son—doesn't vanish. It doesn't dissolve into something soft or noble. But it dims. Like a fire banked down, not extinguished.

I expected the anger to erupt when I saw him. Thought the weight of what she kept from me would crush everything else. Ten years stolen. Ten years of losing teeth, believing in Santa Claus, hell, watching mindless cartoons about dogs and cats. I'll never get that back. Words I never heard him say. Nights, I never stood guard outside his door. That loss is still there, heavy and dull. But beneath it, I feel it: pride.

Unwelcome. Unreasonable. Real.

She did this.

Jenna brought this boy into the world. She carried him. Protected him. Raised him into this. Quietly brave, instinctively kind, worrying about a man who barely looks at him, even while he himself is breaking. He reminds him to eat. He makes sure the adults drink water. He believes—without question—that his mother will come for him. That doesn't happen by accident.

I don't know a damn thing about children. I don't know what they're supposed to sound like, or how much of their parents they're meant to carry. But this boy—my boy—sounds... good. Solid. Whole, despite everything. Instinctively, I know this is her work.

The fury I aimed at her for so long suddenly has nowhere clean to land. It changes shape. I'm still angry. I won't pretend otherwise. She lied. She decided my place in his life without giving me the chance to choose differently. That reckoning hasn't vanished. But it's no longer blind. It's edged now with something dangerous: respect.

She survived. She didn't break. She didn't raise him weak or bitter or afraid of the world. She raised him aware. Observant. Compassionate. Which means that when I face her again, I won't be able to dismiss her as reckless or selfish or cruel. I hate the part of me that understands it.

I look down at Amauri again, memorizing the curve of his lashes, the way his mouth relaxes in sleep. So much like me, it almost hurts. So much like her in ways I can't see yet. Jenna will still answer for what she did. But not the way I thought. Not with rage alone. Because the woman who raised this? She's no longer just someone who took something from me. She's someone who made something extraordinary.

And that changes everything.

Noise from the rear cabin interrupts the moment.

"Where is my wheelchair?" Whitford's voice cracks through the hum of the engines. "I need a phone. I need to call—"

My men bring him forward. They're being careful with him. I haven't told them yet how to handle him. Hell, I don't know how to handle him yet. They're moving him like he's something fragile and unpleasant at the same time. Which I suppose he is.

I watch them approach, I watch Whitford with the same loathing I've always felt for him. He's not really broken, but he's been—reduced.

He's lost weight. His hands shake. His face has that hollow, pinched look of a man who has never had to be brave and who has finally run out of shields. This isn't survival etched into bone like Amauri carries it. This is decay. I feel nothing like pity. I never have. He was never a man. Men don't sell their girlfriends. Men don't offer women up like currency so they can climb a ladder that was never meant to hold their weight.

Playtime, he'd called it. Coach would get his with Jenna, and Whitford would get his on the field, under the lights, with scouts watching and a future bought in bruises and silence.

I remember when I learned what he'd done. The night Jenna and I buried Coach in the desert. That was the moment I decided he would die. I gave her time. Time to leave him. Time to realize she deserved better. Time to walk away from the boy who thought women were stepping stones.

She did. The very next day. Or so she told me.

That was when I put my plan in motion. The memory flickers—

I'm standing on the edge of the field, anonymous in the crowd. Friday night lights. Noise. Heat. Violence disguised as sport.

"It's all set," Jerry assures me, nodding his head towards a boy on the opposing team. He's big. Number 57. "He'll break his neck, get it done. It'll be quick and public. An unfortunate accident." He shrugs. "Happens all the time in football."

I nod my agreement. It irks me that it'll be quick for Whitford, but it's the best I could do right now, flying under my uncle's radar. If the old man found out what I was up to... It's not family business. Hell, it's not business at all, it's personal, and he always warned me to be careful with personal shit. No, nobody can ever find out about this. Least of all, my uncle and his sons. So it'll be quick. Dead is dead, I tell myself as I watch 57 tackle Whitford. Hard. The angle is what matters. Whitford goes down, rolls awkwardly. The crowd is too loud to hear the snapping of his neck. But when the golden boy doesn't get up, it gets really, really quiet on the field.

I hand Jerry an envelope. A hundred grand. I'm not sure how much of that will get to 57, and I don't care. It's done.

Only it wasn't. Paralyzed, they told me. From the chest down. Karma has a sick sense of humor. I didn't demand my money back. It didn't matter. He was nothing but a walking corpse to me until... he married Jenna.

They place Whitford into a seat across from where I stand. He fusses with his legs, the seat belt, and a blanket. I remain still and standing. Fully intending to let the height do the work for me, letting him crane his neck just enough that it irritates him. Petty? Absolutely. Satisfying? Immensely.

He looks up at me with polite confusion, not recognition. That alone is interesting.

"I owe you thanks," he nods, arranging his face into something practiced and political. The smile doesn't quite stick. "Did Kingsley send you?"

He waves down the flight attendant like he owns the aircraft. "Food," he says briskly. "Something light."

I don't stop it. I let him believe, for a few seconds longer, that he's still the kind of man whose gestures matter.

"No," my voice catches his attention again. "Kingsley didn't send me."

He looks up properly now, eyes sharpening, reassessing, brows furrowing. "Then... who?"

He studies my clothes. My stance. My men, strategically positioned without being obvious. The way the cabin seems to orbit me instead of him.

"You're not," he hesitates, then tries again, "some kind of special ops?"

I laugh. It slips out before I can stop it. Low. Genuine. The sound of something being entertained by its own restraint. "No."

I lean back against the seat across from him and cross my arms over my chest.

"Then who?" he presses, irritation creeping in. "Because you're clearly not military. And you're not State. And I don't recognize you."

"I know," I chuckle. "That's my favorite part."

The stewardess returns with a tray. She sets it down in front of him. He's nervous now, sensing the imbalance but not understanding it. Whitford thanks her distractedly, already losing interest in the food. He's lucky he's still amusing me in a strange way. My uncle always said don't play with your victims, but I find the opposite much more entertaining. "I'm the man who paid for the plane. The men. The doctor. The silence."

He frowns. "You're... private?"

"In a way."

He exhales sharply, impatient. "Listen, whoever you are, I appreciate the rescue. Truly. But I need to contact my father-in-law. There are arrangements—"

"Your father-in-law," I interrupt, "figured you're more worth to him dead than alive."

Whitford freezes.

I continue, unhurried. "You sold a woman for a career. You bought a child for cover. And you've been coasting on borrowed authority ever since."

His smile collapses. "That's not—"

"You don't know who I am," I agree. "But you know who *she* is."

I let that sit.

His eyes flick, just once, toward the back of the cabin. Toward the couch. Toward the small, sleeping shape wrapped in a blanket. I step into his line of sight again, blocking it completely.

"You don't get to look at him," my tone is still soft, deceivingly so.

Fear finally arrives—pure, undiluted—as he starts picking up that I'm not here to rescue him.

"Who are you?" he whispers.

I lean down until we're eye level, close enough that he can see there's no anger left in me for him. Just judgment.

"You should have died the moment you touched what wasn't yours." I let that sink in, but it only confuses him further. He's clueless. "I'm the man who ordered you hit on the field." His breath stutters. "I'm the reason you're still alive," I continue. "And the reason your life is about to become very small." I straighten. "My name is Massimo Manetti."

He recognizes the name instantly. It hits him late, but

when it does, it's catastrophic. The color drains from his face.

"Oh," he breathes.

"Yes," I nod. "That's usually the moment."

Carter still doesn't understand. I can see it in the way his brow furrows, the way he keeps searching my face for a role he can recognize.

"But why would you come for me?" he asks, voice thin. "Save me?"

I almost smile.

"Who said I saved you?" I reply calmly. "Your wife asked me to save our son." The word our hits him like a slap. "You were just... part of the package," I continue. "Collateral."

His mouth opens, disbelief flickers into something closer to panic.

"You're lucky," I add, stepping back just enough to gesture at the tray in front of him. "I haven't quite decided what to do with you yet."

I tap the edge of the plate. Then the glass. "So eat. Drink." I let my gaze settle on him, heavy and unblinking. "Until I do decide, you'll keep breathing. "But make no mistake—" I straighten, towering over him again. "You're on my time now."

The words sink in slowly. His hands hover uselessly above the food, appetite gone, power stripped bare.

My phone rings. Perfect timing. I turn away from Whitford without another glance, done for now. Whatever comes next for him can wait. "Enzo?"

"Boss," he greets. His voice is tight. Focused. "We got a name. The Mexican talked."

Of course he did.

"The Oven never fails." It has never failed. Pain, fire, the prospect of a slow death... it works miracles. I move toward the back of the cabin, away from Carter, away from ears that don't deserve context. There's a pause.

"Enzo?" I stop. "Spit it out."

"The Oven might have failed us this time."

I still. "What?"

"It wasn't the Oven who made him talk." His next words give me a chill. "It was Jenna."

Silence slams down so hard I feel it in my chest. "... what?"

"She got him to talk," Enzo continues. "She didn't touch him. She didn't threaten. She just—" He exhales. "She broke him."

I hear admiration in his voice. That stops me for a fraction of a second, because Enzo doesn't give out that kind of compliment freely or often, but then undiluted fury flares so fast it almost blinds me. "Why the fuck was Jenna anywhere near that place?" I snap. "Of all the—"

"Listen to me," Enzo cuts in, calm but firm. He explains what happened. What she did. What she said. The name. The cartel. Joaquín Beltrán. La Orden del Norte. I don't interrupt. When he finishes, I'm standing very still.

"Jenna?" I'm speechless. Not surprised. Not really. In my mind's eye, green eyes inside a bloodied face stare up at me, defiant, strong. She's leaning over a dead body, holding a spike in her hands, dripping blood. Her stance tells me she won't hesitate to attack me next.

"She handled it," Enzo's words cut through the fog of memory. I'd almost forgotten how strong she can be. How unbendable. "Better than most men I know."

That... doesn't help. It should. But what I need right now is something that will slot neatly into the version of Jenna I've been clinging to, the girl who ran, who hid, who chose someone else and built a life without me. The woman who kept my son from me and thought she could manage the fallout.

But this? This doesn't fit that story at all.

Or maybe it fits too well. This is the Jenna I remember. The one who took a situation that should have broken her and ended her attacker. The one who collapsed afterward, yes, but she was eighteen. Bleeding. Alone. Still standing when she had no right to be. Still breathing when men stronger than her would have folded.

That was ten years ago.

Ten years is a long time.

Long enough for empires to rot from the inside. Long enough to rebuild them stronger. Long enough for a woman to sharpen herself into something unrecognizable. Suddenly, I'm seeing her again, not as the mother of my son, not as the woman who lied to me, not as a complication I have to control, but as someone I may have fundamentally underestimated.

She walked into the Oven.

She didn't flinch.

She didn't beg someone else to do it for her.

She broke a man with words and will and the kind of quiet authority that can't be taught.

That changes things.

It makes me wonder how many times she's done that in the last decade. What else she's survived. What else she's hidden. What parts of herself she's buried so deep no one—including me—thought to look.

Ten years.

A lifetime in this world.

The balance shifts. I'm not just furious with her any longer. I'm curious. Dangerously so. Because if Jenna Whitford has been carrying secrets of her own all this time—if she's been building herself into something this formidable—then I don't just want answers. I need to know every skeleton in her closet. Before one of them decides to come for my family.

"Send me everything," I command. "I'll be back in a few hours. Get a meeting organized. We'll plan from there."

"Understood."

He doesn't hang up. "Massimo," Enzo adds. "There's more."

I close my eyes for half a second. "What now?"

"I don't know if it's something or nothing." He's careful now; experience has taught me that heads are about to roll when he gets like that. "Jenna and Bello... they know each other. It was weird. And Bello's been acting off ever since."

My jaw tightens. "How off?"

"Like a man who just realized something he buried isn't dead."

I don't reply. The silence stretches, heavy with implications neither of us is ready to name.

"Any ideas?" Enzo asks, finally.

I do. The memory surfaces slowly, like something pulled up from deep water. Ten years ago. I was barely conscious. Days after the hit. With my bones shattered and skin stitched together without any consideration for the flesh, my pain was so constant it blurred thought.

My phone—the disposable counterpart to the one I shared with Jenna—is gone. Lost somewhere between asphalt and blood and impact.

I can't leave the room. Can't move. Can't even sit up. But Bello is there. standing at my bedside, watching the door like he expects death to walk through it at any moment. "Hang in there, Massimo. You need to survive and get back on your feet quickly. This is your uncle and your cousins' doing. They want you dead. Just like they did your father."

He tells me to survive. He tells me my uncle ordered the hit.

And I believe him.

"If you die," he adds quietly, leaning closer so only I can hear, "everything rots from the inside out."

Panic cuts through the drugs when I think of her. Jenna alone. Jenna thinking I'd vanished. Jenna thinking I'd left her without a word. I force my throat to work. Tell Bello to go to her. Find her. Make sure she is safe. Make sure she knows I'm alive. Make sure she doesn't think I disappeared. He doesn't argue. Doesn't question the timing. Doesn't remind me we were at war. He just nods. Solid. Loyal. Reassuring.

"I'll handle it," he promises.

And then he leaves the safest place in the city to walk straight into uncertainty because I asked him to.

I survived on that. Clawed my way back from death believing she would be there at the end of it. Believing that when I stood again, rebuilt and breathing, she'd know I hadn't abandoned her. I built my recovery on that promise. And he built my war on it.

I fill Enzo in. He grunts on the other end. Unconvinced. "That might be part of it, but there's more."

"I'll have Gabe look into it," I assure him and end the call.

When I turn back, Amauri is still asleep, curled into the couch, his breathing slow and steady. Safe. For now. Behind him, Whitford stares at nothing, finally quiet. Somewhere between the two of them—between what I lost and what I just got back—I feel it. A shift. Jenna wasn't supposed to be part of this world. But the world didn't give a shit about what she was supposed to be.

I look down at my son again, commit the sight to memory. Then I straighten. Because whatever game is unfolding—whatever ghosts are stepping out of the dark—it's no longer just about territory. It's about family, which makes it lethal.

I find Gabe a few rows down, half-turned in his seat, phone low in his hand. His jaw is locked tight, attention split between the plane and whatever obsession currently owns him. He looks up when I stop beside him.

"She mean a lot to you?" I ask, already knowing the answer.

I sit. He doesn't bother hiding the screen. A pretty brunette is stretched out on a couch, legs tucked beneath her, watching television. Comfortable. Safe. Another man's arm is draped around her shoulders, familiar in the way only long practice allows. Domestic.

"She's happy," Gabe sounds wistful, closing the image with his thumb. A rare, unguarded softness crosses his mouth. "I can't take that from her."

I study him. "You could."

His gaze snaps to mine, sharp, flaring. Dangerous. "I know I could. I can do a lot of things." He pauses. Then adds, a note colder, "But I'm not a bastard who destroys other people's lives for sport."

Not yet, hangs unspoken between us. Gabe has always drawn his lines carefully. That's what makes him lethal. He doesn't cross them by accident; he steps over them when he decides the cost is worth it. I glance back at the dark screen in his hand. The woman. The man beside her. The life he's pretending not to want.

"Careful," I tell him. "Men like us don't stay spectators forever."

His mouth curves. Not a smile. A promise. "I know."

Gabe is a complicated man. The problem is that complications in our world always collect interest.

"We got the name," I change the subject. "Of the Mexican cartel that's orchestrated the abduction. Joaquín Beltrán. La Orden del Norte."

His eyes sharpen. "Ambitious bastard."

I nod, then lower my voice. "Enzo feels Bello is acting strange. I need you to dig. Quietly. Dig into everything.

Past, money, loyalties, lies. I want to know what he eats for breakfast and who taught him to lie."

Gabe nods once. No questions. No hesitation. That's how it's always been between us.

Bello has been with us since the beginning. Before the casinos. Before the polish. Before Vegas was mine instead of something I was going to conquer with blood and patience. He bled for this family. He built routes, buried bodies, and closed doors that needed closing. I trusted him with men, with money, with my back.

Trust like that isn't given lightly. And it's not revoked gently. Gabe understands that, too. Just like he understands that Enzo wouldn't put word out like that lightly.

I rake a hand through my hair, jaw tight. If Bello is compromised in any way, then this isn't just betrayal. It's treason. It means he looked me in the eye, every day, and chose to lie. That kind of betrayal doesn't just hurt. It costs.

"I'll find it," Gabe says quietly. "One way or another. It'll stay between you, me, and Enzo."

We both understand what's at stake. If this is nothing, it stays nothing. If it's something...

I don't want to believe Bello is dirty. Men like him don't turn easily. He has as much to lose as anyone else, if not more: status, protection, legacy. But Enzo has never been wrong. Not once. When his instincts flare, it's because something underneath is already rotting. If Bello is rotting, I won't hesitate. History doesn't buy mercy. It just makes the punishment personal.

Finally, I pour myself a bourbon and find a spot alone,

at the rear of the plane. The Stagg's burn steadies me. I sit, watching Amauri sleep a few feet away, curled into a blanket like he's always belonged there. Like the world hasn't already tried to break him.

My son.

That word still feels dangerous.

Uninvited, another memory surfaces.

Jenna—years ago—washing blood off her hands.

"Will this come back to me?" She isn't crying. She isn't shaking. Her voice is steady in the way people get when they've already accepted that fear won't save them.

I kneel beside Coach's body, awkward, young, furious at the world but not yet powerful enough to bend it. "Not if we do this right."

"Tell me what to do." She looks at me. It's not trust in her eyes. It's not desperation, but that's there too. She looks like she's ready to negotiate with me.

She always had guts. I saw it then. I just didn't understand its value yet. Back then, I was a twenty-year-old idiot with a beautiful girl in my arms, trying to impress her with control I didn't yet have.

Now?

Now I'm a man who understands exactly what kind of strength it takes to endure and adapt. I don't feel rage when I think of her anymore. I feel something far more dangerous. Respect.

And now, curiosity.

THE COUCH DIPS BENEATH ME AS I SHIFT, HALF-AWAKE, half-lost. Sleep won't take me fully. It circles. Teases. Drops me back into myself over and over again. I stare at the ceiling, Massimo's ceiling, and let the truth settle where denial used to live. This is the second time I've killed someone.

The first time, I didn't have a choice. Survival stripped it down to instinct and aftermath and shaking hands. This time... this time I chose. I looked a man in the face and nodded, knowing exactly what would happen when I did. I watched him die. The thing that gets me is that I don't regret it.

That's what scares me. There is no line left. Not really. No moral edge I won't step over if it means Amauri comes home safe. If it means he sleeps without flinching. If it means he never learns what the Oven smells like. The thought settles, cold and absolute. With it comes something else. Something I haven't let myself touch in ten years.

Massimo.

Not the man he is now. Not the monster Vegas whispers about. Not the fury and the violence and the way he looks at me like I am a liability and a weakness all at once.

The boy. The man who found me when I was shaking apart. It comes back in pieces at first. Not scenes. Sensations. The smell of citrus, bleach, and men's sweat. And yes, death. I scrubbed my hands raw, convinced I could still feel him on my skin. The way Massimo didn't touch me until I asked. Didn't crowd me. Didn't ask questions I couldn't answer.

Just sat there. Present. Solid.

I remember how grateful I was. God, I was grateful. For his silence. For the way he looked at me like I wasn't broken, or dirty, or something to be pitied. Like I was still... me.

One night turned into another day. Then another day. Grief doesn't respect schedules; it leaks. It followed me. So did Coach's face, which was suddenly everywhere. Missing posters taped to lampposts and grocery store windows. His name scrolled across the bottom of the news like a prayer that wouldn't be answered. Pillar of the community. Beloved mentor.

I saw his wife on TV. She clutched a microphone with shaking hands. I watched his children, too young to understand what missing really meant, only knowing that their father hadn't come home. I remember thinking he was a monster. I remember thinking he deserved everything he got.

And then—God help me—I saw their tears. The waiting. The terrible, human not-knowing. It tore me open deep inside. I would lie awake at night, staring at the ceiling, guilt pressing so hard on my chest I thought it might crack my ribs. Some nights I couldn't breathe. Others, I couldn't stop shaking.

Massimo was there for all of it.

Not fixing. Not judging. Not giving absolution that he couldn't give. He was there when the posters multiplied. When the story shifted from missing to presumed dead. When the world moved on, and I couldn't. He held me when the guilt wrecked me so completely that I forgot how to exist as anything but a wound.

We stopped talking about what happened because we didn't need to. Words would have cheapened it. He didn't treat me like glass. Didn't look at me like something fragile or ruined. He treated me like a woman who had survived something ugly and was still allowed to want things. Allowed to laugh. Allowed to touch. Allowed to feel good without earning it through pain.

At some point between the days and nights he stayed and the mornings he didn't rush away, between the weight of guilt and the quiet relief of being seen, I fell in love with him. I remember laughing with him, real laughter, the kind that sneaks up on you and leaves your ribs sore. Walking through gardens at night, neon bleeding into green, pretending the world wasn't sharp. Him stealing food off my plate and smirking when I pretended to be offended.

I remember the first time he kissed me. Not hungry. Not careless. Reverent.

I had never been kissed like that before. Like he was memorizing me. Like this wasn't just a moment, but a decision. I fell in love slowly. Terrifyingly. The kind of love that doesn't crash so much as settles—quiet and deep and impossible to shake. I let myself believe that maybe I was allowed that. That maybe the worst thing that had ever happened to me wouldn't define the rest of my life. Somewhere along the periphery, I remember breaking up with Carter. Not the next day, I was too shaken, but soon after. Then he had the accident. People looked at me like I should care. I didn't. There was only Massimo.

And then one day...

He was gone.

No warning. No explanation. Just absence where certainty had been. I had folded that memory so tightly, wrapped it in anger and pride and survival, that I almost forgot how much it hurt to lose him. Not just him, but the version of myself I was with him. The girl who still believed someone could choose her and stay.

I swallow hard, chest tight. I didn't let myself grieve him back then. I didn't have time. I was pregnant. Terrified. Cornered by men who saw my body as a strategy. I became efficient. Practical. Hard.

I became a mother.

And now? Now I see what I did today. What I was willing to do. What I will do again if I have to. I finally understand something I couldn't at eighteen. Massimo didn't make me strong.

He just saw it first.

I turn onto my side, pulling the blanket closer, eyes burning but dry. Whatever we were... whatever we might have been... it mattered. Enough that it still echoes.

Enough that I survived losing him and became someone capable of walking into hell and not looking away.

Ten years ago, I loved him. Tonight, I don't know what I feel. But I know this: if he thinks I'm the same girl he left behind? He's about to be very surprised.

Hours blur. I drift in and out, caught in that strange half-place where thoughts dissolve and the body keeps score. My limbs are heavy. My heart won't slow. Every time I close my eyes, I see fire. Ovens. Hands. Amauri's face on the night he was taken, frozen in shock that I couldn't reach through.

"Mummy!"

The sound slices straight through me. I don't move. I don't open my eyes. I don't breathe. Because if this is a dream, I don't want to break it. I don't want to lose the sound of his voice, bright and alive and here. My lips curve into a soft, broken smile against my will. God, it hurts. It hurts so much it almost feels good.

"Mummy!"

Closer this time. Louder. Impatient. Exactly the way he sounds on Sunday mornings when he thinks I've slept too long. Suddenly I feel—weight. Unexpected and familiar. Small knees digging into my stomach, arms flinging around my neck with reckless force. I gasp. My eyes fly open. Impossible. He's here.

Amauri.

Real. Solid. Warm. His hair smells like soap and airplane and something metallic I don't want to think about. His arms are locked around me like he's afraid that if he lets go, I'll vanish.

"Amauri?" My voice breaks completely. It barely makes it past my throat.

"Mummy," he sobs into my neck, the word wet and desperate and whole. "I missed you. I missed you so much."

I wrap myself around him without thinking, pulling him closer, tighter, like I can fuse him back into my bones if I hold hard enough. My hands are everywhere—his back, his arms, his hair—counting, checking, proving. Alive. Breathing. Here.

"I've got you," I whisper over and over, my face buried in his shoulder. "I've got you. I've got you. I'm here. I'm here."

He's shaking. I realize I am too. His fingers knot in my shirt like he's afraid I'll disappear again. His tears soak into my skin, and I welcome every one of them. Let them burn. Let them hurt. This is the pain that means he's alive.

"They were scary," he hiccups. "But I knew you'd come. I knew you would."

That does it. I break. A sound tears out of me, ugly and raw and unstoppable. I rock him like I did when he was a baby, back and forth, pressing my mouth to his hair, his temple, his cheek. I don't care who sees. I don't care where we are. The world can burn down around us.

"You were so brave," I choke. "You were so brave, my love. I'm so sorry. I'm so sorry I didn't get there sooner."

He pulls back just enough to look at me, his hands framing my face the way mine used to frame his when he was small. His eyes are too old right now. Too knowing. It shatters me.

"But you came," he says simply.

"Yes," I whisper fiercely. "I will always come for you. No matter what. No matter who I have to go through. No matter what I have to become."

He nods like this makes perfect sense, then burrows back into me, curling against my chest like he used to do after nightmares when he was little.

I hold him.

I hold him like letting go would kill me.

Around us, the penthouse is silent. The world waits. But none of it matters. Not the danger. Not the blood. Not the lines I crossed to get here. All that matters is that my son is in my arms. This time, I am not letting him go.

I lift my head. He's standing a few feet away, arms folded over his chest, posture rigid, face carved into something unreadable. No triumph. No relief. No demand for recognition. Just watchfulness. Like a man guarding something he doesn't quite trust himself to touch.

Massimo.

For a heartbeat, the room narrows until it's just the three of us; my son, warm and alive in my arms, and the man who brought him back, standing in the shadows like he doesn't know where he belongs in this picture. Whatever I feel for him right now—anger, grief, history, all of it—doesn't matter.

He brought my son back.

Our eyes lock.

There's too much in the look. Ten years. Blood. Fire. Everything we broke, and everything that still refuses to die. His jaw tightens slightly, like he's bracing for something. An accusation, maybe. Or collapse. I don't give him either. I mouth the words instead, because my voice wouldn't survive them.

Thank you.

It's barely a movement. Just breath and intent. Something shifts in his face then. Not softness, never that. But the tension in his shoulders eases a fraction, as if a weight he hadn't admitted to carrying has finally been set down.

He gives a single nod. Nothing more. No words. No crossing the room. No claiming space that isn't his to claim. Somehow, that restraint—that—tells me more than anything else ever could. I tighten my arms around Amauri, press my cheek to his hair, and let my eyes close again.

For this moment, at least, we are all exactly where we need to be. ####

WHATEVER I THOUGHT THIS MOMENT WOULD FEEL LIKE, I was wrong. I expected anger. Vindication. Control snapping back into place like a blade sliding home. Instead, something feral coils low in my chest.

She's on the couch, curled around him like gravity itself bends toward her. Amauri fits against her the way he was built to, small body molded into the curve of her arms, fingers knotted in her shirt like letting go might break the world again.

She looks exactly like she did ten years ago when I found her, shattered, furious, and alive.

Fuck, she's under my skin. Again.

The kid loves her. That much is obvious. The way he clings. The way he keeps touching her as if she might vanish if he doesn't anchor her there. Every laugh, every breath, every quiet reassurance comes from her. She didn't just keep him alive. She raised him right. That lands harder than anything else.

I spent hours with him on the plane. Hours watching him worry about the wrong man. Watching him call Whitford dad with a loyalty that didn't belong to him. Every time the word left his mouth, it tested a restraint I hadn't realized I possessed. I didn't kill Whitford for two reasons: I needed answers, and Amauri was watching. But make no mistake, every second that man stole my place is permanently carved into me, and I'll make him bleed for it.

Now it's quiet. No blood. No shouting. No bargaining. Just the three of us. The way it should have been all along. The realization hits me clean and brutal: I'm never letting this go.

Not him.

Not her.

Not again.

I don't care why she didn't come to me. I don't care what lies she believed or who fed them to her. I don't care if she loves me or I her. Love is irrelevant.

What matters is claim.

What matters is that my son is here—breathing, warm, safe—and she is the axis around which everything in him revolves. Which makes her essential. Non-negotiable. A fixed point in a world that bends to my will.

I want what was stolen from me. I want my child. And I want her. Not because she's weak. Not because she needs saving. Because she's strong enough to survive me, and stubborn enough to try to walk away again.

She won't.

Not this time.

She made her choice ten years ago without knowing all the pieces. That mistake won't repeat itself. I'll make sure of it. She will stand at my side. At my son's side. In my world. Whether she wants to or not.

Because whatever she thinks this is—whatever illusion of freedom she still clings to—there is one truth she will learn again, slowly and inexorably: I keep what's mine.

And she has always been mine.

But now's not the time for lessons.

I don't move closer. I don't interrupt. I don't claim anything. I give them this. Amauri is already half-asleep against her, breath soft, trusting in a way that hurts to witness. Jenna's eyes are glassy with exhaustion, her hand rhythmically stroking his hair like the motion itself is required to keep him here. They need this moment. They've earned it. I step back quietly, the way you do when you understand that presence can be an intrusion. A few hours of sleep. A locked door. Guards doubled. Silence.

I'll give them that.

I still have fires burning elsewhere. Whitford is secured in one of my warehouses. Medical staff on standby, not for comfort, for longevity. He'll live as long as I need him to. No longer.

Enzo's called a meeting. Gabe is digging into Bello. Threads are being pulled, loyalties weighed, old names dragged into the light whether they like it or not. Alessio is checking the streets for word of Joaquin. Damiano is vetting the employees at the club where Mia was killed. The noose is tightening; Joaquín just doesn't know it yet.

I turn toward the door. I should leave now. I should go to Enzo. To the meeting. To the war still unfolding outside this room. This moment is theirs.

Then she looks up. Just once. Her lips move without sound. *Thank you.* Something in my chest cracks. Not softly. Not cleanly. Ten years of silence don't evaporate with gratitude. They sharpen. I stop. Slowly, I turn back. I look her dead in the eyes and throw ten years of fury into her face. "You knew."

Jenna stiffens. Her hand stills in Amauri's hair. "Knew what?"

"You knew I was alive." With every word, I take a step forward. If she had any sense, she would run. "You knew I hadn't disappeared. Bello came to you. He told you I couldn't come because I was hurt."

The words land like a grenade. Her breath catches. Just a fraction. Enough.

"And you still married him," I continue, heat bleeding into my tone despite myself. "You still let another man put his name on my son."

Amauri shifts, frowning. He pushes himself upright, half-awake now.

"Massimo," Jenna says, warning threaded into my name.

Too late.

"You don't get to look at me like I abandoned you," I snap. "You don't get to act like I left, when you were the one who chose—"

"Stop." It's not her. It's him.

Amauri is fully awake now, standing on the couch between us, small fists clenched, jaw set with an expression far too familiar. "Don't say that to my mummy."

The room freezes. I look at him. I don't see any fear in his expression; he's not shrinking from me. There is just plain defiance. Pure and bright and untrained.

"Sit down," I say automatically.

"No," he says, planting his feet wider. "You're being mean."

The word shouldn't hit like it does.

Jenna reaches for him. "Amauri—"

"She didn't do anything wrong," he insists, his voice shaking but steady. "She came for me. She always comes."

Silence swells, thick and merciless. I feel it then, something I didn't expect. Underneath the anger. Guilt. This isn't a fight that should be waged in front of a kid. It's too late now, though. The war has started; I can see it in the fury burning in her eyes. I swallow, jaw tightening, forcing my hands to unclench at my sides.

"Stop." This time, it's Jenna who gives the command. "Both of you."

Her gaze locks on me, unflinching, the kind of look that doesn't ask; it ends things. Then she turns to Amauri, her expression softening without losing authority.

"Amauri," her tone is gentle. He looks up at her immediately. "Do me a favor and go into that room." She nods toward the guest bedroom she's been using. "Turn on the TV so Mummy and Da—" she hesitates, just a fraction, "—Massimo can talk. Grown-up talk, okay?"

Amauri doesn't seem to notice the stumble, but I do. He nods, obedient but alert, already halfway to the room. The pause is small. Almost nothing. And it tells me more than she ever could with words. This isn't new for him. The way he moves. The way he accepts it without fear or confusion. This is routine. Arguments redirected. Tension managed. A child who knows when adults need to be separated from their worst impulses.

Which means she and Whitford fought like this. Often enough that Jenna learned exactly what to say. Often enough that Amauri learned exactly what to do. The realization lands heavy. Not because she handled it wrong. But because she handled it well. And because it means I wasn't the first man she had to protect our son from.

"No, wait. I'm leaving. I'm not doing this here." Amauri pauses at my words. "Not in front of him. Not now."

At least that instinct still works. Amauri watches me closely, suspicious but curious. Like he's filing me away. I meet his gaze. "We'll talk later," I tell him. Not her. Him.

He nods once. Serious. Evaluating.

I turn and leave before I say something I can't take back. Behind me, I hear her exhale, shaky, furious, alive. I refuse to look at her as I stride toward the door. I hear her whisper something to Amauri, but I ignore it. I just need to get out of here. Outside, Max takes one look at my expression and nods at one of the men to call the elevator. The door behind me clicks open. Jenna.

"Oh no, you don't get to walk away from me like that."

I freeze. Her voice isn't loud, but it doesn't need to be. It carries. Controlled fury. The kind that doesn't burn out fast, it waits.

"You said you sent Bello to tell me you were hurt," she fires at me. "To tell me you were alive."

Max and the guards are not even pretending not to listen. I glare at them, and they finally turn away. Thankfully, the elevator arrives. The doors open, and I grab

Jenna's wrist and pull her inside before anyone else can think to follow. I press Lobby, give it a second, then hit the emergency stop before the box can even move. But the doors are closed. Silence slams down.

I turn on her, every instinct screams at me to regain control of a situation that's suddenly tilting sideways.

"What the hell do you think you're doing?" I demand.

Her eyes are blazing. Not scared. Not wavering. Furious in a way that has nothing to do with weakness.

"Well, let me tell you something," she continues. "The first time I met Bello was when I came to your mansion. I stood at your gates like an idiot who still believed in answers."

My chest tightens.

"He had me removed," she snaps. "Told me you didn't want to see me. Told me to go home and to never come back."

The words don't land all at once. They stack. Slow. Relentlessly so. I'm suddenly aware of how loud my own breathing is in the enclosed space.

"That's impossible," the words flow out automatically.

She laughs once. Sharp. Ugly. "Is it?"

My mind is spinning now, gears grinding, timelines snapping into place and not aligning. "You're telling me that Bello told you I didn't want to see you."

"Yes."

"After the attack."

"What attack?"

It's the frank confusion on her face that makes me stop and run a hand through my hair. I turn away from her because, honestly, I'm about to hit something. She grabs the arm of my suit jacket. "What attack, Massimo?"

She's not strong enough to turn me around, but I'm not a coward, so I face her. "I was attacked, run over by a car. I was out for several months." I explain, running my hand through my hair again before I plant my face against the elevator wall, hard enough to send spider cracks through the mirror.

I move forward; she takes a step back until she hits the other side of the elevator. Both of my palms now plant on either side of her face, locking her in. "When I was somewhat able to move, I found out that you married Carter fucking Whitford."

My fury washes over her face, but she doesn't shrink back. She leans forward, meeting me nearly nose to nose.

"Because I was pregnant and left with the choice to either marry the man who sold me out or have an abortion," she spits into my face.

Both our breathing is hard and uneven. Chests heaving, she stares up, and I stare down. Down into the most mesmerizing green eyes I've ever seen. Eyes I had gotten lost in ten years ago and now know I will again.

Her words penetrate my brain. Barely. There will be time for it later. Right now, all that exists are those eyes burning into me with a passion I know all too well. My cock responds in kind.

"Jenna," I rasp.

"Massimo," she breathes, right before her hands knot into my jacket and tie, pulling me down. My arms move from the sides of her face. One to her waist, the other to the back of her head. I pull her against me like a man who is clinging to a lifeboat in the middle of rapids. Our mouths clash. It's not gentle. It's an explosion of emotions that have been pent up and held hostage for ten years.

We're consuming each other. That's the only way to name it. Ten years, a million lies, every mile and minute of separation, none of it matters. Not in this moment, not with her hands desperate on my chest, not with my mouth claiming hers like I'll die if I stop. She bites me. Her nails dig into my shoulder through silk and bone, and it's so familiar, so right, I have to choke down a laugh, or I'll lose myself too fast.

I don't wait. I don't ask. I slide my hand into her hair, fist the strands at the nape of her neck, and pull her up into another kiss, hard, hungry, all the rage and need of ten years channels straight through my mouth. Her lips split against mine, the faint copper tang of blood, but she doesn't flinch. We devour each other, trying to win, to erase, to survive. I want to bite her, to mark her for every night I spent burning for this and every day I hated myself for it.

She meets me head-on, grinding up into my space as if she's desperate to climb inside my skin. My hand works down, rucking her skirt up so fast the seams scream in protest, the sound nearly drowned out by the wet, gasping breaths between our mouths. Her thighs bracket my hips, her muscles flex. God, she's soft, but there's strength I didn't remember, or maybe never saw. She's trembling. I don't know if it's fear, fury, or the simple act of finally being wanted. I don't care. I want all of it. I want to drink her until she shakes apart.

Her fingers are already on my belt. Her hands fumble with my buckle, almost inexperienced, but that can't be, she's been married for ten years. She drags me free, and her hand tightens around my cock, solid and possessive, stroking with just enough pressure that my vision whites out for a second. Her mouth parts, and a hiss escapes.

I push her panties aside—black, lace, a tiny useless scrap that just makes me harder—and run two fingers over her velvety folds, amazed at how wet she already is. She gasps. Her head thumps the back of the mirror, her hair fans out like a halo, her eyes glitter with desire. She meets my gaze, unblinking. "Fuck you," she whispers, voice low and guttural.

"You will," I promise, and mean it. "Count on it."

There's no room or reason to wait. I grip her ass, lifting, shifting so that the tip of me finds her. I want to take it slow, to remember every fucking second, but my body isn't wired for that, not when it's this woman and this moment, when it's everything I've ever denied myself. I want to ravage her, to remake her, to carve my shape into the parts of her Carter Whitford never touched.

She hauls me into place with both legs, locking her ankles at the base of my spine, and I almost lose my grip when she does. She's so small compared to me, but she's pure leverage; she uses my body as a fulcrum to drive me into her. The first thrust is an electric shock, too much and not enough, and I have to grab the wall behind her. The cracked glass bites my palm, and pain spikes up my arm, goading me on.

I bottom out inside her, and we both freeze for a second, forehead to forehead, dripping sweat, the mingled sounds of our breath and our hearts pounding deafening in the small space. Her nails dig into the back of my neck, scraping, and she bites my jaw, hard enough to send a jolt straight to my cock. "Jesus Christ, Massimo," she breathes, but she doesn't tell me to stop.

"Tell me to stop," I rasp. I don't know if I can, but I have to say it.

"Don't you fucking dare."

That's all I need. Every motion is a confession, every thrust an apology or accusation. I fuck her like I'm at war with her, like if I stop, we'll both fall apart. She claws at my shirt, popping buttons, and I do the same to her blouse, yanking it open and freeing one perfect breast. I take her nipple in my mouth, biting until she gasps, then sucking the sting away with my tongue. She arches into me, her whole body straining for more, skin slick with sweat and desperation. For a brief moment, the colors of her tattoo catch my eye, sending a spiral of emotions through me, but I push them aside. I want to break her open, to see what's left inside after all this time. Her skirt is hiked around her waist, her panties bunched at one thigh, and I don't bother slowing down, not even when I feel the sharp edge of the mirror driving deeper into my palm. Blood streaks the glass behind her, bright and vivid, but it barely registers. All that matters is the sound she makes—pure need, guttural and exposed—I ram into her, over and over, taking her higher.

She's close, I can feel it. The way her hips jerk, the way her nails scrabble for purchase on my back, the way her breath comes in little shattered bursts. I remember those. Everything about her comes back to me, making me question how I survived the past ten years without hearing them. I reach down, thumb rough and sure on her clit, and she bucks hard enough I nearly lose my footing. "Fuck—oh fucking hell—" she chokes, and I watch her come apart for me, face contorted, hair wild, lips bitten red and wet.

She tries to fight it. She does. But she's got nothing left; she surrenders. Her whole body convulses, and in the chaos, she buries her teeth in my shoulder to keep from screaming. I feel the bite. I want her to leave a scar so I can remember this every time I look in the mirror.

That's when I lose it. I slam into her, harder, faster, until I'm sure the elevator itself will break, the whole world will break, and it's only us left locked together. The sight of her, ruined and perfect and exactly how I always wanted her, pushes me over the edge. I come so hard the edges of my vision shrivel, and all I see is white, all I hear is her voice, my name, over and over.

We don't move. Not right away. I hold her, arms braced so I don't crush her; her legs are tangled around me, both of us gasping. I can't tell where her skin stops, and mine starts. If the elevator plummeted now, I'd still be inside her when we hit the ground.

Eventually, she kisses my jaw, softer this time, almost gentle. "You're bleeding, idiot," she observes.

I glance at my hand, red. Lines of wet on her neck, her cheek, probably more all over her. It doesn't matter. I swipe it away with my thumb, smear it down her throat, a mark I want the world to see.

She rests her head on my shoulder. For a minute, she lets herself be held. The elevator is silent except for our breathing. We collapse together against the mirrored wall, the web of cracks radiating from the spot where my fist had landed. In the reflection, we're doubled and fractured and inseparable.

She runs her palm up my chest, slow, almost gentle, as if she forgot how to touch without leaving a scar. "If you ever leave me again," she says, "I'll murder you before you even see me coming."

"If you ever leave *me* again," I answer, voice hoarse, "I'll burn the world down finding you."

She leans in and mouths my throat, almost a kiss, almost a warning. I should ask what happens now. I should say something about Amauri, or about her husband, or about the sharks circling outside these walls. Instead, I stay right where I am, holding her, memorizing the weight of her against me.

I force myself to move first. Not because I want to, but because if I don't, I'll stay right here with her until the world outside this elevator becomes irrelevant, and that is a weakness I can't afford. I adjust my jacket, ignoring the blood on my hand, the heat still humming under my skin, and the way her body seems to resist being let go even after I step back. I don't apologize. I don't explain. Whatever just happened between us doesn't need language yet. It needs containment.

This shouldn't have happened before the truth was fully unfolded. I know that. I crossed a line without knowing who put it there in the first place. Bello. Whitford. Her father. Too many hands in a story that should have been simple. I claimed her on instinct, on rage, on ten years of unfinished fire, and now there's no version of this where she walks away untouched by my decisions. Or where Amauri does. That awareness settles into me, heavy and permanent. I don't regret it. But I feel the cost forming.

The elevator hums back to life beneath our feet. When the doors open, I don't look at her again. If I do, I won't leave. And leaving—right now—is the only way I don't turn this into something that destroys us both. I step out first, already recalibrating, already locking the pieces into place. Bello will answer. Whitford will suffer. The lies will be dragged into the light and burned down to the bone.

And when this is over—when every man who thought he could decide our fate is dealt with—there will be no more misunderstandings. Because she's back in my world now. And nothing that's mine ever leaves it, especially not twice.

THE DOORS SLIDE OPEN, AND THE ANTECHAMBER HITS ME like a mirror I didn't ask for. Max's eyebrow lifts—just a fraction—but it's enough. He doesn't need to look me over carefully. The evidence is everywhere. Blood—*Massimo's* —on my throat and collarbone. My hair is a wrecked mess, pulled loose from its careful lie. My pulse is still loud enough to be mistaken for guilt. I know what I look like. I can feel it in the way my skin hums, in the ache between my thighs that hasn't caught up with reality yet.

Massimo sees it too. He growls something low and lethal at his men—Italian, sharp—and before I can open my mouth, his jacket is on me. Heavy. Warm. It smells like him. Dark. It shouldn't feel like safety, but it does. He doesn't ask. He doesn't explain. He just wraps it around my shoulders and steers me forward, palm firm at my back, pushing me toward the suite like he's shielding me from a firing line instead of his own people.

"Inside," he says, and I go.

Before the door closes behind us, he stops me and wipes my face with a handkerchief from his pocket. My eyes are already scanning. Couch. Hallway. Guest room.

Amauri.

"We don't want you to scare Amauri," Massimo nods to himself.

Amauri! He's not where I left him.

My heart drops so fast it feels like freefall. The room tilts. For half a second, my mind is back to when he was missing, echoing the sound of my own breathing in my ears while I counted seconds and prayed I wasn't too late.

"Amauri?" My voice breaks on his name before I can stop it.

I move before I think; panic climbs up in my throat. What kind of mother—what kind of *idiot*—lets herself get fucked in an elevator when her son has just been pulled out of a nightmare? What kind of woman leaves her child alone for even a minute after—

"Mummy."

The word stops me cold. I spin toward the kitchen just as he strolls out, completely unbothered by the apocalypse I've built in my head. He's barefoot. Calm. Nutella smeared across his chin like war paint. A sandwich clenched in his hand, thick and uneven and very obviously self-made.

"Here," he says again, as if he's been standing there the whole time. "I was hungry."

My knees go weak. I cross the room in three steps and drop in front of him, hands already checking—arms, shoulders, ribs—counting breaths, confirming solidity. He smells like chocolate and soap and *home*. Alive. Unhurt. Real.

"Oh my God," I whisper into his hair. "You scared me."

He pats my shoulder, serious as a tiny old man. "You said you'd be right back."

"I know," I choke. "I know."

He pulls back to look at me, eyes sharp, assessing. "You're crying."

I swipe at my face, laughing and sobbing at the same time. "No, I'm not."

"Yes, you are," he contradicts calmly. "And you're wearing *his* jacket."

I freeze. Behind me, I feel Massimo's presence like a weather system. He hasn't moved. He hasn't spoken. He's watching us with an intensity that makes my skin prickle. Amauri follows my gaze. His eyes flick to Massimo, then back to me. Curious. Not afraid.

"He swore," Amauri adds, apropos of nothing.

Massimo exhales through his nose. "I apologized."

Amauri considers this. Then nods, solemn. "Okay."

Just like that. I stare at my son—this small, impossible person who survived hell and still believes apologies matter—and something inside me tightens so hard it hurts.

"I made a sandwich," he offers, holding it up proudly. "There's a lot of Nutella because I like it."

"I can see that," I say, brushing chocolate from his chin with my thumb. "You're a genius."

"I know." Of course he does.

I pull him into me again, slower this time, breathing him in, letting my heartbeat settle against his. Over his head, my eyes meet Massimo's. There's blood on his knuckles. Dried now. There's something unreadable in his expression, possession, yes, but also restraint. Calculation. Something like... recalibration.

I don't thank him. Not for the jacket. Not for pushing

me inside. Not for giving Amauri space instead of interrogations, guards, and questions.

Gratitude is complicated. So is survival.

"I'm tired," Amauri announces into my collarbone. "Can I watch TV?"

"Yes. Pick something quiet."

He nods, already turning away, sandwich in hand. "I like the space one."

"That's fine, just not that one episode with the sehlat." It always makes me cry when the cartoon character remembers his I-Chaya.

"Oh, Mummy, it's just a show," Amauri states with the worldly certainty of a kid who thinks he's seen it all and pads off toward the couch, utterly at ease, leaving chaos in his wake like it's nothing.

When I stand, I don't look away from Massimo.

"This doesn't happen again," I say quietly.

His jaw tightens. "What?"

"Leaving him," I clarify. "For answers. For fights. For you."

Something flashes in his eyes—anger, maybe—but it's gone just as fast.

"You won't have to," he promises.

That's not reassurance. It's a statement of intent.

I step closer anyway, lowering my voice. "You don't get to decide that alone."

His gaze drops to my throat. The marks he left there. The ones I'll have to explain or continue to hide.

"I already did," his words make me shiver, and the expression in his eyes turns my blood cold.

I should argue. I should push back. I should remind him who I am and what I've survived. Instead, I glance toward the couch, where Amauri is already curled into the corner, space cartoons murmuring softly, Nutella abandoned on the table like evidence of a small, perfect rebellion.

"I'm his mother," I iterate. "That's the only thing that's non-negotiable."

Massimo nods once. "Good."

The word settles between us, heavy and loaded. His jaw is locked tight. He studies me like one might a structure under stress, eyes cutting, searching for fractures, for omissions, for the place where I might still be lying to him. It's the look he wears before violence. Or truth.

"I have to go," his voice is clipped, like his mind is already half elsewhere. Then, quieter, deadly precise, "But I need to know something first."

My spine straightens.

"Did Bello come to you," he asks, "and tell you I was in an accident?"

The question hits harder than it should. Accident. The word detonates backward through ten years of grief and fury and abandonment. My breath stutters. He didn't disappear. He didn't choose silence. He was *hurt*. Broken. Taken out of the world the same way I was, without consent.

But there's no time to process that now. I can feel it; this question is loaded. Not emotionally. Strategically. Whatever answer I give him is about to change something far bigger than us. All I can give him is the truth. All of it. With everything I have.

"I swear," I keep my eyes on his and my voice steady even as my chest tightens, "the first time I ever met Bello was at your mansion. I went there looking for you. He told me to leave. He said I wasn't welcome." His eyes darken. His focus narrows. "The second time I saw him," I continue, "was yesterday. At your... Oven."

Silence drops between us like a blade. I want to ask him about the accident—how bad it was, how long he was gone—but I can see it in his face. His mind has already pivoted. This isn't about the past anymore. It's about now. About Amauri. About who decided what for all of us.

I want to ask about Carter, too. About where he is. What Massimo plans to do. Not now. This man doesn't multitask emotion. When he locks onto something, everything else waits, or burns.

"I didn't betray you," I say, stepping closer before I lose the nerve. I rise onto my toes, press a kiss to his mouth. Not desperate. Not apologetic. Certain. "I did what I had to do to keep our son alive."

His hands come up and stop just short of touching me. For a heartbeat, I think he might pull me back. That he'll say something final. Something irreversible. Instead, his hand moves forward, and his palm rests against my cheek. His dark eyes are full of regret and words we don't have time to say. That's when I know how dangerous this has become.

For a moment, I melt the side of my face into his hand. He nods, and I turn back to Amauri just as the soft click of the door sounds behind me. The suite settles into a quiet that feels almost unreal after everything.

Massimo is gone.

For now.

Amauri glances over his shoulder at me from the couch. "Is he mad?"

I smooth my hand over his hair, smiling even though my chest still aches. "No, baby. He just has... work." He nods, accepting this like he accepts too many things children shouldn't have to.

"I'll be right back," I promise and make a mad dash toward the bathroom to wash up before I return to sit beside him, pulling him close. One truth settles in with terrifying clarity: Whatever storm Massimo's about to unleash, we're standing in the middle of it. But Amauri is here. Warm. Alive. Curled against my side like he's done a thousand times before. And Massimo—Massimo didn't leave me. Not then. Not ten years ago. Not the way I thought. He didn't disappear. He was taken out of the world the same brutal way I was. The realization is too big. Too sharp. My chest feels tight, my pulse skidding higher and higher as questions pile up faster than I can grab them.

How bad was the accident?

How long was he unconscious?

Did he wake up and look for me?

Did he know about the baby then—or only later?

How much of my life was shaped by one lie told at the wrong moment?

My heart races like it's trying to outrun the past.

Amauri shifts, pressing closer, his head settling against my ribs. The simple weight of him grounds me. Anchors me back into the present before I float apart. Right. I have responsibilities *right now*.

"Amauri?" I ask quietly. He hesitates. I can feel it in the way his fingers twist into the fabric of my shirt. "Do you want to talk about it?"

He turns to me, his eyes are big, but the question coming out of him is the last I'd expected I'd have to answer now. "Why did Massimo call me *his* son, Mummy?"

My heart drops straight through the floor. Not now. Not yet. I close my eyes for a fraction of a second, cursing silently. Damn you, *Massimo. Throwing words like that into the air and leaving*. Of course, this is what Amauri latches onto. Of course, *this* is the thread his mind grabs and won't let go. Guilt pricks, sharp and immediate. I owe him the truth. I know that. But not like this. Not when his world is still wobbling on its axis.

I smooth my hand over his hair, buying time. "That's... a big conversation," I say carefully. "One we'll have. I promise. Just not tonight."

He studies my face, serious, too perceptive. "Okay."

Bless him for that. I try to redirect, gently. "Do you want to talk about what happened? About how scary it was?"

He looks at me for a long moment, and in that second, I see it, his face, his expression, the tilt of his mouth when he thinks.

"He looks like me."

I squeeze my eyes shut.

Ah, shit.

He takes another bite of his sandwich and chews thoughtfully. Nutella smears a little more across his chin.

"It was scary," he admits. "Dad was really, really scared," he adds, like he's reporting the weather. "I held his hand."

Fuck.

Of course he did.

My little man.

I pull him closer, pressing my lips to the top of his head, breathing him in like oxygen. "You were very brave," I whisper. "I'm so proud of you."

"Is Dad at the hospital?"

I swallow. I have no idea where Carter is, nor do I... care. Not even a little bit. If that makes me a bitch, fine. I can live with that. "Yeah, baby, they're making sure he's okay." I lie.

He shrugs, but he leans into me, accepting the words. Carter went to the hospital quite often; it's nothing new for Amauri and nothing scary. Carter always came back okay.

We sit there like that—him eating, me holding him—while the world outside this suite rearranges itself without my consent. Answers are coming. I can feel it. Storms. Truths that won't stay buried. But for now, my son is safe in my arms. And for now, that is enough. I rock him gently, feeling the steady weight of him against me, the warmth, the proof that he's real and here and mine. His chewing slows. His eyelids droop. He's so small for everything he's already survived.

I press my cheek to his hair and let myself believe—just for this moment—that holding him is enough to keep the world out. I feel something wet between my thighs and know I need to go take a shower. The quick wash-up helped, but it wasn't enough. Unfortunately, for the life of me, I can't summon the will to leave Amauri on the couch. The stickiness between my legs reminds me of another uncomfortable truth, though. I'm not on birth control. I didn't need to be during the last ten years. Ten years ago, I'd just started taking them when... well, we all know how that ended up. His name is Amauri. Somehow, the thought of another pregnancy doesn't scare me, though. Not even a little bit. Not only because of Massimo, but because I know I'm changing. I'm becoming stronger with every moment. I'm turning into the version of Jenna I was always supposed to be.

But somewhere deep in my chest, beneath the relief, something tightens. Because safety, I'm learning, is never permanent. It's something you borrow. And sooner or later, someone always comes to collect.

THE ELEVATOR DOORS SLIDE SHUT, AND THE AIR TURNS thick. It still smells like her. Like heat and skin and the kind of hunger that doesn't fade just because you step away from it. Fuck. My chest tightens. That shouldn't have happened. Not here. Not now. Not before the ground stopped shifting under my feet.

Yet, nothing has felt that good, that *right*, in... Not in years. Not ever.

I brace my hand against the wall, my breath steady but heavy, like I've just surfaced from deep water. My knuckles throb where I shattered the mirror, and blood still dribbles out in places, slick and warm. I take my tie and wrap it around the cut, knotting it hard, willing the pain to anchor me back into control. My jacket is gone. My shirt is ruined. Blood streaks the white silk, and I don't bother fixing it. My shoulder holster is exposed; the gun is visible, unapologetic. Let them see. I don't give a shit.

My men stand behind me, silent. Good. Anyone dumb enough to comment on the state of the elevator—or to speculate on what happened inside it—won't get a warning. They can feel it rolling off me. This is not lust. This is the fallout of something that shouldn't have happened.

But it did.

And now there's no pretending it didn't matter.

Her mouth. Her hands. The way she met me without flinching, without apology, like ten years hadn't tried to grind us down into strangers. It wasn't just sex. It was recognition. It was coming home to a place I didn't know existed.

That's what scares me. Because while my body is still humming with it, my mind keeps snapping back to her words.

Bello.

The name turns acidic in my mouth.

I trusted that motherfucker. Trusted him with something more important than territory. More important than money, blood, or loyalty tests. I trusted him with *her*. With the truth. With the thin thread that tied my past to my future.

With my son.

The realization sits ugly and heavy in my gut. If he lied —if he decided what Jenna deserved to know, what I deserved to lose—then this wasn't a mistake. It was a decision. One that cost me ten years. One that shaped a child's entire life.

The elevator chimes. I straighten, my shoulders lock into place as the doors open. The casino explodes into light, sound, and motion. People stare. Of course they do. Blood on my shirt. Gun in plain sight. My face, still carved raw from whatever I left upstairs. Let them stare. This is my casino. My floor. My world.

I walk through it like I own gravity. Dealers stiffen.

Security snaps alert. Conversations die as I pass. I pull my phone out, dial Enzo without breaking stride. He answers fast. "You're on your way."

"Yes."

A pause. He hears it. "What's up?"

"Make sure Bello is at the meeting."

This time, the pause is on him. During our inner circle meetings, we don't usually bring our seconds. "He's here."

"Keep him there." I end the call and keep moving, boots eating up polished floor, my men fall in behind me like shadows. Whatever just happened between Jenna and me will have to wait. Whatever truth is clawing its way to the surface will be dealt with.

Because if Bello thought he could touch what was mine—rewrite my life, my family, my son—then this isn't just betrayal. Whatever happens next won't be loud. It won't be rushed. It won't be merciful. He didn't start a war. He just forfeited his life.

The SUVs are already waiting in the valet lane. Their engines are idling, dark glass reflecting the neon lights, money, and fear like they always do. Same formation. Same drivers. Same discipline. The meeting is at the Monarch tonight, Enzo's casino. We rotate locations for a reason. Patterns get men killed. And right now, we can't afford even the illusion of predictability.

I slide into the back seat, and the door shuts with a soft, final click. My phone vibrates once in my hand with an incoming text.

OKSANA.

Unfortunately, Aurelio found a very quick end. Silvestre is still talking.

WITH ALL THE OTHER TRUTHS I'M FINDING OUT, AURELIO and Silvestre are so far on the back burner that I'd nearly forgotten about them.

I text back.

ME:

Make it count.

SHE SENDS A THUMBS-UP. I PUT THE PHONE BACK IN MY jacket pocket. Aurelio and Silvestre. They dared take my blood and now pay with theirs for it. Deep down, I should owe them a debt of gratitude; if it wasn't for them, I still wouldn't know about Amauri. That notion is short-lived, however. I don't owe anyone. Least of all the Valverdes. And with the Venezuelans out of the picture, I can turn my full focus on Joaquín and Mexico. The fucker is trying to test my borders, probing my city to see where the seams might split. That will be handled. But first, Bello.

The car barely has time to settle into traffic before we're pulling up again. Short ride. I don't waste it thinking about logistics. Those are already locked in place.

The SUVs stop. Doors open. I'm already moving. Enzo's casino parts the same way mine did. Heads turn. Voices drop. People step aside without being told. Whispering follows me like exhaust. I don't look at any of them. I don't need to. I cross the floor, boots steady on polished marble. Someone says my name. Someone else nods. A cocktail waitress catches my eye and offers a shy smile, hopeful, nervous.

I don't slow. I don't acknowledge it. None of it matters.

The elevator doors slide open. I step inside. The ascent is smooth, silent. Controlled. Exactly how I feel now. At the top floor, security greets me with quiet respect. One opens the door without being asked. Another nods once, tightly. I walk toward the meeting room with my jacket still missing, blood dried dark against my shirt, knuckles bound with a tie. Let them see. This is what wrath looks like.

The moment I step into the boardroom, everything goes silent. All eyes fall on me. Damiano straightens first. Gabe's jaw tightens. Alessio goes still in that dangerous, coiled way of his. Enzo doesn't move at all; he just watches me, eyes sharp, already counting outcomes.

Bello looks like shit. Gray in the face. Eyes sunken. Shoulders heavy in a way that has nothing to do with age. He knows. He's known since the moment I asked Enzo to make sure he was here. Since the moment Jenna said his name. He doesn't look surprised. He looks like a man who, after living on borrowed time for ten years, just heard the collector knock.

I don't sit. I don't speak.

I pull my gun. The sound of it clearing leather is the only thing that breaks the stillness. I cross the room in three long strides, grab Bello by the collar, and slam him into the wall hard enough to rattle his bones. He doesn't resist. Doesn't fight. Doesn't even grunt. I press the muzzle of my gun into his forehead.

Close. Intimate.

"You told Jenna," my voice is cold, even, and terrifyingly calm, "that I didn't want to see her."

His eyes meet mine. There's no fear in them. Only resignation.

"Yes," he admits.

A breath moves through the room. Someone swallows. No one interrupts.

"You were in the middle of a war," Bello continues, his voice steady, old-school to the end. "Vittorio was circling. Your cousins were sharpening knives. You didn't need that kind of distraction."

"That was not your decision to make," I growl.

"If she stayed," he defends quietly, "you would have lost focus. If she stayed, you wouldn't have won. You wouldn't be standing here right now."

My grip tightens.

"You don't get to decide what I can survive," I say. "You don't get to decide what I deserve."

He exhales slowly. "I did what I thought was right for you."

That's the betrayal. Not the lie. The *choice*. I lean closer, the gun never leaving his skin. "You stole ten years from me."

His jaw tightens once. "I know."

"You stole my son's father from him," I continue. "You stole *her* choice. You rewrote my life without permission."

"I knew when I did it," Bello says, finally. "That if you ever found out, I was dead."

Silence crashes down around us.

"The only reason," I say, "that you're not going into the Oven right now... is because you stood by my side when everyone else tried to knife me in the dark." A flicker of something like relief crosses his face. Not hope. Acceptance. "But make no mistake," I finish, "this betrayal is unforgivable." He nods once. No begging. No pleas. No prayers. Just a man standing by the cost of his choices. "Consider this my mercy."

I pull the trigger. The sound is sharp. Final. Bello's body goes slack instantly, sliding down the wall to the floor like gravity finally remembered him. Blood blooms dark against marble. No one moves. I lower the gun, and smoke curls faintly from the barrel. I look around the room.

"This," I state calmly, "is what happens when someone decides they know better than me."

I holster the weapon. The room exhales, barely. No one looks at Bello's body anymore. He's already been filed away as a consequence.

I turn to Damiano. "Did you find the insider at the club where Mia was killed?"

Damiano doesn't blink. He finishes his scotch, sets the glass down with deliberate care, then takes a seat like we're discussing quarterly earnings instead of murder.

"Yes, boss. Two of them. Security guards. They messed with the system, camera loop, and door logs. Both were paid off by a Mexican named José."

"Where is he?"

"Running," Damiano replies. "My men are on him."

"Good."

I shift my gaze to Gabe. He shakes his head once. Clean. No hesitation.

"So Bello was otherwise solid," I say.

"Yes," Gabe confirms. "No leaks. No money out of place. Nothing else compromised."

That lands exactly where it should. Bello's betrayal wasn't rot. It was *choice*. Still unforgivable, but better than more fallout. I turn to Alessio. He's already leaning forward, elbows on the table, eyes bright with something close to satisfaction. "Joaquín is hiding in Mexico, on the northern side. I have his exact location."

For the first time in days, something like alignment clicks into place. Fortuna, it seems, has finally decided to stop laughing at me.

Enzo clears his throat. "We caught five more rats. Hired to poison our coke. All of them folded. Same pipeline. Same handlers."

I nod once. "They won't be missed."

No one argues. The pieces are falling where they belong now. Threads tightening. Noise resolving into pattern. What started as chaos is turning back into something I understand. Something I can control. I look around the table, meeting each of my most trusted men's eyes in turn.

"This ends," I declare. "Now. Anyone who thinks they can bleed us quietly will learn otherwise. Anyone who thinks my house is open season will be corrected."

I glance once—just once—at the place where Bello died.

Then I turn back to my men. "Clean it up," I order.

"What do you want to do with Whitford?" Gabe asks, rising.

The room stills again. Whitford is unfinished business. Everyone here knows it.

"He stays where he is," I command. My voice is calm, measured. Worse than anger. "Alive." A flicker crosses Enzo's face. Damiano's mouth tightens. Alessio doesn't react at all. "For now," I add. "What's his condition?"

"Demanding asshole," Gabe replies. "Comfortable enough to remember every choice he made. Not comfortable enough to forget who owns him."

Whitford is leverage. Not against Jenna. Against truth. Against timelines. Against the men who thought they could move my pieces without asking permission. I do have a few questions left for him. He talked once. He'll talk again. And when he does, it will be because he understands exactly how small he is.

Gabe's expression doesn't change. "And when you're done with him?"

I look at the table. At the men who have bled with me. At the empty space where Bello had stood ten minutes ago.

"When I'm done, Jenna will be a widow."

That satisfies them. I straighten my cuffs, already

mentally moving past Whitford. He's a footnote. A delay. The real threats are still breathing—Mexico, Joaquín, the men who thought Las Vegas was soft because I was distracted.

Not anymore.

"We move south soon," I order. "Quietly. I want Joaquín alive long enough to understand what he started."

Alessio smiles, sharp and eager. "I'll handle it."

"I know you will."

I turn toward the door; the meeting is already over in my mind. "And someone make sure," I add without looking back, "that Jenna and my son are not disturbed tonight. No updates. No visitors. Nothing reaches them unless it comes through me."

"Yes, boss," comes the chorus.

I leave the room without another word. The blood has been paid.

The house is aligned. And now, now I go back to what matters.

Everything else can wait its turn.

I DON'T REMEMBER FALLING ASLEEP. ONE MOMENT, I WAS sitting upright on the couch, every nerve still humming, listening to Amauri's breathing like it was a lifeline. The next, I wake up warm. Not on the couch. Not in the guest bedroom.

I freeze for half a second before memory catches up with sensation. I'm in Massimo's bed. The sheets are dark and impossibly soft. The room smells faintly of him, clean, expensive, something ironed through with danger. My body is angled protectively, instinctively, and when I look down, I see why.

Amauri is curled into my side, one arm slung across my waist, his face relaxed in sleep in a way that makes my chest ache. No tension. No shadows behind his eyes. Just a child, finally safe enough to let go.

Thank you, I think, not sure to whom. God. The universe. Massimo. Anyone listening.

I lie still for a long moment, memorizing the sight of him like this, but my bladder is about to explode. So—carefully, painstakingly—I extract myself. I slide one leg free. Then the other. I ease his arm back onto the pillow, tuck the blanket around him the way he likes it. He sighs, but doesn't wake.

Mission: slide out of bed without waking the kid, part one: check.

I pad out of the bedroom and into the massive bathroom barefoot, my body sore in that deep, familiar way memory immediately explains. Scenes from the elevator flash through me without permission: heat, pressure, the way I forgot how to breathe. I push them aside. Not now. I do what I came here to do, wash my hands, and peek in on my son. He's still out. I contemplate sneaking back under the covers, but the smell of coffee hits me like a punch. Rich. Bitter. Real.

I don't drift in that direction. I follow the scent like a woman who knows exactly what it will cost her and goes anyway. The scent of food adds to the rich aroma of coffee, making my mouth water. It leads me into the kitchen, where I find Massimo standing behind a counter. Sleeves rolled up. His hair is still damp. A cup of espresso sits in his hand like it's an extension of him. The counter is covered in silver domes, the kind hotels use when they want you to feel important. I stop short, unsure.

"I had no idea you cooked." The words come out lighter than I feel.

He glances up at me, something unreadable flickers across his face, making me swallow, and my insides clench at the thought of what we did yesterday.

"I don't," he replies calmly. "I had it sent up from the kitchen."

I should have known. On leaden legs, I move forward,

watching as he lifts one of the domes. Eggs. Fresh fruit. Bread still steaming. Another reveals pastries. One more, something warm and savory that makes my stomach betray me immediately.

"Hungry?" his voice is low and sounds like he's asking something other than the simple word.

I hesitate. Everything about this feels... precarious. The night before hasn't settled yet. The truth hasn't finished rearranging itself in my head. My body remembers him far more clearly than my heart knows how to handle.

"I—maybe," I admit honestly.

He nods, accepting that without comment, and pours another cup of coffee, setting it where I can reach it but not pushing it into my hand. It's a small thing. It shouldn't matter. It does. I lean against the counter, crossing my arms lightly, hyper-aware of myself. Of the faint ache between my thighs. Of the fact that I'm still wearing his shirt from last night. Of how easily this could slip into something I'm not ready to name.

Behind us, down the hall, Amauri sleeps. That's the anchor. The line I won't cross blindly. Massimo watches me over the rim of his cup, not predatory, not soft. Just... present. I squirm because I don't know what to make out of that gaze, what to think, what *he* thinks. And I hate that he's making me feel like an insecure seventeen-year-old. The realization that this morning is going to be harder than the night hits me full force. Because daylight asks questions that darkness lets you avoid.

I take a sip of the coffee. It's good. Strong. Reviving in

the way only coffee can be, like it reaches straight into my bloodstream and flips a switch marked *function*. I let the heat settle and ground me, then reach for a croissant. It flakes under my fingers, the layers peel apart delicately, but I don't actually eat it. I just... pick. Pull. Tear. Something to do with my hands.

Massimo watches me.

Not openly. Not like a predator sizing up prey. More like he's cataloging, taking stock of my tells, my hesitations, the way I'm stalling without meaning to. The silence stretches. I hate it.

"So," I finally break it, lifting my chin. "Now what?"

His lip quirks up, just a little. Amused. That's new. Or at least new since I've seen him again. Up until now, he's been anger and heat and accusation, all sharp edges and pressure. This—this flicker of humor—throws me off balance more than the shouting ever did.

"Now," he says, "we talk."

He gestures toward a small round table by the window. Sunlight spills across it, Vegas glitters below, and the desert stretches endlessly beyond the glass. Power and emptiness, side by side. Fitting. For a moment, I hesitate, then I square my shoulders and walk over anyway. I sit in the proffered chair, back straight, spine stiff, like I'm bracing for impact. Awkward doesn't even begin to cover it.

As he settles into the chair across from me, my eyes betray me. I notice the scar running along his forearm, long, pale against darker skin, disappearing beneath the cuff of his sleeve. My breath catches before I can stop it.

He notices. Of course he does. Without a word, he reaches up and rolls his sleeve down, covering it like a curtain falling. Final. Closed. I clear my throat.

"Bello," he cuts straight to it. "Tell me everything."

The command in his voice hits a nerve I didn't know was still raw.

"Oh," I snap, righteous anger flaring hot and fast. "So *now* you want to hear my side of the story?"

His gaze doesn't harden. It doesn't sharpen. It stays patient. That somehow makes it worse. "Yes. Now."

I open my mouth with a dozen sharp retorts lined up and ready, but then he continues, quieter, grounded. "Jenna, we've wasted ten years." The sadness in his voice gives me pause. "Ten years kept apart by misunderstandings. Lies. Silence." He pauses, keeping his eyes steadily on mine. "I think it's time we clear the air."

My fingers curl into the croissant, crushing it slightly. He leans forward just a fraction. "We owe it to our son."

That does it. The bravado doesn't vanish, but it reshapes. Hardens into something steadier. I lift my gaze to meet his, green to dark, unflinching.

"Fine." He wants to hear the story? I can give him the story. "One day, you didn't show up. I called you. I texted you. Nothing. I didn't know what to do. I had a vague idea of who you really were, Vittorio Manetti's nephew. That name meant something even to an eighteen-year-old. It scared me."

My bravado vanishes at the memory of how scared I was. We had decided to keep our relationship a secret. Me, because it would look bad if I flung my new love into

Carter's face right after the accident, especially since nobody knew anything about what he had done. To everybody else, he was still the golden boy. The hero. And I wasn't ready to be the bitch who left him when he was at his lowest. Massimo, because he was worried about giving his uncle leverage over him. Me. He was afraid of what his uncle might do. Especially given who my father was, the Governor of Nevada at the time.

He listens quietly and patiently, waiting for me to collect my thoughts and get back on track. "I didn't know what to do," I repeat. "I was worried about you, about me. About us. And then... then I figured out that I was pregnant." A single tear falls down my cheek, and his gaze traces it. I see a flicker of anger flaring, but I know it's not meant for me. He leans forward, but before he has a chance, I wipe the tear away. Impatient. Frustrated with myself.

Fuck this is hard. Harder than I thought. Whenever I imagined this scene in my head, it sure as hell hadn't been in a penthouse, sitting across from him like civilized people. No, it had always been accompanied by a lot of shouting, and it always ended with Massimo on his knees, begging my forgiveness. Now I want to scoff. As if. Hell would freeze over before Massimo Manetti would be on his knees.

He sends me an imperceptible nod. *We've got all the time in the world. Take your time.*

"I didn't know what to do. So I went to my mom. I thought... I thought..." I didn't know what I thought. Maybe that, for once, she would wake from her Xanax and

Valium induced fugue and help me? "Mom went straight to Dad, and well... I've already told you the choice he gave me."

I stare defiantly at Massimo, whose jaw locks. "So you married Carter?" he states, this time it's not laced with accusation.

I nod, "Yes, for my son. I already loved him..."

My hands fly to my stomach, where he lived for nine wonderful months. Even though it was scary, heartbreaking, and painful, it was the best time of my life. I loved the baby inside me with all my heart. How could I not? What Massimo and I had shared... it was the world. It was everything. No matter the reason he left me, I carried our love long after the answers disappeared. I swallow hard, fighting the pull of the past, trying not to get dragged back into the emotional quagmire I barely survived ten years ago.

"Days before the wedding," I manage, my voice already fraying at the edges, "I finally worked up the courage to go to your uncle's mansion."

My hands are shaking now. I curl them together in my lap as if to physically hold myself in place. "It was the only place I could think of to go find you. The last door that might still open. I didn't care about consequences anymore. I didn't care who saw me or what it would cost. I just... I had to know why. Why you left..." My throat tightens, "...me." I wipe at my eyes, but the tears keep coming, stubborn and relentless.

God, this hurts more than I thought it would. Because walking up to those gates, I'd still had hope. Stupid, humiliating hope. I laugh weakly; the sound is jagged. "I told myself there had to be a reason. A reasonable one. That maybe you'd been sent away. Europe. Some emergency. Anything." My chest aches as I breathe. "I was willing to believe *anything.* I was ready to forgive *everything.*" Another tear slips free, and I don't bother stopping it.

"If only I'd known you still wanted me," I whisper. "If there'd been even the smallest chance you were coming back, then maybe I wouldn't have had to go through with it." My voice cracks completely now. "Maybe I wouldn't have had to marry a man I didn't love. Maybe I wouldn't have had to stand there and pretend my heart wasn't already buried."

I press my hand to my stomach, muscle memory from a lifetime ago.

"I wasn't asking for forever," I finish quietly. "I was just begging not to be alone."

All the defiance I've been clinging to—every scrap of pride, every hard-earned layer of control—breaks at once. Not cracks. Breaks. Like a dam giving way under too much water, too many years. Suddenly I'm there again. Eighteen. Pregnant. Terrified. Standing on the edge of a life I never chose, about to marry a man I hate because there is no one left to save me from it. The memory hits so hard my knees start to shake. I lose it. My shoulders heave, violently and uncontrollably, like my body has finally decided it's done pretending. The stupid croissant slips from my fingers and hits the floor, forgotten, meaningless. I don't even notice.

Massimo is there instantly. One moment I'm breaking alone, the next he's on his knees in front of me, arms wrapping around me like he's been waiting ten years for this exact second. Strong arms. Solid. Real. Arms I needed so badly back then, it still hurts to remember. For one fragile, treacherous moment, I let myself pretend those ten years never happened. I lean into him, collapse against his chest, and everything I've held inside pours out. I cry the ugly kind of cry, the kind that wrecks your dignity, that comes with deep, shuddering sobs and hiccupped breaths you can't catch. I sound broken because I *am* broken. I clutch at him like he's the only thing left standing in a hurricane, like if I let go, the world will swallow me whole. And he holds me. He doesn't rush me. He doesn't shush me, or tell me to breathe, or try to fix it. He just holds me, tight and unyielding, like he's anchoring me to the ground while everything else falls apart. For the first time in ten years, I'm not alone in the wreckage. And that almost hurts the most.

Suddenly—

"Let go!"

Tiny fists slam into Massimo's back, fast and furious, the blows more indignant than painful but full of absolute conviction.

"Let go of my mummy," Amauri shouts, his voice shaking with fury and fear. "Don't hurt her!"

The world snaps back into focus. Massimo freezes. Not slowly. Not cautiously. Instantly. Like a man who has just realized he's holding something sacred the wrong way. I feel it before I see it, the way his arms loosen, not dropping me, never that, but easing as if he's afraid any sudden movement might shatter something irreparable. I suck in a breath, my sobs stuttering to a stop as I turn. Amauri is standing behind him, chest heaving, fists clenched so tight his knuckles are white. His eyes are blazing. Protective. Wild. Too old for his small face. My heart breaks all over again.

"Amauri," I whisper, reaching for him.

Massimo moves at the same time, but he stops himself, catches the instinct mid-motion, and sinks back onto his heels instead. He turns slowly, deliberately, bringing himself down to Amauri's level like a man approaching a skittish animal.

"I'm not hurting her," he explains in a rough voice that has been stripped of command. "I would never hurt her."

Amauri doesn't lower his fists. He steps in front of me instead. Full shield.

"I heard her crying," he says, chin lifting defiantly. "You made her cry."

That lands harder than any accusation in the world. Massimo swallows. I see it, see something old and dangerous and helpless flicker across his face.

"I didn't mean to," He admits quietly.

I pull Amauri into my arms, pressing my face into his hair, breathing him in until my hands stop shaking.

"It's okay," I murmur. "I promise. I'm okay. Massimo didn't make me cry."

He doesn't fully relax, but he leans into me, one arm still angled outward like he's ready to fight if he has to. Massimo watches us, really watches this time. Not as a don. Not as a man reclaiming territory. But as a father. I watch the realization hit him with brutal clarity: his son learned how to protect *me* long before anyone taught him how to protect himself.

"I'm sorry," Massimo says again, and this time the words are for both of us. Amauri studies him, weighing something far too heavy for a child to carry.

"It wasn't Massimo's fault," I kiss Amauri's forehead. "Mummy just remembered something painful from the past, and Massimo tried to make me feel better."

Amauri's eyes search my face with an intensity that makes my breath hitch. It's uncanny. The focus. The weighing of truth. It's the same look Massimo wore earlier, measuring, deciding, unafraid of what he might find. Goosebumps rise along my arms.

"Is that true?" Amauri asks quietly, looking from me to Massimo.

The room holds its breath. Massimo doesn't hesitate. He crosses himself, solemnly, old-world, deadly sincere. "The whole truth," he says. "I swear."

Amauri studies us both again, deep in thought, like a tiny judge presiding over something far bigger than pancakes and cartoons. For a long second, I don't dare move. Then he nods. Satisfied.

He lets go of me, and the tension drains out of his small body as quickly as it came. His gaze shifts past us; his eyes light up. "Are those pancakes?"

And just like that, the world exhales.

MASSIMO

My head is still reeling. It's not what she said; I already knew the facts. I'd reconstructed them piece by piece, stripped them down to bones, timelines, and lies. That part I could handle.

What I wasn't prepared for was *how much she'd carried alone*. Ten years of grief that she never let show. Ten years of believing I betrayed her. That I *left*. Walked away. Chosen absence over her and the child growing inside her.

The thought hits like a blunt instrument. She thought I fucking abandoned her. The realization sits in my chest, heavy and corrosive. Not guilt, something worse. Loss compounded by misunderstanding. A wound that never had the chance to scab because it was never seen.

And then there's Amauri.

The kid just clawed his way back from hell. Kidnapped. Imprisoned. Watched men with guns decide his fate. And what does he do the moment he hears his mother cry? He shields her. No hesitation. No calculation. Just instinct. That bond between them is ferocious. Built in the dark. Forged by fear and love and survival. It's something to be envious of. Something that sparks jealousy, low and sharp in my gut. And something I admire the hell out of.

I force my breathing to steady. Clamp down on everything in me that wants to pull Jenna back into my arms, that wants to rage at the world for taking ten years I'll never get back.

For him, I stay calm.

"Yes," I say evenly, keeping my voice light, grounding. "Those are pancakes. And waffles."

Amauri's eyes go so wide I think they might actually fall out of his head.

"Both?" he asks, reverently.

I nod once. "Do you like those?"

His head bobs up and down so eagerly, and his eyes are so huge, it does something to my chest that I refuse to name.

"Go ahead," I tell him. "Have some."

That's all the permission he needs.

He attacks the food like a starving animal, climbing halfway onto the chair, shoveling pancakes onto his plate with zero concern for dignity or syrup distribution. It's chaotic. It's loud. It's... life.

I look up and catch Jenna watching him. She's wiping at her eyes, smiling through tears, pride radiating off her like heat. Fierce. Exhausted. Unbroken. A deep, primal part inside me *recognizes her*. This is still her. After ten years. After the betrayal she believed to be real. After fear, and sacrifice, and surviving men who should never have touched her life, she's still the same woman who loves without half-measures. I feel it. Not a snap. Not a return. A *click*. Like something long dislocated sliding back into place. And instead of fighting it—instead of resenting the vulnerability—I let it settle.

There are still bills to call due. Kingsley, for one. For what he did to his daughter. For the choices he forced on her when she was barely more than a girl. That debt hasn't even begun to accrue interest yet.

Mexico still waits. Enemies still breathe. Blood will still be spilled. But for this moment—this fragile, impossible morning—I watch my son eat pancakes like the world never tried to break him. I stand in my kitchen with the woman who should have been here all along. Whatever was taken from us is being reclaimed. Slowly. Brutally. And this time I'm not letting it go.

Breakfast settles into something almost normal. Plates clink softly. Syrup drips. Amauri's chewing is enthusiastic, messy, and unapologetic. The chaos of earlier fades into a hum, replaced by coffee, sunlight, and the sound of a child eating like he hasn't eaten in days.

In between bites, Amauri looks up at me. Not casually. Carefully.

"The bad men are gone?" he asks, mouth still half full, voice low like he's testing whether saying it out loud will make them come back.

The question lands square in my chest.

"Yes," I assure him. "They're gone." Praying he won't ask for details.

He watches my face the way Jenna did earlier, searching for cracks, for doubt. I keep my expression steady. Certain. He nods once, absorbing that, then goes back to his plate. Two bites later, he adds, quieter, "The helicopter was really cool."

Jenna stills beside him.

"But," Amauri continues, shoulders hunching just a little, "it was also... really, really scary."

My jaw tightens. I say nothing. I let him finish.

"I always wanted to fly in a helicopter," he continues, poking his pancake thoughtfully. "Just... not like that."

Something sharp twists under my ribs.

"Maybe," I try carefully, "I can take you one day. Just for fun." I pause, watching his eyes lift. "I have one. If you'd like."

His fork freezes midair.

"Really? You have a helicopter?" his voice jumps an octave.

Jenna shoots me a look. Sharp. Warning. "Massimo—"

"What?" I pretend innocence, lifting my hands. I can't help it. I wink at her.

"He's cool, Mummy."

She snorts despite herself.

"And," Amauri adds solemnly, "he has soldiers working for him."

That one... that one hits different. I don't correct him. I don't glorify it either. I just nod once, slow and careful, like I understand the weight behind the words. I feel all the empty places inside me—the quiet spaces I carved out just to survive—start to fill. Not with rage. Not with vengeance. With something I spent ten years hating because it reminded me of what I'd lost.

Love.

Unavoidable. Relentless. Territorial in ways no empire ever was or will be.

I watch my son drown pancakes in syrup like it's his birthright. I watch Jenna watch him, pride and worry braided tight in her expression. And I let it happen. Because for the first time in a decade, the space in my chest doesn't feel hollow. It feels claimed.

After breakfast, Jenna nudges Amauri gently from his chair.

"Go take a shower," she tells him, brushing syrup from his chin. "And brush your teeth. Properly. I'll be right here."

He groans like this is the worst injustice of his life, but he slides off the chair and pads down the hall anyway, already calling back, "I *did* brush them, last night!"

She waits until the bathroom door closes before she turns back to me. And then everything spills.

"I need to get back to my house," the words tumble over each other. "I—I need to get it cleaned up. I need my phone. I need to call his school..." Her eyes widen as panic catches up to her. "Oh my God. His school. I haven't even called them. They'll think Amauri is tardy and—"

I step forward and place my hands on her shoulders, firm, anchoring. "Breathe, Jenna. Breathe."

She looks up at me, and those eyes—those damn eyes—hit me straight in the chest. I could get lost in them. I did, once. Lost everything.

"Jenna," I continue, and my insides tighten, "I swear to you—had I known. About Amauri. Had I been able to... get up... I would have taken care of you." Her breath stutters. "Both of you, I would have never let you go." Her eyes well instantly, and I feel her shoulders begin to shake beneath my hands. "You've always been the love of my life." There's no point hiding it now. "Always."

She breaks then, just a little, and I pull her closer without thinking, forehead resting against hers. "You're not alone anymore. Not ever again." I pull back just enough to look at her, to make sure she hears every word. "I'll send people to your house. We'll get your things. Amauri's things. I'll have it cleaned properly. Your phone will be back in your hands today." I don't pause. I don't give her time to spiral again. "I'll call the school. I'll tell them Amauri is sick. I'll find a therapist for him, one who understands trauma, not someone who'll look at him like a case file."

Her lips part, and she draws a stuttered breath.

"I will right the wrongs," I say firmly. "The ones done to you. To me. To us." Then I add, just as firmly, "But I'm telling you right now, you're not going back to that house."

Her eyes sharpen. She opens her mouth to argue. I lift a finger and rest it gently against her lips. "You and Amauri will stay here. Where you belong. With me."

She stares at me, torn between instinct, fear, and a lifetime of surviving on her own.

"I love you," I breathe softly. "I always have. And I always will." Her breath trembles. "Let me take care of you."

The words are not a command, they're a promise.

Leaving them in my penthouse is the hardest thing I've ever done. Harder than pulling a trigger. Harder than burying men who once stood at my side. Harder than waking up broken and learning the world kept spinning without me.

Amauri's laugh still echoes in my head as I step into the elevator. Jenna's eyes—soft, terrified, hopeful—burn behind my ribs. Every instinct I have screams to stay. To plant myself between them and the world and never move again. But there are things that need to be done. The doors close, and the descent begins. I pull my phone out before the box starts moving.

First call: the school. Polite. Vague. Amauri is sick. Family emergency. Everything handled. They say they saw it on the news, and they ask if Amauri and Jenna are okay. That one touches me the most. They care about her, too. Enough to ask about her.

Second: a therapist. Not just anyone. Someone vetted. Trauma-informed. Discreet. Someone who understands that some children grow up too fast because the world doesn't give them a choice.

Third: clean up Jenna's house. Everything removed that shouldn't be there. Everything restored that can be. Packing her things and Amauri's. No traces. No reminders. Her phone recovered, charged, and delivered.

Promises kept.

By the time I reach the lobby, my voice is steel again. The SUV door opens. I slide inside, the familiar cocoon seals shut, and just like that, emotion gets locked away. What's left is precision. I still have an empire to run. It matters now more than ever; it has to stand. Because it is the wall that keeps safe what matters most to me in this world.

No.

Not most.

The *only* things that matter.

Jenna and Amauri.

I make the next call. Alessio. "What do we know about Joaquín?" I greet him.

"I'll know more in five minutes, something's going down. I'll let you know, Boss."

"Stay sharp. I want eyes on him at all times." I end the call and dial Enzo.

"I need you to smooth things over with the New York family," I tell him without preamble. "They're about to lose one of their biggest assets."

Enzo doesn't ask which one. He already knows.

"Kingsley," he guesses quietly.

"Yes."

"Find out what it costs," I continue. "Pay it."

A pause. Then, "Yes, boss."

The phone buzzes again before I can pocket it.

Alessio. "We got the bastard."

I lean back, eyes on the tinted window as the city slides past.

"He'll be in L.A. tomorrow. I'll have a welcoming committee ready."

A slow smile curls in my chest. Cold. Precise. "I'll be there." I glance once at the reflection of my own eyes in the glass, dark, focused, unyielding. "We'll lay a trap for him."

The SUV pulls into traffic, carrying me back into the world I rule. And this time, I'm not doing it for power. I'm doing it for family.

JENNA

THE DAY SETTLES INTO SOMETHING ALMOST GENTLE. AMAURI sprawls on the floor in front of the TV, half-watching a cartoon while we work on a puzzle that's supposed to be for ten-year-olds but is clearly designed by a sadist. We argue about edge pieces. He cheats. I let him. At some point, we abandon the puzzle entirely and switch to a board game, then back again when he decides the rules are unfair. It feels... normal. Too normal, considering everything.

Then things start arriving. First, my phone. I stare at it for a long second before I touch it, like it might bite. I walk into the room to find it fully charged, sitting neatly on the counter, as if it never disappeared in the first place. Massimo doesn't do half-measures. I should've known.

Amauri looks up. "Is that your phone?"

"Yes," My throat is so tight it comes out as a croak. "Yes, it is."

Not even ten minutes later, there's another delivery.

"Amauri," I say slowly, blinking. "Is that—"

"My hamster!" he yells, already off the couch and sprinting toward the carrier like Christmas came early. "Mummy, you forgot him!"

"I did not forget him," I lie weakly.

The hamster—miraculously alive, fluffy, and indignant—blinks up at us, no worse for wear. We clean his cage together, fresh bedding, food, and water. Amauri narrates every step like he's hosting a documentary. We let the hamster run around in a plastic ball, and he bumps into furniture with reckless confidence. My laugh sounds rusty. During a quiet moment, I step aside and finally unlock my phone. It explodes. Missed calls. Voicemails. Text messages stacked so deep that I have to scroll for several seconds to hit the bottom. Friends. Acquaintances. Numbers I barely recognize.

My father.

Marianne.

Over and over.

My pulse picks up.

Before I can spiral, I call the school.

They answer immediately, voices gentle, sympathetic. They already know. Massimo called. Of course he did. They saw it on the news anyway—*how terrible, how frightening, how are you holding up, what can we do to help.*

"Take all the time you need," they tell me. "Just let us know when Amauri is ready to come back."

I thank them and hang up with shaking hands.

The TV hums softly in the background. Amauri is lying on his stomach now, chin propped in his hands, talking to the hamster like they're old friends. I watch him for a long moment. And then—inevitably—my thoughts drift back to Massimo. To his kitchen. To the way he stood behind me, solid and certain.

To the promises he made like they were already facts.

My life feels like it's tilting, rearranging itself without asking permission. Ten years of survival-mode instincts are struggling to catch up to the reality of having someone else take the weight.

I look back down at my phone. More messages light up the screen. My father's name sits there, heavy and unavoidable. So does Marianne's.

I don't answer any of them.

Not yet.

For now, I sit back down on the floor with my son, help him find a missing puzzle piece, and let the world wait a little longer.

Inevitably, the phone rings. Marianne.

I stare at the screen. Sooner or later, I'll have to talk to someone, and I'd rather it be Marianne than my father. I answer.

"Jenna—oh my God." Her voice spills out fast, breathless, practiced panic. "I was so worried. That shooting—are you okay? Are you hurt?"

I close my eyes. She didn't waste a second hauling ass out of there.

"I'm fine," I lie flatly.

"Oh, thank God," she exhales. "I've been sick with worry. Truly. Have you... have you considered what I said?"

I sit up straighter. Amauri looks over at me, curious, then goes back to lining up puzzle pieces by color.

"What you said about what?" I ask.

"I can help you," Marianne presses. "I can help you get Amauri out. We can make arrangements. Quiet ones."

My stomach drops. They don't know. They don't know Amauri is free. They don't know about Carter either, and —*oh shit*. Carter. I haven't thought about him. Not really. Not since the world cracked open and rearranged itself. He's the only father Amauri has ever known. And technically—the thought skids.

I cheated on him.

Except... it doesn't feel like cheating. Not when the marriage was arranged like a transaction. Not when my heart never belonged to him. No matter how hard I dig, I can't find a shred of guilt.

Only inevitability.

"Hello?" Marianne's voice sharpens. "Jenna? Are you still there?"

"Yes," I say slowly. "I'm here."

"Good," she sounds, relieved. Too relieved. "Because we need to talk. Your father is worried. He wants you home."

There it is.

"Why?" I ask. "Why does he want me back so badly?" A pause. I watch dust motes drift through the sunlight. Amauri hums under his breath, pushing the hamster ball with his foot. "Did my father set this up?" I continue, my voice calm, my pulse anything but. "To get me to come home? Was Sean there to take me if I refused?"

"What?" Marianne laughs nervously. "No—no, you've got this all wrong. I just want to help you. We all do."

Her voice stutters. Just a fraction. Too much.

"Who is that, Mummy?" Amauri asks suddenly, looking up at me.

"Marianne," I respond, keeping my eyes on the window.

He wrinkles his nose immediately. "I don't like her."

Marianne's voice spikes in my ear. "Is that—?"

"She and Sean are always sneaking about," Amauri continues, quieter this time. He's crouched on the floor now, guiding the hamster ball carefully away from the couch leg. My stomach tightens.

Marianne's voice sharpens in my ear. "Who is that, Jenna?"

I ignore her. My entire focus is on my son. Amauri rolls a different ball towards me. "People whisper when they don't want kids to hear," he frowns at the puzzle piece in his hand. He tries to force it where it doesn't belong, gets annoyed, and tries again. "That's what they were doing."

My chest tightens.

"Who, sweetheart?" I ask, even though I already know.

"Sean and Marianne," he says immediately.

The room goes very still.

"They were arguing," Amauri continues, clearly offended on someone else's behalf. "Sean was mad. He said Grandpa had to pay up now."

My breath stutters.

"Pay for what?" I ask quietly.

Amauri shrugs, little shoulders lifting. "I don't know. But Marianne got really angry. She said, *No. Absolutely not. You've already been compensated.*" He pauses at the word and scowls, like he's trying to figure out what it means. "She was mean about it."

Something cold and precise slides into place inside my chest. *Compensated.* Something nags at the back of my mind. The ledger entry to *Northstar Advisory Group,* the company that belonged to Sean before he came to work for my father. The thirty grand the day before Massimo vanished.

Amauri looks up at me, earnest, troubled. "I didn't like it. It sounded like Sean was trying to take money from Grandpa. That's not fair."

Sunlight pours through the windows, bright and oblivious to the dark storm raging inside me. Amauri goes back to the puzzle, already done with the subject, justice satisfied in his own small way.

"Jenna?" Marianne presses. "Who is that child?"

My phone vibrates in my hand. Another incoming call. Aunt Celeste. I don't pick it up.

I close my eyes.

"That's Amauri," I fill Marianne in, just to hear her reaction.

The silence on the other end is instant. Then—too carefully— "...Amauri?"

"Yes."

A sharp inhale. Not concern. Shock.

"Oh my God," Marianne whispers. "He's... he's back?" Then right after, without a breath in between, she asks, "You have him with you? Right now?"

Amauri looks up at me, sensing the shift. I smile at him reflexively, even as my pulse roars in my ears.

"Yes," I also don't pause, and I'm unable to keep some smugness out of my tone, "I do."

Another pause. I can practically hear Marianne thinking. Recalculating.

"And Carter?" she asks carefully. "Where is Carter, Jenna?"

I don't answer. I don't know how. I don't know what to say. That I haven't given the asshole a second of thought since he and Amauri were taken? The sunlight is too bright. Amauri hums to himself, lining puzzle pieces into neat rows. Another text flashes across my screen—my father this time. Then Kelly, the mother of a boy Amauri sometimes plays with. Then a number I don't recognize.

Marianne's voice drops, tight and urgent. "Jenna, listen to me. You need to be very careful right now."

I almost laugh.

"Why?" I ask softly. "Careful of what?"

"Careful of Massimo. He's dangerous. I don't like the way you went to him, I—"

"Marianne?" I interrupt.

"Yes?"

"I don't give a shit what you like or don't like. Tell my father that Massimo freed Amauri and Carter and that I know the truth."

"The truth? What? What do you know?" She sounds almost panicked now.

"I'll call you back," I tell her.

"Jenna—don't do anything rash," Marianne pleads in a high-pitched voice. "Please. We just want to help you."

I end the call.

The quiet that follows is heavy, electric.

Amauri looks up at me, eyes wide. "Is she mad?"

"Probably," There is no reason to lie to him about this. I pull him close, my heart pounding with thoughts I don't want to acknowledge just yet, with the things I said and meant.

"Amauri," my mind is wandering to places I need to explore. "Can you play by yourself for a little while?"

He looks up from the puzzle, suspicious. "Why?"

"Mummy has to work for a few minutes," I explain. "And Hammie probably needs a nap."

The hamster squeaks indignantly as if on cue. Amauri considers this, then nods with exaggerated seriousness. "Okay. But not too long."

"Not too long," I promise.

We put Hammie back in his cage together, fresh bedding smoothed down, water bottle checked twice. Amauri gives him a sunflower seed as a peace offering, then drags his toys back to the carpet and settles in front of the TV.

Only when I'm sure he's absorbed do I open Massimo's laptop. My hands are steady. My heart is not. I pull up the old ledger entry, the one I've never been able to explain away, no matter how hard I tried. It sits there, neat and bureaucratic, the kind of line item designed not to invite scrutiny.

Northstar Advisory Group.

I copy the name and start digging again.

At first, it's nothing. A clean website. Vague language. Corporate buzzwords. Strategy. Risk mitigation. Advisory services. Then the cracks appear. A lawsuit quietly settled and scrubbed. A former *consultant* charged with obstruction. Shell companies that dissolve and reappear under new names. Security contracts that don't quite add up. My pulse picks up. I dig deeper. And then I see it.

Kingsley.

Not loud. Not obvious. Just... present. Pulling strings. A charge dropped here. An investigation redirected there. A judge who suddenly recused himself. A problem that vanished overnight.

Northstar didn't survive on its own.

My father kept them afloat.

Worse, he pulled them out of deep trouble. The kind that would've buried a smaller man. The kind that requires influence, not money. I sit back slowly, the room suddenly too quiet. I don't know exactly what this means yet. Not fully. But I know enough.

I close the laptop just as Amauri laughs at something on the TV, bright and unbothered. My hands start to shake. Because whatever this is, it's bigger than me. And there is only one person who understands this world well enough to tell me what I'm looking at.

I don't call him—yes, I saw his name and number programmed into my phone, right on top. Every instinct I have wants to, but I don't. He's at *work*. Whatever that means in Massimo's world. I keep myself busy instead. Too busy. We make lunch out of snacks. We watch half a movie and abandon it for a game. I help Amauri with homework that he insists on doing even though no one asked him to.

The sun dips low. The city lights come on. Then the door opens.

"Hey," Massimo calls easily, like this is any other evening. "I'm back. Are you guys hungry? We can order something from the kitchen—or go out."

Amauri doesn't even answer. He launches himself at Massimo with the kind of force only a ten-year-old can manage, arms wrapping around his waist like he's afraid he might disappear again.

"I got Hammie back!" he announces, breathless. "Do you want to see him? Have you seen my dad? Is he okay?"

The questions tumble out all at once. Massimo stills, just for a fraction of a second. His eyes meet mine over Amauri's head. *We need to talk about that.*

"Your... dad is okay," Massimo chooses his words carefully, one hand coming up to steady Amauri, the other resting at his back. "He's recovering."

Amauri nods, satisfied enough for now. "Good." Then —already moving on—"What can we eat? Mom and I had chips and cookies and pretzels."

"Whatever you pick," Massimo sends an apologetic smile at me.

That seems to delight him. Amauri grabs Massimo's hand and drags him toward the guest bedroom without another word. "Come on, I want to show you Hammie."

I follow, quietly. Amauri launches into a full demonstration, hamster ball, cage setup, food, and toys. "Look," he says proudly. "Isn't he cute? He can stuff his mouth like this—" He pantomimes dramatically, cheeks puffed out.

Massimo smiles. Really smiles. It looks strange on him. Like a muscle he hasn't used in a while.

"Amauri," I interrupt gently, catching his eye. "Can you give Massimo a minute? He's probably going to want to take a shower."

He considers this, glancing at Massimo, then at me. "Sure. Yeah." He brightens. "But don't forget about Hammie."

"I won't," Massimo promises.

For a heartbeat or two, an awkward silence ensues, then Massimo excuses himself to take a shower. I sigh in relief that he caught my cue. I give him a minute, then make an excuse to Amauri and follow. This is the best way to talk alone for a few minutes.

When I step into Massimo's suite, he isn't there. But I can hear the shower. Steam curls into the bedroom, warm and faintly scented, and before I can stop myself—before common sense catches up—I follow the sound.

Really? I think. *Really?* He must not have understood the cue that I wanted to talk. The shower was just a ruse. I push the bathroom door open.

And freeze.

"Oh my God—you're *naked*," I blurt, heat rushes straight to my face. Massimo whirls, startled, his eyes flash wide for half a second before instinct kicks in. "Shit—" He reaches for a towel, grabbing it off the rack and wrapping it around his waist in one sharp movement. "Didn't you—Jenna, get out."

But it's too late. I saw.

Not him—*him*—but what his body carries.

Scars.

So many of them.

Long ones. Jagged ones. Pale seams cut across muscle and skin like a map of violence. His shoulder. His ribs. His side. Marks that don't fade because they were never meant to.

"Massimo," I breathe, the word slips out without permission.

His jaw locks. "Get out," he hisses, turning slightly, angling his body away from me like he can undo what I've already seen. Giving me a view of more scars on his side. I take a step closer.

"Was that..." My voice wavers. "Was that because of the accident?"

He reaches for the towel, pulling it tighter, trying to cover what can't be hidden. "I don't need your pity," he snaps. "Get. Out."

"What happened?" I ask softly. "What did they do to you?"

That stops him. Not because he wants it to, but because the question lands somewhere deeper than anger. He exhales sharply, hands braced on the counter now, shoulders rigid.

"You weren't supposed to see this," he mutters.

I don't touch him. I don't crowd him. I just stand there, heart in my hands, staring at the evidence of everything he never told me.

"I thought you left," I say quietly. "And all that time you were—"

"Stop," he cuts in, voice rough. "I survived. That's all you need to know."

But his reflection in the mirror tells a different story. This isn't about survival. It's about what it cost him. Finally, I understand that the man who walked back into my life didn't just lose ten years. He paid for them in flesh and blood.

"I'm not here to pity you," I assure him gently. "I just... didn't know."

He finally looks at me. For a split second, the anger fractures.

Then he turns away.

"Get out, Jenna," he says again, quieter now. "Please."

I back out slowly, closing the door behind me with shaking hands. But the image stays with me. So does the knowledge that whatever we're rebuilding now stands on scars, not ashes.

MASSIMO

FUCK. SHE *TOLD* ME TO TAKE A SHOWER. THE REALIZATION hits as I brace my hands on the sink and lean my forehead against the mirror; the steam is starting to fog the glass, almost as if it's trying to hide me from myself.

Why did she follow?

No—wrong question.

Why did I think she *wouldn't*?

Nobody has seen me like that in years. Nobody. I made sure of it. For years, every woman I fucked, I fucked from behind—my control, my rules. In the dark. No questions. No looks, greedy or, even worse, pitying. I didn't allow intimacy because intimacy invites curiosity, and curiosity leads to scars, and scars lead to explanations I refuse to give.

It was fine. It worked.

I didn't need more.

But Jenna—

Shit.

It's been inevitable since the second she walked back into my life, hasn't it? Bound to happen the moment she stopped looking at me like a monster and started looking at me like a man she once loved. Until she saw them.

The look on her face when I snapped at her.

Not fear.

Hurt.

That same fucking hurt I put there ten years ago without knowing it.

"Fuck," I breathe, already moving.

I adjust the towel around my waist and stride out of the bathroom without thinking; the water is still running. "Jenna."

She's sitting on my bed. Still. Straight-backed. Like she's been waiting for me. Like she knew I'd come after her. That sight hits harder than any bullet ever has.

"You shouldn't have seen that," my voice is rough, uselessly defensive.

She looks up at me slowly. No tears now. Just that steady, devastating calm.

"I didn't follow you to hurt you," she explains quietly. "I followed because I needed to talk to you. And I thought... I thought you understood."

"Understood what?" I ask, genuinely thrown. "You told me to take a shower."

She makes a small sound, somewhere between a scoff and a laugh. "The cue," she says. "I needed to talk to you alone. *Go take a shower.*"

I rake a hand through my still-dry hair, irritation mixing with something dangerously close to amusement. "I'm sorry," I apologize flatly. "I don't think I speak *parent* just yet."

That gets me a smile. Not polite. Not cautious. Real.

"You will," she promises simply.

Two words. That's all. They hit me harder than the car that ran me over. Something in my chest jumps, sharp, uninvited. Hope is a dangerous thing in my world. I learned that young. I learned it with blood. But standing there, half-dressed, stripped down in ways I never allow, I feel it anyway. It's not fear or anger. It's something staking a claim.

I don't answer her right away. I just look at her, really look at her, and suddenly I get it: This woman isn't asking permission. She's stating a future.

I take a step closer, then another, stopping just short of her. My hands curl into fists at my sides, and my knuckles are white from the strain. I feel stripped bare in a way no nakedness ever accomplished.

"I don't want you to see me like that," I admit finally, the truth rips itself out of me before I can stop it. "Broken. Marked. Like something that survived instead of something that lived."

She stands. Slow. Careful. Like she's approaching a wounded animal that might bite.

"You think the sight of your scars will scare me?" she asks softly. "You think I don't understand what survival costs?" That lands. Hard. "I spent ten years thinking you left me," she continues. "Thinking I wasn't enough to make you stay. And now I find out you were paying to stay alive, piece by piece."

My throat tightens.

"I told you to get out," I remind her hoarsely.

"I know."

"And you didn't."

She shakes her head once. "No. I didn't."

I close my eyes for a second, clenching my jaw, the weight of it all crashes down at once, the car, the lies, the years, the way she still stands here instead of running. When I open them again, she's close enough that I can feel her warmth.

"I'm not ashamed of what they did to me," I reveal slowly. "I'm angry that you saw it before I was ready."

She nods. "Fair."

I swallow. "But don't ever mistake my scars for weakness."

Her gaze lifts, fierce now. Unafraid. "Like there is a chance in hell for that with you."

Something inside me gives. Not breaks. *Gives.*

I reach out—not to pull her close, not to claim—but to rest my hand against her cheek, just once, grounding myself in the fact that she's real. That she's here. That she didn't look away.

"I don't let anyone see me," I disclose quietly.

"I know."

"I'm not good at this," I add. "At being... seen."

She leans into my touch, just a fraction. "Then we'll be bad at it together."

Dark. Dangerous. Uncertain.

Underneath the soft touches, the words, the glances, something vast and dangerous simmers, an undercurrent of desire powerful enough to redraw the world if we ever stop holding it back. It's like the very air around us is filled with electricity. Heavy, loaded.

"Mummy? Massimo? I'm hungry." Amauri calls

through the closed door from the living room. Reality snaps back into place like a rubber band.

We order food from the kitchen. Plates covered with silver domes arrive, and steam escapes when they're opened. Plates are passed around. The TV comes on, and Amauri insists on *Toy Story*. He wedges himself firmly between us on the couch, as if this is the most natural arrangement in the world, which somehow... it is.

I watch the screen, but I'm only half there. I'm acutely aware of Jenna beside me, the warmth of her thigh, the brush of her arm when she reaches for her drink. Amauri's head eventually tips against my side, heavy, trusting. Jenna's hand smooths over his hair absentmindedly, the gesture automatic and intimate.

I've commanded rooms full of armed men. This feels harder.

When Amauri finally falls asleep, I don't move right away. I let the moment exist. Let myself memorize the weight of him, the quiet, the fragile peace I don't trust yet but desperately want to. After a little while, I lift him carefully and carry him down the hall. Jenna follows without a word. I lay him in the guest bed, pull the covers up, and tuck him in the way he clearly expects. He sighs softly in his sleep. This—*this*—is how it was always supposed to be. And soon he'll have the best bedroom any little boy could want.

I turn, and Jenna is standing in the doorway, watching us like she's afraid the moment might vanish if she blinks. She takes one step inside. I close the distance in two.

"Oh no," I murmur, low and certain. "We're not done."

Her breath catches. She backs up on instinct, not fear, something else. Something that recognizes where this is going and doesn't entirely want to stop it. I keep moving forward, she keeps moving back, that way I guide her gently, inexorably, out of the room. Not rough. Not rushed. Just inevitable. Into my bedroom.

"Massimo," she protests softly as we go, and my name frays at the edges. I shake my head once, never breaking eye contact. Not tonight. Tonight isn't about explanations or apologies or the past. Tonight is about gravity finally being allowed to work.

She lets me close the door behind her and guide her to the edge of the bed. Her eyes catch the city glow bleeding through the blinds, the pools of shadow on the navy sheets, the black suit jacket forgotten from earlier when I tossed it to the floor, carelessly, making space for her. She sits, legs close together, hands braced behind her on the mattress, her face lifted like she's about to take a punch and has decided to suffer it beautifully. That's the bravest part of her, always choosing pain over cowardice, always daring me to do my worst.

I kneel in front of her, bring my face level with her knees, and part them with slow, deliberate pressure. She lets me, doesn't flinch. I palm her calves, fingertips skating the tendon and soft skin, push her skirt up inch by inch until the backs of my hands are flush with the heat of her thighs. She watches every move, wild-eyed and silent, mouth parted.

"Don't look away," I tell her, and she doesn't. Not once. Not even when I pull her in closer, and the tips of my fingers find bare skin beneath the lace, so wet it makes me want to destroy her.

She tries to say something, but I silence it with two fingers on her lips. Then I thumb away a smudge of dessert left from dinner. She licks the pad of my thumb, and I almost lose it right there.

I take her blouse apart, button by button, slow enough to be cruel. The fabric parts like water around her, exposing collarbone and shoulder, the tattoo beneath her breast—black and red ink, *Forever in Pain. Forever in Death.* When we got them, we had no idea what pain was. I run my tongue under the arch of it, trace the line with the flat, wet from my mouth, and she shudders.

"You kept it," I observe, reverently, but she refuses to give up the upper hand even now.

"You kept yours," she observes, and its accusation and confession at once, a dare to take everything she's been guarding for the last decade.

I don't bother with slow, not now. I slide both hands down her hips, taking her skirt with them, yanking it clean over her knees and off her legs in a single, practiced motion. Her panties go next, black, delicate, thin enough to tear, but I make a point to roll them down inch by inch, my knuckles skimming her skin, letting her feel every moment of surrender. She never takes her eyes off my face, like she's measuring the risk, like she's hoping I'll blink first. I don't. I bring the panties up to my nose, inhale her scent deeply, and close my eyes just for a moment to appreciate the sweetness of her. Memories flood back in. They say they come the strongest with scent, and they aren't wrong. I pocket the panties like I should have done back then. Never again will I take one single moment with her for granted.

She's bared for me now. For a moment, I just look at her. Time hasn't taken from her. It's marked her. Claimed her in ways I wasn't there to witness. My hand slides down her stomach, slow, reverent, until I feel it. The faint ridges beneath my fingertips. She stiffens.

Her hand moves instinctively, like she wants to cover herself, a small, almost defensive motion. "Don't..." she murmurs, her voice barely there. "They're—"

She doesn't finish. She doesn't have to. I know. I still her hand gently, my fingers closing around her wrist.

"No," I order.

My thumb traces the lines again. Not hiding them. Not ignoring them. Honoring them. "They're mine."

Her breath catches. I lower my head, pressing my mouth against her skin, right over the soft, pale marks. Slow. Intentional.

"They're beautiful," I murmur against her. "Every one of them." She lets out a shaky breath. "They're what your body did for me," I continue, in a rougher, emotion-filled voice, because fuck, she got those bearing our son. "For our son."

I kiss another one, softer this time. "They're not something to hide."

Her fingers slide into my hair, hesitant at first, then tightening. I move lower—and then I see it. The scar. Clean. Faint. But there. My hand stills. My gaze lifts to hers. She flinches before I even say a word.

"C-section," she explains wryly, like she needs to get ahead of it. "He... he didn't want to come out."

There's a fragile attempt at humor in her voice. It breaks halfway through. Something tightens in my chest. Hard. Violent. I lower myself without a word, pressing my mouth to the scar. Gentler than I've ever touched anything.

"That must have been terrifying," I observe against her skin.

She nods.

I feel it in the way her body shifts beneath me.

"Yeah," she whispers. "I... I've never wanted you by my side more than in that moment."

The words hit like a blade. Because I wasn't there. Because someone made sure I wasn't there. My hand fists at her hip, not enough to hurt, just enough to ground myself. Rage coils, already finding direction.

"They took that from me," I breathe, controlled. Deadly. "From us." I lift my head, meeting her eyes. "They'll answer for it."

Her breath hitches. I press my forehead to her stomach for a moment, closing my eyes, letting the weight of it settle. When I look up again, there's nothing soft left in me. Only certainty.

"You'll never be alone again," I vow. "Not for a single moment."

My hand slides back over her stomach, over the marks, over the scar. "Anyone who ever tries to take me from you again..." My jaw tightens. "They won't live long enough to regret it."

Her fingers brush my face, softer now, searching.

"I guess..." she whispers, "we both have our scars."

Something in me fractures at that. Not from weakness. From truth. I take her hand, pressing it flat over my chest, over the damage that never fully healed.

"Then we wear them together," I murmur.

And this time, when I kiss her, it isn't just hunger. It's a promise I seal with a kiss before I continue my journey down her body. She doesn't stiffen this time. This time, when her thighs tense, it's not embarrassment, it's anticipation. She's waiting for me to lose control; she wants to see if I'll devour her, worship her, or both. I kneel at the edge of the bed, spreading her legs with both hands, thumbs pressing into the flesh until she shudders. Her hands fist in the sheet. She's breathing shallow, fast, her heartbeat is visible in the hollow of her throat. I want to mark her, claim her, erase every memory of the bastard who put a ring on her finger. But mostly I want her to know the difference, to know what it means to be truly wanted.

I duck down, my lips ghosting over her inner thigh. My tongue leaves a wet line but never quite touches her where she wants it most. I savor the way her hips buck, the way her breathing hitches when I pause just shy of her heat, letting my breath tickle her until she curses me under it. I smile against her skin. I pin her thighs with my elbows, anchoring her open and helpless, and then finally —finally—I taste her.

She's hot and slick and trembling, and the shock of it makes her head thump back against the mattress. I listen for that little sound she makes, the gasp she tries to swallow, the one that always meant she was losing her grip. I go straight for the spot, tongue working slow circles, relentless, patient, keeping her right at the edge. Her hands are in my hair now, her nails are digging, yanking hard enough to make my eyes water. I don't stop.

She says my name once, then again, her voice sounds like it's breaking. Her whole body arcs, either trying to break free or force me closer, I can't tell which. I hold her down, sealing my mouth to velvety skin, my tongue is working harder, faster, finding every old map and every new place that makes her quake. She starts to plead, the words chopped by moans, but I don't let up. I want her wrecked. I want her ruined for anyone else.

She comes apart, finally, a shattering and beautiful thing. Her thighs lock around my head, her hips try to jerk away, but I'm stronger, I hold her there and drink every second of it. She sobs, a real sob, and then she's limp, spent, eyes closed, mouth open. I don't let go. I keep kissing her, softer now, cleaning her up, gentling her until she whimpers from the sensitivity and pushes at my shoulders.

Only then do I rise; my heart is pounding. I shrug out of my shirt and kick off my pants, she gazes at me with that same gentle awe she had ten years ago, as if my scars are something beautiful she wants to memorize. "You've gotten bigger," she whispers.

I grin, slipping off my socks and shoes. "After all those hours in the gym, I sure hope so, sweetheart." I lean down and kiss her collarbone, fingertips grazing the curve of her hip. The tremor under my touch sends a thrill through me.

There's a moment when I'm so hard it hurts, when she's clutching at my back and drawing me down like she'll never let me go again. I press her into the sheets, carefully and possessively all at once, and lower my weight so she feels every inch of me, real, scarred, and hers. The way her thighs tense around me, the way she arches up and guides me, makes the years of violence and loneliness collapse in a blink. I'm inside her before I know it, slow and tight, and the heat of her is making me dizzy. She tastes sweet and salty at her throat, her moaning is ragged, and she's breathing me in like oxygen.

She wraps a leg around my waist, locking us together, and I drive deeper, impossibly slow, savoring the friction and the way her body fits mine. Each thrust is a negotiation, a question she answers with a tightening gasp or a shudder, her hands tangling in my hair, down my flank.

"You're mine," I claim her.

She meets my eyes, and even in the half-light I can see the tears gathering, unfallen, fragile as glass.

"I've always been yours," she cries in a thready voice, and my heart—my whole fucking chest—nearly caves in. I don't dare read into them what I hope they mean. Not now. Not yet. This is our moment.

I want to grind my soul into her bones, fuse our aching pieces together until we're something new. But I hold enough back, enough control, to cradle her head and kiss her cheeks and smooth her hair away as I move. Her walls flutter around me, grip and pulse. Her moans get louder, reckless, and I watch her shatter.

When she comes, it's like a dam breaking. She spasms around me and sobs out my name, nails digging so hard I'm sure I'll wear the marks for days. I last a second longer —just long enough to see her break, to taste the salt of her tears as I press my mouth to her lips—and then I lose myself, emptying into her with a groan that sounds like her name and a curse in the same breath. I collapse and gather her up, my arms a cage, a promise.

She buries her face in my neck, panting, her hair sticking to my lips and jaw. I stroke her back, gently now, tracing the line of her shoulder blades and the rise of her spine, memorizing the shape of her in my arms. We stay like that, the two of us, until our breath slows and the sweat cools on our skin. My heart hammers so loud I'm sure she hears it, and her hand presses there, palm flat, like she needs to confirm I'm real.

We lie tangled, bodies lined up seamlessly, and her pulse matches mine even as it gradually settles. I nuzzle her hair, nip gently at her ear, and she laughs, a real one, breathless and unguarded. She rolls her eyes, but holds me tighter.

"You okay?" I murmur, thumb tracing lazy circles over her hip.

She snorts. "I can't feel my legs. Is that normal?"

I grin into her neck. "You'll get used to it."

She shifts, sliding her thigh over my waist, pinning me. "I'd better not." Her mouth finds mine, hungry, and we kiss again, less desperate but no less intense. When she pulls away, her eyes are open and unafraid.

"Does it hurt?" she asks, brushing her fingers over the old scars on my ribs. "Be honest."

The question is unexpected. "Not as much as it did," I admit, and it's mostly true. My body throbs in a dozen places, but being with her dulls every ache. "You take my mind off the pain."

JENNA

My head rests on his chest, right over his heart. I listen to its slow, steady, settling beat until it finds that familiar rhythm I remember from years ago. Strong. Sure. Alive. The sound wraps around me like something I thought I'd lost forever. It's the same. And it's not. Old and yet new, like a song you loved once and forgot how much until you hear it again and realize it never really left you.

Massimo's arm tightens around me slightly, an unconscious gesture, protective even in rest. His fingers trace idle patterns against my shoulder, like he's reassuring himself I'm still here.

"I used to fall asleep like this," I murmur, my voice barely louder than the hum of the city outside. "Counting your heartbeats. It made everything else quiet."

He exhales softly, his chest rising beneath my cheek. "You always did that," he agrees. "Like you were memorizing me."

"I was," I admit. "In case I needed to remember."

His hand stills for a moment, then resumes, gentler now. "I never forgot you," he reveals, roughness creeps into his voice despite how calm he's trying to sound. "Not once."

I lift my head just enough to look at him. His eyes are half-closed, dark lashes cast shadows, and his face is stripped of armor in a way I've never seen before. Not even back then. He presses his lips to my hair, not rushed, not claiming, just there. Present.

"I don't want to sleep," I whisper. "I'm afraid I'll wake up, and this will feel like a dream."

His arm tightens again, unmistakably solid. "Then don't sleep," he murmurs. "Stay right here. I'm not going anywhere."

The words settle into me, deep and warm. I nestle closer, my body fitting itself against him as if no time has passed. Outside, Vegas glows and pulses, loud and merciless. In here, everything is quiet.

I trace one of his scars with my fingertips, slow and reverent, like I'm reading a language my body understands even if my mind doesn't. The skin there is different, tight, unyielding, earned.

"Do you want to talk about it?" I ask softly.

"No." His breath leaves him in a long sigh, the kind that carries weight. "But you should know."

I still.

"My uncle hired someone," his voice doesn't give away the betrayal he must have felt. "Ran me over with a car. Made it look like an accident."

"Your uncle?" I frown, the word snagging. "Why?"

A muscle in his jaw tightens. "I guess he finally gave in to my cousins' whining about me trying to take over."

"Were you?" I ask carefully. "Trying to take over?"

He lets out a humorless breath. "They were fools. They always were. My uncle knew it. So did I."

Something inside me pauses, listening. He feels it. I know he does, because his chest stills beneath my cheek. "What?"

"I don't know," I lift my head to look at him. The words feel fragile in my mouth. "I don't know if it means anything. Or if it's just... timing."

"Just say it," he nudges. "No more secrets between us ever again, Jenna. Nothing kept back. No matter how small." His hand comes up, steady, anchoring. "Nobody will ever come between us again."

The promise lands heavy. Comforting. Terrifying. My mind flickers, news headlines from years ago, read with shaking hands. The deaths. His uncle. His cousins. The quiet certainty that followed when Massimo took over. The world had called it inevitable. Clean. A succession. I swallow. The question rises anyway, sharp and undeniable. *Did you do that?*

I don't ask it. I'm not sure I'm ready for the way truths change you the moment they're spoken aloud. I'm not sure I'm ready to meet that version of him yet. Or the version of myself who might not flinch from it.

I rest my cheek back on his chest, listening to his heartbeat, steady, unrepentant, alive.

"I read about what happened," I say instead. It's not a question. It's an acknowledgment.

"Yeah, you probably did," he replies.

We lie there, the silence not empty but full—of what we've survived, of what we've done, of what we might still do to protect what's ours. I realize something then, quietly, without judgment: the dark doesn't scare me the way it used to. Not when I recognize its shape in myself, too.

He shifts slightly beneath me, like he feels the hesitation building before I even speak.

"What is it you want to tell me?" he asks quietly.

I draw a breath and lift myself just enough to look at him. His face is calm now, unreadable in that way that has always meant he's bracing for impact.

"I found something," I begin, keeping my voice low, aware there will be no taking back the words I'm about to say, and afraid they might rearrange the entire board. "I'm not sure if it means anything or if I am forcing connections that aren't there." He doesn't interrupt. "There was a ledger entry," I continue. "From years ago. Before Amauri. Before everything fell apart." My throat tightens.

His body goes still.

"A payment," I continue. "From my father. To Sean's company. Northstar Advisory Group." His eyes don't leave mine now. "The date," I whisper, because this is the part that still makes my stomach turn, "was the day before you were hit."

Silence spreads between us, vast and cold.

"It's labeled as something harmless. Administrative. I told myself it was nothing." He exhales slowly through his nose. Controlled. Measured. "Today," I go on, "Amauri said something. About Sean and Marianne arguing. About being *compensated*. And suddenly—I saw it. All of it." I swallow. "My father paid Sean," I conclude. "And Sean... Sean was connected to Northstar. And Northstar—" My voice wobbles. "Northstar isn't clean, Massimo. I looked. They fix problems. They make things disappear."

I don't say the rest. I don't have to. He closes his eyes for a brief second.

"And there was something else. I never told my father who got me pregnant. But he knew. When we argued after the kidnapping, he called Amauri your son." I leave the bastard part out. I can't say the word. "When you were hit," I finish softly, "I don't think it was just your family trying to stop you."

His gaze sharpens when he looks back at me. Dangerous now. Focused.

"You think your father ordered the hit," he summarizes.

I nod miserably. "If he knew about us... he wouldn't have been happy about it. He always wanted Carter to be his son-in-law. Even more after the accident. Even after I told him what Carter did." His arm tightens around me, his fingers brush over my skin, leaving goosebumps in their wake. Reassuring, there. But my mind goes to the connections I made and hadn't fully been able to admit to myself yet. Saying it out loud... it feels like a verdict. I know what I'm saying. I know to whom I am saying it. And I am fully aware of the consequences.

"I never thought he would be capable of this... but I found other things... he's not the man I thought him to be and yet," I shudder, admitting the truth to myself, "he's exactly the man I always knew he was. Deep down."

The words hang there, poisonous and undeniable. For a moment, I'm afraid he'll pull away. That the darkness of it—*my* blood tied to his near-death—will finally be too much. Instead, his hand comes up to cradle the back of my neck, grounding, certain.

"You didn't do this," he says firmly.

Tears burn behind my eyes anyway. "But he did."

"If he did, I'll find out." He promises.

I swallow, "And then?"

"Then your father will answer to me."

I rest my forehead against his chest again, shaking now, grief and fury tangling together.

"I don't know what that makes me," I whisper.

His arm tightens around me, protective in a way that feels absolute.

"It makes you honest. And brave enough to tell me."

I listen to his heartbeat, steady, but faster now. Calculating. And somewhere deep inside me, I know with terrifying certainty: This wasn't the end of the past catching up to us, but it was the moment it finally stepped fully into the light.

I don't know how, but eventually I relax to the sound of Massimo's heart and his breathing. I know he's awake, thinking, plotting, calculating, but sleep claims me. In his bed. In his arms. And it feels right.

Time feels suspended, but Amauri's shrill scream rips me from deep sleep. With a mother's instinct, I'm already out of bed, only to hit a brick wall by the entrance to the bedroom. Massimo. Naked. Gun in hand.

"Stay here." He orders in a deadly voice that doesn't leave room for argument.

My heart beats a hundred miles an hour; every

instinct in me calls me forward to the sound of my son's voice, but I force myself to stay behind Massimo, at least long enough to grab his shirt off the floor and fling it over myself. I catch up with him in the living area, where he's conducting a fast, measured scan of the surroundings. The front door is open, and my heart races even faster.

Max and two of the guards are already inside when I register what's happening. My heart slams into my throat. Guns are up. Movement everywhere. Dark shapes cut through the low light like something out of a nightmare. Déjà vu hits me like a cement truck. Fear doesn't stand a chance against the rush of adrenaline pulsing through me, though. *Not again*, is all I can think. *I'll die before I let anything happen to Amauri again.*

"Stop," Max says sharply, holding up a hand as he reaches the guest bedroom door. His voice drops immediately. "He's having a nightmare."

Everything pauses. The guards lower their weapons in one smooth, practiced motion. Massimo's hand presses lightly between my shoulder blades. "Go," he murmurs.

I don't hesitate. I rush to Amauri's side just as he jerks awake, tangled in sheets, eyes wild with terror. He latches onto me the second he sees my face.

"Mummy," he sobs, fists clutching my shirt. "Mummy."

"I'm here, baby," I whisper, crawling onto the bed and pulling him into my arms. "It's okay. You're safe. I've got you."

I don't notice the guards filtering out. I don't even notice Massimo leaving the room. All that exists is my son shaking against me, his breath hitching, his fingers digging in like he's afraid I'll disappear. I kiss his face over and over, murmuring nonsense and promises. "It's okay. It's okay. Mummy's here."

When I finally look up, Massimo is back. He's donned joggers, but is still barefoot, making his movements quiet. The gun is nowhere to be seen. He stops a few feet away, watching us with an intensity that makes my chest ache.

"And Massimo," I add softly, smoothing Amauri's hair, "see? He won't let anything happen to you."

Amauri peeks out from my shoulder. Then, without warning, he stretches his arms toward Massimo. My heart leaps into my throat. Massimo doesn't hesitate. He steps forward and lifts Amauri effortlessly, settling him against his chest like it's the most natural thing in the world.

"It's okay, champ." His voice is low and rough with emotion. "I've got you." Amauri buries his face in Massimo's shoulder. "Nobody will ever hurt you again," Massimo continues quietly. "I swear it. They'll have to come through me first."

The honesty in his words—and in his voice—is impossible to miss. It brings tears to my eyes. I still have no idea how to untangle all the strings holding the three of us back, threatening to pull us under. But I know this much: Massimo will find a way. With precision. With patience. With brutal force, if necessary. And God help me; I'll be right there with him.

"And me," I add for good measure. Looking at Massimo. "I'll be right there with you. By your side."

MASSIMO

The next morning...

Jenna's words stay with me long after she falls asleep again. Not the fear in them. Not even the resolve. The certainty. *I'll be right there with you. By your side.* That should comfort me. It should feel like victory. Instead, it disturbs something deep and buried, something I thought I'd already dissected and put to rest. Because if she's stepping fully into my world, then every lie, every omission, every half-truth becomes a fault line.

I don't sleep after that.

Morning comes gray and quiet; the noise of Vegas is hushed behind the glass like it's holding its breath. Jenna and Amauri are still asleep when I slip out of bed. I stand by the window for a long time, coffee untouched, jaw tight, thoughts circling one name.

Bello. Again.

The memory comes without warning.

Pain first. Always pain. Crushing. Wet. Everywhere. I'm floating in and out, drugged and heavy, lungs burning like I've swallowed fire. Machines beep. Voices blur. Light hurts. Darkness hurts worse. There's a taste of blood in my mouth I can't spit out.

Enzo is there.

I know it's him because he smells like smoke and leather and home. His voice cuts through the fog, low, controlled, but tight around the edges. "Easy, boss. Don't move."

I try to speak. My chest seizes instead. Time doesn't make sense. Days blur into nights. Weeks maybe. I wake and sleep and wake again, trapped in a body that doesn't answer to me anymore.

One night—or day—Enzo leans closer.

"I found out who ordered it," he tells me quietly.

My vision swims. I focus on his face like it's a target.

"Bello overheard it," Enzo continues. "Your uncle. He gave the order himself."

The memories land slow. Heavy. Impossible.

Bello overheard it.

Bello.

Always Bello.

I try to lift my hand. It barely twitches.

"Your cousins pushed," Enzo adds. "But the call came from him."

I remember thinking—through the morphine, through the haze—that at least the rot was contained. Family business. A clean line. A betrayal I could understand. I trusted Bello's ears. I trusted Enzo's voice. I built everything that followed on that foundation. The memory snaps loose. I'm standing in my kitchen now, knuckles white around the mug I never drank from.

Jenna's father. Kingsley.

Northstar.

The money.

The date.

And Bello—again—standing right at the point where truth bends. My jaw tightens until it aches. If Bello lied then—if he *filtered* what he overheard—if Enzo knew more than he said… The implications are catastrophic. From a drawer, I pull a notepad with the hotel's icon on it and scribble a hasty note for Jenna.

Jenna,

I had to leave for some business
but I'll be back soon.

Call me if you need me—
I put my number in your phone.

The kitchen will bring you and
Amauri anything you want.

Love you.

Massimo

I'm just about to pull my phone out when I hear the *tap tap tap* of little feet. Amauri stands in the doorway, looking devastatingly adorable in his dinosaur pajamas and sleep-tousled hair. A big yawn nearly splits his face in half.

"Good morning, buddy, you're up early."

"I'm thirsty," he declares and, without fanfare, shuffles into the kitchen, opening the industrial-sized fridge. I watch him pull out a chair, climb on top of it—while resisting the urge to help—and pull out the orange juice. He's a resourceful little man. Pride swells my chest. I decide to intervene when he goes for the glasses and hand him one down.

"Thank you," he mumbles, impressing me with his manners as well.

"You're welcome. You want something to eat too?"

He shakes his head and drinks down the juice in big gulping swallows. An idea occurs to me. "Hey, if you could decorate your own room, what would it look like?"

He wipes his mouth with the back of his hand, and I hand him a napkin. He tilts his head, deep in thought. "Whatever I want?"

"Anything." I agree. If he wants a damn slide down into his bed, I'll have the roof cut open and get it done. My little man deserves nothing less than everything.

"I saw something..." he looks at me, "Can I have your phone?"

Curious where this is going, I hand it to him. He scrunches his forehead up as he looks through it. "You don't have Pinterest."

"Pin... what?"

He taps like a little madman, then hands me the phone, "I need your passcode."

He's resourceful, too, it seems. I take it, type in the code, and hand it back. A few moments later, he has something pulled up on it and shows me the screen with the biggest grin I've ever seen.

There is a wall, made to look like a forest. On it run several clear tubes in different colors. A giant cage stands in the center of it, and the tubes all interconnect, some with little balls in between, and I realize it's a large running place for hamsters.

"That looks... awesome," I hedge. I like his hamster, because he likes the rodent, but having vermin in my house has never occurred to me before. "Do you think Hammie needs friends?"

My son looks at me with a *duh* expression. "Hamsters are solitary animals."

Oh, thank fuck.

"I'll see what I can do about that," I promise.

"That would be cool." He nods, yawns again. He puts my phone on the counter. "I'm going back to bed."

I watch him return to his room, while pride swells in my chest. I give myself a minute to just relish the moment before I grab my phone, already moving. Enzo answers on the first ring.

"Boss."

"We need to talk," I greet in a calm voice. Too calm. "Now."

A pause. Just a fraction too long.

"I'm on my way," Enzo replies.

"Meet me in the boardroom." I don't want Jenna or Amauri anywhere near what might happen. I end the call.

Whatever Enzo tells me next will decide something irreversible. Because if the truth I built my empire on is compromised, then I've been standing on a lie for ten years. And I don't forgive that.

Not of anyone. Not even Enzo.

The elevator doors slide shut behind me with a muted thud, sealing off the penthouse, sealing her off, sealing my son off.

The boardroom level opens, all glass, dark wood, and quiet authority. Enzo isn't here yet. It'll take him fifteen minutes, give or take. I don't sit. There's too much pent-up restlessness in my body for that. Too much motion with nowhere to go. I pace the length of the long table once, twice, then drift toward the window.

My city stretches out below me. Las Vegas doesn't pretend to be innocent. She advertises her sins in neon, wears excess like perfume, dares you to underestimate her because you think you've seen it all before. People come here believing the rules don't apply. They're half right.

This city was chaos when I took it, fractured crews, borrowed power, men confusing noise for strength. I didn't tame it. I aligned it. Every street, every club, every casino now hums to the same rhythm. Mine.

My uncle ruled with fear and spectacle. Public punishments. Loud reminders. His sons would have done the same, broken bones in daylight, headlines as warnings. They believed power had to be seen to be respected.

I learned differently. Vegas thrives on illusion, but underneath it's built on control. Timing. Pressure. Knowing when to let people think they're winning.

I press my palm to the glass. Somewhere down there, people are waking up, making bad decisions, falling in love with strangers, losing money they don't have. They don't know how close they are to the machinery that keeps them safe from worse men than me.

This city knows me. It responds to me. It bends because it understands the cost of resisting. For years, that was enough for me. Power. Order. Expansion. The quiet satisfaction of an empire that works. But now, now there are two more lives tied to it. Jenna and Amauri. Suddenly, Vegas isn't just something I rule. It's something I have to protect them from.

That changes everything.

My city—my beautiful, dangerous city—will feel the shift long before anyone else realizes it's happening. Because when a king stops ruling for himself... the ground always moves.

I pull my phone from my pocket and call Alessio.

"What time are we wheels up?" I ask, already pacing the length of the room again.

"Two," he answers without hesitation. "Everything's arranged. Private terminal. No noise."

Good. That gives me time. A few hours with Jenna. With Amauri. Enough time to remind myself why I'm doing all of this. The call ends. I don't waste a second before dialing Damiano. "How's our guest?"

A low chuckle comes through the line. "Still breathing. Still bitching. Louder by the hour."

I can picture it. Whitford, chained to a chair, pride bleeding out of him one complaint at a time.

"Can I shut him up yet?" Damiano asks.

"Gag him if you need to," I reply coolly. "He doesn't get comfort. He gets time."

"Understood."

An expression from Whitford's face returns to me. The one he wore on the plane when I told him who I was. I'm confident I can peg a liar a hundred miles away, and he didn't wear the mask of one. He really didn't know who I was. But my name rang a bell. Not that it wouldn't. Everyone in Vegas at least knows *of* me. The fear I saw could be from that, or from what he knows. Only one way to find out.

"Actually, why don't you have a chat with him?"

"About?"

"About what he knows about the hit and run ten years ago. About what Kingsley told him or how and why he might have been involved."

I can hear a thousand questions on the other end, but Damiano doesn't ask them. He knows I'll tell him when I'm ready. The boardroom doors open, and Enzo walks in with a calm expression and eyes sharp enough to cut glass. He takes one look at my face and knows better than to open with small talk.

"I've got to go," I tell Damiano, ending the call. The line clicks dead. Then my attention shifts fully to Enzo.

He nods once. "Everything ready?"

"Yes," I nod, "But things just got... complicated."

That gets his full attention. I move to the head of the table, palms braced against the polished wood, jaw tight.

"Sit," I tell him.

Enzo takes the chair across from me like he's done a thousand times before. Calm. Unhurried. He pours himself a drink without asking, the sound of ice too loud in the stillness. I stay standing, hands braced on the edge of the table, my reflection looks fractured in the polished wood.

"Remind me, what Bello told you. Exactly. About my uncle."

Enzo's hand pauses just long enough to notice. He gives me a puzzled look. Then his brows knit in concentration as his mind goes back ten years. He doesn't ask what this is about. "He said he overheard a conversation. Your uncle and one of your cousins. Cesar was complaining. Again." He takes a sip. "Said you were pushing too hard. That you were moving pieces without permission."

"And?" I press.

"And your uncle said it was time to put a stop to it," Enzo continues. "That you were becoming a liability."

I turn my head slowly. "His words."

Enzo meets my gaze. Steady. "Those were Bello's words."

I nod once, like I'm filing paperwork. "And Bello said he heard this himself."

"Yes."

"Not from someone else."

"No."

"Not inferred."

"No."

Silence stretches. I walk around the table, slow,

measured, stopping behind Enzo's chair. Not looming. Just present. Letting the weight settle.

"And Bello told you this when?" I ask.

"After the hit," Enzo replies. "When you were still... not awake."

"Not awake," I repeat softly.

I rest my palms on the back of Enzo's chair now. I don't squeeze. I don't threaten.

"Did Bello ever mention anyone outside the family?" I ask. "Any third party. Any money changing hands."

Enzo exhales through his nose. A controlled sound. "No," he shakes his head. "He was very clear. This was internal."

I hum quietly, considering. Enzo turns the glass slowly in his hand, ice clinking once before he stills it. He's watching me now, not defensive, not wary. Just attentive. The way he's always been.

"What is this about?" he finally wants to know.

I don't answer right away. I walk back around the table and stop across from him, close enough that he can see my expression clearly. I want him to. I need him to.

"A reliable source came to me," I explain evenly, not wanting to bring Jenna into this. "Someone I trust. A large sum moved out of Kingsley's account the day before the hit-and-run."

Enzo blanches. Not guilt. Shock. "Kingsley? That doesn't make sense." He looks up at me, his scars pulling tight across his face as the implication settles. "You think Kingsley was involved."

I don't answer that. Not right away. I lean my hands on

the table and look him dead in the eye. "Bello lied about Jenna. Didn't he?"

The words hit like a gunshot. Enzo's brows knit together slowly, pieces clicking together in his head. He stares at me, then shakes his head once. "I swear to you, boss—I had no idea about that."

"I know," my response comes immediately. The certainty in my voice surprises even me.

A long breath leaves my chest, slow and heavy, carrying something I hadn't realized I was holding onto, and relief settles into its place. Because if Enzo had been part of it—if he'd filtered the truth, protected someone, shaped the lie—I would have had to put him down the same way I did Bello.

But Enzo...

Enzo is blood in every way that matters. He taught me how to read men. How to survive power. How to build something that lasts. Killing him wouldn't have been justice. It would have been a loss.

"But why would he—" Enzo starts, then stops. He turns fully in his chair now and locks eyes with me.

I straighten and finally say what I've been holding back. "Jenna and I were together. Back then. It wasn't a fling. Not a distraction. It was serious."

Enzo's face changes from surprise to understanding as the pieces click into place.

"She was... important to you," he guessed slowly.

"She was everything," I reply. "Kingsley would've hated it. His daughter with a man like me." I give a short, humorless exhale. "He would've seen it as a threat. To his image. To his control."

Enzo leans back, running a hand over his hair. "You think Bello and Kingsley worked together?"

I shake my head. "I don't know yet." But I will.

"If this is true," Enzo mutters, staring at the table, "if your uncle didn't—" He breaks off, drags a hand down his face. "Fuck."

"I know," I agree quietly. "I killed them all for nothing."

The words sit between us, heavy and irreversible.

Enzo falls back fully into his chair. "Fuck," he exhales again, softer now.

We look at each other—two men who've buried enough bodies to populate a small city—and for once, neither of us knows what to say.

After a moment, Enzo lifts his gaze. "Go ahead," he invites.

I frown. "What?"

"Shoot me," his voice is flat. "Get it over with. This is as much my fault as it was Bello's."

The thought twists something ugly in my chest. I shake my head. "I'd have to shoot myself then, too."

That stops him. We sit in silence for a moment longer, the air thick with ghosts. We both trusted Bello. Fucking Bello.

"The hit may have been framed as family," I continue. "But the money doesn't lie. Kingsley paid someone. Bello made sure I never looked in that direction."

Bello didn't lie outright; he filtered. Passed on what

suited him, buried the rest under *handled* and *no further action needed.* Silence settles between us. Heavy. Shared.

"So what now?" Enzo asks.

I straighten slowly.

"Now," I say, "we pull the thread Bello tried to bury. And we do it quietly."

Enzo nods once. No hesitation. No questions.

"Good," I add. "Because if Kingsley thought he could buy his way into my world and walk away clean—"

I let the sentence hang. Enzo finishes it for me. "He forgot who you are."

And for the first time since this began, I know one thing with absolute certainty: The rot didn't come from my house. But I'm the one who's going to burn it out.

"There's always noise around a hit," Enzo reminds me. "People try to attach themselves after the fact."

"They do," I murmur. "Damiano is working Whitford over. I need you to get your hands on a woman named Marianne and a man named Sean. Both work for Kingsley. I want them brought to the Oven. I'll talk to them tomorrow. This afternoon, Alessio and I have business in LA with Joaquín."

"Alright." He comes over to me and puts a hand on my shoulder. "For all it's worth, your uncle, your cousins... they had it coming."

I nod. They did. But I would have liked to deal with them on my own time instead of being pushed into it. For a moment, the image returns. A house lit from the inside out. Windows glowing like furnaces. My uncle's voice, gone long before the roof surrendered. Fire is cleaner than bullets. It leaves no witnesses.

Just the slow, sharp crack of timber under pressure, the controlled collapse of something that believed it was permanent. I didn't watch until the end. I didn't need to. Blood built that house. Ash finished it.

Enzo straightens and walks to the door.

"One more thing," I stop him. "When Bello told you this... did he seem nervous?"

Enzo thinks about that longer than I like. "No. He was more resigned. But that could be me now, reading into things after."

That lands. I nod again. "Thank you."

I turn toward the window, my city gleaming below, and speak without looking back.

"If Bello filtered what he heard," I say quietly, "or protected someone who didn't deserve it, then everything I built on that truth becomes suspect."

Enzo doesn't answer. He doesn't have to. The silence does enough talking for both of us.

JENNA

I FIND THE NOTE ON THE KITCHEN COUNTER. CREAM PAPER. Heavy. Elegant. His handwriting is unmistakable, decisive, slanted slightly forward, like he never hesitates even when he's saying something gentle.

I read it once. Then again. Then I press it to my chest like an absolute idiot and laugh softly at myself, a small, breathless sound that feels... young. Ridiculous. Lovesick.

God. I haven't done that in years.

It reminds me of the notes he used to leave me. Folded into my bag. Slid under my door. Sometimes just a word. Sometimes a sentence that meant everything. We used to joke that we'd leave each other breadcrumbs across the city. Those notes are still at the house. The thought hits me out of nowhere.

Massimo's people were thorough, I know that. Clothes. Documents. Amauri's things. Everything obvious. But there's a box they wouldn't have found. Hidden under the loose floorboard in the closet. Pictures of us, printed and faded at the edges. An old disposable phone I never had the heart to throw away. Messages saved like talismans. Notes he wrote me that I couldn't risk keeping out in the open. A past I buried, not erased.

"Mummy!" Amauri's voice pulls me back. "There is a *pool*."

I smile automatically. "There is?"

He grabs my hand and drags me toward the balcony like it's a matter of urgency, pointing wildly the moment we step outside. I smile to myself, assuming he must have discovered the rooftop pool. But no. That's not what got him so fired up.

"There," he says, practically bouncing. "Down there!"

I follow his finger. Below us, tucked between towers, is something that makes me blink twice.

"Oh my God," I laugh. "That's not just a pool, that's a waterpark."

Slides. Blue and white with curves that catch the sun. Splash zones. A lazy river. It looks like something out of a dream.

"Can we go?" he asks, already hopeful. "Please?"

"You bet," I say without hesitation.

His grin could power the city. As he launches into a breathless plan involving races and slides and something he calls *the big splash of doom*, my mind wanders just a little. To Massimo. Maybe I could talk him into opening it just for us tonight. Just the three of us. No crowds. No noise. Amauri would lose his mind.

"I wish we could live here," Amauri sighs happily, leaning against the railing. "Forever."

Something in my chest tightens. I tuck the note back against my heart, smiling into the sunlight. Maybe. A knock at the door startles me. I open it to find an older woman standing there, posture relaxed, despite the several guards in the foyer. Her eyes are kind but observant. The kind of presence that doesn't demand trust, but invites it.

"Jenna Whitford?" she asks gently. "I'm Esther Bonnet." She holds up a card. *Therapist.* "Mr. Manetti sent me," she adds, like she already knows how much that matters.

My chest tightens. Of course he did.

Amauri appears at my side immediately, peeking around my leg with open curiosity. "Are you a doctor?"

Esther smiles at him, warm and unthreatening. She looks like she's in her fifties, with the warmest eyes I've ever seen. "Something like that. I talk with kids. And grown-ups too, sometimes."

Amauri considers this. "Do you fix nightmares?"

"Sometimes," she replies honestly. "And sometimes I just help people understand them."

He nods, satisfied enough. I step aside to let her in, and emotion swells unexpectedly in my throat. Massimo has so much on his shoulders right now—enemies, betrayals, ghosts clawing their way back into the light—and still, he thought of *this*. Of Amauri.

Of his son.

The contrast hits hard.

Carter would never have done this.

The thought comes sharp and unwelcome, and I shudder despite myself. He wasn't cruel to Amauri. Not overtly. Not in ways that would leave bruises or headlines. He was something worse. Distant. Like Amauri was a guest in his own home. Tolerated. Ignored. Always *other*.

The memory surfaces unbidden.

"You said you wanted a son," I throw into his face, frustration spilling over after another weekend of excuses. "That's why you agreed to marry me."

He doesn't even look up from his phone. "For image, yes," he replies coolly. "That doesn't mean I have to tolerate the bastard."

The word hits like a slap.

"He's a child," I snap. "Your child."

"He's not mine," Carter states flatly. "And don't confuse obligation with affection."

I stand there, hands shaking, realizing with brutal clarity that this is the line. That if he ever crosses it—if he ever aims that coldness directly at Amauri—I will leave. Consequences be damned. Reputation. Politics. Money.

None of it will matter.

I blink myself back into the present. Esther is kneeling now, eye-level with Amauri, asking him about his favorite games. He answers cautiously at first, then with growing animation. I watch him, how he leans in, how his shoulders slowly relax.

It makes me think of Massimo. Of the way he scooped Amauri up without hesitation. Of the way he swore, with his whole being, that no one would ever hurt him again. My eyes burn. I'm starting to understand something I never let myself see before: I'm not the only one to just survive my marriage. Amauri did too. And now—finally—he doesn't have to anymore.

Esther straightens and looks at me gently. "Would there be somewhere private I could talk with Amauri?" When I instinctively tense, she adds, "You're welcome to stay if you'd like. But it's often easier if I speak with him alone first. Just for a little while."

I glance at Amauri. He's listening, serious, taking this in the way he always does when adults talk around him instead of to him.

"That okay, baby?" I ask.

He nods after a second. "Can I bring Hammie?"

Esther smiles. "Of course you can."

That settles it. I watch them head toward the guest bedroom, Esther unhurried, Amauri clutching the hamster carrier like it's armor. The door closes softly behind them. I tell myself I trust Massimo. I wouldn't have let this happen otherwise. He wouldn't send just anyone. Still, the habit of vigilance is hard to shake. I grab my phone and type in *Esther Bonnet, therapist*. The results come back almost immediately. Highly recommended. Trauma-informed. Decorated. Discreet. Trusted with children in high-risk situations. Article after article. Parent testimonials. Professional accolades. Nothing even remotely questionable. Easing the tightness of my chest.

The door opens behind me.

Massimo.

He steps inside, taking in the room in one sweep, eyes sharp, posture loose but ready. He spots me immediately.

"She's with him," I say before he can ask. "Esther."

He nods once. "Good."

I don't say anything else. I just walk up to him and kiss him. Not careful. Not hesitant. "Thank you."

He stills for half a second, then his hand comes up to my jaw, grounding, familiar.

"For thinking of him," I murmur against his mouth. "For not forgetting."

"I never will," simple words, but I don't think he knows how much they mean to me.

I believe him. Somewhere down the hall, my son is talking to someone who knows how to listen.

"I'll have to leave for a few hours," Massimo fills me in, adjusting his cuff as if it's nothing more than a scheduling detail. "Around one-thirty. Business."

My chest tightens instinctively, but he's already shaking his head. "I'll be back in time for dinner. I promise."

I nod, trusting that promise more than I ever thought I would.

"In the meantime," he continues, "I've arranged for a decorator to stop by. I want you to change the penthouse however you like. Make it yours." His gaze softens just a fraction. "Amauri can pick any of the guest bedrooms for himself."

Something warm blooms in my chest. "Massimo..." I start.

He shrugs lightly. "He needs a space that's his."

The simplicity of it nearly undoes me. Because everything is moving so fast, I can barely get my footing. One moment I'm surviving—holding things together with duct tape and stubbornness—and the next I'm standing in Massimo's penthouse, watching him plan a future like it's the most natural thing in the world.

My chest tightens. I don't know what to think. Not really. I know what I *feel*, and that's the problem. I want him. Not in the dizzy, reckless way people talk about wanting. Not in a way that ignores reality. I want him because losing him once nearly destroyed me, and finding him again feels like something I don't get to squander. We've already lost ten years. Ten years of silence and wrong assumptions and pain that calcified into habit. I don't want to waste another day pretending I don't know what I want when I finally do.

I want to be with him.

Finally.

There are also the practicalities to consider—to pacify my logical mind.

If we didn't stay here, where would we go?

Back to my house? The thought makes my stomach twist. That place is heavy with ghosts, arguments whispered behind closed doors, cold dinners, and Amauri learning how to make himself small. I don't want to drag my son back into a space where every corner holds a memory I worked so hard to survive.

Take him somewhere else? A temporary place? Another in-between? We've lived in limbo long enough. Moving in here—into Massimo's world, his penthouse, his life—feels inevitable and terrifying all at once. Not because I don't want it, but because it makes everything *real*.

The real question is: who do I owe an explanation to? My father? A dark chuckle escapes me. Friends who watched me build a life they never really understood? Or do I finally get to choose without having to justify myself to anyone? My gaze drifts to Massimo—already thinking three steps ahead—and something steadies inside me. He isn't rushing me. He's making space. For Amauri. For me. For whatever comes next.

I don't have the answers yet. But I know this: I'm done living half a life. Done planning around absence. Done choosing safety over truth. Whatever this becomes—wherever we land—I want to walk into it with him and never let go. Before I can think too deeply, I grab his hand and pull him into the kitchen.

"Sit."

He raises a brow but obeys, settling onto one of the stools, watching me with open amusement as I move around the counter on autopilot. Bread. Mustard. Pastrami. Pickles.

"You're still in love with pastrami?" I ask over my shoulder.

"As if there's any better sandwich," he replies solemnly, making me laugh. The sound is easy, familiar. God, I've missed this. I set the sandwich onto a plate and slide it across the counter to him.

"Eat," I order. "You look like you've already had a hard morning." He hesitates, just a beat. "No secrets," I remind him gently. "That goes both ways."

He studies me for a moment, then nods.

"I had a talk with Enzo this morning; he's clean," he fills me in. "He acted on what Bello told him. Nothing more."

Relief loosens something in my shoulders.

"And..." he adds carefully, "Damiano is questioning Whitford."

My stomach drops.

"Questioning," I repeat, because it's easier than saying what I'm actually thinking. I know what that word means in his world. I've lived adjacent to power long enough not to be naïve.

I'm also acutely aware of him watching my face, gauging, measuring. Waiting to see where I'll flinch. Where I'll fold. If I want to be his partner in this, I can't. I have to man up, so to speak. I have to be willing to cross lines I never thought I would. I know he'd happily shield me, keep me comfortable, insulated, living a life of luxury and carefully curated ignorance. But it's a path that would have to be paved with lies. And lies always rot eventually.

If I want him, really want him, I have to take *all* of him. The good. The bad. And the very ugly. The thought of what that means for Amauri tightens something deep in my chest. But the truth is, I already made that choice the moment I asked Massimo to save him. I changed my son's life irrevocably that day. There is no world where Massimo lets me walk away with Amauri now. And if I'm honest, I don't think I want to. Not even for Amauri. Or maybe *because* of him. Because if everything that's happened has taught me anything, it's this: there is exactly one man capable of keeping us safe in the world we're standing in now. That man is currently eating my fucking pastrami sandwich. I swallow and straighten my spine.

"Who is Damiano?" I ask calmly.

It's not denial. It's a choice. Massimo's gaze sharpens into respect. "One of my capos. You'll meet them all."

I nod once. My hands curl briefly against the counter, then relax. "Okay."

That's it. No flinching. No retreat. He exhales slowly, like he didn't realize he'd been holding his breath. He takes a bite of the sandwich, eyes never leaving me.

"Thank you." We both know it's not for the food.

I lean against the counter, watching him eat, feeling the strange steadiness settling between us. We're not pretending anymore. We're learning how to stand in the truth, together.

"So," I ask, leaning against the counter like this is casual, like my pulse isn't already picking up. "Where are you going this afternoon?"

Massimo doesn't sugarcoat it. He never does.

"L.A. The Mexican cartel has been giving us trouble, especially a man named Joaquín." My stomach tightens, but I don't interrupt. "He's been connected to some of the shit hitting my business lately," Massimo continues. "And tomorrow morning, I'll have a long conversation with Sean. And Marianne. And Whitford."

The names land one by one, each heavier than the last. He watches me closely now. Not testing. Waiting. I feel it all at once, the fear, the anger, the urge to retreat, and the equal, opposite urge to burn everything down. My hands curl slightly against the counter to keep them from shaking.

"I want to be there." The words surprise me with how steady they sound. His brow lifts a fraction. "If they're involved," I continue, forcing myself to keep eye contact, "if my father had anything to do with what happened ten years ago, I have a right to know."

My chest tightens, my breath is shallow, but I push through it. "And if so, I have just as much revenge to dish out as you do."

There it is. Raw. Unfiltered. I'm terrified. Of what I'll hear. Of what I'll confirm. Of the version of myself that might emerge once the truth is spoken out loud. But underneath the fear is something harder. Resolve. I've spent too many years being managed, redirected, and protected from ugly truths like a fragile thing. I'm done with that. Done being spared at the cost of my agency. I swallow. My voice is softer now, but no less firm. "I'm asking you not to shield me. I'm asking you not to shut me out."

My gaze flicks, unbidden, toward the hallway, toward Amauri.

"I've already crossed the line," I add quietly. "The moment I asked you to save our son. I'm not pretending otherwise." I straighten, meeting Massimo's eyes fully now. "I'm scared," I admit. "But I'm not backing down."

Whatever comes next—whatever truths crawl out into the light—I won't face them blind. Not anymore.

THE JET HUMS BENEATH MY FEET LIKE A LIVING THING. NOT loud. Not showy. Controlled. Purpose-built. Leather, brushed steel, low light that never quite lets you forget you're airborne. I've always liked that about planes; you're never allowed the illusion of permanence. Everything is temporary at thirty thousand feet.

I loosen my cuff and settle into the seat opposite Alessio. The city lights of Las Vegas fall away beneath us, shrinking into glitter, then darkness. Home recedes. Responsibility doesn't.

The flight attendant pours me a drink without asking. Stagg bourbon. Neat. She's been with me long enough to know to keep herself unobtrusive. The first sip burns slow and deep, familiar as muscle memory. It settles my nerves without dulling my edges. I need both this afternoon.

We're heading to L.A. with a small army and a narrow window. Joaquín thinks he's clever. He thinks proximity equals safety. He's wrong. California isn't neutral ground; it's a marketplace. And I owe favors for Enzo contacting Antonio DeLuna—one of the New York capos—as a courtesy to let him know a shitstorm is about to land in his territory. And to assure him that I'll clean up the mess.

Alessio spreads the tablet between us, satellite images glowing faintly in the dim cabin. "He'll be at the Avalon warehouse by nightfall," he points at a set of nondescript buildings. "Light security. He's been moving like he doesn't expect resistance."

I snort quietly. "They never do."

We go over the plan, intercept, isolate, and collapse the perimeter before he realizes he's already lost. It's clean. Efficient. My kind of work. Alessio talks. I listen, ask the right questions, and make small adjustments that turn good plans into fatal ones. But even as we talk, my mind keeps circling back.

Jenna.

The way she stood there in my kitchen, spine straight, fear present but not steering. The way she didn't flinch when I told her about Whitford. The way she claimed her place without asking permission. She won't just be a queen. She'll be a partner. The realization settles in my chest, heavy and undeniable. I've ruled alone for a long time. Trusted men. Relied on loyalty, fear, and structure. It worked. It always has. But watching her piece things together—watching her see what I missed, connect what I dismissed—made something shift. Without her, Kingsley would still be a shadow. Oh, he would've died eventually —men like him always do—but Bello and my uncle, the lie I built an empire on? That rot would've stayed buried. I owe her. Not in blood. Not in favors. In truth.

That doesn't mean I'll show her everything. Some ugliness serves no purpose but to stain. But tomorrow—tomorrow she has a right to be there. To hear it from their mouths. To look her *husband* in the eye when the illusion finally breaks. I take another sip of bourbon.

Alessio finishes his rundown and leans back. "You okay, boss?"

I glance at him, then out the window. The sky is endless. Indifferent.

"She's stronger than I thought," I say finally.

He nods once. "It sounds like it. I'd like to meet her."

"You will."

The plane dips slightly as we adjust course. Somewhere behind us, men check weapons, review routes, and prepare to do what they do best. Joaquín will learn that he miscalculated. But the real reckoning is waiting for morning.

I roll the glass between my fingers, watching the amber catch the light.

The jet touches down without ceremony. No applause. No wasted movement. The engines idle while doors open and men move. We don't announce ourselves. Black SUVs swallow us whole and spit us back out miles later, closer to the industrial spine of the city where the rules thin, and the lights stop pretending.

The warehouse sits exactly where Alessio said it would. Concrete. Corrugated steel. Sodium lights buzz overhead like insects. The kind of place people use when they don't want to be seen or remembered. I study it from the shadow of the SUV, taking in exits, sightlines, the lazy rhythm of men who think they're safe. We receive confirmation from one of our men that Joaquín is inside.

"Positions," I murmur.

Men peel off soundlessly, becoming angles and blind spots. Time compresses. Every sense sharpens. This is the moment before a storm breaks, when the air goes still, and everything holds its breath. The first man dies without knowing why. A shape in a doorway, a soft crack, a body folding in on itself before it hits the ground. Another goes down near the loading bay, reaching for a weapon he never gets to use. There's no shouting. No chaos yet. Just the quiet removal of obstacles.

Ultimately, someone notices. A shout cut short. A gunshot answered immediately. That's our cue to move.

I breach with two men, muzzle up, eyes tracking. Inside, it looks like any other warehouse. Crates are stacked high, shadows everywhere. Movement flickers and disappears. One man fires wildly. The shot slams into my chest hard enough to knock the breath clean out of me. The impact throws me backward a step, and then Alessio is there, a solid hand at my shoulder, keeping me upright before I can even think to fall.

Fucking Kevlar vest. It's not the first time one of them saved my ass. I suck in a sharp breath. Pain is already blooming across my ribs, hot and deep. That's going to be one motherfucker of a bruise.

I don't give the asshole time to celebrate. I raise my weapon and return fire, controlled, precise. The man jerks once and drops, the sound of his body hitting concrete lost beneath the ringing in my ears. For half a second, I do nothing but breathe. Then I straighten, roll my shoulders, and nod once at Alessio.

"Keep moving," I order.

Pain is temporary. This isn't. Nothing important got hit.

These motherfuckers won't get a second shot at me. Gunfire blooms and dies in short, controlled bursts. No wasted ammo. No hesitation. They scatter, then try to regroup, but panic makes them stupid. Panic makes men predictable. More bodies hit the floor, one by one.

I spot Joaquín at the far end of the warehouse, trying to slip through a side office. He looks smaller than I expected. Older. Desperation has a way of shrinking men.

"Take everyone else," I order calmly into the comm. "He's mine."

He makes it three steps before someone clips his leg. He goes down hard, skidding across concrete, screaming now, finally loud enough to hear. By the time I reach him, the warehouse is quiet again. The quiet of death.

My men secure the perimeter while Joaquín crawls backward, blood slicking the floor beneath him. His eyes lock on mine and widen with recognition.

"Massimo," he breathes, like saying my name might save him.

Which it won't. I crouch in front of him, take in the wreckage, the ruin. Everyone else in the warehouse is dead. Exactly as planned. I grip Joaquín by the collar and haul him upright just enough to meet my gaze.

"This is where you stop running," I tell him quietly.

He curses something I don't bother translating. I stand and gesture once. "Bag him."

Hands descend. Joaquín is dragged away, still alive,

still breathing, still very much conscious. The warehouse will be empty by morning. Cleaned. Sanitized. Forgotten.

I step back into the afternoon, blood on my shoes. My mind is already moving ahead to later this evening. Jenna, Amauri.

"We'll interrogate him on the plane, then drop him somewhere over Arizona," I order, and don't bother watching as someone patches Joaquín up long enough so he can answer some questions, then throws him in the back of one of the SUVs. There is no sense in wasting time here. I have a hot date planned.

JENNA

KNOWING MASSIMO IS OUT THERE SOMEWHERE—ARMED, hunting, in danger—keeps my nerves stretched thin. I try not to picture it. Try not to imagine steel and gunfire and blood. It doesn't work. Every creak of the building, every distant siren, makes my pulse spike. I tell myself he's done this a thousand times. That he's built for it. That worrying won't bring him back any faster.

None of it helps.

Esther is good with Amauri. Better than good. They spend nearly an hour together, talking, drawing, and—at one point—playing a card game I don't recognize. I watch from a distance, pretending to be busy, soaking in the sound of my son's laughter like medicine. When Esther finally asks to speak with me alone, I brace myself. But she's gentle. Grounded. She tells me Amauri is a tough kid. That he's processing in his own way. The worst thing I could do is rush him or force language onto feelings he's not ready to name yet.

"Let him talk when he's ready," she advises. "Your job is to make sure he knows he *can*."

I nod, absorbing it all. I'm tempted—so tempted—to ask her how she thinks I should handle the Carter situation. The words sit right at the back of my throat. What do I say when the man he's always known as his father... disappears? What do I say if the truth is darker than silence? But I don't ask. Not yet.

Esther is smart. She would give me an answer. But some things don't need to be solved this minute. And the truth is, Massimo is already stepping into the role without forcing it. Without posturing. Amauri gravitates toward him naturally, like he senses something solid there. We'll figure it out. We have to. Still, the thought I can't quite outrun curls cold in my stomach: I'm almost certain Carter will see his last sunrise come morning. I don't know how. Or where. I also don't know what—if anything—I'll tell Amauri.

Life is complicated. Mine especially.

I sigh and look out over the city, watching the light shift as afternoon drags toward evening. Somewhere far away, Massimo is doing what he does best, clearing paths through darkness.

The door finally opens just after dusk. He's there, filling the doorway like a presence of power nobody dares to touch. Massimo.

Relief hits me so hard my knees almost give. For a heartbeat, we just look at each other. He looks tired. Not wounded, not broken, just spent, the way men look when they've carried too much weight without setting it down. I cross the room without thinking and throw my arms around him. He holds me immediately—strong, familiar—and for a moment everything feels so *normal* it's almost dizzying. Like this is how it's always been. Like the world hasn't been trying to tear us apart. Then he inhales sharply.

I pull back instantly. "Massimo—"

"It's nothing," he says too quickly, his jaw tightening. "Just a bruise."

A bruise from what? Before I can ask, Amauri barrels into him like a missile. "Massimo!"

He scoops him up automatically, laughter breaking through his fatigue, then there's another brief wince, almost imperceptible, but I see it this time. My stomach tightens. He's upright. He's steady. I don't see blood. Whatever it is, it's not catastrophic. *Be patient,* I tell myself. *Not now.*

Amauri wraps himself around Massimo's neck like an octopus. "You're back! You promised!"

"I did," Massimo says, pressing a kiss to his hair. "And I keep my promises."

I watch them together, my chest aches with how right this looks. Then Amauri's eyes light up with a new thought. "So," he tries for nonchalant like he's not been thinking about it all day, drawing the word out, glancing between us with unmistakable calculation, "Mummy says that waterpark down there is *yours*?"

Massimo arches a brow, amused. "She did, huh?"

"And she said we could go," Amauri adds quickly. "Like. Soon."

He fixes Massimo with his most devastating weapon: wide, hopeful eyes.

I cross my arms, trying—and failing—not to smile. "He's been talking about it all afternoon."

Massimo looks at me over Amauri's head, something warm and dangerous in his gaze.

"Well," his face doesn't give anything away, as if considering a high-stakes negotiation, "that sounds like something we should discuss over dinner."

Amauri gasps. "That means yes."

Massimo laughs softly. "That means *maybe*."

Amauri beams anyway, clearly counting it as a win. Then he looks back at Massimo, and the smile on his face could melt an iceberg instantly. "The decorator was also here, she said she could make me an awesome Hammie wall."

I lean against the counter, watching the two of them, and the weight of the day finally eases from my shoulders. Whatever storms are still waiting for us—whatever truths tomorrow brings—this moment feels real. Good. Earned. For now, it's enough.

MASSIMO

The next morning...

Morning comes sharp and unkind. Max is already on Amauri duty when we leave: quiet competence, eyes alert, a presence that reassures without hovering. Esther will be back later. Everything is covered. Everything *except* this. Jenna slides into the car beside me without hesitation. The door closes. The city starts to move.

"Are you sure you want to be there for this?" I ask, keeping my voice level.

She nods. "No," her words contradict the gesture. "But I need to."

I lace my fingers through hers, feel the steady warmth, the faint tremor she doesn't try to hide. "If it gets too much—"

"I'll tell you," she assures me. "I'll leave."

I glance at her. "You don't have to prove anything."

She exhales, almost a laugh. "Don't worry. I won't make a scene in front of your men."

That earns her a look. "I'm more worried about you," I clarify.

She meets my gaze, then says quietly, "Call me."

I frown. "What?"

"That's what he said," she continues, eyes forward now. "After he delivered me to the coach. He leaned in and said, *Call me.*"

The car goes very still. She shakes her head once, as if clearing it. "Trust me. Whatever you're planning for the bastard, it's more than deserved."

Silence settles between us, thick but not strained. I keep my hand in hers, grounding myself in the present, even as my mind drifts backward. To yesterday. To Joaquín.

He screamed. He begged. He broke in all the expected ways. But when he said the name—*El Recaudador*, The Collector—everything changed. His bravado didn't just crack. It *evaporated.* His hands started to shake. Not from pain. From memory.

"You don't understand," he whispered hoarsely. "You don't know him."

I leaned closer, certain he was finally breaking. He shook his head, eyes glassy with something that was more than terror of death.

"You don't. You think you're the monster in this room. You're not."

That made me pause. Intrigued, I made him continue.

"He doesn't rush. He waits. He *collects.*"

I leaned in closer, letting him feel my breath. "Everyone bleeds," I told him.

Joaquín shook his head. "Not him."

That wasn't fear of death. That was fear of *memory*. He

was more terrified of the man who wasn't in the room than of me, standing right there, breaking him piece by piece. That kind of devotion—or leverage—doesn't come cheap. It's personal. And personal is dangerous.

There's always a bigger threat. I've lived long enough to know that. But this one doesn't feel like ambition or territory or power for power's sake. This feels like a man who's been waiting for a name to come back around: *Mine.*

The car slows as we near the perimeter.

Jenna shifts, studying my face. "You've been quiet."

I glance at her. "Thinking."

"About yesterday." It's not a question. The woman knows me too well, so I don't even try to deny it. "You don't have to protect me from it," she adds gently. "I want to be part of this."

I squeeze her hand once. "You already are."

She nods, resolute. Outside, my world waits, concrete, steel, men who understand orders without questions. Inside the car, something else settles into place. Partnership. Whoever El Recaudador is, whatever he thinks he's collecting, whatever ghosts he thinks he can cash in, he's welcome to come and try. I don't run. And I don't lose what's mine.

"Let me talk to you about this later," I look into her eyes, letting her know I mean it. "Let's get this done first."

She nods, but the color has drained from her face. Too pale. Too still. I should have made her stay home. The thought hits hard and late, the way regret always does. She turns to me, her eyes lift, steady despite everything.

"Call me," she repeats as if she can read my mind.

The words land like a strike to the chest. For a split second, I'm not here. I'm not walking into another reckoning. I'm back there—years ago—*in a locker room that smelled like bleach and blood and panic. I see her shaking hands. The way she can't stop apologizing. The way I hold her while she cries until there is nothing left in her but resolve.*

I was there.

I saw the aftermath.

I helped her clean up.

I helped her get rid of the body.

That was the night everything changed. The night lines were crossed that can never be uncrossed. She doesn't blink now. The fire in her eyes is still there. It always was.

Her lips press together, satisfied, and for a moment I see it clearly: this is not a woman who needs shielding. This is a woman who knows exactly what the cost is and chooses to stand anyway. I squeeze her hand one more time before letting go. We step out of the car. Steel. Concrete. Men waiting for orders. And somewhere in the back of my mind, a thought settles in with grim amusement: Nobody had better ever ask how we met.

Because if they do, there's no version of that story that doesn't end in silence or blood.

The Oven is already humming when we enter. Low heat. Controlled. Clinical. Everything exactly where it should be. Whitford is strapped to the gurney in the center of the room, wrists and ankles bound, head immobilized. The dead body beneath him—some man scheduled for today's burn—serves its purpose without needing explanation. Consequence, made literal. The message is unmistakable.

Marianne and Sean sit facing each other, chairs bolted to the floor, ropes tight around their torsos. Gags in their mouths. Terror has already stripped them of composure. Sean has sweated through his collar, and Marianne is pale and shaking, her eyes darting wildly as if escape might materialize if she looks hard enough.

Damiano approaches us. His eyes linger curiously on Jenna, but he doesn't say anything. "Whitford didn't know about you or the hit on you."

I nod. It doesn't matter; he's still a rat. Jenna takes a short intake of breath. I send a worried look at her, but her expression doesn't change.

Enzo steps out of the shadows, calm as ever. "We're ready."

Marianne sees Jenna. Her muffled scream pierces the room, high and frantic. She jerks forward in her chair, eyes huge, pleading, fixated on Jenna like she's the last lifeline left. Jenna stiffens beside me, but she doesn't step back. That woman's spine is made of steel.

I move forward slowly, letting my presence settle over the room like a weight. "This," I announce evenly, "is where lies end."

I stop in front of Whitford first. He's already crying. Silent, shaking sobs he can't stop. He looks smaller like this. Reduced. The man who once thought himself untouchable. I don't address him yet. I don't raise my voice. I don't have to. I lift two fingers instead.

Enzo gives a barely perceptible nod. The sound of the soft scraping of metal wheels against concrete as Whitford's gurney shifts closer to the heart of the Oven is the only sound in the room. Not into it. Not yet. Close enough that the heat changes, that the air grows thick and oppressive, that fear sharpens into something feral. Whitford starts to whimper. I turn back to Marianne and Sean and step between them slowly, making sure they can both see Whitford. Making sure they understand exactly where this is going.

"Here's how this works," I say calmly. "He goes first."

Sean's breathing turns ragged. Marianne lets out a broken sound, halfway between a sob and a prayer. "But," I continue calmly, "one of you will not be next." Their heads snap up in unison. Hope—raw, desperate—flares in their eyes. "The one who tells me," I keep my voice conversational, "how you were involved in the hit on me. And why."

I let that sit. I don't say *saved*. I don't say *free*. I don't say *alive*. Just *not next*. I gesture once. The gags come off. Sean breaks immediately.

"It wasn't my idea," he blurts, words tumbling over each other. "I was hired—consulting, security, logistics, nothing violent at first—"

"Sean," Marianne gasps, panic-stricken. "Stop—"

He doesn't even look at her. "It started small," he continues desperately. "Background checks. Quiet intimidation. Kingsley paid well—"

Marianne cuts in, voice shrill. "Oh, don't give that bullshit, you were willing to do anything for money. You beat people up and worse before I came to you!"

Her eyes flick to Jenna again, pleading. Begging. As if Jenna could still save her. I don't intervene. This is exactly what I want.

"Kingsley told me to find someone," Marianne blurts, shaking. "He demanded I find someone to get rid of... of *him*." Her gaze flicks to me. "He said his daughter was involved with a man who would ruin her."

Jenna stiffens beside me. Marianne sees it and latches on. "It wasn't personal," she insists, tears streaming now. "It was about protecting you. Protecting the family."

I feel Jenna's breath hitch, but she doesn't speak.

"She found my firm," Sean snaps bitterly. "Northstar. She hired us. Kingsley quickly realized how useful we were." He laughs weakly, hysterical. "One job became another. And another. Until I wasn't a contractor anymore. I was on staff."

"And the hit?" I ask softly.

Sean swallows hard. "Kingsley ordered it. Paid for it. He wanted you gone before you could—" He stops himself, eyes darting to Jenna. "Before things got complicated."

The room hums. The Oven breathes. Whitford lets out a thin, broken scream as the heat inches closer, reality finally landing.

Marianne sobs openly. "I didn't know it would become this," she whispers. "I didn't know anybody would die."

I tilt my head slightly and laugh dryly, "Everyone says that."

I nod at Enzo. Whitford sees it and guesses the meaning immediately. "No, oh God, no, please. Jenna! Jenna."

Jenna steps forward, and I don't interfere. Whatever she decides here, I will stand behind her. I owe her that much.

JENNA

I WATCH IT ALL. I DON'T LOOK AWAY. I DON'T FLINCH. I don't cover my ears or close my eyes like some fragile thing that needs to be spared. I stand there and let it carve through me, because if I don't face it now, it will own me forever.

My father did this. The truth quietly locks into place revealing something that has always been there, waiting for me to be strong enough to name it.

Ten years. Ten years stolen. Ten years of silence, lies, and choices that were never really mine. Ten years during which Amauri never knew his real father. Ten years where Massimo suffered—alone, broken, furious—because of a decision made in a room I wasn't allowed into.

And *they* knew.

All three of them. If not all of it, then parts. Enough to have eased my pain. Enough to have given Amauri his rightful father. They watched my life rot in slow motion and called it necessary. Called it protection. Called it *for my own good.*

Marianne is the worst. She was there on my wedding day, adjusting my veil, telling me how beautiful I looked. Smiling. Lying. Pretending she didn't know the marriage was a farce, that I was being sacrificed to preserve a reputation, a career, a legacy that was never mine.

She fucking knew!

She knew I loved Massimo. She knew he wasn't gone by choice. She knew I was pregnant and terrified and cornered. And she smiled anyway while she fed me lies. Something inside me goes cold and sharp. Carter screams my name, and it barely registers. He is nothing now. Less than nothing. A footnote in a story that never belonged to him in the first place.

When I step forward, it isn't hesitation that moves me. It's clarity. Massimo doesn't stop me. He doesn't reach for me. He lets me choose. That matters more than he'll ever know.

I look at Marianne. Really look at her. At the woman who stood beside me and watched me burn. And in that moment, I understand something with terrifying calm: this isn't just about what was taken from me. It's about what was taken from *him*. From *us*. From our son. Ten years of lies don't get forgiveness.

They get reckoning.

It's time they paid the piper.

"Jenna, please. Please. I swear, I didn't know. I didn't." Carter pleads as the gurney moves closer to the oven.

"Maybe you did, maybe you didn't. It doesn't matter. Don't call me." I nod at Enzo, and he pushes the button.

Call me. Call me. Echoes inside my head. *Carter leads me down a corridor, our footsteps echo off the walls lined with glass shelves filled with sports trophies where they're not plastered with team photos, championships, smiling athletes, Coach*

Brent Cafferty with his arm around players, grinning like a man who owns the world.

We stop outside the heavy locker room door. Carter swallows hard. "Ready?"

"Sure," I say, even though something inside me whispers don't go in there.

He reaches for the door. It opens before he touches it, and Coach Cafferty greets us with a wide smile. "Hey, kids."

"Hey, Coach." Carter nearly squeaks, and I shoot him a funny look. Coach steps aside to let us in.

"Ladies first," his voice is smooth as snake oil.

Nervousness overcomes me. Something is off. Something isn't right. "Carter?"

He lifts his hands, not touching me, just raising them as if surrendering. "I'm sorry," he breathes. His eyes shine, like he might cry. "I'm so sorry. I love you. It'll be okay. I swear. Call me."

Those were his parting words as he left me with his coach. As payment for playtime on the field, the coach got to play with me. Carter knew exactly what was about to happen. He didn't stumble into ignorance or hide behind misunderstanding. He made a *choice*. The man I thought I loved. The man I *trusted*. He *sold me out,* not for money, not for survival, but for minutes on a field and the illusion of a future he wanted more than he wanted me.

To his coach.

For playtime.

The memory slams into me now with brutal clarity, and the old indignation snaps back into place so hard it steals my breath. How *dare* he? How dare he use me like an object he could barter away? How dare he strip me of my fear, my consent, my humanity, and call it a transaction? What kind of man does that?

I was a virgin. He knew it. We had talked about waiting, about wanting it to mean something, about choosing the moment together. I *trusted* him with that. With *my body*. With *my first yes*. And he was prepared to throw it away like loose change. Not because he didn't understand what it would cost me. But because he did and decided it was worth it. That realization is the cruelest part. Not that I was hurt. But that my pain was *calculated*. Accepted. Written off as collateral damage for his ambition. Standing here now, watching the truth crawl out of their mouths, I don't feel weak.

I feel burningly alive.

Because whatever they took from me that night, whatever they tried to reduce me to, they failed in one crucial way: I survived. And the man who thought he could trade me like property?

He's finally about to learn what that decision was worth.

Carter screams. The sound rips through the room, raw and animal, as he's moved forward. He thrashes, begging now, all the arrogance and entitlement stripped away in seconds. Whatever he thought he was—husband, protector, man—burns off fast.

Marianne breaks. Her sobs are loud and ugly, collapsing her in on herself. Sean fights the bindings, his chair rattles against the floor, and curses spill out of him in a frantic stream. The stench of fear fills the room as he loses control completely. The man who manhandled and drugged me countless times, who touched me whenever and however he thought he could, is reduced to fear so great he pisses himself. I should feel pity for him. For Marianne. I don't. They not only knew. They collaborated to have Massimo killed. My Massimo. And if they had succeeded, I would have never known. Amauri would still be a prisoner of the Venezuelans, a sacrificed pawn in my father's game. They deserve every ounce of pain coming to them.

"Her next," Massimo orders calmly. "Then him."

"No—no, no," Sean wails. "You said— you said if I talked, I wouldn't be—"

"Next," Massimo corrects coldly. Sean freezes as understanding blooms.

"And you're not," Massimo continues, unhurried. "You're not next after Whitford." Relief flashes across Sean's face, brief, pathetic. "You're next after her."

The meaning lands. Sean breaks down completely, screaming, pleading, bargaining with anyone who might listen. Marianne's cries rise to match his, desperation feeding on desperation.

Massimo turns to me.

"Ready?" he asks, holding out his hand.

I'm trembling. There's no denying that. My hands shake, my heart pounds, and every nerve in my body feels raw and exposed. But I straighten my spine. I don't let them see it. I won't give Marianne the satisfaction of my tears. I won't give Sean the comfort of my fear. Whatever emotions are tearing through me stay locked behind my ribs, contained, controlled.

"Ready," I nod once, taking his hand. His grip tightens, solid, grounding, a silent promise that I am not alone in this.

We move forward together, and I understand something with absolute clarity: This isn't mercy. This is consequence. And I will not look away.

The car door shuts behind us, sealing away the noise, heat, and screaming like it never happened. The city slides past the windows, indifferent.

"Are you okay?" Massimo asks.

I shake my head. "No." My voice doesn't wobble. I'm past that. "But I will be."

He nods once, accepting it.

Then I turn the question back on him. "Are you?"

He exhales slowly and drags a hand through his hair; the gesture is tired, unguarded in a way I haven't seen before.

"I killed my uncle. And my cousins. Over this lie."

The words hang in the air between us, heavy and

irrevocable. I don't know what to say. First, the fact that he's telling me this at all, not just admitting it, but offering it, trusting me with something that raw, that damning? That's monumental, almost eclipsing the words themselves. Then I think of the lie. How big it was. How far it spread. How many lives it warped. How much blood it cost.

"I don't know what to say," I admit quietly.

He nods again, like he wasn't expecting absolution.

"It was inevitable," he admits after a moment. "Really." Then his mouth twists, just slightly. "But I don't like someone setting my terms for me."

That, I understand too.

I glance at him, something dark and familiar settling in my chest. "Yeah," I say softly. "I get that."

"Now what?" I ask after a few seconds.

He lets out a short, humorless chuckle and finally looks at me. "You're asking *me*?"

I lift a brow, unsure of his meaning. He shrugs lightly, but his eyes are serious. "He's *your* father." A pause. "What do *you* want to do?"

The question lands heavier than anything else today. Because for the first time in my adult life, it's actually mine to answer. I don't answer right away. The truth is, I don't know. Not yet. The question is too big, too layered, to unwrap in the space between traffic lights. My father's face flashes through my mind, not the monster from today, but the man who lifted me onto his shoulders when people were watching, smiling for the cameras like I was something to be proud of. The man who once fixed my broken toy at the kitchen table, silent and focused, like it mattered more than he ever let on. The man who decided, somewhere along the way, that my life was a problem to be managed.

"I don't know," I concede finally. "I just know I don't want him deciding anything for me ever again."

Massimo nods once, like that's enough for now. Maybe it is. The car rolls on in silence, but it's not empty. It's full of things unsaid, of futures pressing in from all sides. My hands rest in my lap, still trembling faintly, and I curl my fingers into fists until the shaking subsides. I think of Amauri. Of his laugh. His stubbornness. The way he believes promises matter.

"I promised him the pool." The words are meant to distract.

Massimo glances at me. "Then we keep the promise."

Something in my chest loosens at that. Not relief—resolve. We'll go back to the penthouse. We'll let him be a kid for a few hours. The rest—the truth about his grandfather, about his father, about the world he's been pulled into—can wait. For now, my choice is simple. I choose my son.

We pull up at the hotel a little while later. The elevator ride feels endless, and my nerves hum just beneath my skin, but the moment the penthouse doors slide open, everything else fades. Amauri spots us instantly.

"Mummy!"

He launches himself across the room, a blur of limbs and momentum, arms locking around my waist. The impact knocks the breath out of me and gives it right back. I drop to my knees to hold him properly, bury my face in his hair, breathing him in like oxygen after a long, suffocating dive.

"Hey, my brave boy," I murmur, pressing kisses into his curls.

He pulls back just enough to grin past me at Massimo, and he receives his hug. Then his eyes widen as he remembers something important. Very important.

"Are we still going to the pool?" he asks, gaze flicking between us, hopeful and insistent all at once.

I look up at Massimo.

He doesn't hesitate. "Yes."

Amauri whoops, grabbing both our hands at once, clutching them like anchors, like if he holds on tight enough, nothing bad can happen. In that moment, the rest of the world—the lies, the blood, the choices waiting down the road—falls quiet.

The pool deck is empty when we arrive. No shrieking kids. No tourists with neon drinks and sunburned shoulders. No noise beyond the soft rush of water. An oasis in the middle of a humming city. Massimo had it cleared completely; security is posted discreetly at every access point, eyes alert but unobtrusive.

For a split second, guilt pricks at me. All those tourists in the hotel, spending their money, expecting the full experience. And here we are, alone in paradise because we can. But then Amauri lets out a delighted gasp and bolts forward, shoes already half-off, and the guilt dissolves. Security for my son comes first. Always.

And if I'm honest—truly honest—I feel a flicker of something else too. Enjoyment. This kind of quiet luxury. This kind of protection. This kind of *being chosen*? It's something I could get used to. Easily. Would I want it every day? No. Amauri needs other kids, scraped knees, noise, chaos. He needs normalcy, too. But for right now? This is perfect.

Amauri doesn't wait for instructions. He barrels straight toward the water slide like it personally insulted him by existing without him. "I'M GOING FIRST," he announces, already climbing.

Massimo laughs—a real one, unguarded. He looks at me, and I realize he doesn't know what to do. Because of his scars. He doesn't like to show them even now, even with the waterpark emptied of people. With a shrug, I peel out of my dress, a little self-conscious about the bikini I got at the boutique. My stretch marks are on full display, and so is the scar from the C-section. Defiantly, I raise my chin, and Massimo's smile deepens as he shrugs out of his shirt and follows Amauri at a more reasonable pace. It seems today is the beginning of a new life for all of us.

I freeze for half a second. God. The scars are there. Faded and angry, old and new all at once, mapping battles

I only know pieces of. But instead of detracting from him, they somehow make him *more*. More real. More dangerous. More earned. And infuriatingly—unfairly—he's only gotten more handsome in the last ten years. Taller than I remember. Broader through the shoulders. His body has settled into its power, muscle carved by use rather than vanity. He doesn't look like a man who works out to be admired; he looks like a man built to endure, to protect, to destroy when necessary. The kind of body that doesn't ask for attention but commands it anyway.

Sunlight catches on his skin as he steps closer to the pool, highlighting the planes of his chest, the strength in his arms. There's no hesitation in him, no self-consciousness. He just *is,* solid, grounded, lethal. I swallow, heat pools low in my stomach, and I briefly resent the universe for this particular injustice.

Ten years apart. Ten years of hell.

And somehow, he gets to look like *that*.

I tear my gaze away just as Amauri comes flying down the slide, reminding myself that now is not the time, but filing the image away anyway. For later. Much later.

"Did you see that?" Amauri beams. "Did you?"

"I did," Massimo says seriously. "Ten out of ten. Excellent form."

Amauri puffs up like he's just won an Olympic medal, then his eyes flick back to Massimo's chest. He squints, curiosity knitting his brow in that very particular way kids have when they notice something that doesn't fit their understanding of the world.

"Massimo?" he asks.

"Yes, champ?"

"What are those?" He points, vague but earnest. "The lines."

My breath catches. I hold it without meaning to. Massimo doesn't hesitate. He glances down at himself, then back at Amauri, calm and unbothered.

"These?" he points lightly. "These are from times I got hurt doing my job."

Amauri considers this. "Did it hurt a lot?"

"Some of them," Massimo admits. "But I'm okay now."

Amauri nods, satisfied with that answer. Then, after a beat, he adds solemnly, "You're like a superhero."

Massimo's mouth twitches. "Not quite."

"But superheroes get hurt too," Amauri insists, then brightens suddenly. "And they still win."

Massimo meets my eyes over Amauri's head, something deep and unspoken passing between us.

"Yeah," he agrees quietly. "They do."

Amauri grins, already distracted as he scrambles toward the ladder. "I'm going again!"

He takes off, fearless, and I finally let myself breathe. I realize—with a mix of awe and aching gratitude—that Massimo didn't just answer the question. He taught my son something important—that scars don't mean broken, they mean survival. When Amauri comes flying down for the second time, we move on to the lazy river. Amauri insists Massimo sit behind him in the inflatable, explaining the rules in grave detail. Massimo listens like this is the most important briefing he's ever received. I hang back a little, watching them drift. Amauri talks. Not just chatter, but real talking. About the helicopter. About how scary it was, but also kind of cool. About how Carter yelled a lot when he was scared, and how he didn't like holding his hand because it got sweaty.

Massimo doesn't interrupt. Doesn't correct. Doesn't defend. He just listens.

"That must've been confusing," he commiserates gently.

Amauri nods. "But you don't yell."

"No," Massimo agrees. "At least not when I'm afraid."

Something in my throat tightens. I drift closer, resting my arms on the edge of the float. Massimo looks at me, and for a second, the world narrows to just the three of us, water lapping softly around our legs. After a while, Amauri goes back to the slide, and while he's gone, Massimo reaches out, fingers brushing mine beneath the surface. A quiet, stolen touch. Nothing overt. Everything loaded.

"You okay?" he murmurs.

I nod. "Yeah. I just... didn't know it could feel like this."

His thumb presses lightly against my knuckle. "Neither did I."

Amauri comes flying back into the pool, demanding we both watch again, and Massimo releases my hand without regret, turning all his attention back to him. That's when I realize, watching them, how natural it is. How unforced. How Amauri leans toward him without hesitation, how Massimo adjusts instinctively, already anticipating needs he's only just been introduced to. This isn't pretending. This isn't a role. This is a bond forming in real time. The sun dips lower. Amauri's laughter echoes across the empty deck. For a few stolen hours, the past loosens its grip.

I know the darkness hasn't gone anywhere. But here, in the water, with my son laughing and Massimo steady beside us, it feels like we're building something strong enough to stand against it.

MASSIMO

AMAURI IS ASLEEP BEFORE I MAKE IT ALL THE WAY DOWN THE hall. One moment he's talking—murmuring something about slides and superheroes and whether Hammie needs a night-light—and the next his weight goes slack against my chest, breath evening out, fingers still curled in the fabric of my shirt like he might fall if he lets go. I stop walking. Just stand there for a second, holding him. He's heavy in the way only sleeping children are. Trusting. Unaware. Completely certain the world will still be there when he wakes up. I never expected this.

I always assumed there would be children one day. An arranged marriage. Practical alliances. Sons raised to inherit, daughters married off strategically. That was the shape of the future I'd accepted early on. But this?

This quiet, bone-deep pull in my chest when I look at him. The instinct to shield, to soften, to *stay*.

My son.

The word still feels unreal. And inevitable. Like something my body knew long before my mind caught up. I lay him down gently, tugging the covers up to his chin. He sighs in his sleep and turns onto his side without waking. I stand there longer than necessary, memorizing the way his face relaxes when he feels safe. I have to force myself to leave the room.

Jenna is in the kitchen, sleeves pushed up, washing dishes like this is any other night in any other life. The sight of her hits me harder than it should.

Normal.

Domestic.

Mine.

I step up behind her and nuzzle into the curve of her throat, breathe her in.

"Don't," I murmur. "We have people for that."

"I don't mind," she replies, leaning back into me like it's instinct. Like her body remembers mine. "It helps me think."

I reach around her anyway, take the plate from her hands before she can protest, and set it gently in the sink. Turn her. Frame her face with my hands. Up close, I can see the exhaustion in her eyes. The aftermath. The weight she's carrying without complaint.

"You did well today," I praise her quietly.

She blinks. "That feels like a strange thing to say."

"I know." My thumbs brush her cheekbones. "It's still true."

She studies me for a long moment, like she's searching for cracks, for distance. She doesn't find any. Neither do I.

"I didn't know I wanted this," I admit. The words come easier than I would expect them to. "This life. This feeling. I thought I understood power. Control. Legacy." My voice drops. "Turns out I understood nothing."

Her hands slide up my arms, grounding, warm. "Does that scare you?"

"Yes," I say without hesitation. Then, softer, "No."

I rest my forehead against hers, let myself be still. Let myself be here. I study her face up close, the familiar lines, the strength she's always carried, even when the world tried to bend her. And for the life of me, I can't understand how I ever let myself hate her. Resent her. How I convinced myself she'd betrayed me. The thought turns sour in my chest. I should have known better. Should have trusted the woman who stands in front of me now, the woman who faced hell today without flinching, who chose truth even when it cost her everything. Jenna would never have walked away from me if she'd known. Never would have kept my son from me out of spite or fear or convenience.

The fault lies with me. I was too busy sharpening my knives. Too busy building a vengeance that I thought righteous. A rage that gave me direction, purpose. I needed someone to blame, and she was silent and unreachable, and therefore, easy. That vengeance carried me for ten years. And now I know it was built on a lie.

The realization doesn't undo what I did. My uncle is still dead. My cousins are still dead. Blood answered blood, and I can't pretend otherwise. I told myself it was inevitable—and maybe it was—but knowing *why* I did it doesn't settle easily anymore. I don't know what to do with that yet.

I don't know how to reconcile the man I was with the man standing here, holding the woman he once swore he'd never forgive. The man who thought power meant control, and who is only now learning it might mean restraint.

My hands tighten slightly on her face, not to trap her —never that—but to anchor myself.

"I was wrong," I say quietly. Not an apology yet. Just the truth, laid bare.

Her eyes soften, not triumphant. Not relieved. Just... present. Making something inside me shift. The vengeance that defined me doesn't vanish, but it loses its center. It no longer has her face. No longer has her name carved into it. Whatever comes next—El Recaudador, Kingsley, the reckoning still circling—I'll face it differently. Not fueled by a lie. But by the certainty of what I almost destroyed... and won't lose again.

I kiss her. It's not urgent. Not claiming. Just... necessary. When we break apart, I don't step away. I stay right there, my forehead resting against hers, my breath still tangled with hers.

"Thank you," I say quietly.

She blinks. "For what?"

"For you," I answer without hesitation. "For Amauri. For the truth. For everything."

Before she can respond, I scoop her up, effortless and familiar, and she lets out a soft laugh of surprise as she slings her arms around my neck. She fits against me like this was always the shape we were meant to take.

"Thank you," she says back.

I smile, unable to stop myself. "For what?"

"For being you," she replies simply. "For being who you

are. For bringing Amauri back to me. For loving him. For taking care of us."

Each word lands heavier than the last.

"You deserve that," I tell her, my voice rough now. "And so much more, Jenna."

She looks at me like she believes it. Like it's obvious. Like it's not unraveling something deep and structural inside me. She has no idea what she's doing to me. No idea how close I am to breaking under the weight of being seen like this, not as a king, not as a weapon, not as a consequence, but as a man worthy of love. Worthy of a family.

I carry her down the hall, past the quiet rooms, past the place where our son sleeps, safe and exhausted and whole. For the first time in my life, I don't feel like I'm taking something. I feel like I'm being given everything.

In the bedroom, I set her down with care. The lights are low, and gold and indigo shadows spill against the floor. For a moment, neither of us moves, and then she tilts her head, like she's waiting for a verdict, or maybe for me to admit I'm making a mistake. I'm not. I'm exactly where I want to be. And I'm not leaving it to chance again. Yesterday, between meetings, blood, and business, I walked into a private jeweler and bought a ring that could anchor a continent. Not subtle. Not delicate. A stone that catches light like it owns it. Like she does. I didn't ask for advice. I didn't compare options. I saw it. I knew.

It's in my pocket now. Heavy. Solid. A promise I intend to keep this time. She won't walk away from me again. Not because I'll cage her. Because I'll give her no reason to.

I reach into my pocket. Her breath stills. The velvet box is small in my palm. Unassuming. It doesn't need spectacle. I flip it open. The diamond catches the light immediately. Big. Unapologetic. Cut to command attention. Her eyes widen.

"Oh my God, Massimo—"

"Now that you're a widow," I state calmly, "I believe I'm allowed to correct an old mistake." Her lips part. I don't kneel. I don't need to. "I should have put this on your finger years ago," I continue. "Before politics. Before fear. Before anyone convinced you that you belonged anywhere but with me."

My thumb brushes her jaw.

"I won't lose you again. Not to silence. Not to pride. Not to anyone else's ambition. I made that mistake once; I learned my lesson." My voice lowers. "You are mine, Jenna. Not as a possession. As a choice. As a partner. As the only woman I have ever loved."

Her breath shudders.

"I built an empire. But you are the only thing I would burn it for."

Her hands come to my chest.

"Yes," she whispers immediately. "Yes, of course—"

I slide the ring onto her finger. It fits. It always would have. She's smiling up at me like the world just rearranged itself. Then she blinks.

"Oh," she says.

I narrow my eyes slightly. "Oh?"

"You have to ask the other man first."

The temperature in the room drops.

"Other man?" I repeat.

She winks. "Amauri."

I stare at her. Of all the battles I've prepared for, of all the enemies I've faced, I would rather walk unarmed into a rival compound than negotiate with my ten-year-old son about marrying his mother. I exhale slowly.

"I'd prefer a shootout," I mutter.

She laughs, wrapping her arms around my neck. "He likes you."

"That's not the same thing," I reply darkly.

But I pull her close anyway, my hand settles at her waist, and the ring flashes between us like a promise carved in stone.

"I'll ask him," I promise. "And he'll say yes."

She smiles against my mouth. "And if he doesn't?"

I kiss her, slow and certain. "He will."

I kiss her again, deeper. My hands slide into her hair, fingers threading through the soft strands like I'm learning the texture of forgiveness. She gasps into my mouth, just enough to let me know I can take whatever I want, just enough to let me know she wants it too. I move slow. It's new to me, this patience. My body aches for her, but it's not the hungry, mindless kind I remember. I want to savor this. To watch her unravel and know that I'm the reason.

Her hands find the buttons of my shirt, and she fumbles a little—she always does—and I think about the first time she undressed me, the clumsy urgency of it. This is different. No hurry, no threat, no time bomb ticking down on the wall behind us. Just her breath, her hands, her skin.

"You're beautiful," I say. It sounds idiotic; it isn't enough. But she flushes at the words, her eyes turn soft and disbelieving, like no one's ever told her that before. Or maybe no one's ever told her and meant it.

"I'm a mess," she tries to laugh it off with a nervous edge in her voice.

"You're perfect," I correct, and slide my hands under her shirt to trace the curve of her waist, the silk-smooth skin warm beneath my palms. With one motion, I lift her and lay her back on the bed, following her down, every inch of me pressed to every inch of her.

Her mouth parts. She breathes my name. I lose track of time. I worship her slowly. It isn't a word I ever understood—worship—but now I do. It's the careful way I unbutton her blouse, deliberate, slow, watching her chest rise and fall with every snap. It's the reverence in my lips as I follow the shallow line of her neck, the sharp clavicle, the hollow at the base of her throat. She clings to me, nails digging into my shoulders, but she lets me set the pace. I strip away everything between us, not roughly, but with purpose. I want her skin on mine. I want the heat. I want to see her come undone.

When she's naked beneath me, I pause. I take her in. She tries to cover herself, shy and beautiful and aching, but I won't let her. I pin her wrists above her head and hold her there, my mouth at her ear.

"Don't hide from me," I whisper. "Not ever."

Her breath shudders out. She closes her eyes.

"I want to watch you," I tell her, lips just grazing her jaw. "I want to see what I do to you, Jenna. Every sound, every muscle, every fucking inch."

She bucks up against me, desperate, and her eyes fly open.

"Tell me what you want," I growl, and it comes out harsher than I mean it, but she only bites her lip and stares me down.

"I want you inside me," she whispers.

My hand moves between her legs. I find her already wet, so fucking wet for me.

"Is that for me?" I ask softly, my mouth brushing her skin, lingering at the place where her pulse betrays her. It's racing. For me.

"Always," she whispers, swallowing hard. "It's always been you. Only you."

I still.

The words echo in my head, too big, too dangerous to touch without breaking something. I lift my head slowly and meet her gaze. Her eyes are glossy, pupils blown wide, the green around them reduced to a thin halo like the last ring of a dying star.

"What do you mean?" I ask, even as something inside me already knows. It's been ten years. Ten long, empty years. Of course, she would have... lived. Loved. Found someone else. Anyone else.

Her throat bobs again. "Carter couldn't," she says quietly. "After the accident. The paralysis."

The air leaves my lungs in a rush. A dark, visceral satisfaction flares before I can stop it, sharp, vindictive, ugly. The bastard deserved that and worse. I'd hated him for existing in her life, for taking a place that was never his. But the feeling dies as fast as it came. Because this isn't about him.

"What about others?" I need to hear it said. Need it to be real.

She shakes her head. Slowly. Absolutely. "No. Never."

Something inside me finally gives way. I rest my forehead against hers, breathing her in like oxygen, like the only thing tethering me to the ground. Ten years collapse into a single moment, everything I lost, everything I thought was taken from me, everything I told myself to survive.

Nobody.

Not ever.

Her first. Then. And now. Always.

The realization breaks through me with a force I wasn't prepared for. Not pride. Not possession. Reverence. She didn't wait because she had to. She waited because she chose me.

"I thought I'd lost you," I whisper, the confession tearing out of me before I can stop it.

She lifts her hand to my face, thumb brushing my cheek. "You never did."

That's when I understand it fully, not as power, not as ownership, but as something far more terrifying and sacred. I am not one choice among many. I am *the* choice. It undoes me completely.

I ease into her slowly, watching her the whole time. Her eyes never leave my face, and when I fill her, she moans, a helpless, hungry sound that shreds my composure. It almost breaks me, how much I want her. How much I want this. I move slowly, dragging it out, letting pleasure build in long, steady increments. Every thrust is a promise: I'm not leaving, not running, not disappearing. I'm here for every second of this.

She meets me, stroke for stroke, her legs wrapping around me until we're impossible to separate, her hands fisted in the sheets, in my hair, on my back. I fuck her like I mean it. Like I need her more than air. And I do. I do.

"You're so fucking beautiful," I whisper into her mouth. "I want you to come for me, Jenna. I want to feel you come all around me. Can you do that?" My hand moves to cover the scar on her belly. "I'm going to fuck a baby into here."

She nods, frantic. Her body is wound tight, her thighs quivering, her eyes wild and begging me not to stop.

I slow myself, just for a second, pinning her with my hips and my words. "Look at me," I order. "Don't look away, not when you come."

She doesn't blink. I shift just enough to hit that perfect angle, and her body shatters. She screams—quiet, desperate—and I catch her sound with my mouth, swallowing it whole. Her pussy clenches so hard I almost lose it, and I fight to hold back, to give her every last second. When she starts to come down, I press her wrists harder into the mattress, holding her there, helpless, open, mine.

I fuck her until I can't think, until there's nothing but heat and friction and the animal satisfaction of being wanted this much. Everything else disappears. No past. No war. No ghosts. Just her. Just this. The way she feels around me drags something primal out of my chest, something I buried the night I thought I lost her.

Mine.

The word pulses through me, raw and unrelenting. I move harder, deeper, chasing it, needing it, needing her to feel exactly what this is. What we are. She's not slipping away from me again. Not this time. Never again. The thought sharpens, turns from want into something darker. Something rooted.

I should have had this. I should have been there the first time. Every moment. Every breath. Every second of it. Her belly rounding with my child. Her hand reaching for mine. Her pain. Her fear. Mine to carry.

Stolen.

Rage coils tight in my chest, feeding the rhythm, driving me harder, until there's nothing left but instinct and need and the overwhelming certainty of what I'm taking back. What was always mine. And this time, this time, no one takes it from me. Not her. Not my child. Not this life.

When release hits, it tears through me, sharp and absolute, dragging a rough breath from my chest as I hold her close, grounding myself in the reality of her beneath me. Of us.

I stay there for a moment, forehead pressed to hers, breathing her in, anchoring myself. Beneath the fading edge of it, the thought settles in, quiet, dangerous, immovable. Let it take. Let it root. Let it grow.

This time, I'll be there for every second.

My hand slides to her stomach, instinctive, possessive,

lingering there. Guarding something that isn't even there yet.

But will be.

She wraps herself around me, holding me together while I fall apart inside her.

We stay like that for a long, silent minute, just the sound of our breaths and a slow, shared heartbeat. Eventually, I roll over and drag her on top of me, tucking her head under my chin. She's shivering. Not from cold, just the aftershock. I hold her close and don't let go.

For the first time in years, there's not a single thought in my head about power, or revenge, or anything except the miracle of having her here with me. She belongs to me. And I belong to her. I never believed in fate, but this feels close enough.

I wake sometime later, tangled in a mess of sheets and Jenna's limbs. Her hair is a wild snarl across my chest, one thigh hiked over my hip, her arm heavy and possessive around my waist. I'm hard again; the night's pleasure echoes through my body in slow, lazy waves.

Her breathing is deep and even. She's exhausted, and I can't blame her. I kept her up for hours. I should let her sleep now, but I can't resist the urge to touch her again. I slide my hand down her back, palm flat, slow. She stirs, mumbling nonsense, but doesn't wake. I keep going, tracing the curve of her ass, the warm crease of her thigh. I want to wake her up gently, but I'm starving for her. I want her every way I can have her.

I ease her onto her back and settle between her legs. She blinks awake, groggy and annoyed for half a second, then she sees me and her expression shifts, soft, languid, hungry. Her hands find my hair, pulling me down for a kiss. Only when she reluctantly releases me do I lower myself to feather kisses, gentle but insistent, along the inside of her knee, then move up to the warm, sensitive skin of her thigh. She goes from sleepy to shivering in a heartbeat. I want her to feel worshipped, adored, drenched in awe. I want her to understand with every nerve ending she has that she's the only thing I will ever hunger for. She's still sleep-fuzzy, blinking in the half-light, but I don't let up. My hands bracket her hips, slow and careful, and I press my mouth between her legs, tasting the salt and heat of her even before she's fully awake.

She arches, a low, broken sound humming through her as I work her open with my tongue. She's swollen and sensitive, still throbbing from the last round. I want to leave her raw from pleasure, ruined for anyone but me. I take my time, savoring every gasp, every involuntary flutter of her stomach. My fingers dig into her hips, holding her steady while I lap and tease, circling her clit slowly, never quite giving her what she wants until she's panting, nails carving crescents into my shoulders.

She tries to speak, to protest or beg, but all that comes out are little whimpers, the kind that make my chest ache with something savage and ancient. I look up at her, and her eyes meet mine, dark, wild, pleading. She's never looked at me like this, and the sight nearly undoes me. This is the real her, the core of her, unguarded and desperate. I want to memorize it.

I slide a finger inside her, gentle and slow, and she chokes on a moan, thighs clamping tight around my head. I keep going, patient and relentless, working her until she's shaking all over, sweat slicking her skin. With every surge of pleasure, she calls my name, voice breaking, and I drink it in. I want her to remember this, the way I touch her, the way I break her apart and hold her together at the same time. I want this to be the standard she measures all other touch against, for the rest of her life.

She comes once, hard, her whole body curling tight as a bowstring. I don't stop. I keep licking, coaxing every last tremor out of her, pushing her higher and higher until she's sobbing with the force of it. I love her like this, unfiltered and raw, not hiding behind armor or anger. Just need.

When she can't take anymore, I crawl up her body, trailing kisses over her stomach, her rib cage, the tattoo twin of mine, her breasts, the fluttering pulse at her throat. She's limp and shaking, a mess of tangled hair and flushed skin. I crush my mouth to hers, letting her taste herself on my tongue, and she kisses me back with a kind of reckless gratitude that splits me open.

She wraps her arms around my neck, pulling me down until our bodies are flush, and I can feel every tremor of her aftershocks rippling through her. My hands are everywhere—her hair, her jaw, her breasts—mapping her all over again, greedy for new territory. She clings to me, nails raking down my back, urging me closer, deeper, more.

I line up against her, slow and deliberate, and push

inside. She's so slick and tight I nearly lose it right there, but I grit my teeth and force myself to go slow. I want to remember this night for the rest of my life. Her legs come up around my waist, and she pulls me in, hips rolling to meet mine. It's different this time, less hunger, more ache. The kind of ache that's almost unbearable, because it's not just about getting off; it's about giving her something she can't get anywhere else.

She comes twice more before I pull out, flip her over, and put her on her hands and knees, her face buried in a pillow to muffle the sounds. I make it last as long as I can, but she's too tight, too hot, and I'm too far gone. I finish hard, clutching her hips, grinding deep until I'm sure she knows who she belongs to.

After, I collapse next to her, pulling her onto my chest, kissing the sweat off her forehead. She laughs, breathless, and pushes at my shoulder.

"You're insatiable," she whispers.

"I've waited a decade for you," I say, and it's only half a joke.

She kisses me, slow and sweet, and then we both drift for a while, lost in the warm dark.

She sleeps. Curled into my chest, trusting in a way that feels almost violent after the day we've had. I keep my arm around her, fingers resting lightly at her waist, afraid that if I move too much, I'll wake her, or worse, discover this isn't real.

I don't close my eyes. My body is spent. My mind is not. I listen to her breathe and think about how easily everything I've ever wanted fits into this one quiet moment. Her. Our son, asleep down the hall. The illusion —no, the *promise*—of something like peace. And the beginning of a new life inside her. Inside the only woman I ever loved. It will be like I finally get something back from what was stolen from me. I'll make every second up to Amauri. I swear. And her.

It's enough to make a man careless. So I don't let myself sink into it. My thoughts slide backward instead, to the hum of engines and cold air rushing past an open hatch door in the compartment room of the jet—a room installed just for this purpose. To Joaquín, bound and broken, no longer screaming. No longer bargaining.

That was when he finally talked. Not when the pain peaked. Not when fear did its usual work. But when he realized he was already dead and nothing he said could change that.

Right before we pushed him out, he lifted his head and laughed, a wet, disbelieving sound. "You think this ends with me. That's what he wants you to think."

I remember leaning in, close enough that he could see his reflection in my eyes.

"He?" I asked. I had an idea who he was talking about; he had already mentioned him, but I had to hear it again.

Joaquín swallowed. Hard. "El Recaudador."

The name tasted like ash.

"He knows about your family," Joaquín went on. "Not the ones you killed. The ones you *made*." His gaze flicked, pointed, knowing. "He's not interested in territory. He's interested in *choice*."

I told him he was stalling.

He shook his head. "No. I'm warning you."

The wind roared louder then, drowning out the rest, but not before he said one last thing, quiet, certain, almost reverent. "He doesn't collect the past. He collects what men would burn the world to protect."

The memory sits heavy in my chest now. I look down at Jenna, at the soft line of her mouth, the way her brow smooths when she sleeps. I think of Amauri, sprawled across his bed like the world has never hurt him and never will. I understand it then.

There is no way that Joaquín or El Recaudador—what a ridiculous name—knew about them. Not yesterday. No, he was talking about my *other family*. The one that took a decade to build. With Enzo, Alessio, Gabe, and Damiano at the top.

This isn't about revenge. Or expansion. Or power.

This is about leverage.

I press a kiss into Jenna's hair, careful not to wake her. El Recaudador will find out about her and my son. Likely not today. Maybe not even tomorrow, but it will be sooner rather than later. Let him come, I think, the resolve settling in cold and steady. If El Recaudador wants what I'd burn the world for, he's welcome to try.

But there are lines you cross only once. And this time, I won't be the one paying for someone else's lies.

The sky is just beginning to pale when I step out onto the balcony. Las Vegas stretches below me, restless even at dawn. Neon still burns in places it shouldn't. The city never truly sleeps; it just pretends to. There is a lull right about this time, when normal people get up. I rest my forearms on the railing, breathe in the desert air, and let the cool seep into my bones. Once, this view meant dominion. Control. A kingdom I built with blood and patience and an unshakable belief that I understood every moving piece.

Now it means something else. Behind me, Jenna sleeps. Down the hall, our son dreams. The city looks the same as it always has, but I don't. The phone vibrates in my hand before it rings. Gabe.

I answer without speaking.

"There's something you need to hear," he announces. No preamble. No wasted words.

I straighten slightly. "Go ahead."

"I got a call." His voice is tight. Alert. "Unknown number, probably from a burner, no ID."

I straighten slightly, premonition filling my bones. "And?"

"It was a man. The guy knew who he was calling. Knew who *I* worked for." A beat. "I've already got Alessio tracing it. He's pulling everything: latency, relay points, ghost servers. Whoever this is didn't come in sloppy."

"What did he want?" I demand, wishing Gabe would get to the point and dreading it at the same time.

Gabe exhales. "It wasn't a threat."

That makes my jaw tighten.

"It was an offer," he adds carefully.

I close my eyes.

"Let me guess."

"*Join me*," Gabe's voice drops, "*and live. Stay with Manetti... and die.*"

The words settle over me like frost.

"He give a name?" I ask, though my pulse has already shifted.

A pause. Then, quieter, "Yeah."

I open my eyes and look back out over the city as the first line of sun cuts across the skyline. Already guessing his answer.

"El Recaudador."

Of course.

"When?" I ask.

"No deadline," Gabe replies. "Which feels intentional. Like he assumes you'll understand the urgency on your own."

I almost smile.

"He knows me," I wager.

"Yes," Gabe agrees. "That's one of the things that worries me."

"*One* of the things?" I repeat, dragging the words out.

There's a pause on the line. Too long. I shift my weight and lean back against the railing, the cool metal biting into my spine as the city wakes below me. Of course there's more.

"Gabe," I say quietly.

He exhales. "I wasn't the only one who got the call."

I close my eyes for a beat. "Who else?"

Another pause. Then, flat. Controlled. "Everyone."

My fingers tighten around the edge of the railing. "Define everyone."

"All four of us, Me, Enzo, Damiano, and Alessio," He fills me in. "From there, it kept going. Lieutenants.

Runners. Dealers. As far down as we can trace it." My jaw locks. "Further," he adds. "Strippers. Hookers. Cocktail waitresses. Anyone even loosely tied to your operation."

I let out a short, humorless breath. Not a laugh. Not quite. "Jesus Christ."

Gabe lets out a nervous laugh. "Whoever this fucker is, he's thorough."

I open my eyes and stare out at the Strip, watching the sun climb higher, gilding the very thing someone is trying to shake apart.

"He's not just trying to get my attention," I conclude. "He's rattling the foundation of my empire, seeing what cracks first."

"Yes," Gabe agrees. "He wants you to look over your shoulder and not trust anyone."

I rake a hand through my hair. "Any idea who it is? Voice recognition? Accent? Anything?"

"If I had that," Gabe snaps, then catches himself. "If any of us did, I would've led with it."

I let the comment go. He's on edge. I have a feeling we all will be until this fuck is found. And we will find him.

"Alessio's still tracing?" I ask.

"He hasn't stopped."

I look back toward the glass behind me, where Jenna sleeps, where my son is dreaming, unaware that the ground beneath us just shifted. This isn't about territory. It isn't even about me. This is about destabilization. About planting doubt. About making every single person under my roof wonder if loyalty is a death sentence. And fuck me—it's working.

"Listen to me," I order finally. "No one moves. No one responds. No one gets clever."

"Understood."

"He wants a choice," I continue. "I'm not giving him one."

I end the call and stay where I am, gripping the railing as the city fully wakes, bright and loud and deceptively intact. The bastard isn't just coming for my kingdom. He's trying to make it eat itself from the inside out. As much as I hate to admit it, he picked the right pressure point. But not for long. I turn back inside. War is coming. And I have a feeling it's going to get ugly.

THE NEXT MORNING...

Breakfast is already cleared when the tutor arrives. Amauri is thrilled at first—someone new, someone who treats him like he's fascinating—but I can tell he's still a little off, still recalibrating after everything. I hover longer than I mean to, smoothing his hair, kissing his temple, watching him settle with the quiet intensity he gets when he's trying to be brave.

Massimo watches from the doorway, arms folded, unreadable.

He looks up as I approach and says, "I don't want this to be permanent. Just for now."

I keep my voice low so Amauri won't hear. The tutor is already engaging him. "I had no idea you did this. And I appreciate it. I really do."

Massimo's gaze doesn't waver. He's listening. I don't want to seem bitchy, "But, there's one thing that needs to be clear between us." Something in his expression shifts, not anger, not resistance. Attention. "You don't get to make decisions about our son without talking to me first," I state calmly. "Not even good ones."

His jaw tightens, but he doesn't interrupt.

"I know your instincts are to protect," I go on. "And I'm grateful for that. But Amauri isn't a territory to secure or a problem to solve. He's our child. And I need to be part of every choice that affects him."

For a heartbeat, the room feels very small. Then Massimo exhales slowly, like he's recalibrating rather than retreating.

"You're right," he agrees after a pause. The words carry more weight than any argument would have. "I didn't mean to cut you out," he adds. "I saw a risk and moved."

"I realize that," I concede softly. "That's why I'm saying this now. Before it becomes a habit."

He studies my face, searching for accusation, for fear. Finding neither.

"You won't have to remind me again," he nods. "We decide together."

Something in my chest loosens at that.

"Thank you," I reply.

He steps closer, lowering his voice further. "I'm still learning how to do this," he admits. "How to be... more than just the man who fixes things after they break."

I meet his eyes. "So am I."

From the table, Amauri looks up again. "Are you done talking?"

Massimo's mouth curves. "Sorry, bud."

Amauri nods, satisfied, and goes back to his work. Massimo takes my arm and directs me to his office to give Amauri and the tutor some privacy.

"Well, I guess now would be the time to tell you that I pulled some strings and enrolled Amauri in the best private school in the valley."

I stare at him.

"Private. Smaller. Better security." He keeps talking.

I turn to face him fully. "His school *is* private."

"Not enough," he counters immediately. "I've looked into it."

Of course he has.

"His friends are there," I argue. "His routine. He's already been uprooted enough."

Massimo exhales through his nose. "His classmates are the sons and daughters of politicians."

I lift a brow. "And?"

"That makes them targets."

I cross my arms. "What's so bad about a politician's daughter?" I ask, cool and deliberate.

He opens his mouth. Then closes it. We stare at each other for a beat, and I can almost see the gears turning as he realizes he's walked straight into it.

"I'm one," I add mildly.

His mouth quirks despite himself. "You're not exactly a *selling point* for your argument."

I snort. "I survived."

"That's not the standard I aim for," he counters.

"I know," I reply. "But Amauri needs more than safety. He needs continuity. People who knew him before all of this."

Massimo studies me for a long moment, weighing risk against something he's still learning how to value.

"Let me increase security," he negotiates. "Quietly. No uniforms. No disruption."

I consider it. Then nod. "That's... reasonable." I have no idea how the school will feel about that, but I imagine a large donation will keep any objections under closed lids.

He steps closer, lowers his voice. "We revisit this if the ground shifts."

"When," I correct gently.

A beat. Then he nods again. "When."

Massimo shifts, and the air between us changes.

"Have you decided," he asks evenly, "what to do with your father?"

I still. The question lands harder than I expected it to, like it's been waiting for me to stop moving long enough to catch up. I look past him, toward a painting on the wall.

"I..." My voice falters. I clear my throat. "I don't have that kind of power."

Massimo steps closer. Gently—always gentle with me—he takes my chin between his fingers and tilts my face up until I'm forced to meet his eyes.

"You have me," he reminds me quietly. "And through me, all the power in the world." There's no arrogance in it. Just fact. "Say it," he adds. "And it will be done."

My heart starts to race.

I swallow hard. "I don't want him to die."

The words surprise me with how much they hurt to say. Because the truth is—I do. And I don't. I want him punished. Exposed. Stripped of the authority he used to bend my life into something unrecognizable. I want him to *know* what he took from me. From us.

But he's still Amauri's grandfather.

I'm already standing on the edge of one impossible conversation, already trying to figure out how to explain that the man Amauri called *Dad* is gone. Forever. How to frame that kind of absence without breaking something fragile inside my son. I can't add another body to that reckoning.

"I don't want his blood on Amauri," I say softly. "I don't want my son growing up with that kind of legacy hanging over him."

Massimo doesn't let go of my chin. His thumb brushes my jaw, grounding, steady. Emotions move over his face I can't read, but there is something like recognition and realization. This father role, this responsibility, is new for him too, and he has to figure out how to navigate it against his killer instincts.

"What do you want," he asks, slower now, "instead?"

I close my eyes for a second, letting the answer take shape.

"I want him removed," I say. "From power. From influence. From my life." I open my eyes again. "I want him to live long enough to see everything he built taken apart. Quietly. Legally. Completely." A pause. "And," I add, voice barely above a whisper, "I want him to never be able to speak to Amauri again."

Massimo studies me, not for weakness but for resolve. When he nods, it's once. Decisive.

"Done," he agrees.

No qualifiers. No conditions. Relief and grief crash together in my chest, messy and overwhelming. I lean into him without thinking, pressing my forehead to his shoulder, breathing him in.

This is the hardest choice I've ever made. But it's mine.

Two days later...

Massimo comes into the bedroom without knocking. I know what it is before I see it. He doesn't sit. Doesn't soften it. He just holds out a burner phone, his expression is as steady as ever, his eyes search my face one last time.

"It's time," he announces.

I nod. I've known this was coming. I've rehearsed it in my head, told myself I'm ready. Still, my chest tightens the moment my fingers touch the phone. I feel clumsy when I press dial. Massimo doesn't ask *are you sure*. He already knows the answer. He presses a kiss to my temple instead—grounding, solid—and steps back, giving me space but not distance.

I draw a breath. It rings twice.

"Who is this? My father's voice comes sharp and annoyed, already defensive.

"It's me."

"Jenna? Do you have any idea how much trouble you've caused me? Running off, disappearing, do you know what people are saying?"

I close my eyes for a second. How did I not see this earlier? Well, I did, but back then, I chose to ignore it.

"I do," I respond calmly. "That's kind of the point."

There's a pause. A recalibration.

"So," he scoffs, "you finally call. Let me guess, this is about that man. The mobster. Of course it is. I warned you about him."

"No," I reply. "This is about you."

His tone hardens. "Watch yourself."

I straighten, even though he can't see me. "Carter is gone." Silence follows that statement; I let him fill in what I mean with *gone*. "Same as Marianne and Sean," I continue. "So before you start pretending you don't know what I'm talking about—don't."

"You think this scares me?" he snaps. "You're running with criminals now, Jenna. Is that what you want? To throw your life away for—"

"I know everything," I interrupt.

That finally does it.

"What exactly do you think you know?" he demands, but the edge is gone now. Replaced by something thinner.

"I know you ordered the hit on Massimo." I'm glad I don't have to see his face right now. "I know you paid Sean. I know Marianne facilitated it. I know how long they've been cleaning up after you."

"You don't have proof," his response is quick. Too quick.

I smile, though my eyes burn. "That's where you're wrong."

Another pause. I imagine him standing in his office, jaw clenched, already calculating exits.

"Oh," I add lightly, "and just so you know, Amauri is

safe. He's happy. He's surrounded by people who actually love him." I let that sink in. "You will never see him again." Not that I imagine he would want to, but I need to say the words. I need to reclaim my power and control.

His voice rises now. "You don't get to do this to me. I'm your father."

"No," I disagree softly. "You were my father. You stopped being that when you decided my life was collateral."

I hear something in the background then. Muffled voices. A knock.

"What's going on?" he demands, sharp with irritation.

I glance at Massimo. He's watching me closely, ready if I need him. I don't.

"You should answer that," I advise. "That would be the FBI knocking."

"What—"

"I sent them everything," I continue calmly. "The payments. The emails. The witness statements. The women who finally felt safe enough to talk. Enough to bury you for the rest of your life."

He starts to speak. To threaten. To bargain. I push end call.

My hand shakes as I lower the phone. For a second, I just stand there, breathing, existing, letting the weight of it crash through me. Widow. Daughter no more. Survivor.

Massimo is there instantly. He takes the phone from my hand, sets it aside, and pulls me into his chest.

"It's done," he assures me quietly.

I close my eyes, press my face into him, and let the

tears come, not loud, not dramatic. Just honest. For the first time in my life, the past has no hold on me. And the future?

The future is finally mine.

Life doesn't snap back into place all at once. It settles. Slowly. Carefully. Like something fragile learning how to trust gravity again. Amauri is back in school. Not the way it was before, not entirely. Massimo insisted on extra security, and now there's a man at the school who pretends to be an aide. Clipboard. Neutral clothes. Polite smile. No one who looks at him for more than two seconds believes the act. But no one openly questions it either.

The other parents whisper. The kids stare. Amauri pretends not to notice, but he does. He always has. Still, he goes. He laughs again. He brings home drawings, spelling tests, and stories about friends who argue over Pokémon cards and who got tagged during recess. The nightmares haven't vanished. Some nights, he still crawls into bed with Massimo and me, small hands clutching my shirt, his breathing uneven.

But they've softened and become less frequent. Esther says that's progress. That trauma doesn't disappear; it loosens its grip. She comes twice a week now, and Amauri trusts her. Talks to her in that sideways way kids do, circling the truth until it feels safe enough to touch.

Massimo's and Amauri's bond is growing in ways I never could have planned or forced. It's in the way Amauri looks for him when he's unsure. The way he mirrors Massimo's posture without realizing it. The way Massimo lowers himself—physically and emotionally—to meet him where he is.

I finally told Amauri about Carter.

That he was gone.

There were tears. Of course there were. Carter had been *there*. Flawed, distant, wrong in ways Amauri couldn't articulate, but present. Grief doesn't ask whether someone deserved love. It just arrives. I held him while he cried. Massimo held him, too. Finally, when the tears stopped, when Amauri curled into Massimo's side and stayed there, something settled quietly into place. Not replacement.

Belonging.

Some days, when Massimo comes home, and Amauri runs to him without hesitation, when the three of us end up tangled on the couch watching something ridiculous and animated, it almost feels... normal.

Not the life I imagined at eighteen. But the life I would have chosen had I been given a choice. The one I fought for. The one that survived. I don't know what the future will demand of us. I know Massimo's world is dangerous. I know shadows don't disappear just because you drag them into the light. But I also know this: I am no longer alone. My son is safe. And the man beside me doesn't just promise protection, he lives it.

I look at the ring on my finger sometimes, simple and heavy and real, and think about everything we lost. Then I look at Amauri. At Massimo. At the family we're building from the wreckage. And I know—with a certainty that feels like peace—that this is not the end of our story. It's the beginning of the one we finally get to write ourselves.

Amauri knows the version he needs to know. That there were bad men. That Carter didn't make it. That Massimo is his father.

He took it the way he takes everything, quietly, without breaking.

Esther helped smooth the edges. Gave it shape. Something a ten-year-old can hold onto now, with space for the rest later. And somehow... he's okay. More than okay. He's already attached to Massimo in a way that feels natural, inevitable. Like something that was always meant to find its place.

Massimo gives him the kind of attention Carter never did. Steady. Present. Uncomplicated. The two of them are already thick as thieves. And every time I see them together, it feels like my life is finally settling.

Carter's death is already public knowledge. The official story is that he was killed in Venezuela by the Cartel. Massimo used his FBI contacts to spin the story that they rescued Amauri, but were not in time to save Carter. There is no body, but it's enough for a Justice of the Peace to declare me a widow. Enough for the country to mourn him. Enough for it to turn on me for not mourning him long enough.

Massimo keeps the worst of it out of the papers. Keeps Amauri's name out of their mouths. But he can't stop all of it, can't stop people from counting the days between Carter's death... and our wedding. There was a time when I would have cared. That time is over. As long as Amauri is safe from the gossip, I'm fine with it, and the school is doing an excellent job shielding him when he's there.

This weekend, we're getting married. Quietly. No spectacle. No press. No politics. Just us. Massimo's *friends* will be there, the other capos I haven't met yet, but will tonight at our long-overdue dinner party. I purposefully kept the affair informal. Massimo told me about his friends, how they met, how they took over the city, and how they saved each other's lives more than once. I feel a deep sense of gratitude towards each of them. They kept Massimo alive in more ways than one, and that already gives them a big place in my heart. I've ordered the long dark wood table to be placed and set by the terrace—because God forbid, I so much as fold a napkin—the doors open to the warm Vegas night. Candlelight. Just food, wine, and whatever kind of men survive loving someone like Massimo.

Somewhere in the background, the city hums like it always does — unaware of the men who run it.

Amauri is practically vibrating beside me.

"They're soldiers, right?" he whispers.

"Friends," I correct gently.

The elevator chimes. Massimo appears from the hallway first, followed by two men. I recognize Enzo.

Scarred. Controlled. Authority wrapped in calm. I've spoken to Amauri about how he might look scary to him, but all Amauri can think to say is, "Wow, you survived a lot. Just like Massimo."

Enzo tries to smile. On his ravaged face, it looks grotesque, but Amauri doesn't flinch away. He shakes Enzo's hand like a pro. Then Enzo shakes mine. "Good to see you again, Jenna."

"Enzo," I nod, smiling. I like him. I like his quiet demeanor filled with confidence. I have a feeling there is no deceit in the man. You'll know if you get on his bad side. Fast.

Behind him, another man enters. I've seen him before, at the Oven when Carter, Sean, and Marianne were... laid to rest. But I never caught his name.

"Jenna, this is Damiano Ferrante. Damiano, Jenna." Massimo introduces.

"Nice to meet you." We shake hands, his is strong, and his dark eyes bore questioningly into mine.

"The woman of steel, I'm told," Damiano winks. "And after meeting you, I can confirm the rumors."

"What rumors?" Massimo demands.

Damiano laughs, "Easy, boss. Nothing bad, only that the men are in complete awe of her and already intimidated."

Blood rushes to my face. It was never my intention to make some kind of impression on Massimo's men. "I..." The word hangs there, fragile and utterly useless.

Massimo's hand slides to the small of my back. Not

possessive. Not restraining. Anchoring. I straighten my shoulders instead of shrinking.

"What exactly did you hear?" Massimo asks again, but there's less edge in it now. More curiosity than warning.

"That she walked into our world," Enzo answers smoothly as he pours himself a drink, "and didn't flinch."

"That she stood by the Oven," Damiano adds quietly, "and didn't break."

The air shifts. Not heavy. Just aware.

Blood still warms my cheeks, but I refuse to let it feel like embarrassment.

"I broke," I correct softly. "I just didn't fall."

Silence for half a breath. Then Damiano nods once. Slow. Respectful.

"Steel," he repeats.

Amauri looks between us, frowning thoughtfully. "Mummy doesn't break," he announces with the absolute certainty only children possess. "She bends. Like in karate."

A laugh ripples through the men. Massimo crouches slightly toward him. "Your mother is more dangerous than karate."

I nudge him with my elbow. "Careful. I might start believing you."

He leans closer, voice low enough for only me. "You should."

Thankfully, the arrival of Gabe with another man I don't know ends the awkward situation. Gabe seems taller than I remembered. Broad. Quiet. The kind of man who looks like he'd rather be underestimated.

The other man nods at me, "So this is the woman who's been rearranging our Don's priorities," he says warmly.

"And improving them," I answer without missing a beat.

His laugh is genuine. Massimo introduces him, "Alessio, Jenna."

He's different from the others. I can't quite put my finger on it. But his edges seem sharper. His eyes seem to calculate before they blink. If Damiano is brute strength and Enzo is strategy carved in stone, Alessio is precision.

Then it's Gabe's and my turn to shake hands. "Nice to see you again, Jenna. You look," he throws a look at Massimo, "better."

Massimo pulls me against his chest. "Let's get some drinks."

Amauri bounces from one man to the other like he's known them all his life. Chatting and, for some reason, really latching on to Enzo, peppering him with questions. Before the food arrives from the kitchen, Enzo leans back in his chair and looks over Gabe's shoulder at the phone in his hands. "Did the suburbs survive the drive over?"

Gabe doesn't look up. "Traffic was light."

Alessio lifts a brow. "Because you already know the traffic patterns."

Damiano pours wine. "Cameras help."

I glance at Gabe. "Cameras?"

He finally looks at me. Calm. Unbothered.

"Monitoring," he corrects.

"For what?" I ask curiously, I wouldn't have pegged

him for the suburban type. He studies me like I'm testing him.

"Stability."

Enzo smirks. "In someone else's marriage?"

Massimo says nothing, but I feel the amusement vibrating under his skin. Gabe's jaw tightens just slightly.

"She's happy," he says quietly.

There's something in the way he says it. Not envy. Not resentment. Restraint. I'm still confused, "And you're... observing? What? Whom?"

"For now." Enzo's words hang in the air. Amauri looks between them all, confused but fascinated.

"Is he a spy?" he whispers loudly.

Damiano coughs into his drink. Gabe actually smiles. "Something like that."

Dinner is brought up, interrupting the confusing conversation. Plates are set down. Steak. Potatoes. Wine for the adults. Sparkling water for Amauri, who insists on clinking glasses like he's part of a secret council. The stories shift. No details. Just pieces of shared history meant to entertain—even though they are somewhat questionable for the ears of a ten-year-old.

"The night we took the north side," Damiano starts.

Massimo arches a brow. "You mean the night you got stuck on a fence?"

Alessio laughs. "He did. Tore his pants clean open."

"It was strategic," Damiano protests. "Distraction."

"You screamed," Gabe says mildly.

"I did not."

Amauri's eyes widen. "Like a girl?"

The entire table loses it. Enzo wipes his mouth with a napkin. "No one screamed. But someone definitely got chased by a dog."

"That dog was trained," Damiano mutters.

"It was a Pomeranian," Alessio corrects.

Even I laugh.

"The time Enzo nearly died," Massimo begins, but his tone is lighter now.

"I tripped," Enzo interrupts. "On a pallet. Don't let him dramatize it."

"You lost a lot of blood," Gabe corrects flatly.

"Paper cut," Enzo waves it off.

"That's a lie," Damiano says. "He passed out and hit his head on a crate."

Amauri gasps like that's the most thrilling thing he's ever heard. "Did you get stitches?"

"Four," Enzo admits grudgingly.

"Five," Massimo corrects.

They argue over the number. The tension dissolves. Alessio gets his turn.

"I once hacked a rival's entire computer system in under an hour."

Amauri leans forward. "Like in the movies?"

Alessio considers. "Less explosions. More coffee."

"And more crying," Gabe adds.

"You made someone cry?" Amauri asks, impressed.

"Only financially," Alessio bends over to my son conspiratorially.

That earns another round of laughter. The stories aren't about violence. They're about stupidity. Luck.

Loyalty. How Damiano once got so drunk he tried to climb a palm tree and fell into a decorative fountain. How Gabe once spent three hours tracking a *security breach* that turned out to be a raccoon.

"It was persistent," Gabe defends.

How Massimo once miscalculated a deal and had to swallow his pride and ask Enzo for backup. Amauri listens like they're knights around a round table. And maybe they are. Just darker, not the kind from the storybooks. They aren't bragging. They're remembering. Massimo relaxes in a way I've never seen before. Shoulders lower. Voice warmer. His hand rests on my thigh under the table, not to control me, but to anchor himself. Amauri eats like he's at a superhero convention. At one point, he leans toward Massimo and whispers, "Are they always this scary?"

Massimo glances around the table. "They like to think so, but they're softer than Hammie's bedding."

The men laugh. Something shifts inside me. These aren't just capos. They're the men who kept him alive when I couldn't. That gives them a place at this table. And maybe, eventually, in my life too. Gabe sits across from me. Watching. Not me. His phone. I narrow my eyes. Enzo notices.

"What's she doing now? Taking a shower?" Enzo asks casually.

That earns him a scorching look from Gabe, "I'm not some... pervert." He lowers his voice at the last word, looking at Amauri, whose ears instinctively pick up.

Damiano snorts into his drink.

"I said monitoring," Gabe mutters.

Amauri's head pops up immediately. "What's a pervert?"

Every adult at the table freezes. Massimo answers without missing a beat. "Someone who doesn't mind his own business."

Amauri nods thoughtfully. "Oh. So like when I read Mummy's messages?"

"Exactly like that," I jump in quickly.

Gabe exhales through his nose. "I mind my business."

"From a distance," Enzo adds.

"With surveillance," Alessio corrects mildly.

Gabe shoots him a look. "You hacked your ex-girlfriend's thermostat."

"That was climate control," Alessio says smoothly. "And she was wasteful."

Amauri looks between them, delighted. "You guys are weird."

"That," Damiano says solemnly, raising his glass of water toward Amauri, "is the nicest thing anyone has ever said to us."

The tension dissolves into laughter. I glance at Gabe again. He's pretending not to care, but there's a faint color high on his cheekbones now.

"She's really that happy?" I ask quietly, keeping my tone neutral.

His expression shifts, not soft, exactly. But guarded in a different way. "She has a good life."

"And you're... what? Making sure it stays that way?"

A spark flickers in his eyes. "Something like that."

Massimo leans back in his chair, studying him. "Just don't confuse protecting with hovering."

"I don't hover," Gabe replies.

"You installed cameras," Enzo reminds him.

"For security."

"In her house?"

Gabe doesn't answer.

Amauri gasps again. "You *are* a spy!"

Gabe looks at him seriously. "If I were a spy, you wouldn't know."

Amauri's eyes go wide with admiration. "That's so cool."

I shake my head, smiling despite myself. The banter keeps rolling after that, lighter, easier. Stories about bad haircuts in the early days. A deal that went sideways because someone wore the wrong shoes. Damiano once getting locked out on a balcony in nothing but dress pants.

"It was a tactical retreat," he insists.

"It was a sliding door," Enzo corrects.

Massimo's hand settles over mine under the table. Warm. Solid.

I look around at these men—dangerous, powerful, ridiculous in flashes of humanity—and realize something unexpected. They aren't just testing me. They're letting me see them. Sometime, between steak and sarcasm, between Gabe's questionable *monitoring* habits and Damiano's balcony incident, this stops feeling like a summit of crime lords. It feels like family. Complicated. Slightly unhinged. But family all the same.

The laughter dies down eventually, replaced by the comfortable clink of silverware and low conversation. Amauri is halfway through dessert when Enzo leans back in his chair, swirling his wine.

"So," he asks casually, as if he's asking about the weather. "How did you two meet?"

The table goes still. Not dramatically. Subtly. I feel it before I see it. Massimo stiffens beside me. Not much. Just enough. His hand rests loosely on the table, still. His jaw tightens a fraction. A flicker of warning passes through his eyes.

Oh.

I fight a smile.

Amauri perks up immediately. "Yeah! Mummy never told me!"

Massimo's eyes cut to Enzo in a way that, under different circumstances, would have resulted in someone reconsidering their life choices.

Enzo lifts both hands. "What? It's a normal question."

Is it though?

I beam sweetly. "He helped me get rid of a body."

Silence. Utter silence. Massimo turns his head toward me very slowly. His eyes scream: *Are you fucking serious*?

"A body?" Amauri echoes, eyes enormous.

I widen mine right back at him. "A raccoon," I correct lightly. "I accidentally ran it over."

The men stare at me. Not buying it. Not even a little. Gabe's mouth twitches. Damiano coughs into his napkin to hide a grin. Alessio watches me like I just passed some kind of unspoken test. Massimo closes his eyes briefly, shaking his head. I feel his amusement before I see it. He leans closer, his voice low enough that only I can hear. "I love you."

I turn to him fully, my heart hammering in my chest, and the candlelight catches in his dark eyes. "I love you too."

It slips out easily. Naturally. Like it was never gone. Across the table, Enzo exhales softly. Damiano smirks into his wine. Gabe looks away, as if suddenly very invested in his phone again. Amauri looks between us, suspicious. "You guys are being weird."

Massimo ruffles his hair. "Get used to it."

Later, when we have a moment, I ask Massimo about Gabe. His strange obsession is quietly bothering me.

Massimo shrugs, utterly unconcerned. "We all have our tics."

I stare at him. "That's not a *tic*."

That finally earns me a glance. A small, knowing smile. "Depends who you ask."

I look back across the room. Gabe is leaning against a pillar, phone in hand, expression unreadable. He types something, pauses, then pockets the device as if whatever he needed to know has just been confirmed. I briefly consider warning her.

Whoever *she* is.

Then reality settles in. I don't know her name. I don't know where she is. And I don't know what version of the truth she's already living inside. Also, I have enough on my plate. Because whatever this is, it isn't casual. It isn't accidental. If there's one thing I've learned living in Massimo's world, it's this: Some men don't need proximity to possess. Some men claim from a distance. And once they do... they don't let go. I don't dwell on it. This world is full of choices made long before anyone realizes they had one. And I've finally learned where my responsibility ends.

The weekend arrives sooner than I thought. On my side, there will only be a handful of people. Amauri, of course, he will walk me down the aisle—since my father is, has been, and will be incarcerated for the foreseeable future. He's also my best man. Then there's Esther. And my cousin Philippa, who lives in England, far enough away that we could maintain a *close* relationship without her ever seeing the cracks. The secrets. The shadows.

I haven't let many people close over the years. After I dropped out of college, after everything that happened, it was easier to keep my distance. Easier to be composed, contained, unknowable. Too many secrets made intimacy feel dangerous. But I'm learning something new now. Secrets don't have to be isolating. They can be shared. Held. Protected. I'm learning to live *with* them instead of hiding inside them.

The guest list on Massimo's side more than makes up

for the lack of people on mine. What started with a handful of invitations snowballed fast. In addition to his capos, Massimo invited the three people who helped get Amauri out, Stephano, Raffael, and Stephano's wife, Oksana, along with Raffael's wife, Sophia. That opened the door for more of the New York family. Enzo brought his daughter Violet and her husband, Marcello, to Vegas, and once they were included, the rest followed. Enrico Sartori and his wife, Cat. Antonio DeLuna and his wife, Scarlet. Friends. Extended family. Allies. Suddenly, we're looking at close to a hundred people. More than enough to remind me exactly how alone my side of the aisle still is.

The day comes without fanfare. No crowds. No press. No spectacle. Just sunlight spilling through tall windows, soft and golden, and the low murmur of voices that matter. I stand at the altar in a dress that is objectively ridiculous—custom, silk, worth more than my first car—and for once I don't feel like I'm wearing a costume. I feel like myself.

Amauri stands a few steps away, solemn in a suit he's already wrinkled, clutching the rings with a seriousness that makes my chest ache. Esther smiles at me from the front row. Philippa dabs at her eyes like she knew she would. Behind them sit an entire clan of people who all seem to get along well, but who I have yet to properly meet.

And then there's Massimo. Waiting. Tall. Still. Dressed in black like he always is, but softened somehow, stripped of armor in a way only I can see. His eyes are locked on mine, unblinking, like I'm the only fixed point in the room. I don't think about danger. Or consequences. Or the life we're choosing. I just know—deep in my bones—that this is right.

When it's my turn, I say *I do* without hesitation. No tremor. No doubt. The words feel like an anchor dropping into place.

Then it's Massimo's turn. He doesn't reach for a prepared vow. He doesn't look at the officiant. His gaze never leaves mine.

"For most of my life," he begins in a low and steady voice, "I believed love was a liability." A faint, self-aware smile touches his mouth, gone as quickly as it appears. "I was taught that love makes men weak. Predictable. Easy to break." His eyes never leave mine. "So I became something else."

The room is silent now. Every breath feels suspended.

"I became ruthless," he admits simply. "I learned how to take. How to survive. How to sin without remorse." A pause. "It worked."

My chest tightens.

"Then I met you." His voice softens—not weaker, never that—but stripped bare. "I didn't understand you then. I didn't understand why you unsettled me. Why you made the world feel... less certain." He swallows. "But I knew I didn't deserve you."

Tears blur my vision.

"I tried to convince myself I could walk away from you," he continues. "That I could bury what I felt and still be whole. I told myself I hated you. I told myself you betrayed me." His jaw tightens. "I was lying to survive."

A ripple moves through the room. Someone inhales sharply, Philippa, maybe.

"I never stopped loving you," he continues. "Even when I became a man you shouldn't have forgiven. Even when I didn't want to. Even when loving you felt like the most dangerous sin of all." His eyes shine now, unguarded. "I am a merciless sinner," he acknowledges quietly. "I have done things that cannot be undone. I carry blood and guilt and ghosts that will never leave me."

My heart feels too big for my chest.

"And still," he goes on, "you survived without me. You protected our son without me. You built a life in the ruins you were left behind in. And when I came back broken and late... You let me come home." He steps closer, as if distance itself is unbearable. "I don't ask for forgiveness I haven't earned," he says. "I don't ask you to forget who and what I am." He takes my hands in his, warm, steady, anchoring. "I vow this instead," he kisses my fingers. "I will spend the rest of my life proving that loving you is the one thing I will never fail at again."

Tears spill freely now.

"You are the one," his dark eyes shine with severity. "The only one. You were before I understood it, and you are now, and you will be until my last breath." His thumb brushes my knuckles, grounding me. "You are my truth," he finishes. "My family. My redemption. My home." His voice drops, fierce and reverent all at once. "And whatever darkness waits for me in this world will never touch you or our son without first going through me."

There isn't a dry eye left.

Massimo Manetti—Don, king, merciless sinner—looks at me like this vow is the only absolution he's ever believed in.

"I do," he finishes.

The moment he slides the ring onto my finger, I know something with absolute certainty: I didn't marry power. Or protection. Or a kingdom. I married the man who chose love and let it change him. And that choice?

It was the bravest thing either of us has ever done.

Later, after dinner, the atmosphere shifts. The long banquet tables are cleared, the candles are burning lower now, casting everything in a softer glow. The tension of the day dissolves into laughter, music, the easy hum of people who have survived too much together to stand on ceremony for long.

Massimo takes my hand without a word. He doesn't ask. He never does. The room quiets just enough as he leads me onto the dance floor, that quiet awareness that follows him everywhere settling over the crowd. Conversations pause, glasses lower, eyes track us. His thumb brushes over my knuckles, grounding, possessive.

"Don't think," he murmurs, pulling me closer. "Just follow me."

I huff out a quiet breath. "I hate when you say that."

A corner of his mouth lifts. "You never listen anyway."

The music swells, something slow, familiar, and he moves like he was born to it, sure, controlled, guiding me with an ease that makes it impossible to do anything but fall into step with him. Around us, the room begins to stir again. Someone whistles. Enzo, I think.

"About time," a voice calls out, amused.

Massimo ignores it, his focus entirely on me. Which only makes the commentary worse.

"Careful, Jenna," another voice chimes in, teasing. "He gets territorial when people watch."

"He already is," I mutter under my breath.

Massimo hears it. Of course he does. His hand tightens at my waist, pulling me closer, a silent confirmation. I don't fight it. For once, I let myself sink into it. By the time the first song ends, the dance floor fills. Couples drift in, laughter loosens the edges of the room, conversations overlap, glasses clink. The formality of earlier fades into something warmer, more chaotic, more real. This is his world. And mine, because it doesn't feel like I'm standing outside of it any longer.

Violet, Marcello's wife, is the first to approach me. She's striking in a quiet way, with observant eyes that seem to miss nothing. Marcello stays close, his hand resting possessively on her back like he's not entirely convinced she won't disappear if he lets go. "Congratulations."

There's something steady about her. Grounded.

"Thank you," I reply, smiling.

My gaze flicks briefly to Marcello, to the way he watches her, like she's something fragile and unbreakable at the same time. There's history there. Heavy. Violet follows my gaze, a hint of amusement touching her lips.

"I used to be his nurse," she explains, like she already knows the question forming. "He was... difficult."

Marcello huffs. "I was dying."

"You were stubborn," she corrects calmly. "There's a difference."

I blink, surprised. "You saved him?"

"Twice," she says simply. Marcello's hand tightens at her waist. Like he remembers every second of it. Like he'll never forget. Something about that settles deep in my chest. The way these men love. It's not soft. But it's absolute.

I move through the room slowly, meeting people in pieces rather than all at once. Enrico and Cat share easy laughter, with sharp eyes that take everything in. Antonio and Scarlet. Scarlet is warm, vibrant. Antonio watches her like she's the only thing in the room that matters. There are threads between all of them. Stories I don't know yet. But I really want to. Sophia approaches me. She is the wife of the New York Don, Raffael DeSantis. "I hope we're not overwhelming you on your wedding day."

I say honestly, "It would be, if all of you weren't so nice and warm. Thank you so much for coming."

She hugs me and presses something surreptitiously into my hand, a card. She winks. "You can read it later. It's an invitation to our The Real Mafia Wives Club. We do all kinds of fun things, like dig out past histories." She winks again, making me think there's a bigger story, but I'm still giggling over the name of their club. "The card contains links to our texts, emails, and groups. I hope you'll join us. But beware, the initiation is gruesome."

"Oh, don't let her fool you," Scarlet links an arm through Sophia's and shakes her head. "The initiation is bringing desert to the next meeting."

I laugh. "That I can do."

A movement to my left draws my attention to Enzo. He's watching someone. A woman. Older. Fuller. Soft where the others are sharp. There's something warm about her, something unbothered, as if she exists outside the rules everyone else follows. I blink to focus on an object in her hand. Is that... yep, that's a kitchen towel. At a wedding.

"Who is that?" I ask quietly.

The women follow my gaze. Violet, Enzo's daughter, joins us and laughs, lifting her hand to her mouth like she's trying to contain it. "Oh, that is Zia Rosa."

"Zia...?"

"Marcello's aunt," she clarifies. "And don't let the towel fool you."

As if on cue, the woman—Zia Rosa—reaches out, swats one of the men upside the head with it, and keeps talking like nothing happened. I stare. Violet leans closer. "They got... very close last time he was in New York."

I glance back at Enzo. At the way his usual sharp edges have softened. The way he watches her, not like prey, not like strategy. Like something entirely different.

"Really?" I murmur.

Violet nods, her eyes are dancing. "He's completely gone," she whispers. "Didn't stand a chance."

Zia Rosa says something across the room, gesturing

with the towel. Enzo straightens immediately. I bite back a smile.

Behind me, Massimo's hand finds my waist again, pulling me back against him, like it's instinct. Like he's always aware of where I am.

"What are you smiling about?" he murmurs against my hair.

I glance over my shoulder, tilting my head toward Enzo. "Apparently, your right-hand man has a weakness."

Massimo follows my gaze. There's a pause. Then, he mutters, "God help us all."

For a moment, I just watch him. The room still hums around us—music, laughter, the low murmur of conversations, but everything feels... lighter. Softer.

Like we made it through something. Like maybe we get to keep this. I lean back into him, letting myself breathe.

That's when Enzo appears, moving with the kind of purpose that never means anything good. He doesn't waste time. The second he's close enough, he lowers his voice. "Someone took Gabe's girl."

"Shit," Massimo mutters, already going still behind me.

My chest tightens for her. I know exactly what that feels like, being *taken*, being powerless while someone else decides your fate. "Massimo, we need to do something."

Enzo glances between us. "This is your wedding. Damiano, Alessio, and I have it handled. We'll keep you in the loop, boss."

I feel the hesitation ripple through Massimo, the pull

between here and there, between me and them. I hate the idea of him leaving. But this is the life I chose. And Gabe, Gabe is family.

"If you need to go..." I start.

Massimo shakes his head before I can finish. "No. Enzo's right. They can handle it."

It's not dismissal. It's trust. The kind that runs bone-deep between men like them. Enzo nods once and disappears as quickly as he came. The music swells again. Voices rise. Glasses clink. Like the world didn't just tilt. Like something terrible isn't already in motion somewhere else. I let out a breath I didn't realize I was holding.

Then, because apparently this is who I am now—standing at the center of a mafia wedding while someone is being kidnapped—I murmur, "I know this isn't romantic, but I have to pee."

Massimo goes very still behind me. Then his hand tightens at my waist, like he's anchoring himself there, like he needs the reminder that I'm here. Safe.

"Now?" he asks.

I tilt my head back to look at him. "Yes, now. It's a thing people have to do."

His eyes narrow slightly. Calculating. Hopeful. Suspiciously hopeful. His fingers tighten around mine. "You don't go anywhere alone," he says quietly.

"Come."

I blink. "Massimo—"

But he's already moving, pulling me with him through the crowd, not even bothering to hide it.

"Massimo," I hiss under my breath, trying not to laugh. "We're at our wedding."

"Exactly," he says, not slowing. "Good timing."

I stare at him. "You are unbelievable."

He glances back at me, completely serious. "You could be pregnant."

I open my mouth. Close it. Then laugh despite myself as he pulls me toward the elevator.

By the time we reach the penthouse, I'm half laughing, half shaking my head.

"This is getting ridiculous," I tell him as he pushes the door open.

"You say that every time," he replies calmly.

Because this isn't new. For the past week, there's been a test. Every morning.

Every. Single. Morning.

I swear the man has never been more disciplined about anything in his life. He lets go of my hand long enough to reach for the drawer. I don't even have to look. I know what's inside. A small, perfectly organized stack. I cross my arms. "You bought them in bulk."

He doesn't even try to deny it. "Efficiency."

"Obsession."

"Preparation."

I snort. "You're impossible."

"And yet," he murmurs, holding one out to me, "you married me."

I take it, shaking my head.

"Give me a minute," heading toward the bathroom.

He follows. Of course he does. I stop in the doorway, turning slowly to face him. The look I give him is the same one I've given him every day for the past week. He pauses. Considers. Then lifts his hands slightly in surrender.

"I'll wait."

I raise a brow.

He doesn't move.

"...Outside," he adds.

"Thank you."

"I'm a reasonable man."

I shut the door in his face.

A minute later, I step back out, test in hand. He's exactly where I left him. Pacing. I don't even try to hide my smile.

"Relax," I soothe, setting it down on the counter.

He looks at it like it might explode. Then at me. Then back at it.

"Is it...?"

"It takes a minute," I remind him.

He exhales slowly, dragging a hand through his hair. For a man who commands an entire city, he looks wildly out of his depth right now. I slip my hand into his. He laces our fingers together immediately, his grip tight, grounding.

We stand there. Waiting. Neither of us speaks. The seconds stretch. Longer than they should. Long enough for my heart to start beating a little faster. For the weight of it to settle. What this means. What this could mean.

Massimo's thumb moves over my knuckles, slow,

steady. A quiet reassurance. Or maybe he needs it as much as I do.

Then—

A shift. I see it before I fully process it. My breath catches. Massimo's grip tightens.

"Jenna," he breathes loudly.

I look at him.

Then back at the test.

Pregnant.

The word feels unreal for a second. Like it belongs to someone else. I laugh. A soft, breathless sound that turns into something brighter. Real. And so different from the last time I stared at a test in desperation.

"It worked," I whisper.

Massimo doesn't say anything at first. He just stares at it. Then at me. Like he's making sure this is real. His hand comes up to my face, rough and gentle at the same time.

"Again," he says, voice low. I smile, tears already burning behind my eyes. "Again."

His forehead presses to mine, breath warm against my skin.

"I won't miss this," he murmurs. "Not a second."

I shake my head, smiling through it.

"You'd better not."

His mouth curves slightly.

"I won't."

And I believe him.

"Come," he says after a moment, already reaching for my hand again.

"Where are we going?"

His eyes darken, something softer underneath. "To tell our son he's going to be a brother."

My heart flips. I squeeze his hand. "Okay."

This time, when he pulls me forward, I follow.

EPILOGUE

The city sleeps differently when you own it. Las Vegas at night isn't quiet—never has been—but there's a rhythm to it now that I recognize. A steadiness. Order restored, at least on the surface. I stand on the balcony of my penthouse, jacket draped over a chair behind me, the glow of the Strip bleeding into the glass like a living thing. Inside, Jenna sleeps.

My wife.

The word still lands heavy. Sacred.

Amauri is down the hall, sprawled sideways across his bed, one arm flung over a stuffed animal that looks like it's seen better days. The sight of him like that—safe, unguarded—does something permanent to a man like me. This is what they'd take from me if they could.

Which is why they won't.

The phone in my hand vibrates once. Gabe. He's been busy lately taking care of the freshly widowed Audra Hale. I'm not crazy about the war he started with one of the Mexican cartels, but if anyone can understand the crazy shit love makes you do, it's me. I answer without a word.

"You're not going to like this," he warns.

A corner of my mouth lifts. "I rarely do."

"Alessio finished peeling back the layers on the call network," Gabe continues. "El Recaudador didn't just reach out to our people. He's trying to buy them."

That gets my attention. "Explain."

"He's recruiting," Gabe says flatly. "Not aggressively. Not loudly. He's planting seeds. Offering exits. Futures. Protection." A pause. "Choice."

I look out over the city again, jaw tightening. "And?"

"And someone answered," Gabe hisses through his teeth. "No one from our inner circle. Yet. But close enough to matter." His voice sharpens. "This isn't a power move, Massimo. This is a test."

"Of you," I say.

"Of loyalty," he corrects. "And of me."

That's when I understand what he hasn't said yet.

"El Recaudador didn't call you because he wants my empire," I conclude slowly. "He called because he wants one of *you*. He wants to infiltrate my inner circle. He wants to turn my friends against me.

"Yes," Gabe confirms quietly. "He's trying to get to you through us."

I close my eyes for a brief moment. The Collector doesn't deal in territory. Or money. Or even revenge. He deals in people.

"I want everything," I command. "Every whisper. Every offer. Every name he's circling."

"You'll have it," Gabe replies. Then, after a beat, "This changes things."

"Yes," I agree. "It does."

I end the call and remain where I am, the desert air cool against my skin. Behind me is the life I fought for. Ahead of me is a shadow that understands exactly where to press.

El Recaudador thinks he's patient. He thinks he can wait. I smile to myself, slow and dangerous. He's wrong. Because the moment he reached for what's mine, he stopped being a rumor. And the moment he made Gabe his next move, he declared himself my enemy. The city flickers below me, bright and alive. Inside, my family sleeps. Somewhere out there, the Collector waits and is counting debts. He'll learn soon enough. I don't owe. I collect.

The phone vibrates again. Not Gabe this time. Enzo.

"Is it done?"

"It's done," he confirms.

Two words. Efficient. Final. I lean one forearm against the balcony railing, eyes still on the Strip. "How bad?"

A pause. Not hesitation. Measurement. "Every major bone," Enzo replies. "Arms. Legs. Ribs. Hands. Our men were... thorough." Good. A satisfied grin spreads over my face. "He's alive. Doctors say he'll recover. Eventually."

Eventually. I picture Preston Kingsley in a hospital bed. Tubes in his throat. Casts encasing limbs that once pointed at people and called it power. The same sterile lighting. The same helplessness I had.

"Make sure the records say mugging," I tell him.

"They do."

"And the guards?"

"Bought."

Enzo doesn't do anything by halves. I close my eyes briefly. Ten years ago, I woke up in a bed with shattered bones and no memory of impact, only the certainty that someone wanted me erased. I rebuilt myself piece by piece. Metal and fury. I learned how long bones take to heal. How many weeks before you can stand. How many months before pain stops being blinding and becomes... companionable. Kingsley will learn that, too.

"Jenna doesn't know," Enzo guesses quietly.

"She doesn't need to," I confirm.

A beat. I told her she could choose what happens to him, but incarceration is not consequence, it's inconvenience. And not nearly enough for what he'd done to me. To her. To our son. To what he would have done to her and our son. She might forgive. I won't.

Silence stretches. Enzo understands me better than most.

"As soon as he heals," I continue, voice calm as the desert night, "it happens again."

No emotion. No heat. Just math.

"Yes, boss," Enzo confirms.

"And again. For as long as I decide."

An eye for an eye would've been merciful. Kingsley didn't just try to kill me. He stole ten years. He fractured lives. He set wars in motion. He let Jenna believe I abandoned her. He let my son grow up without knowing my name. Pain is the only language men like him understand. I straighten, looking out over my city. "He'll live. But he won't ever walk without remembering me."

Enzo exhales slowly. Approval, not hesitation.

I remain on the balcony long after. Jenna shifts in her sleep inside. A soft sound. A dream. She asked me to let her choose, and she did. I only added a little something extra. There are parts of war she doesn't need to carry. Like she won't ever know that it was me who ordered Whitford's accident. She has enough on her plate.

Soon we're going to tell Amauri more. Esther agreed it's time. The truth is no longer a weapon; it's an inheritance. He needs to know about the responsibility that comes from being my son. What it means to carry my name. I don't fear that conversation. I fear the one after.

The moment my son understands what kind of man I am. The moment he realizes I break bones not out of rage, but because I believe in balance. Just like I did with Whitford. Just like I will continue to do with Kingsley.

I rub my thumb over a faint scar along my wrist. The Collector is circling.

My men are being tested.

My empire is being measured.

Let them measure.

Let them test.

I am not the man they tried to kill ten years ago.

I am a husband.

A father.

A king who learned that love does not make you weaker—

It makes you precise.

Below me, Vegas pulses like a living organism.

Inside, my family sleeps. And somewhere in a hospital room, Preston Kingsley is learning what it means to survive something he cannot control.

He'll heal. I'll make sure of it. Because suffering is only meaningful if it lasts.

And I collect in installments.

The end of Book One in Empire of Sin

Start book two HERE

If you've made it this far, I'm guessing you enjoyed Massimo's story 🖤

I would truly appreciate it if you could take a moment to leave a review on Amazon—your support helps other readers discover the *Empire of Sin series.*

And if you're not quite ready to leave this world just yet...

The next book is already waiting for you.

Gabe and Audra's story is coming next.

What can I say? Some men don't fall in love...

They *consume.*

For two exclusive bonus scenes—including what really happened to Jenna and how it all began—subscribe to my newsletter. HERE

Please note: these scenes contain a foiled SA situation and may be sensitive for some readers.

ALSO BY BELLA RAY

Savage Kings of New York

1. Savage King
2. Dangerous King
3. Wounded King
4. Shadow King
5. Ruthless King

Companion Novella with newsletter signup

The King's Blade Vito and Gigi's story

Empire of Sin

1. Merciless Sinner
2. Possessive Sinner

ABOUT THE AUTHOR

Bella Ray writes dark, addictive mafia romance where power is everything, loyalty is lethal, and love comes at a cost. Her stories are packed with morally gray kings, dangerous obsession, and heroines who know how to draw blood and boundaries. When she's not plotting betrayals or forbidden kisses, she's rewatching Dexter for *research*, and walking her German shepherd or catering to an unnamed number of felines.

Her husband is far from a Mafia boss, but just as loyal and protective. They've been married for many years and enjoy life in beautiful Arizona.

Find her website and other social links here:

BellaRayBooks.com

facebook.com/BellaRayBooks
instagram.com/bellarayromance
bookbub.com/authors/bella-ray
pinterest.com/bellaraybooks

www.ingramcontent.com/pod-product-compliance
Lightning Source LLC
LaVergne TN
LVHW041051080826
845145LV00007B/1536

* 9 7 8 1 9 7 1 3 9 5 0 2 9 *